Though the Heavens May Fall

E.V. Thompson

SPHERE

First published in Great Britain in 2007 by Sphere
This paperback edition published in 2008 by Sphere
Reprinted 2008
Reissued by Sphere in 2011

Copyright © 2007 by E.V. Thompson

The moral right of the author has been asserted.

*All characters and events in this publication, other than those
clearly in the public domain, are fictitious and any resemblance
to real persons, living or dead, is purely coincidental.*

A CIP catalogue record for this book
is available from the British Library.

ISBN 978-0-7515-4512-8

Typeset in Palatino by Palimpsest Book Production Limited,
Grangemouth, Stirlingshire
Printed in the UK by CPI Mackays, Chatham ME5 8TD

Papers used by Sphere are natural, renewable and
recyclable products sourced from well-managed forests and certified
in accordance with the rules of the Forest Stewardship Council.

Sphere
An imprint of
Little, Brown Book Group
100 Victoria Embankment
London EC4Y 0DY

An Hachette UK Company
www.hachette.co.uk

www.littlebrown.co.uk

E. V. Thompson was born in London. After spending nine years in the Royal Navy, he served as a Vice Squad policeman in Bristol, became an investigator for British Overseas Airways (during which time he was seconded to the Hong Kong Police Narcotics Bureau), then headed Rhodesia's Department of Civil Aviation Security Section. While in Rhodesia, he published over two hundred short stories before moving back to England to become a full-time award-winning writer.

His first novel, *Chase the Wind*, the opening book in the Retallick saga, won the Best Historical Novel Award, and since then more than thirty novels have won him thousands of admirers around the world.

Let justice be done though the heavens may fall
William Watson, c. 1559–1603

1

1856

When the knock came on the schoolroom door in the Cornish coastal village of Charlestown it was answered by the girl occupying the nearest desk. She opened the door to reveal John Mitchell, a constable appointed by the parish of St Austell, of which Charlestown formed a part.

Ill at ease as the bearer of tragic news to someone he knew, and discomfited at being the focus of attention of more than forty young girls whose ages ranged from seven to seventeen, Mitchell remained in the doorway and addressed the young teacher who stood in front of the blackboard.

'Miss Kernow, I am afraid we have found your father. What I mean is . . .'

He faltered and Talwyn Kernow said, 'What do you mean . . . you are afraid? Has he been hurt? Where is he, Mr Mitchell? I shall dismiss the class and go to him this instant.'

Clearly agitated, the parish constable said, 'Unfortunately it is more serious than an injury . . . I am very, very sorry.'

As her pupils gasped in horror, the piece of chalk Talwyn was holding dropped unnoticed to the floor. Looking at the constable in disbelief, she said, 'You don't mean . . . He's not . . . dead?'

John Mitchell's agonised expression made a reply unnecessary. For a moment, the room swam about Talwyn and she needed to reach out and seek support from the table beside the blackboard.

'Are you all right, Miss Kernow? Can I call someone to come to you . . . your mother, perhaps?' Cornwall had no county police force and Mitchell earned a living by deputising for wealthier members of the parish when they were called upon to perform the onerous and unpaid duties of a parish constable. He was keen on his work but this was an obligation of the post he had never before been required to fulfil.

The room ceased its motion, and, regaining control of herself with great difficulty, Talwyn said, 'No, my mother has not been well. She must not hear of this until I am able to tell her myself . . . but I need to know all the facts first. Will you wait for a moment, please, Mr Mitchell?'

Turning to the class of wide-eyed girls and struggling to maintain control of her voice, she called, 'School is over for today, girls – and will you pass the word to anyone you know who may be affected that there will be no boys' school this evening. You may go now . . .' Her voice broke and she added, 'Please hurry.'

There was a scramble for the doorway which forced

2

John Mitchell to stand aside. One of the youngest pupils paused for a moment with the intention of asking a question of Talwyn, but a none-too-gentle shove in the back from an older girl propelled her swiftly to the door.

When the last of the girls had collected her coat and passed from the porch of the small schoolhouse, Talwyn approached the man who had brought the tragic news.

'Where was my father found, Mr Mitchell? What happened to him? My mother and I realised something serious must have occurred when he failed to return after evening school yesterday. He always came straight home after the last class, so when he did not I came out to look for him, thinking he might have had to stay late for some unexpected reason. When I got here the school was in darkness and locked. I came inside and checked, but everything seemed to be in order, so I went home once more, collected a lantern and returned here again, this time checking the verges and hedgerows along the way. There was no sign of him and so I went up to the manor and told Sir Joseph Sawle. He said he would send word out to the constables.'

She was fighting back tears. 'I stayed up all night. When morning came and he still hadn't returned I knew something dreadful must have happened. I took my mother to stay with one of her sisters and came to open the school. I suppose I should have closed it for the day, but Father would have been cross had there been some reasonable explanation for his not coming home . . . besides, I didn't know what else to do, especially as Sir Joseph sent word to say he had ordered all his men out to make inquiries about him.'

3

Sir Joseph Sawle was lord of Penrice manor and, as senior magistrate for the district, was responsible for appointing parish constables and the maintenance of law and order.

Despite all her efforts, tears were streaming down her cheeks as she asked, 'Where was he found, and where is he now? Does anyone know what happened?'

Mitchell seemed more at ease now he was no longer under the scrutiny of the young pupils, but instead of answering her questions he asked, 'What time was it usual for your father to end his classes in the evening?'

'That depended upon what he happened to be teaching – and how hard the boys had been working. If they had been fishing, or working a shift in the mine, they sometimes had difficulty staying awake, but as they each paid fivepence a week for their lessons they expected value for their money. Father never liked to end too early, but he would not keep them after ten o'clock.'

'You said he always came straight home . . . are you quite certain of that?'

'Of course I am! Sometimes, if I had nothing else to do, I would come to Charlestown to meet him and we would walk home together . . .'

Her voice broke and, apologetically, Mitchell asked, 'Your home being the cottage in the grounds of Sir Joseph Sawle's home at Penrice?'

He accepted her nod as a reply and, after a few minutes, she added, 'Sir Joseph had the schoolhouse built for my father and let us have the cottage rent free because he is keen that as many local children as possible

4

should receive an education . . . but you still haven't answered my questions. Where was my father found? How did he die – and why didn't *I* find him when I was looking for him last night? Was he taken off by someone after an accident on the road home?'

'No.'

Talwyn had formed the impression that the parish constable was reluctant to go into details about the death of her father and it made her more determined than ever to learn exactly what had happened . . . but the constable was asking yet another question.

'Did your father always take the same route home – or might he have taken the path that goes along the edge of the cliffs?'

'Not in the dark,' Talwyn replied. 'It would have been far too dangerous.'

'Then perhaps he might have arranged to meet someone there?' the constable persisted.

'There would have to be a very good reason for him to go anywhere near the cliffs after dark. It was something he always warned me against when I was a young girl. He certainly would not have gone home that way. Why do you ask? Is that where he was found?'

'Yes,' the constable eventually admitted. 'Sadly, his body was discovered by the coastguard on the rocks at the foot of the cliffs. Another half an hour and the tide would have come in and carried him away, probably never to be recovered.'

Talwyn shuddered at the image conjured up by his words . . . but there were still things that needed to be said and questions to be asked. 'Father would have had no reason to be anywhere near the cliffs. He *always* came straight home to talk about the next day's lessons with me so that I would not be too late going to bed. I need to be up in plenty of time to open the school and prepare everything before the girls arrive for their lessons. No, Mr Mitchell, if he went to the cliffs instead of coming straight home something must have been happening there. Something unusual, which he believed was important enough for him to break his routine. Are you aware of anything that might have been going on there last night?'

Evasively, Constable Mitchell said, 'That's a question you will need to put to the coastguard, Miss Kernow. Something *was* going on, I believe, but they keep such things to themselves.'

'You mean . . . my father probably went to see what was happening and slipped over the cliff?' She shuddered at the thought of it. 'Was the cliff high at that point? I mean . . . is it possible he was lying injured at the foot of the cliff for a long time?'

The tears began once more and, embarrassed, Mitchell said, 'No, Miss Kernow. That's one thing I can tell you for certain; he wouldn't have suffered at all. In fact, he would have been dead before he went over the cliff edge. You see . . . somebody shot him.'

2

The ageing wooden stairs of the old house in Great Scotland Yard gave warning of the approach of someone making their way to the attic room. Here, Detective Constable Amos Hawke was fighting a losing battle against the light from a single, diamond-paned window in order to complete the report he was writing.

Thinking the unwelcome visitor was one of the cleaners who descended upon the offices of the Metropolitan Police's detective branch offices at the end of each working day, Amos looked up from his desk with the intention of telling him to clean the other offices first. He needed to complete his report before going off duty.

To his great surprise, it was not the cleaner who entered the room, but Detective Inspector Marcus Carpenter, the officer in charge of the detective department.

Hurriedly pushing back his chair and rising to his feet, Amos's irritation at being disturbed disappeared.

As far as he was aware, this was the first time Inspector Carpenter had paid a visit to this part of the building. His suite of executive offices occupied half the ground floor accommodation of the adjacent house. After normal working hours the career-minded detective inspector was more often to be found in the fashionable clubs of London, or the houses of men of influence, than in the dingy Scotland Yard police offices.

Waving Amos to his seat, he said, 'It's all right, Hawke, be seated.' Looking unsuccessfully around the room for another chair, he perched himself gingerly on a corner of the large desk on which Amos was working.

Frowning at the lack of light in the room, he said, 'Is that a report you are writing? How on earth can you see to work in this light? It's almost dark . . . don't you have a lamp?'

'No, sir,' Amos replied. 'There are candles in the cupboard, but Sergeant Tremlett keeps a tight rein on expenditure. He forbids their use before seven o'clock – it's only a quarter past six now.'

Sergeant Tremlett was the clerk in charge of the detective office stores and he was notoriously mean about issuing candles and any other items from his storeroom. He had carefully recorded the time it took a candle to burn itself out and refused to issue another if he felt they were being used unnecessarily.

'What are you working on?' Carpenter asked. 'Are you heavily involved in anything in particular?'

'I have a few minor cases to investigate,' Amos said, indicating a sheaf of documents that half filled a wooden tray marked 'IN', 'but I need to complete this report first. It's on the arrest and conviction of Jeremy McCabe.'

'Ah yes, the highwayman who was hanged this morning. You did well to take him. The Metropolitan Police were after him for years . . . as were the Bow Street thief-takers. He'd become something of a legend.'

'That's his neckerchief over there, on the mantelshelf,' Amos said. 'He gave it to me this morning, on his way to the scaffold. May God rest his soul.'

Looking at Amos sharply, the detective inspector said, 'Don't tell me you had any sympathy for McCabe . . . he was the scourge of the Great West Road.'

'True,' Amos agreed, 'and his fate was well deserved, but he accepted it with more dignity than a great many villains I have taken. I respected him for that.'

'Well, you have more experience with villains than most,' Inspector Carpenter conceded. 'In fact, your record is most impressive since you joined us here. I understand you also excelled yourself in the Royal Marines before joining the police?'

'I received a commission in the field during the Crimean war,' Amos admitted modestly.

'For outstanding gallantry, I believe,' Carpenter persisted. 'Why did you not remain in the Marines, where your future would have been assured?'

Amos shrugged. 'To make a successful career as an officer in the Royal Marines requires sufficient money to keep up appearances. I had only what I earned. I joined the Royal Marines as a drummer boy when I was thirteen. My mother had died, my father had married again and I didn't get along with my stepmother – or her two sons. It was an easy way out for me. Then, while I was in the Crimea, I received a letter from an aunt – my father's sister. My stepmother had died, her two sons had been taken to Australia by an uncle and it seemed my father was drinking himself into an early grave. She begged me to come home and see if I could do something about it. It was another six months before I returned to England and was able to resign my commission and go to Cornwall – to Mevagissey – to see what was going on, and in the meantime my aunt had also died and my father had left the village. There were lots of rumours. That he had fallen over a cliff into the sea; had taken a boat to go fishing – there was a small boat missing from the harbour about that time; had returned to the mines where he had worked for many years – or had simply taken off because he had run up a great many debts. He certainly owed a great deal of money. I settled his debts, and spent an unsuccessful month in Cornwall trying to learn what had happened to him. By that time I had realised there was little left in Cornwall for me, so I came to London and joined the Metropolitan Police. When the detective branch expanded I was lucky enough to be chosen for the work.'

Amos had thought the detective inspector's visit to be no more than a routine call by the head of the branch on one of the many offices occupied by his men in the houses surrounding Great Scotland Yard. However, Carpenter's next words told Amos he had not found his way to the attic office by chance.

'I have been looking at your personal file, Hawke. I was interested to read that you had experience in commanding a police force during your service with the Marines in the Crimea.'

'It sounds grander than it actually was,' Amos explained. 'When we captured a Russian town in the Crimea I was left behind with a couple of platoons of marines to keep law and order there.'

'And carried out your duties so well you were commended by the commander-in-chief, I believe?'

'That is so.'

'I am at a loss to understand why this was not taken into consideration when you were recruited into the Metropolitan Police, Hawke. You should have entered with the rank of inspector – or, at the very least, sergeant.'

'I had been led to expect that would be the case,' Amos said, 'but I am not complaining. I enjoy my work as a detective.'

'I am very pleased to hear you say so, but due recognition should have been given to your experience as a commissioned officer in the Royal Marines – and Commissioner Mayne agrees with me.'

Commissioner Mayne was in command of the Metropolitan Police and Amos felt a thrill of excitement at Inspector Carpenter's words . . . but there were more than five thousand men in the London police force. He could not understand why he had been singled out for special attention by the detective chief.

Inspector Carpenter was quick to enlighten him.

'There have been three murders in your home county in recent months, Hawke. The earliest two, some months ago now, were of Excise officers going about their duty, but the latest victim, only this last week, was a schoolteacher and for some reason the magistrate who gave this information believes the three deaths are connected.

11

Unfortunately, Cornwall does not yet have a county-wide police force and still relies upon the old system of parish constables and watchmen. They are neither as efficient nor as non-partisan as they should be and the Cornish magistrate who wrote to the commissioner is concerned at the lack of progress in the investigations. He and his colleagues on the bench have requested that a senior detective officer from the Metropolitan Police go there and lead the investigation, preferably with a colleague to assist him. Commissioner Mayne has asked me to take on the task and agreed I should take a detective sergeant with me. I believe that Cornishmen, even more than the residents of other counties, have a very strong sense of community and are likely to resent having an outsider come in to sort out their problems. For this reason I would like you, as a Cornishman, to help me in my investigation. You will be made up to sergeant immediately, and the promotion will be permanent. I would also like to add that this investigation is not only extremely important from the point of view of bringing a murderer – or murderers – to justice; it will set a precedent for future investigations and show what can be achieved by an established detective force, such as we have here at Scotland Yard. In so doing it might also persuade the authorities in those counties which are dragging their feet that it is time to employ an efficient police system. What do you say, Hawke? Will you come to Cornwall with me as soon as you are able to settle your personal affairs here in London . . . or would you like time to think about it?'

Amos knew that such an investigation, if successful,

would reflect very well upon the expertise and efficiency of the Metropolitan Police detective branch – and greatly boost the promotion prospects of Carpenter – but it would not be easy. Cornish people *were* suspicious of strangers, the fishing communities particularly so – and he believed that whoever had killed the Excise officers probably came from such a community. There had been similar killings in the past, when smuggling had been almost a part of everyday life for those who earned a living from the sea.

Times had changed and much had been done to eradicate the activities of the 'freebooters' since John Wesley had condemned smuggling in the previous century, but Amos was aware there were a number of diehards who believed they had a right to continue such activities. It seemed there were also some who were ready to kill in order to exercise that right. He was also aware that Detective Inspector Carpenter would be given no assistance from anyone in the tightly knit fishing communities without the help of someone like himself, who could claim kinship with at least some of their own.

There was also the possibility that during the course of such an investigation he might be able to discover something to throw light upon the disappearance of his father . . .

'Well, now you know the details, I will leave you to think it over, Hawke. Let me know when you have reached a decision.'

'I have no need to think it over, sir. I will be delighted to assist you in every way I can and I have no pressing personal matters to attend to. When do we leave?'

3

The London streets were in darkness when Amos completed his report. Locking up his small office, he made his way down the creaking stairs and headed across the open space that gave its name to the detective headquarters. Bidding goodnight to the uniformed constable on duty at the yard entrance, Amos passed through an archway to the street beyond.

He had taken only a few paces when a powerfully built man standing a head taller than Amos fell into step beside him. It was Harvey Halloran, an ex-Royal Marines colour sergeant who had been second-in-command of Amos's small force when he took over the policing of a captured Russian town during the Crimean war. They had met again in London soon after Amos had been transferred to Scotland Yard's detective force.

Without slowing his pace, Amos said, 'Hello, Harvey. Have you been waiting for me?'

'I have, Mr Hawke, sir, and I seem to have been hanging around outside the Yard for so long I was beginning to fear I would be arrested for loitering.'

Amos grinned. 'I doubt very much whether there are enough policemen on duty at the Yard to successfully arrest you.'

'I don't fight policemen, Mr Hawke, you know that,' Harvey said seriously. 'The fact is, I often wish I'd been able to stay in the Royal Marines, and that's the truth.'

'I have no doubt the Marines felt the same when you left them. Unfortunately, because of your wounds they had no alternative but to discharge you.'

'That's true . . . but I'm fit again now,' Harvey insisted.

'You have certainly made a remarkable recovery,' Amos agreed, 'but the Marines weren't to know you would do that – and they did give you a generous pension.'

'Yes, and it's very welcome,' Harvey admitted, 'but I want to be fully active again . . . that's why I went to see the Metropolitan Police recruiting sergeant today, to try to join them, like you.'

Harvey's statement brought Amos to a halt. 'You've spoken to the recruiting sergeant . . . ? What did he say? Did you tell him you had been given a medical discharge from the Royal Marines?'

'I showed him my discharge certificate and told him I had fully recovered, but he said the medical examination would make no difference.'

'So . . . have you been accepted?'

'No . . . but it had nothing to do with my fitness. It was because of my prizefighting days, before I joined

15

the Marines, when I was bound over to keep the peace, in order to stop me fighting.'

'But that was years ago,' Amos said indignantly. 'You were a marine for more than fifteen years and one of the foremost heroes of the Crimean war. Surely that counts for something?'

'It would seem not,' Harvey said gloomily. 'They don't want me in the Metropolitan Police ... I don't suppose you can do anything to help me, by putting in a good word ... ?'

'Much as I would like to, I am afraid I am going to have no opportunity to do so in the near future,' Amos said. 'I am going to be away for a while. Detective Inspector Carpenter wants me to go with him to ... wants me to go out of London with him. A senior magistrate has requested the help of Scotland Yard detectives in solving a series of murders.'

'How long do you think you'll be away?'

Amos shrugged. 'Your guess is as good as mine. For as long as it takes, I suppose.'

'What is Joyce going to think about your going?'

Amos winced at Harvey's question. Joyce Pemble was the daughter of Amos's landlady. Despite all his attempts to distance himself from her, she had become increasingly possessive, assuming a relationship which had no substance in reality. The situation was made more complicated by the fact that Joyce's mother was the widow of a Metropolitan Police superintendent.

It was usual for Metropolitan policemen to live in quarters at their various stations, but such accommodation was severely limited. Most of the detectives lived

16

in Scotland Yard itself, but when Amos was appointed there had been no rooms available and he was boarded on the superintendent's widow, who occupied a house with Joyce, her only child.

Harvey knew the family because he was occasionally employed by them to carry out gardening and other odd jobs. He found Joyce's pursuit of Amos highly amusing.

'I don't think Joyce's mother is going to be happy either,' he added. 'She has already decided you are to be her future son-in-law.'

'She is going to have to find someone else to take Joyce off her hands,' Amos retorted. 'When I move out of the house it will be permanent. I will need to find lodgings in my new posting. I can't pay two rents – and Joyce and her mother can't afford to keep my room vacant while I am away. It might be for many months.'

Amos's explanation of the financial situation was not entirely accurate. Detective Inspector Carpenter had told him that the Cornish magistrate who had requested the presence of the two Scotland Yard detectives had also offered to assume responsibility for all their expenses during the time they were in Cornwall, but Amos had become increasingly embarrassed by the bold advances of his landlady's daughter and her proprietorial attitude towards him. This would be the best opportunity he was ever likely to have to escape from the one-sided relationship without hurting Joyce – and he did not want to hurt her any more than was absolutely necessary. She was a nice enough young girl, but at seventeen years of age she was ten years younger than Amos and still immature. Besides, he knew he could never return the

17

feelings she believed she had for him. This was the best way out of the situation – for both of them.

Harvey broke in upon his thoughts once more, saying hopefully, 'Perhaps this place you are going to might have a place in their police force for an ex-Royal Marines colour sergeant?'

'Unfortunately, they don't yet have a police force, Harvey – although a law has recently been passed in Parliament ordering every county to establish one. If it looks as though they are about to recruit I will recommend you to them.'

'God bless you, Mr Hawke, sir . . . and good luck with your dealings with Joyce and her mother.'

4

A week after the visit of Detective Inspector Carpenter to the office occupied by Amos, and with his departure from the house occupied by a tearful Joyce and her mother safely behind him, Amos and the detective inspector arrived by train in Plymouth. There the men made their way to the bank of the River Tamar, from where they would cross into Cornwall by ferry. Standing on the edge of the river that formed the border between Devon and Cornwall for the whole of its length, they were in the shadow of the spectacular skeletal framework of the railway bridge towering above them, which was being constructed to the design of the brilliant engineer, Isambard Kingdom Brunel.

Once across the river the two men would no longer be travelling together. Before leaving London they had decided that, initially at least, Amos would work 'undercover', not revealing his true identity until Carpenter deemed the time to be right. Until then, Amos's story would be that he had returned to Cornwall in another attempt to locate his missing father. In this way he might be able to obtain information that would not otherwise be forthcoming.

'Are we quite certain we each know what we are doing, Amos? It is very important that we make no mistakes . . .' Detective Inspector Carpenter put the question as the ferry approached from the far shore.

'I am quite confident, sir,' Amos replied, but, aware of the importance the detective inspector put on solving this case, and in order to put the other man's mind at ease, he repeated the plan that had been agreed between them. 'You will be staying with magistrate Sir Joseph Sawle, in his mansion at Penrice, and openly carrying out an official investigation into the murder of the school-teacher. Travelling separately, I will purchase a horse and make my way to Charlestown, which is not far from Penrice, and take lodgings at an inn there until I can find somewhere else. I too will be trying to obtain information about the murderer – or murderers – but we will initially keep my part in the investigation a secret. Should anyone need to know, the reason I shall give for being back in Cornwall is a renewed attempt to find my father. Once a week, on a Friday, we will meet an hour after dark at the crossroads by Lobb's shop, on the St Austell to Pentewan road – I have marked the spot on your map. There we will exchange any information we may have obtained.'

Satisfied, Marcus Carpenter nodded. 'Good! We both know exactly what we are doing – but take no chances,

Amos. We are obviously up against ruthless men and if – as Sir Joseph Sawle seems to think – the schoolteacher's murder is somehow connected with the killing of the Excise officers, then we are dealing with particularly vicious smugglers, who value illegal profits more than the lives of their fellow men. I believe we will be carrying out this investigation in the best possible way, but I will not be entirely happy until we can do away with the subterfuge and both work openly to secure the arrest and conviction of the guilty parties.'

By now the ferry was close to the shore. Parting company, they joined the other passengers and moved forward to the ferry's berth.

When the train arrived at St Austell railway station, Sir Joseph Sawle was waiting on the platform to meet Inspector Carpenter. Amos witnessed the warm welcome given to the detective chief, but studiously ignored the two men. He had remembered that the following day was market day in St Austell and, as a result, had decided to remain in town in order to attend the auction of livestock.

By noon next day he was the owner of a fine, if somewhat skittish, four-year-old mare, together with a saddle and all the necessary tack. Then, with his baggage packed in two saddlebags, he set off for the tiny port of Charlestown. Finding comfortable accommodation in the Rashleigh Arms inn, he spent the remainder of that day rediscovering the countryside of his childhood.

That evening, after partaking of a somewhat mediocre meal in the dining room, Amos adjourned to the inn's public bar. It was fairly quiet and most of those drinking here were local men. He enjoyed listening to the soft Cornish dialect that until his return in search of his father he had almost forgotten, but was aware that his presence was attracting attention. He pretended not to notice when landlord Thomas Stephens was summoned to the busiest table in the room and entered into a low-voiced but animated conversation with the Cornishmen seated there, during which many meaningful glances were cast in his direction.

Shortly afterwards, Amos signalled to the landlord that he would like another drink, and when it was brought to him he was not at all surprised when Stephens began wiping off the wooden top of the already spotless table with a damp cloth and engaged him in conversation.

'I believe that when you arrived you said you had come to St Austell yesterday evening, after coming to Plymouth on the London train.'

'That's right, landlord. I would have come straight to the Rashleigh Arms there and then, but as today is market day I stayed on in St Austell to buy myself a horse – and I am well pleased with my purchase. It came far cheaper than London prices.'

'I'm pleased to hear it, sir, but . . . talking of London, you would have been travelling in good company from there yesterday. There was one of they police detectives from London on the train with you. He was met at the station by Sir Joseph Sawle and is staying up at Penrice manor with him. He's not been wasting any time, either; he's already been to Charlestown today, asking questions. From what I hear he's a top man up there in London.'

'I can't say he stood out from the other passengers,' Amos said, with apparent disinterest, although the landlord's words had reminded him how difficult it was in Cornwall for anything to remain secret for very long. It was a fact he hoped might be turned to the advantage of Carpenter and himself in the near future. He added, 'I wonder what such a man is doing in these parts? He must be a friend of this Sir Joseph. There wouldn't be anything to require his professional attention hereabouts.'

'Ah! Now that's where you're wrong,' landlord Stephens declared. 'We had a very nasty murder only last week. A very nasty murder indeed and one that shocked everyone hereabouts. Someone shot and killed Edward Kernow, the schoolteacher, right here in Charlestown . . . heaven knows why. He was one of the most inoffensive men you could ever wish to meet. As far as anyone knew, he didn't have an enemy in the world – but this isn't the only murder we've had in Cornwall this year. There were two others, all in the space of a couple of months.' Lowering his voice and looking about him before he spoke again, he added, 'Mind you, the other two were both Excise officers, and they have never been very popular in Cornwall.'

Resisting an urge to comment on the implication that the killing of Revenue officers was not of particular importance, Amos said, 'The Excise service isn't for men who want to be popular, but it's one thing not to like a person – and quite another to kill him.'

'Perfectly true,' agreed Stephens. Increasing the speed of the cloth he was wielding, he added, 'You've got a

23

Cornish accent, sir, but I can't say I've seen you in these parts before.'

'You wouldn't – although I was born near here, at Mevagissey. I joined the Royal Marines as a drummer when I was thirteen and spent most of my service overseas. When I came back I learned my father had disappeared and no one was able to tell me where he had gone. As there was little work for me in Cornwall, I went to London. That was a couple of years ago. Now I've managed to put a little money by and decided to come back and make more inquiries about my father. I'd like to find him again after all those years away.'

'What's his name . . . and what did he do?' the landlord asked, with what seemed to be a genuine interest.

'His name is Hawke . . . the same as mine. *Doniert* Hawke. He was born into a mining family, up on Bodmin Moor. That's why he was given his Christian name. He was born in a house not far from where King Doniert was drowned in the River Fowey, about a thousand years ago.'

'I know nothing about any King Doniert,' Stephens said, 'but if your father was a miner up on the moor why are you looking for him down here?'

'He was working on a mine at Crinnis, just up the hill from here, when he met my mother. She was a fisherman's daughter and when work was slow on the mines he would go out fishing with her family. They lived in Mevagissey.'

'Then wouldn't you be better staying in Mevagissey rather than here?' the landlord queried. 'Not that I'm trying to lose business,' he added hastily. 'I'm merely curious, that's all.'

'That's where I *was* looking for him as soon as I left the Marines,' Amos explained. 'Unfortunately, my father fell out with my mother's family when he married for a second time. They didn't want anything to do with him and I'd been away for so long I felt like a stranger in their company. Then someone in the village told me that when his second wife died they thought my father had signed on as crewman on one of the clay boats, out of either Charlestown or Pentewan, so I thought I'd start my second search for him here.'

'Doniert Hawke, did you say he's called?' Stephens mused. 'I can't say I've ever heard the name mentioned – and I've had the Rashleigh Arms ever since it first opened, six years ago. But a great many boats come in to load china clay so I won't have seen every man who's ever sailed on 'em. If you like, I'll pass the word around that it's the reason you're here. You never know, someone might know of him.'

'I'm much obliged to you, landlord. I trust you will draw an ale for yourself and charge it to my bill.'

'I'll do that, young sir, and thank you. I'll drink to the success of your search for your father.'

Shortly after leaving Amos's table, the landlord returned to the local Charlestown men and it was quite apparent to Amos that he was passing on the information he had learned about him and his reason for being in the small village. Now, the glances that were cast in his direction showed sympathy instead of mistrust and Amos knew he would be able to roam the area observing what was going on and even asking discreet questions without arousing too much suspicion.

Evidence that his story had been accepted by Thomas Stephens, at least, came shortly before Amos left the bar room. The landlord came to his table and, putting a tankard in front of him, gave a conspiratorial wink before whispering, 'Here, young sir, take this with my compliments. I've put it in a tankard so it won't excite the curiosity of anyone who might take an unhealthy interest in it. It's not ale, but some of the finest brandy you're likely to taste anywhere – and all the more enjoyable for coming straight from France without the contamination that comes from the inside of a Customs shed.'

Savouring the brandy, which was all that Stephens had claimed for it, Amos knew that he would be able to confirm to Inspector Carpenter that his theory about smugglers being active in the area was correct.

It might prove to be the first lead in their murder investigation.

5

When Amos rode along the narrow lane to keep his first rendezvous with Detective Inspector Carpenter a quarter-moon was playing hide-and-seek with cirrus cloud that peppered the night sky.

As he approached the Lobb's shop crossroads a small section of the moon showed itself. It was sufficient for Amos to see a mounted figure allowing his horse to crop the grass on a flat verge close to the junction.

It was Inspector Carpenter and he had seen the approaching horseman.

'Is that you, Amos?' he called softly when Amos neared.

Having confirmed his identity and shaken hands with his superior officer, Amos said, 'Shall we ride back towards St Austell, sir? Two horsemen riding at night will excite no interest, even if we were to be seen, which is unlikely. The lane is very quiet.'

Detective Inspector Carpenter agreed and as they set off, riding side by side at a slow walk, he asked, 'Have you learned anything of interest while you have been at Charlestown?'

When Amos told him of the conversation he had had with the landlord of the Rashleigh Arms on the first night of his stay at the Charlestown inn, and the brandy Stephens had given him, the inspector commented, 'So much for Sir Joseph Sawle's magisterial assurance that smuggling is a thing of the past. His suggestion is that we should be looking for a criminal who has returned from transportation bearing a burning grudge against Excise officers.'

'It's an interesting theory,' Amos commented, 'but, as we now know, there *are* smugglers operating in the area and I believe we are most likely to find the killer of the Excise officers among them – although it doesn't explain the murder of the schoolteacher. But it is possible, albeit unlikely, that his murder has no connection with the other two.'

'Unfortunately that is not the case,' Carpenter replied. 'Although Sir Joseph's theories may not be entirely accurate, he is a very efficient magistrate. He had the bodies of the murdered men examined by a surgeon and the bullets removed. All three were examined by a highly experienced armourer from the thirty-second regiment, which is stationed at Bodmin. The armourer declared the bullets to be of a type used in a large calibre pistol, such as that carried by cavalrymen some years ago, but which is now obsolete. Apparently the gun was never extensively issued, but after careful examination of the bullets he is of the opinion that they were all fired from the same weapon.'

'Oh!' Somewhat disconcerted, Amos asked, 'Is there any known association between the dead schoolteacher and the murdered Excise men?'

'That is something we need to find out,' Carpenter replied. 'Since the murder of the schoolteacher there have been no lessons for the boys of Charlestown. I obtained their names and addresses and have already interviewed some of them, but they could not – or would not – tell me anything. You might do better when you come out into the open, but I doubt it.'

They had reached the entrance gate to the Penrice estate where the inspector was staying. He brought his horse to a halt, and as Amos followed suit Carpenter added, 'Of course, it could be that Kernow saw something he wasn't meant to see and recognised someone involved in whatever was going on. However, in order to pursue that line of inquiry we need to know a great deal more about the murdered schoolteacher and I think I know a way this might be achieved – by you.'

'I can't go around asking questions about the schoolteacher's family and his habits without revealing who I am,' Amos protested. 'To do that would make our investigation even more difficult than it already is.'

'Sir Joseph Sawle has provided us with a possible answer to that problem,' Detective Inspector Carpenter replied and Amos thought he sounded irritatingly smug. 'It seems the murdered schoolteacher, Edward Kernow, has a daughter who teaches a class of girls in the mornings, while he taught boys in the evenings.

The arrangement meant that the boys were able to put in a reasonable day's work before gaining some education at night. Unfortunately, in order to keep the school running it needs two teachers, one male and one female, but if Miss Kernow has to pay another teacher out of the income the school generates it will be only just viable. Should anything unfortunate occur to reduce the number of pupils at the school, such as a mine closure, or even a brief epidemic, things would become extremely difficult for Kernow's widow and daughter.'

Alarmed by what he thought to be Carpenter's implication, Amos said, 'You're not asking me to become a teacher? No, sir. I'm willing to try my hand at most things, but not that.'

Detective Inspector Carpenter gave an amused laugh. 'I am not suggesting you should become a schoolteacher, Amos. Sir Joseph Sawle has put it to the widow Kernow that she might take in a lodger to supplement her income. Now, if *you* were to become that lodger, you should be able to learn a great deal about the habits of the murdered man from the two women in his life without appearing too inquisitive. They will no doubt *want* to talk about him.'

While Amos digested the inspector's suggestion, Carpenter said, 'You have said yourself that you should not remain at the Rashleigh Arms for too long because if the landlord and his customers had more time to get to know you they might become more inquisitive about your background and things could become awkward. As it is, you have made yourself known to them and, should it be necessary, you will be able to call in and renew your acquaintanceship without any unwanted questions being raised.'

'That's quite true,' Amos admitted, but with a recent experience of being boarded upon a widow and her impressionable daughter fresh in mind, he added, 'I am not too happy about the thought of taking lodgings with a spinster schoolteacher and her newly widowed mother. If we are after a gang of smugglers our investigation is going to involve a great deal of after-dark work. That might be difficult to explain to them.'

'Nonsense!' Carpenter said. 'I will ask Sir Joseph Sawle to recommend you as a prospective lodger and say that you came to him inquiring after your father. Your search for him is likely to cover a fairly wide area and following up leads will necessitate spending many evenings visiting taverns and similar establishments. The travel involved will mean occasionally returning to your lodgings at an hour when most respectable men and women are in bed. Naturally, you will do your best to keep any disruption to their routine to a minimum and will, of course, be prepared to pay a little more than would a lodger with a more regulated way of life in order to compensate for any inconvenience your comings and goings may cause.'

Amos still had reservations about the whole idea and repeated his earlier misgivings about taking lodgings with a widowed woman and her spinster daughter. 'I won't feel comfortable in such company,' he said, finally, 'and I doubt very much whether they will be at ease having me in their house.'

'We did not come to Cornwall seeking "comfort",'

the inspector retorted. 'We are here to solve three murders. I will inform Sir Joseph that you are in agreement and will call on him tomorrow for his approval. You will tell whoever answers the door to you that you have come seeking Sir Joseph's help to find your missing father. Servants' gossip will ensure that the story of your visit to Penrice, and the reason for it, is generally known – and accepted, as will be your move to take lodgings with widow Kernow. I will leave you to agree with Sir Joseph the amount you pay for your lodgings. He will be providing the money from county funds.'

Their business settled, the two men were about to part company when Carpenter called softly, 'Wait, Amos. I almost forgot. I have something for you.' Edging his horse closer to Amos's mount, he reached into a saddlebag and lifted out a flat box, which he handed to his subordinate.

The box was very heavy, and before placing it in his own saddlebag Amos asked what it contained.

'It's a Beaumont-Adams revolver, an improvement on anything you will have used in the Royal Marines. Carry it with you whenever you go out at night – and use it if you need to. We are dealing with a ruthless man who has killed three times already. I have no wish to have to report to Commissioner Mayne that you have become our murderer's fourth victim.'

6

Following Detective Inspector Carpenter's orders, Amos made his way to Penrice the following afternoon. He had intended going earlier in the day but it had been raining heavily. The rain had now stopped, although the clouds scudding in off the sea were black and heavy and streams of water ran along the narrow lane and filled the ditches on either side.

Reaching the impressive manor house, he dismounted and tethered his horse, securing the reins through a ring set into a heavy block of granite to one side of the pillared entrance porch.

After tugging on the bell-rope hanging beside the front door, he was required to state his business to a maid who must already have been in the hallway. Because of her uncertainty that the matter was important enough to disturb Sir Joseph Sawle, he was asked to repeat it to the butler.

Eventually, Amos was escorted by that august figure to the study to meet the St Austell magistrate. Here, the elderly baronet shook hands and invited him to seat himself in one of the leather armchairs placed conveniently about the spacious dark-panelled room.

When the door closed behind the butler, Sir Joseph said, 'So you are the young man who is helping Inspector Carpenter with his investigation. He speaks very highly of you. I understand you were commissioned in the field while fighting with the Royal Marines Light Infantry, in the Crimea?'

'Yes, Sir Joseph.' Amos did not feel called upon to amplify his statement.

Nodding approval, Sir Joseph said, 'My late father was a seagoing man – an admiral, but that would have been considerably before your time. Why did you leave the service? Having received a commission in such a manner future promotion would have been assured for you.'

'Possibly, sir, but . . .' Amos gave Sir Joseph the explanation he had given to Detective Inspector Carpenter when he asked the same question.

'That's the damnable thing about money,' the baronet commented when Amos had finished. 'It's supposed to be beneath one's dignity to discuss it . . . but it's a sight more demeaning to be without it – and that's the problem facing poor Edward Kernow's widow and daughter. The pair of them were in here talking it over with me only yesterday. Poor widow Kernow was in tears. She came from a good family background, but married for love, and not for security. It was my suggestion that taking a paying guest might help them out for a while. Talwyn, the daughter, agreed somewhat reluctantly and I said I would try to find a suitable person for them. When I mentioned the discussion to Inspector Carpenter he immediately suggested it might prove useful to have you living in their household. I think it a first class idea, for very many reasons, but said I would like to meet you first. They have suffered a dreadful tragedy and the last thing I would want is to billet an unsuitable lodger upon them. I feel I owe that to poor Edward Kernow. He was a good man, honest and dedicated. He did not deserve to meet his end in such a tragic manner.'

Lifting a small wooden box from his desk, Sir Joseph took out a cigar, then, as an afterthought, proffered the box to Amos. When Amos declined with a shake of his head, Sir Joseph lit his cigar with a taper he drew from the fire before continuing, 'Now I have met you I am satisfied you will prove a suitable addition to the household of a recently bereaved woman.'

Although Sir Joseph was satisfied, Amos still entertained the misgivings he had voiced to Carpenter and he said hesitantly, 'I am happy that you think so, Sir Joseph, but I am not at all certain the irregular hours I shall be obliged to keep will fit into the routine of a widowed woman and her spinster schoolteacher daughter.'

An expression momentarily came to Sir Joseph Sawle's face in which Amos thought he detected amusement, but when the baronet replied all he said was, 'I am quite certain you will make allowances for each other and have no doubt the arrangement will prove convenient for you, for widow Kernow – and for her spinster daughter.'

Once again Amos thought he detected a glint of unexplained humour in the baronet's expression . . . but Sir Joseph had more to say. 'Besides, they must be aware that as they live so far out of town it will not be easy to find another suitable lodger. I will speak to them later today. I suggest you call on them tomorrow . . . shall we say early afternoon? You will see their cottage among the trees on the left as you go out along the driveway. If tomorrow is not convenient for them I will send word to you at the Rashleigh Arms.'

Mounted once more, Amos thought it looked as though the rain was moving in from the sea again and he put his horse into a trot in order that he might beat it to the Rashleigh Arms.

He had almost reached the end of the long driveway that curved away from the house when a young woman he took to be a servant from Penrice came through the open gateway from the lane carrying a basket laden with provisions.

Amos immediately slowed his mount so as not to alarm her, but as he did so a large dog that he had earlier observed running loose among the trees in the park with its nose to the ground suddenly leaped on to the driveway, barking, and greeting the young woman with tail-wagging enthusiasm.

The exuberant animal startled Amos's horse, causing it to rear up unexpectedly. As Amos fought to bring the animal under control he was aware that the young woman was dangerously close. He maintained his seat with some difficulty but by the time he had his mount under control they were in the lane. Looking back, he was dismayed to see the young woman sitting on the wet ground inside the gateway, trying to ward off the dog, which was enthusiastically licking her face, provisions from her basket strewn about her.

Concerned for her well-being, Amos hurriedly dismounted and, leading his horse, went back through the gate.

'Are you all right?' he asked anxiously.

Struggling to her feet, she looked behind her to where mud and water stained the back of her cloak, the wetness having soaked through to her skin. 'Yes, I am all right,' she replied, 'but it is no thanks to you – or your horse. It might be suitable for a hunt meeting, but it is certainly not safe to be near people.'

'That's quite unfair,' Amos protested. 'What happened was most unfortunate, but it was a pure accident – and if any blame is to be apportioned, then it has to be the dog's fault. Had it not barked and run in front of my mount this wouldn't have happened.'

'A well-trained horse would not have been startled by a dog,' she retorted. 'It wasn't aggressive.'

'I wouldn't argue with that,' Amos agreed, 'but I have only owned the animal for a few days and know very little about its habits. Not that it changes anything in any way at all. It was entirely the fault of the dog ... But let me help you pick things up. If anything is seriously damaged, tell Sir Joseph Sawle I will reimburse him.'

'I can manage quite well on my own, thank you,' she said angrily. 'If you really want to do something useful

37

then you can take that horse away before it goes crazy again.'

The young woman was already retrieving the provisions that were scattered on the ground about her and, in truth, Amos's horse did seem to be unsettled by the presence of the dog, which was now enthusiastically investigating the contents of the basket. Amos repeated his apology and his offer to pay for any damage, before leading the horse away. A short distance along the lane, he looked back and saw the young woman hurrying along the driveway towards Penrice manor, her bonnet askew and a large muddy patch staining the rear of her pale blue cloak.

7

The day after Amos's meeting with Sir Joseph Sawle was a Sunday, and he set off for the cottage of widow Kernow and her daughter in a less than positive mood. Despite all that had been said by Detective Inspector Carpenter and by Sir Joseph, he was still not convinced that taking lodgings in the home of the two women was a good idea.

The cloud and rain of the previous day had disappeared and it was now warm and pleasant, with only an occasional white cloud drifting leisurely across an otherwise unmarred blue sky. Because it was such a fine day Amos had chosen to walk to the Penrice estate. Along the way he paused to gaze out to sea and admire a merchantman under full sail, which could clearly be seen hugging the Cornish coast, en route to the Atlantic Ocean.

He was in no particular hurry to reach the Kernow

cottage, but once he entered the wooded grounds of the manor house he squared his shoulders and told himself this was just part of the work necessary to solve another case – and one that had already brought him an unexpected and welcome promotion.

Halfway along the woodland path to the cottage he met the dog that had caused his horse to rear with such unfortunate results on the previous day. Today, although seemingly pleased to see him, the animal was less exuberant and trotted happily alongside him until, within sight of the Kernows' cottage, a rabbit suddenly bolted from cover. The dog took off after it, leaving Amos to go on his way alone.

He had half hoped the occupants of the cottage might be absent, but arriving at the cottage gate he saw a small and motherly woman on her knees at the edge of a flower bed in the front garden, digging out weeds and dividing clumps of primroses.

When she saw Amos she climbed stiffly to her feet to greet him. She was younger than he had expected her to be, perhaps in her early fifties, but she appeared tired and careworn.

'Mrs Kernow?' Amos paused at the gate.

'That's right – and you will be Mr Hawke. Sir Joseph Sawle said you would be calling today about taking up lodgings with us ... with my daughter and myself. Unfortunately, my daughter is not here at the moment. She is taking a Sunday school class at Charlestown church.'

'Oh! If you would prefer her to be here I can come back another time ...'

Maisie Kernow had been studying Amos as he spoke and she hesitated for only a moment before saying, 'No, she should not be very long now – and you come with Sir Joseph's recommendation.'

'It is very kind of him to recommend me to you but, as I told him, I am not at all certain that the hours I must keep will be suitable in a household of two ladies. You see, I am trying to find my father and my inquiries are taking me to inns and taverns along the coast hereabouts where the men I wish to speak to are usually only there late in the evenings.'

Maisie Kernow had again been scrutinising him closely as he spoke and now she said, 'Yours is an honourable quest, Mr Hawke, and so long as you conduct yourself with consideration for my daughter and myself and do not come home the worse for drink, your comings and goings should present no problems – not that I am suggesting total abstinence. I have no objection to a man's taking a drink and would occasionally enjoy one with my late husband. As for disturbing us with your comings and goings, my daughter and I sleep in the two front bedrooms. If I gave you the back bedroom and the key to the back door we would hardly hear you. It is probably not necessary to lock the doors – we never did when my husband was alive – but now my daughter and I are alone . . .'

She did not complete the sentence and Amos said quickly, 'I was very sorry to hear of your tragic loss, Mrs Kernow, and quite understand. As for my drinking habits, I can assure you that I will *never* return to the cottage having had too much to drink.'

Uncomfortably aware of his deception in keeping secret his real reason for seeking lodgings at her cottage, Amos was grateful to be able to express the truth about something that mattered to her. Although his investigations would entail drinking, it would of necessity be in moderation. Although he hoped that drink might loosen the tongues of others, *he* would need to be alert at all times. Both the investigation and his career as a detective were dependent upon his sobriety.

Maisie Kernow had already decided that she liked this young man. Quietly spoken, he was also extremely personable. Making up her mind, she said, 'Would you like to come in and see the room I can offer you? Then, if you think it would suit you, we can sit down and discuss details over a cup of tea. I . . . I have never had a lodger before. It has never been necessary, so I am not quite certain what needs to be settled . . . but my daughter will soon be home. She is a very bright girl and will have thought about such things.'

Accepting the offer, Amos followed her into the cottage and was struck by the unexpected air of comfort and cleanliness in the stone-floored interior. The bedroom she had to offer impressed him too. It was larger than he had expected it to be and was light, clean and fresh. It even had a small desk upon which he could work. From the window there was a view over a fair-sized vegetable garden that was as neat as the house and Amos guessed correctly that Maisie Kernow was the gardener. At the end of the garden was an orchard and beyond that open fields which sloped away to give a view of the sea beyond Charlestown. There were also a couple of outbuildings, one of which looked as though it had once been a stable.

Despite his earlier misgivings about lodging here, Amos was forced to admit to himself that it was a most attractive room – and he said so to Maisie Kernow.

'I am so pleased that you like it. Now, would you like to come down to the kitchen? I will make a pot of tea and you can tell me something about yourself . . .'

Not only was Maisie Kernow a good listener, but she had an ability to ask pertinent questions. As a result, Amos found himself telling her far more about himself, his service with the Royal Marines, and his childhood in Cornwall than he had intended, although he succeeded in saying very little about the time he had spent in London since leaving the Marines. In fact, he believed he had probably given his listener the impression that his service career had ended only recently.

After he had drunk two cups of tea and answered all the questions that Maisie put to him, there was a lull in the conversation – and Talwyn Kernow had still not returned to the house.

Maisie was quite happy with the thought of having Amos as a lodger, but she would not make a firm commitment until the arrangement had been approved by Talwyn. For his part, Amos had reconciled his earlier doubts and believed he would be comfortable in the homely and well-kept little cottage. They agreed he should call at the house again later that same evening in order to meet Maisie's daughter.

As Maisie was letting him out of the cottage, still

engaged in conversation, there was the sound of the garden gate shutting and Amos looked up to see the young woman who had been knocked over by his horse advancing towards him along the garden path. Behind her, shut out on the far side of the gate, was the dog which had been the cause of the previous day's unfortunate incident.

'Ah . . . here she is. Here *is* Talwyn . . .' Maisie Kernow said.

Her daughter was not listening. Her gaze fixed firmly on Amos, she said angrily, 'What are *you* doing here? I hope you have come to apologise properly for knocking me over yesterday and to pay for the damage you caused – not to mention injuries to myself. I have a bruise the size of a saucer . . . !'

Suddenly remembering where the bruise was situated, she stopped short and blushed, but the embarrassment served only to fuel her rage. 'I bought six eggs in the market but when I got them home I found five had been broken – and they cost me a penny each. That isn't all. When I tried to wash the mud from my cloak it took most of the colour from it and now it's unwearable. If you don't believe me, you can look on the line behind the house. It's there – with the dress I was wearing. That cloak cost me four and sixpence only last fair day – and I certainly won't be able to afford another for a long while . . .'

Suddenly remembering *why* she was unable to afford another shawl and choking on the uncharacteristic anger which seemed to have come out of nowhere, Talwyn felt her throat constrict, and, pushing between Amos and her dumbfounded mother, she fled into the house.

'I am *so* sorry, Mr Hawke,' said Maisie, sounding thoroughly confused. 'I have never known Talwyn behave in such a manner. I know the loss of her father has been a terrible shock to her . . . to all of us . . . but she has been so strong until this moment. She has truly been my rock. I must apologise to you.'

'There is no need,' Amos said. 'I really do understand how she must be feeling.'

'But . . . I don't even know what it was all about.'

Amos gave her brief details of what had occurred at the entrance to Penrice the previous day. He ended his tale by pointing to the dog which was whining outside the garden gate. 'That dog played a part in it, but your daughter is quite correct, it *was* my fault. I should have been able to control my horse.'

As he was talking he had been feeling inside a pocket of his waistcoat and now his hand came out with a silver crown held between two fingers. It was more than he could really afford to give away but, holding it out to Maisie, he said, 'Please give her this to reimburse her for the broken eggs – and to pay for a new cloak the next time the fair comes round.'

When Maisie began to protest, Amos took her hand and, placing the coin in her palm, curled her fingers round it. 'No, you *must* take it. I promised her yesterday that I would pay for any damage that may have been caused. As I said before, I should have been able to control my horse. Go into the house and make another cup of tea, for Talwyn – and for yourself too. I think she has been holding her emotions in for too long. She will need comforting.'

'You are very kind . . . and thank you.' Hesitantly, she added, 'Will you be calling on us later this evening?'

Amos shook his head. 'I don't think that would be a very good idea. In view of what has happened I think we must forget any idea of my coming to lodge with you. Now, go to Talwyn. She needs you.'

Walking along the driveway towards the road Amos thought of what had occurred. Contrary to the emotions he had entertained on his way to the cottage, he now felt very real regret at not being able to lodge with the widow and the schoolteacher. Recalling an angry Talwyn seated on the wet grass, bonnet awry and provisions scattered about her, he gave a wry smile. She was not at all how he had envisaged Maisie Kernow's daughter would be. Talwyn was both spirited and attractive. He believed that had they not had such an unfortunate first meeting he might have found it both comfortable and interesting lodging with Maisie Kernow – and her spinster daughter.

8

When she did not find Talwyn anywhere on the ground floor of their cottage, Maisie climbed the stairs and knocked upon the door of her daughter's bedroom. There was no reply but she could hear sounds from inside the room and gently opened the door.

The sounds she had heard were muffled sobs. Talwyn was slumped in an armchair in a corner of her room, hands covering her face and her shoulders heaving.

Dropping to her knees beside the armchair, Maisie gathered her daughter in her arms, holding her close for the first time since Talwyn had been a young girl. 'It's all right, Talwyn. Just let it out, my love. I've been expecting this since we lost Daddy. It had to happen – you have been far *too* brave.'

Even as she was comforting her daughter, tears were coursing down Maisie's own cheeks, but she wept silently today. The noise of her grief had occurred in the quiet of an empty cottage, when Talwyn was away teaching in the Charlestown school.

Gradually, Talwyn brought her anguish under control, and when she raised her head and saw tears on her mother's cheeks she remembered guiltily that she was not the only one grieving for her dead father. Suddenly remorseful, she said, 'I am so sorry . . . I have upset you too. I never meant to do that . . . but I never intended this should happen to me, either.'

'I am glad it has,' Maisie replied. 'Especially glad that it has happened here, with me close at hand to comfort you. I was concerned you might suddenly break down at school, in front of all those young girls.'

'Yes, that would have been dreadful,' Talwyn agreed. As she spoke she plucked a handkerchief from her sleeve and pressed it against each eye in turn. 'It was bad enough allowing myself to become so cross with that man outside in the garden – even though he deserved it.'

'Are you quite certain of that?' Maisie asked gently. 'He told me what happened yesterday, at the gate to the lane. He accepted full responsibility for the unfortunate incident but I can't help feeling that Skellum was the real culprit.' Skellum was the name of their dog, which had been obtained as a small pup from a Dutch ship trading into Charlestown. 'Anyway, whether Mr Hawke was at fault or not, he asked me to give you this.' Handing the silver crown to her daughter, Maisie added, 'He said you were to use it to buy a new cloak at the next St Austell fair.'

Maisie was relieved to have something to say that

48

would take Talwyn's mind off the grief she felt over the death of her father – and her words certainly did that.

'Mr Hawke?' Talwyn exclaimed. 'Isn't that the name of the man Sir Joseph recommended to us as a lodger? You don't mean . . . ? Oh, no! We couldn't possibly have him living here. He is quite unsuitable.'

'Had you not met him in such unfortunate circumstances I think your opinion of him would be very different,' Maisie declared. 'I had a long talk with him before you came home and found him to be a very likeable young man. In fact, he originally came from these parts.'

'If he has family in Cornwall, what is he doing around here, looking for lodgings?' Talwyn asked suspiciously. 'And what is his connection with Sir Joseph?'

'He has come back to Cornwall to look for his father, who left Mevagissey while he was out of the country,' Maisie explained. 'He seems to have disappeared rather mysteriously and Mr Hawke is very concerned for him.'

'I still don't understand why he should want to find lodgings,' Talwyn persisted, determined not to agree with her mother about Amos. 'He must be staying somewhere at the moment.'

'He is at the Rashleigh Arms in Charlestown – very close to the school,' Maisie explained, 'but staying at an inn is expensive and he expects to be in Cornwall for some time. When he visited Sir Joseph to inquire whether his father had ever come to his notice during the course of his magisterial duties, he happened to mention that he was looking for lodgings.' Looking speculatively at her daughter, Maisie added, 'Sir Joseph must have taken

49

a liking to Mr Hawke, or he would not have recommended him.'

'Be that as it may,' Talwyn said, 'I don't suppose our cottage would suit him. If Sir Joseph likes him so much why doesn't he offer to put him up there?'

Ignoring the question, Maisie said, 'In fact, Mr Hawke thought our cottage would suit him very well. He said so when I showed him the back bedroom. He would have taken the room there and then, but I told him you must approve him first. As you weren't home at the time he said he would come back to speak to you this evening.'

'He is coming back?' Talwyn was dismayed. 'No, Mother. He is not suitable – and I don't want to speak to him again.'

'You won't have to,' Maisie said. 'The arrangement was made before you arrived home. After your tirade he said that in view of what had happened yesterday you would not want him staying here.' Despondently, she added, 'It is a pity . . . a *great* pity, because I like him and would have been happy to have him about the house. I doubt if we will find a prospective lodger I like more . . . that's if we succeed in finding anyone at all. I can remember talking to Emily Dunne on the subject . . . she was a spinster who lived just up the lane, by Lobb's shop, when you were no more than a baby. When her ninety-three-year-old father died, she was desperate to find a paying guest, so that she could afford to stay in the cottage where she had lived since the day she was born. Unfortunately, those who did come to look at the house went away again, saying it was too far away from anywhere. In the end she had to leave and it broke her heart. She was dead herself within three months.'

'Well, at least it hasn't come to that for us.' Talwyn spoke without conviction. She was well aware there was barely enough money coming into the house for her and her mother to live on.

Maisie was fully aware of the situation too . . . more so than her daughter. 'We might not be in that situation *yet*,' she said grimly, 'but it won't be long before we are. Your father was a wonderful man, but accumulating money was never important to him. As long as we were comfortable, he never felt the need for anything more. Any spare money went straight back into the school – to buy books, or pencils – or even to subsidise those children whose parents were going through a bad patch.'

'I still have the girls to teach,' Talwyn said, determined to be optimistic. 'So we are not likely to starve.'

'That is unfortunately not true, Talwyn. You have been too upset to fully realise the situation we are in. When Daddy was alive we had money from both the boys' and the girls' schools coming into the house and were able to manage quite comfortably, but now that income has been halved. Even if we *are* able to find a teacher for the boys, we will need to pay him almost as much as he makes. If we do not, and fail to keep the boys' school open, we are in very real trouble. Families will not pay for their daughters to have lessons while their sons have none. Daddy found it difficult enough as it was to convince many of the parents that their daughters needed educating at all. So, you see, if we don't have a boys' school the number of girls attending your classes in the mornings is going to fall away alarmingly. If that happens Sir Joseph will think twice about letting you keep the school going for no more than a handful of girls. Without a school there is no reason why he should allow an out-of-work schoolteacher and her mother to live rent free in one of his cottages. We must be able to pay for a teacher in the boys' school – and we need to have him there as a matter of great urgency!'

Talwyn realised that all her mother had said was true, but she said stubbornly, '*I* could take on the boys' school, Ma . . . for long enough to ensure both schools remained open, anyway.'

Maisie shook her head. 'That might work if we were talking only of *young* boys, but some of them are as old as sixteen – and I believe Daddy had some pupils even older than that. At that age they are not boys, but young men – and you are not very much older. They would not take discipline from you and I doubt if their parents would accept you as their teacher. It would not be proper. No, Talwyn, if we are to keep the school running as Daddy would have wished, we must have a man to teach them. If we are to afford that and not live like paupers as a result, we need to take a lodger. Amos Hawke not only would have fulfilled that role, but was also prepared to pay a little extra because of any inconvenience he might have caused by the hours he keeps in the search for his father. In other words – he would have been the perfect lodger.'

9

Later that evening, Amos was seated in the bar room of the Rashleigh Arms making a pint of ale last as long as was possible without drawing attention to himself, when he saw a shabbily dressed man enter the room and look about him at the customers.

The landlord saw him too and moved quickly to intercept him. There was a brief conversation between the two men and then, to Amos's surprise, the landlord turned and pointed in his direction before returning to where the ale casks were stowed behind the bar. He continued to watch the shabbily dressed newcomer suspiciously as he made his way across the room to where Amos was seated with a tankard held to his lips.

Coming to a halt beside the table, the scruffy newcomer waited until Amos lowered his drink before saying, 'Is it you who's asking around after Doniert Hawke?'

Feeling a sudden surge of excitement, Amos replied eagerly, 'That's right – do you know where he is?'

'Not exactly . . . but talking's a thirsty business and nothing's passed my lips all day . . .'

The landlord was still looking in their direction and Amos signalled for him to bring two tankards of ale to the table before saying to the man standing before him, 'A drink is on its way. Sit down and tell me what you know of my father . . . but, first, what's your name?'

There was an aroma exuding from the other man that Amos recognised from his days as a uniformed police constable in the poorest areas of London. The odour of an unwashed body and the filthy clothes worn by a man who 'slept rough', spending his nights in derelict houses and other unsavoury places.

'My name doesn't matter,' said the malodorous stranger, 'and it would mean nothing to you if I told you. I've answered to a great many names in my time, so you can call me whatever you like. I'll tell you what I know about your father – but I warn you right away, it ain't much.'

'Whatever it is, it will be more than I've learned in Cornwall so far,' Amos replied. 'He might have disappeared into thin air for all anyone round here seems to know about him . . . or care, for that matter.'

As he was speaking the landlord arrived at the table, ale overflowing from the two tankards he carried in one hand. Placing them on the table between Amos and his anonymous companion, he left after giving the latter a disapproving glance.

Reaching out for one of the tankards, the unkempt

stranger downed half its contents before lowering it to the table and returning his attention to Amos. 'Are you the son Doniert used to talk about? The one who went to sea as a drummer boy in the Marines?'

The doubts Amos had entertained about this man's ever having met his father disappeared and he felt a sense of pleasure at his words. 'He spoke of me? Where was this . . . and how long ago?'

'Quite a while – but don't ask me exactly *how* long. Time hasn't meant much to me for a long time now, but I was in regular work when we first met. We were both mining for copper at the Wheal Notter by Henwood village, up on Bodmin Moor. Me and your father worked on the same pare together for a while.'

Aware that 'pare' was the Cornish miners' word for 'team of workers', Amos asked, 'Why did you leave? Was my father still working there when you left?'

The stranger shook his head. 'The lodes began to run on to Wheal Phoenix ground – and they were a lot bigger and richer than the Wheal Notter. There was trouble up there and when they threatened to take the Wheal Notter to court the owner called it a day and closed the mine down. By then many other mines in Cornwall were cutting back – especially in the far west. Miners began flocking to the moor to find work that just wasn't there. I've seen a hundred miners clamouring for every job that came up and things got very nasty, especially when the western men hit on the idea of setting on moorland miners, deliberately breaking arms or legs in order to apply for the crippled men's jobs. I'm not saying all western men were the same, but there was a hard core that would stop at nothing to make a living – and some of 'em are still around.'

By now the ex-miner had emptied his tankard of ale and was becoming garrulous. Amos suspected he was drinking on an empty stomach, but he wanted to keep him talking. 'What happened to my father when Wheal Notter closed? Did he stay on the moor?'

Looking down into his empty tankard, Amos's companion said slyly, 'Talking so much makes a man thirsty.'

Pushing the second full tankard across the table, but keeping hold of it, Amos said, 'Here, you can have this. I still have some left in my own. But when did you last eat?'

'I don't know,' was the vague reply. 'Sometime yesterday . . . I think.'

Beckoning to the landlord, who had seldom allowed his gaze to wander far from their table, Amos ordered one of the large pasties that he knew were kept warm in the kitchen behind the bar.

The landlord was not at all eager to serve Amos's dirty and badly dressed companion, and he said, 'You can have a pasty for him, but I want him out of here when the bar begins to get busy. The smell of him will put customers off their food and drink and I'll lose money.'

'I don't think it will take him long to tell me all he knows about my father,' Amos said. 'So the sooner you bring the pasty the quicker he'll be gone.'

When the grumbling landlord had left the table, Amos turned to his companion and said, 'Right! You have a second drink, and there's food coming up for you, but before you get either I want a name I can call you. Whether it's the right one or not doesn't much matter, just as long as I can call you something.'

For a moment it seemed the other man might argue, but then he shrugged. 'You can call me Cap'n Billy. It's what your father called me.'

Amos looked at 'Captain Billy' in disbelief. 'You were a mine captain?'

'No – but I was a shift cap'n for a while,' his companion corrected him. 'That was before I grew too fond of this.' He pointed to the tankard of ale Amos held.

Just then the landlord returned to the table with a hot pasty and two thick hunks of bread and butter resting beside it on a battered pewter plate. Explaining his unexpected generosity, he said, 'By the looks of him he hasn't eaten for a while and this is yesterday's bread. It won't keep for another day.'

When the landlord had gone, Captain Billy's gaze was riveted on the plate which held the bread and pasty. Amos finally released the tankard, but said, 'You'd better get that food down before you have any more to drink. While you're eating you can tell me what you know of my father after you both left the Wheal Notter.'

Before Amos had finished talking, Captain Billy had taken two large bites from the pasty. Seemingly finding some difficulty in swallowing, he washed the mouthful down with a large draught of ale.

'I'm waiting,' Amos said unsympathetically. 'Perhaps I should take the plate away until you've told me what I want to know.'

Half choking on the food, Captain Billy croaked, 'There's not much more I can tell you. I came down this way, to the mines over at Polgooth, hoping to find work underground, and the last I heard of your father was that he had fallen in with a bad crowd. I can't tell you any more than that.'

Amos was convinced he was being lied to, but at that moment his companion glanced towards the door and his eyes opened wide with what Amos later decided was sheer terror.

Turning round quickly, Amos saw half a dozen men entering the bar room led by a black-bearded giant of a man. All were dressed roughly, in clothes of a type worn by miners rather than fishermen, and Amos's interest increased when the landlord hurried across the room to meet them. Despite their unprepossessing appearance, Stephens greeted them with a deference that bordered upon servility.

As the new arrivals sat down the large bearded man cast a glance around the room. When it fell upon Amos the detective turned back to Captain Billy – only to find he was no longer there. The remains of the pasty had disappeared too, along with the bread, although a half-full tankard of ale remained on the table.

There was a door at the end of the room farthest from the entrance and Amos knew it led to a small yard at the back of the inn. From here another door opened on to the cobbled alleyway which ran beneath the window of the room he occupied. Captain Billy must have made his exit by that route – and in a great hurry. Amos realised that his companion's precipitate departure from the bar room had something to do with the sight of the bearded man and his companions, and he wondered what it was.

Soon after the bearded man and his party had received their drinks, the landlord came across the room to where Amos was seated and gathered up the empty pewter plate. Pushing the half-empty tankard left by Captain Billy towards him, Amos said, 'You can take this too. It was left by the man who was supposed to be telling me what he knew of my father. He left in something of a hurry.'

'Before finishing his drink?' the landlord said. 'He *must* have been in a rush to leave. What did you say to him?'

'I didn't have an opportunity to say anything,' Amos replied. 'I'd turned round to watch the men who'd just come in and when I looked back he was no longer here!'

'Then I suggest you check whether you still have your purse,' the landlord said cynically.

'It will still be here,' Amos declared, aware that Captain Billy could not have stolen it from his pocket, 'but I felt he could have told me more than he did about my father. When he disappeared I was looking at that black-bearded giant you were just serving. I have a feeling I might have seen him somewhere before . . . is he a Cornish wrestling champion? What's his name?'

Amos was sure he had never seen the man before but he wanted to know the man's name and perhaps learn the reason why Captain Billy should have been so frightened of him that he would want to escape from the bar room without being seen.

'I don't know,' Stephens replied quickly, and Amos knew instinctively that he was lying. 'As landlord of an inn I've learned not to ask too many questions of my customers. He's a miner who occasionally comes in here with his friends. All I need to know is that they're prepared to spend their money freely. Now, would you like another ale?'

Amos ordered another drink and made it last for the time in which the bearded man and his friends had another five or six rapidly downed rounds. During the course of their drinking they became noisier and Amos recognised the accent of at least two of them as being that of Bodmin Moor. His curiosity grew and he was determined to remain in the bar room as long as they did and try to see where they went when they left.

It was not going to be easy. Even though the men had grown noisier with drink, he was aware they were also taking more than a passing interest in *him*. In a repetition of what had occurred on Amos's first night at the inn, the landlord was called upon to answer questions about his presence in the bar room and what he was doing in Charlestown, but on this occasion Amos had the impression that the men were not entirely satisfied with the landlord's explanation.

Eventually, at about 10.30 p.m., the bearded giant rose to his feet and the others quickly downed what remained of their drinks and followed suit. The party then made their way to the door, offering no words of farewell to the landlord, or to anyone else, but as they went their leader gave Amos a searching, sidelong glance.

When they had gone, Amos drained the last dregs of

ale from his tankard and, trying to appear unhurried, made his way to the door.

As he reached the doorway another customer was leaving and Amos let him pass out first. Then, stepping into the unlighted street, he looked up and down to see if he could make out the black-bearded miner and his friends.

He saw them almost immediately, silhouetted in the light from numerous oil lamps burning around the harbour where, despite the late hour, ships were still being loaded and unloaded. In the same instant, he realised that although six men had left the Rashleigh Arms together, there were now only five of them walking away.

The inn customer who had pushed past Amos was walking in the same direction. He was quite a way behind the others when a man suddenly stepped from the deep doorway of a fisherman's loft and confronted him.

After a brief exchange of words between the two, the lone customer continued on his way towards the harbour, the man who had accosted him stepping back into the shadow of the loft entrance once more.

With a thrill of excitement, Amos realised that the black-bearded man had been suspicious enough of *him* to leave one of the party behind to check whether he would attempt to follow them. It made him more determined than before to learn the identity of the big man, but he wondered what would have happened had it been *he* and not the other man who had been accosted?

One thing was quite certain: the miners were up to no good – and they were extremely wary of strangers. Amos decided it would be foolhardy to try to follow them tonight, but he would make discreet inquiries about them – the big, bearded man in particular.

He returned to the bar room once more. Thomas Stephens appeared to be startled to see him and, cheerily, Amos said, 'It's smoky in here tonight, landlord. I needed to step outside for some fresh air before going to bed. I'll see you at breakfast. Good night to you.'

Much later that night, Amos was awakened by noises in the alleyway beneath his open window. He heard low voices and what sounded like hooves slipping on the cobblestones. They were followed by quick and uncertain footsteps, as if something heavy was being carried from the lane to the yard at the back of the inn, via the door which must have been used by Captain Billy when he fled from the bar room.

Then Amos heard the low voices again, and this time was able to distinguish the accent: it was moorland Cornish. He believed at least one was a voice he had last heard coming from the table where the bearded man sat with his friends.

There were more sounds before he heard a bolt being thrust home on the inside of the yard door. Amos had no doubt that a firkin or two of smuggled brandy had just been delivered to the Rashleigh Arms.

He might or might not be closer to solving the murders of the Excise men and schoolteacher Kernow, but he realised he had confirmed that smuggling was definitely taking place on this part of the Cornish coast. He also believed that in the bar room of the Rashleigh Arms that evening he had looked upon the men involved.

10

The next morning Amos was first down for breakfast. As soon as he had eaten, he collected his horse from the inn stables and took a ride along the coast to the west of Charlestown for about half an hour. When he was satisfied there was nothing to be found in that direction he retraced his route and headed eastwards from his original starting place. Here, at the far end of a long sandy beach, within sight of Charlestown, he found what he was looking for.

Around high tide mark the sand had been recently – very recently – churned up by the hooves of many animals that might have been donkeys or horses, but Amos believed to be mules, the pack animals favoured by mine owners – and smugglers. The hoofprints led him to where there was a track up the slope of the nearby cliff.

Amos led his horse up the steep path, then remounted and followed the hoofprints across the rough ground away from the cliff. At first he believed them to be leading him to a mine complex situated nearby, but very soon the tracks bypassed the mine, heading inland.

He continued following the trail for some hours, losing it more than once, usually at a spot where the animals had left the poorly maintained road to avoid passing through a village, but searching doggedly back and forth he found it again. He estimated that there must have been at least thirty and possibly as many as forty animals in the group, and there were the footprints of almost as many men. Men who wore the type of stout, wide-soled boots made to stand up to the rigours of work underground.

Mules had long been used to carry ore from the mines to ports or railway sidings. Although replaced by narrow gauge railways on many of the larger mines, they were still used by some smaller or more remote workings, especially on Bodmin Moor – and the longer Amos followed the trail, the more convinced he became that this was the destination of the men and animals whose trail he was following.

He was equally convinced this was smuggling on a very large scale. If the contraband was brandy then each mule was capable of carrying the equivalent of a barrel-load, split up into smaller barrels, or ankers. Brought in on a regular basis, it could make someone very rich. Rich enough to kill if such an act became necessary in order to remain in business.

Following the smugglers' trail took far longer than Amos had anticipated. He had still not arrived on Bodmin Moor by late afternoon and rain clouds were beginning to gather over the high ground of the moor. Once the rain arrived it would wash away all trace of the route taken by the mules and, in addition, he had no waterproof clothing in his saddlebags, so he decided to head back to Charlestown.

He managed to reach the Rashleigh Arms before darkness fell, but he did not beat the rain and arrived there thoroughly soaked. After stabling his horse and instructing the ostler to dry the animal off before feeding it and settling it down for the night, he entered the inn and went straight to his room to change into dry clothes.

Instead of going down for a meal immediately, he pored over a map of the area which he had purchased in St Austell on his arrival in Cornwall. Tracing the route he had taken that day, he contemplated the possible destination of the smugglers. He felt certain they would have a safe hideaway for their contraband goods and believed the most likely place would be a disused mine. However, searching for it would be dangerous, even though Captain Billy had provided him with a reason for being on the moor by telling him his father had once worked there.

As a result of his labours, Amos was much later than usual going down to supper that night and was well into his meal before the landlord took time off from the bar room to check on the dining room and saw him eating.

Disappearing again for a few moments, he returned bearing an envelope which he handed to Amos, saying, 'This was delivered for you this morning. I would have given it to you earlier, but I wasn't aware you'd returned to the inn.'

'I went straight to my room when I came in,' Amos

explained. 'I stayed out too long and got soaked. I needed to change everything before I caught a chill.'

The landlord made duly sympathetic noises, and added, 'Before you retire for the night bring your wet clothes down and I'll get one of the maids to dry and iron them ready for you in the morning.'

'That's very kind of you,' said Amos, but his mind was not really on what Stephens was saying. He was puzzled by the envelope, on which was written, in very neat handwriting, 'Mr Hawke'.

'Who can be sending me a letter?' he asked. 'I don't know anyone in the area well enough for them to write to me.'

'Well, there is only one way to find out,' the landlord said. 'It was delivered this morning by one of the girls from the school. She said that Miss Kernow, the teacher, had asked her to bring it to you.'

'Ah!' Amos felt suddenly enlightened. 'It will no doubt be a thank you note. I was passing her in the lane when a dog frightened my horse. It caused her to fall over and muddy her cloak and break some eggs she was carrying. She was very angry about it at the time, so yesterday I called at her cottage and left some money with her mother as compensation.'

'That was very kind of you, Mr Hawke,' said the landlord. 'She's had a lot to cope with, what with her father being sadly murdered and all. She's a very pretty young woman – but a couple of our workers in the kitchen here have young daughters at the school and they say she has quite a temper on her and will take no nonsense from the older girls.'

'I shouldn't think she would take nonsense from anyone,' Amos replied ruefully. 'Not girls, boys or men. But it is very sad about her father's death. I believe it's something of a mystery. What do *you* think happened?'

The landlord looked startled. 'Me? I don't have any idea . . . and I don't want to know. Even if I did I'd keep my mouth tight shut. The secret of being a good landlord is to forget everything you see and hear, and say nothing that matters to anyone. But I've been away from the bar room long enough. I'd best be getting back in there.'

So saying, he hurried away. Amos was left with a feeling that the question he had put to the landlord had perturbed him far more than should have been the case had he really known nothing about the murder. Then, remembering the letter lying on the table in front of him, he opened it, expecting, as he had told Thomas Stephens, it to be a thank you for the money he had left for Talwyn.

Instead, much to his surprise, it was a brief note asking him to call and see her at the school at one o'clock that day, when school ended.

Wondering why she wanted to see him, he momentarily thought of going to the cottage to speak to her now, but when he looked at the grandfather clock standing in the dining room he saw it was almost eleven o'clock, far too late for a social call. It was also still raining outside and he had already soaked one set of clothes that day.

His response to Talwyn Kernow's unexpected letter would need to wait until she ended lessons at the Charlestown school the following day.

11

While Amos was reading Talwyn's letter at the Rashleigh Arms, the writer was washing up supper dishes in the Kernow cottage, helped by her mother, prior to preparing for bed.

They were late retiring because they had once again been discussing the omnipresent problem of their finances. Maisie had returned to the criticism she had made intermittently throughout the evening: 'If only you had been able to control that temper of yours our troubles would be over now. At least, they would be for long enough to let us take on a teacher for the boys and so ensure the future of the school. We'll not find another lodger like Mr Hawke . . . indeed, we'll be lucky if we're able to get anyone at all.'

Exasperated by her mother's constant praise of Amos and her reminders that the fault lay with her, Talwyn took her hands out of the washing-up bowl and placed them on her hips before turning to face her mother.

'I am becoming tired of hearing how I frightened away your paragon of all lodgers,' she declared. 'Yes, I *was* angry with him – but the fact that he parted with his money so easily shows he accepted that what happened *was* his fault. What's more, it might interest you to know that I sent a note to him at the Rashleigh Arms this morning, asking him to come and see me after school. I intended to apologise for my ill-temper, offer to give him his money back, and say that if he wanted to come here as a lodger I would work as hard as you to ensure his stay with us would be both pleasant and comfortable. I waited for an hour after school ended, but he neither put in an appearance nor sent a reply to my note. So now you can stop blaming me for his not coming here as a lodger – and you also know the real reason why I was late coming home today.'

Talwyn had told her mother she had stayed at school to mark some work produced by her pupils.

'You would have done that . . . apologised and invited him to come here?' Maisie was taken aback. She had complained many times that her daughter's major fault was a stubborn pride that would not allow her to apologise when she was in the wrong . . . about anything.

'That's right. I would have swallowed my pride and done exactly that. I know just as well as you do that we are in desperate need of a lodger and that you are particularly taken by this Mr Hawke – although I am at a loss to know why. But now we have got to face up to the fact that he is *not* coming and think of something else.

I will go into St Austell tomorrow and speak to the reverend. He can spread the word that we are looking for someone to take board and lodging with us.'

Amos was waiting outside the Charlestown school at one o'clock the next day when more than thirty chattering young girls spilled out through the doorway of the building, noisily celebrating their freedom from the strict discipline imposed upon them in the classroom by Talwyn Kernow.

When Amos was satisfied they had all left, he ventured inside. Passing through a small entrance hall which was painted chocolate brown and studded on either side with double rows of iron coat pegs, he entered a spacious room in which stood rows of simple, locally made school desks, each with its equally utilitarian stool.

Talwyn stood at the far end of the room, her back to him, cleaning the blackboard with a chalk-stained duster and he found himself admiring her trim appearance. Amos said nothing for a few moments, waiting until she had cleaned every mark from the blackboard. Eventually, her task completed, she turned and, seeing him standing just inside the entrance to the schoolroom, gave a start of surprise.

Amos was the first to speak. 'I apologise for not calling on you yesterday,' he said, 'but I was late returning to the Rashleigh Arms and your letter wasn't given to me until eleven o'clock last night. Do you still wish to see me?'

Recovering from her surprise, Talwyn said, 'Yes. I would like to thank you for the money you left with my mother for me. It was kind of you . . . but it *was* your horse that caused the damage to my clothes and the eggs.'

Inclining his head briefly, Amos said, 'I could dispute which animal was the cause of the unfortunate mishap you suffered, but I have already apologised for what happened and there is no reason to call me here to thank me for making good the damage that was caused. Your mother has already done that.'

Talwyn's instinctive reaction was to pursue the issue of whether horse or dog was to blame for the accident, but she succeeded in controlling her impetuosity. There was too much at stake to risk an unnecessary argument.

'That is not the only reason I wished to speak to you,' she said. 'I was extremely impolite to you when we met at the cottage and now it is my turn to make an apology. I am very sorry for such unforgivable rudeness.'

'An apology is quite unnecessary,' Amos replied. 'You and your mother have suffered a grievous loss, in the most appalling circumstances. My heart goes out to you . . . to you both.'

It was a generous acceptance of her apology, but it caused tears to spring to Talwyn's eyes. Inexplicably, it was not gratitude she felt towards Amos, but anger. Anger that she should have once again shown emotional vulnerability in the presence of a man who was still a stranger to her. She was therefore more abrupt than she had intended to be when she said, 'If you are still looking for lodgings my mother would make you very welcome in our cottage.'

Aware that she had chosen her words very carefully,

71

Amos asked, 'How about you . . . does my staying there meet with your full approval?'

'My mother is head of the household now,' Talwyn said evasively. 'Such decisions are hers to make, but we have talked it over and I have no objection to having a lodger in the house.'

Amos sensed that having *him* living as a lodger in the Kernow cottage did not meet with Talwyn's full approval, and he accepted that they had not made the most auspicious start to such an arrangement. However, he believed Talwyn would probably have resented the intrusion of any other stranger to the household, if only for the constant reminder of the reason why he – or she – was there. Slightly to his surprise, he found it was important to him that her objection should not be a personal one.

'Thank you,' he said. 'I will call at the cottage this evening to discuss the details with your mother.'

12

Talwyn was not at home when Amos called at the Kernow cottage early that evening. Her mother explained that she had gone to St Austell to meet a teacher who had come to the Charlestown school some weeks before, hoping to find work. Edward Kernow had still been alive then and there had been no vacancy. Now, things had changed dramatically.

When Amos made apparently discreet inquiries about the man they hoped to employ at the school, Maisie told him the prospective teacher was young and single and that, after a brief period working in a so-called 'ragged school' in the slums of Bristol, he had spent the last two years teaching at a private school for boys in the same city. That employment had come to an end when the headmaster, who also owned the school, retired and sold the house to a purchaser who intended returning it to its original state as a large dwelling house. The young teacher, whose name she said was Andrew Elkins, had returned to St Austell where he had been born and his parents still lived.

Amos felt guilty when Maisie Kernow declared her delight that Amos was coming to live with her and her daughter, and said he must look upon the cottage as his own home for as long as he remained with them – and she hoped that would be for a very long time. He eased his conscience with the thought that the murder investigation was likely to take some time. Hopefully, when it was concluded she would have the satisfaction of seeing the murderer of her late husband brought to justice and so forgive his deception.

His discussions with Maisie Kernow satisfactorily concluded, Amos returned to the Rashleigh Arms to inform Thomas Stephens that he would be moving from the inn the following day.

Much to his surprise, the landlord seemed genuinely sorry that he was leaving. He even offered to give him a 'special rate' if he stayed on at the Rashleigh Arms for the remainder of his stay in Cornwall. However, he reluctantly admitted that he could not compete with the terms offered by Maisie Kernow for full board and lodging.

'Not that I would want to,' he added. 'It's being rumoured around the village that unless the Kernows can find enough money to pay for someone to teach the boys they will have to close down the school – and I have a personal interest in the school's future. I have a boy there already and hope to send my daughter when she's old enough, next year.'

'Then I'll be happy in the knowledge that I'm contributing to something worthwhile for as long as I remain in Cornwall,' Amos said. 'What is certain is that whoever murdered Mrs Kernow's husband so callously cared nothing for the welfare of Charlestown and those who live in the area. I hope he is soon found and dealt with as he deserves.'

Amos was watching Stephens closely as he spoke and he felt the innkeeper was distinctly uncomfortable as he replied, 'Well ... we none of us know the rights or wrongs of what happened to Edward Kernow, but there's no one hereabouts who would be happy if the school were to close as a result of it.'

It was still early in the evening and Amos decided he would go for a walk around the small harbourside village before returning to the inn for supper. As he stepped out of the door to the street, he was just in time to see a figure disappear into an alleyway a short distance up the road. He believed it to be 'Captain Billy'.

Sprinting up the road, he reached the mouth of the alleyway in time to see the man enter the last of a row of diminutive terraced cottages, and now he was quite certain. It *was* the ex-Bodmin Moor miner.

Hurrying over the litter-strewn cobbles of the narrow thoroughfare, Amos reached the last house and knocked hard on the flimsy, plankboard door. When there was no immediate response he knocked again, this time more forcibly.

There were sounds from inside the house and the door opened to reveal a drab, tired-looking woman wearing a dirty, threadbare dressing gown – and very little else.

'All right, all right,' she grumbled. 'There's no need to knock the door down.' Looking him up and down, she frowned and said, 'I've never seen you 'ere before. Which of the girls do you want?'

'None of them. I want to speak to Cap'n Billy,' Amos said, aware he had stumbled upon a bawdy house.

'I don't know no Cap'n Billy,' said the woman. She attempted to close the door, but Amos's hand stopped it.

'I saw him come in here,' he said, pushing the door open against the pressure she was applying to it. 'Now, if you tell me which room he's in I'll just go there and find him. If you don't, I'll go through the house trying every door.'

'Who are you? What d'you want with him?' the woman demanded.

'I think he'd be the first to say that names don't matter . . . and why I want him is none of your business. I just want to talk to him, that's all. Now, do you tell me where he is, or do I find him for myself?'

Aware that Amos meant what he said, the woman capitulated. 'If he's in he'll be in the next door along the passage . . . but I haven't seen him.'

'Thank you.' Pushing past her, Amos strode to the door she had indicated and, not bothering to knock, pushed it open.

The windowless room was illuminated by a single cheap candle, whose flame rose and fell as it spluttered uncertainly. In its light Amos saw Captain Billy, who had retreated fearfully to a far corner of the room when the door crashed open without warning.

Seeing Amos, the ex-miner was visibly relieved, but there was no welcome in his voice when he said, 'Oh, it's you! What do you want?'

'I want to finish the conversation we were having the other evening, when you ran out on me.'

'I'd already told you all I know,' Captain Billy replied, his confidence returning. 'There was no reason for me to stay there.'

'There was a half-flagon of ale left on the table,' Amos said. 'That would have been sufficient to keep you there, had something – or someone – not frightened you off.' A sound from outside in the passageway reminded him that the woman who had answered the street door to him was still within hearing and he said, 'Would you like to go somewhere else to talk . . . back to the Rashleigh Inn, perhaps?'

'No! We'll talk here.' Crossing the room, Captain Billy went to the door. Addressing the woman who was listening outside, he said, 'It's all right. This gentleman is in Cornwall searching for his father who I used to work with. We were talking about it the other evening when we were interrupted. I'll see him out when we've finished talking.'

'Make sure you do,' the woman ordered. 'Lily said you could use her room while she's away – but she said nothing about you having visitors.'

As the woman departed, Captain Billy came back inside the room and said to Amos, 'I used to work down a mine with the husband of the woman who has this room. He was killed in a roof fall and she was left with a couple of young 'uns and no money to keep 'em. One died within a fortnight of his pa and the other is living with his grandma, but she's a widow woman too and ... well, someone has to bring money into the house. Lily's gone off on one of the ships for a few days and said I could use her room while she's away.'

Amos did not doubt the truth of Captain Billy's story. It was one he had heard with minor variations many times before during his police service and he accepted it without comment ... but he wanted information from the other man.

'Why did you run off so suddenly the other evening when the big, bearded man came in? Unless I am mistaken he is a miner too, probably from Bodmin Moor. What's his name?'

For a few moments it seemed as though Captain Billy would not give Amos a reply but then, licking suddenly dry lips, he said, 'It's Hannibal Davey ... a miner who originally came from down west, but he's been up on Bodmin Moor for some time now and he doesn't like being talked about – especially not by strangers.'

'Then we'd better not let him know we've been talking about him,' Amos said. 'Would he have known my father?'

Captain Billy nodded his head. 'We all worked together up at the Wheal Notter for a while ... but I doubt if he would talk to you about it, even if he knew anything.'

'Why not?'

Again there was a pause while Captain Billy considered whether he should say any more. Then, making up his mind, he said, 'Davey and his brother killed two men from the Wheal Phoenix while they were working at Notter. They got away with it because they were able to produce witnesses – *their* witnesses – who told the coroner a different story about how the men died. Those who really knew what happened were either too scared to say anything against the Davey brothers, or had disappeared before anyone could ask them.'

Amos mulled this over for a while before asking, 'Did you see what happened?'

Captain Billy hesitated. 'No, but I've made quite sure I stayed out of Hannibal Davey's way ever since, in case he thought I had.'

Amos did not believe him, but he did not pursue the matter, asking instead, 'What about my father ... did he see the fight?'

'He was there with me.'

'Was that why he disappeared?'

'I don't know. Your father was still around for a while afterwards, so I'm not saying Davey had anything to do with his disappearance. I'm not saying that.'

'You don't have to,' Amos said grimly. 'I can draw my own conclusions.' Suddenly changing the subject, he asked, 'Did Hannibal Davey ever serve in the army?'

Surprised, Captain Billy said, 'He was in the army for a couple of years, but I believe he got into trouble and was thrown out. I've heard it said his back bears the scars of a lashing that would have killed any other man, but I've not seen it for myself.'

'When he was in the army ... was he a cavalryman?'

'Hannibal Davey a cavalryman?' Captain Billy

scoffed. 'It would have needed a dray horse to carry his weight. No, he was a guardsman. It was his brother Pasco who was a cavalryman – and although he's a lot smaller than Hannibal, he's not a man to cross either. In fact, there's a streak of madness in Pasco. If you take my advice you'll stay out of the way of both of them. Now, I've done more than enough talking for one night. I suggest you forget all about the Daveys and look else-where for your father. He probably left to get out of their way. You do the same.'

Amos had gained more information than he had expected from Captain Billy, especially concerning Hannibal Davey's brother and his connection with a cavalry regiment. He knew he would get no more that night. 'All right, I'll leave you in peace now. Have you eaten today?'

'No . . . but I've the chance of half a day's work on the harbour tomorrow. I'll eat then.'

Handing the other man a shilling, Amos said, 'Take this and find something to eat tonight – but don't spend it all on ale.'

Walking away from the bawdy house, Amos thought of all that Captain Billy had told him. There was a great deal about the Davey brothers that was interesting, particularly in respect of his father . . . but of far more importance to the investigation that he and Detective Inspector Carpenter were in Cornwall to carry out was the information that Pasco Davey had once served in a cavalry regiment. He would pass the information on to Carpenter in the hope that he could discover which cavalry regiment it was – and whether the regiment had been issued with the type of pistol that had taken the lives of the three murdered men.

Amos was so engrossed in his thoughts as he exited the alleyway that he failed to see Talwyn Kernow, who was walking from the Charlestown school in company with Andrew Elkins, the young man she had employed to teach the boys.

Amos did not see either of them ... but Talwyn saw him and she was horrified. The alleyway from which Amos had emerged was for some reason known locally as 'Chinatown'. It contained only eleven run-down houses ... and every one was a brothel.

13

Amos's first dinner at the Kernow cottage was a somewhat subdued and strained affair. It was a meal which
would have been served at midday in most households,
but as Talwyn's classes were not over by then, it was
put on the table at one o'clock. Maisie had told Amos
she was quite prepared to serve his dinner at the normal
time, if he would prefer, but he assured her that on the
occasions when he was there for the midday meal the
later time would be quite convenient.

Amos had been lodging in the cottage for only two
hours when the meal was served and he told himself
the awkward silence that prevailed at the meal table was
only to be expected. He had already accepted that
Talwyn resented the need for a stranger's presence in
the house she shared with her mother.

Nevertheless, as the meal progressed it seemed to him
there was more than mere resentment in her attitude

towards him. Her manner bordered on actual antagonism. He believed Maisie recognised it too and was trying hard to make conversation, asking questions about his father, when he had last seen him, and the reason why they had lost touch over the years.

When this subject was exhausted she questioned him about life in the Royal Marines. Talwyn seemed to take a little more interest in this subject, but she asked no questions of her own, and when Amos tried to draw her into the conversation her replies were mainly monosyllabic.

The meal over, Amos excused himself and made his way to his room. He needed to make a report of all he had learned to present to Detective Inspector Carpenter at their meeting on Friday evening. When he had left the table, Maisie took her daughter to task about the way she had behaved towards Amos during the meal.

'Why, what did I do wrong?' Talwyn demanded defensively. 'I answered his questions whenever he addressed them to me. What more was expected of me?'

'You were never *actually* rude,' agreed her mother, 'but neither were you polite. Had you still been a young girl, instead of a grown woman, I would have sent you up to your room and said you could come down again when you felt you could add something to the conversation and not bring it to a halt every time you opened your mouth.'

'You have just agreed I was not rude to him,' Talwyn retorted, 'and I *won't* be, but I don't have to like him and *I* don't have to behave as though I think he is the most wonderful person ever to come into our lives –

because I don't believe he is. You like him . . . let's leave it at that.'

That evening, Andrew Elkins called in at the Kernow cottage to ask Talwyn a few questions before going on to the school to take his first class. It was quite apparent that he was nervous of what lay ahead of him, and Talwyn showed a side of her nature Amos had not witnessed before.

He had been invited down from his room by Maisie to have a cup of tea and meet Andrew. Seated at the kitchen table, Amos saw Talwyn displaying a charm she had never shown to him, in order to put her fellow teacher at his ease. He tried hard not to allow her preference for the other man to upset him, telling himself that her approval was of no importance to him.

When Andrew said it was time he set off for Charlestown, Amos unexpectedly offered, 'I'll walk with you. There's someone I want to speak to there.'

Talwyn frowned and for a moment Amos thought she was going to raise an objection to his suggestion, but it was Maisie who spoke. 'What a nice idea. Having someone to talk to along the way Andrew won't feel so nervous. Not that he has anything to be nervous about, of course. Edward used to say every one of his boys at Charlestown was eager to learn all he could teach them. I have no doubt at all that you'll find the same, Andrew.'

The two men set off, and although Talwyn was effusive in wishing the new teacher well, she said nothing at all to Amos. As soon as the door closed behind them,

Maisie commented sharply on Talwyn's differing attitude towards them, adding, 'It was so marked that I found it quite embarrassing.'

'I didn't behave any differently from the way I usually am with either of them,' Talwyn replied coolly. 'I find Andrew extremely easy to get along with.'

'Which is another way of saying you don't like Amos,' Maisie retorted. 'You carry on the way you are with him and he'll be packing his bags and finding somewhere else to stay. There is no shortage of lodgings around these parts. Remember, if he goes then Andrew will have to go too and, easy or not, you'll need to get along *without* him – and without the school too. I don't know what we would do then, with no money coming into the house.'

'I suppose I could always go and work in Chinatown,' Talwyn retorted. 'The trouble is, I would doubtless have to put up with Mr Hawke there as well.'

Maisie was shocked by what her daughter had said. 'Well brought up young women don't even *know* about such places, far less *talk* about them in such a fashion – and I can't imagine a man like Amos ever going there.'

'No? Then I suggest you ask him what he was doing coming out of Chinatown last night, as Andrew and I were walking back from the school.'

Chinatown was the subject of discussion between Amos and Andrew too, as they walked together along the lane towards the Charlestown school.

It was Andrew who introduced it unintentionally by saying, 'It is very kind of you to walk to Charlestown

85

with me on my first night at the school. Having someone to talk to does help to calm my nerves.'

'I doubt whether you have anything to be nervous about,' Amos said. 'I am sure the boys will be very well behaved. Talwyn has a reputation for being a strict disciplinarian and I think she must have learned it from her father. But I am not being particularly altruistic. There is someone I want to see in Charlestown, although I am not particularly looking forward to returning to the place where I found him last night. It's a dingy little alleyway, just behind the weighbridge.'

Andrew looked startled. 'You are talking about Chinatown ... Charlestown's notorious place of ill-repute?' Coming to a sudden halt, he asked, 'Were you there yesterday evening ... at about seven to seven-thirty?'

'Yes, it must have been about that time. Why do you ask?'

'Because I was with Talwyn, coming from inspecting the school at about that time, and we saw someone coming from the alley. I didn't recognise you then, of course, because I didn't even know you – but I am certain Talwyn did. We were talking when suddenly she stopped and looked startled, and she was looking at the man – it must have been you – coming out of the alleyway. That would explain her behaviour towards you at the cottage just now. I could not help noticing her off-hand manner ... rudeness even ... in the way she behaved towards you.'

Amos looked aghast. Struggling for words, he said, 'You don't mean ... ? She thought ... ?'

86

'That you had been frequenting a bawdy house? Most probably. There is not much else to do in that particular part of Charlestown.'

'There was for me.' Amos gave his companion a carefully worded version of his first meeting with Captain Billy and of his sudden disappearance when he saw someone he had no wish to meet, adding, 'Last night I saw him going into the alleyway and ran to the entrance in time to see him go into one of the houses. It was quite obvious to me when I got there that it was a bawdy house, but the man I wanted to speak to was occupying one of the rooms while the woman who rented it was away for a few days. He was able to give me some information about my missing father, but having thought over what he told me I'd like him to clarify one or two things. That's why I am going to see him again now.'

'I wish you luck,' Andrew said, 'but I suggest you find some way of telling your story to Talwyn, or your stay at her cottage is likely to be a very uncomfortable one.'

'Our relationship didn't exactly get off to the best of starts,' commented Amos ruefully, 'and whatever I say now will probably not be believed . . .'

He went on to tell his companion of his first meeting with Talwyn and the young teacher was still chuckling when they parted company, leaving Amos to go on to Chinatown, while Andrew went inside the Charlestown school for his first session with the pupils.

14

When Amos returned to the Kernow cottage later that evening, he was in time to join the two women in a supper which consisted of the leftovers from the midday meal made into a pie, plus bread and cheese, washed down with a choice of either milk or tea.

Talwyn sat at the table saying nothing, but Maisie, who had adamantly refused to believe that Amos had been in Charlestown visiting the bawdy houses, served him his meal and said, 'Had Andrew overcome his nerves by the time he arrived at the school?'

Amos nodded. 'Yes, he'll be all right. He has had a great deal of teaching experience and is obviously a clever man. I think you are lucky to have found him.'

'No doubt your own "business" went equally well?' Talwyn asked, her voice heavy with sarcasm.

'As a matter of fact it didn't,' Amos replied, choosing to ignore the sarcasm. 'The man I went to see had moved on. It's a great pity. Last night he was able to give me some information about my father, but it was rather vague. I was hoping he would be able to tell me more, but I was out of luck. Unfortunately, I doubt if I'll ever see him again.'

'Where was this man living?' Talwyn asked. 'We know a great many people in Charlestown. If some of them were neighbours of this man they might be able to tell us where he's gone.'

The question was asked in an apparent attempt to be helpful and Maisie looked at her daughter in surprise, but Amos thought he knew the reason for her question.

'I doubt if you would know anyone in the street where he was staying,' he said amiably. 'I believe it is known locally as Chinatown, and he hadn't been there very long. He was occupying a room loaned to him in the absence of a woman he had known when they were both enjoying better times, but she returned today and reclaimed the room. He has apparently returned to living rough, so he could be anywhere. It's a great pity. Since I arrived back in Cornwall he's the only man I've met who admits to having known my father.'

As Amos repeated the story he had given to Andrew to explain how he had met Captain Billy, Maisie gave her daughter a look that clearly said, 'I told you so.' His reason for being in Chinatown had been fully explained to *her* satisfaction, at least.

Talwyn was more sceptical. Looking pointedly at the clock, she asked, 'Has it taken all this time to learn he was no longer staying in Chinatown?'

'No. I've been in the Rashleigh Arms having a drink

with the landlord, and then I returned via the school and listened outside for a few minutes to make sure there wasn't a riot going on in there. When I was satisfied all was quiet, I came on home . . . and yes, Maisie, I *will* have some of that pie. It smells delicious.'

He had seen the glances that had been exchanged between the two women and realised that Talwyn must have told her mother of seeing him leaving Chinatown. He retired for the night satisfied that his story had been accepted by the older woman, at least. He doubted whether Talwyn had believed him . . . but he was beginning to think that nothing he did would ever meet with her approval.

The next day dawned bright and warm and Amos decided it would be a good opportunity to ride to Bodmin Moor and pay a visit to the Wheal Notter. As it involved a return journey of some forty miles, he informed Maisie he would not be back for the midday meal, explaining that he was going to visit the mine where he had been told his father had once worked.

Some hours later he was approaching Henwood village, where a small mining community occupied a huddle of houses nestling between Notter Tor, the hill which had given its name to the nearby mine, and Sharp Tor, a craggy peak that could be seen for many miles around. There were a number of mines still working in the vicinity and smoke rose from a dozen tall chimneys. He was also aware of the clatter of ore stamps, the steady thud of a beam engine and a variety of other noises emanating from the nearby busy Wheal Phoenix mine complex.

The village itself had little more to offer the visitor than a scattering of granite miners' cottages, with a whitewashed Methodist chapel and an air of having known better days. From here the buildings of the Wheal Notter could be seen standing silent on the slopes of the tor, the engine house already a ruin, surrounded by sagging wire and battered sheets of rusting corrugated iron lying half buried beneath rubble and mine waste. Someone had made a half-hearted attempt to fence off the gaping hole that had once been the mine's main shaft but much of the wire fence was missing now, leaving the remainder broken and bent.

Although the mine was derelict, when Amos reached it he was quickly made aware that it was not entirely deserted. After dismounting, he was leading his horse round the buildings when two men wearing the garb favoured by miners appeared from a hut constructed from wood and corrugated iron. It was immediately clear that Amos's presence was not welcome.

'What are you doing here?' demanded the more power-fully built of the two men. 'You are on private property.'

'I've come seeking news of someone I believe was once a miner here,' Amos replied, adding, 'Were you here when the mine was working?'

'That's none of your business,' came the belligerent reply. 'Strangers aren't welcome round here ... especially nosy strangers.'

'Who is it you're looking for ... and why?' The second man spoke for the first time and, although not exactly friendly, his manner was less aggressive than that of his companion.

'I'm looking for my father, Doniert Hawke. He was living in Mevagissey when I went off to join the Royal Marines some years ago, but he's not there any more. I was told he'd been working on the Wheal Notter, so I thought I'd come up here and see if I could learn anything about his whereabouts now.'

The two men had exchanged glances when Amos mentioned his father's name, but as soon as he had finished talking the first man said, 'I've never heard of him. There's no one of that name living in these parts, so there's nothing to keep you here.'

Choosing to ignore him, Amos spoke to the second man. 'How about you? Does the name mean anything to you?'

To Amos's surprise, the man nodded. 'I've heard the name . . . and think I can put a face to it, but he's not round here now. He left at about the time the Wheal Notter closed, when a great many miners were leaving the moor. I did hear he was going to try his luck in Australia . . . or some such place.'

The first man was frowning at his companion. Amos said, 'I thank you for your information. Is there anyone in the village who might know more?'

The smaller of the ex-miners shook his head. 'He didn't stay in the village – and when he went drinking it would have been up here, in one of the kiddlywinks that catered for Wheal Notter men. The alehouse in the village was used by Wheal Phoenix miners in those days – and we weren't welcomed by them after the dispute about the Wheal Notter's overrunning on to Phoenix ground. These days the Wheal Phoenix men favour the

Cheesewring inn at Minions and the Henwood alehouse does so little business you'd learn nothing there.'

Pretending to be satisfied with what he had been told, Amos said despondently, 'Oh well, it looks as though I'm going to have to look elsewhere. If you do happen to hear anything more of my father perhaps you could get word to Thomas Stephens, landlord of the Rashleigh Arms at Charlestown. He'll pass it on to me. Thank you for your time.'

As Amos rode away, the larger of the two miners rounded upon the other. 'What were you doing telling him you knew his father? You should have said nothing and let me scare him away.'

'You heard what he said about being in the Marines,' retorted his companion scornfully. 'He didn't look the sort who would scare easy . . . but thinking has never been your strong suit. Sending him off your way would, as likely as not, make him think we had something to hide. He'd have gone down to Henwood village asking questions and might have heard something Hannibal wouldn't want him to know about. By telling him what I did, he'll go off without asking more questions in this area.'

Contrary to the ex-miner's belief, Amos left the Wheal Notter with a firm conviction that the two men he had just left knew far more about his father than they had disclosed. What was more, he was convinced that he was coming closer to the man he and Detective Inspector Carpenter had come to Cornwall to find.

He had already guessed that the smugglers were

93

using a derelict mine in which to store their contraband – and the Wheal Notter would be ideal for the purpose. It was far enough from the coast to avoid the attentions of the increasingly efficient coastguard and Excise services and those who lived on Bodmin Moor had a traditional mistrust of strangers, especially official strangers. Even if Excise officers were to find their way here, they would learn nothing from the moorland dwellers.

On his way to Henwood, Amos had studied the lie of the land around the Wheal Notter. He believed that if it was being used to store contraband, the most likely place to hide it would be in an 'adit', a tunnel driven into the lower slopes of the tor to drain the mine workings of water. Such a tunnel would be at the lowest possible place in order to avoid the need for excessive pumping.

Now, on his way from the derelict mine buildings, Amos rode down the slope, circling Notter Tor – and just out of sight of the village he made an exciting discovery.

Grazing in a large, free-stone walled field, just off the moor, were a great many mules. He put their number at about fifty. It *was* possible, of course, that they were the property of the Wheal Phoenix, but it was not probable. The Wheal Phoenix had a narrow gauge railway linking it to the port of Looe, on Cornwall's south coast. They would have no need of mules.

Minutes later he came across the adit from the Wheal Notter. It was exactly where he had expected it to be, but unlike the broken fence around the main shaft, which did little to preserve anyone from danger, the stout wire fence enclosing the entrance to the adit was higher than the average man, with a gate that was securely padlocked.

There was also a large sign which declared KEEP OUT. DANGER OF ROOF FALLS.

Despite such precautions, Amos thought he detected movement inside the adit as he approached. There was no one to be seen as he rode past, but had there been they would have detected no interest in the adit from him, and he resisted the temptation to look back as he rode on towards Henwood village.

15

Amos had a great deal to tell Detective Inspector Carpenter when they met the next night, and he handed him a lengthy report that he had spent much of the day compiling. It ended with a list of questions, to which he hoped the inspector might be able to obtain answers through official sources.

Two of the questions were about the service records of the two Davey brothers – and it was of these the inspector spoke as he and Amos walked their horses side by side along the quiet lane close to Penrice.

'If this informant of yours is right about Hannibal Davey having scars on his back from a flogging there will be something about it on his service record,' the detective inspector commented. 'For it to have left him permanently scarred he must have committed a particularly serious crime.'

'Not necessarily,' Amos replied. 'If the army is anything

like the navy then the degree of punishment is left to the whim of a man's commanding officer. Some are more ready to resort to the lash than others. Having said that, Hannibal has a reputation as being a violent man. Cap'n Billy is certainly terrified of him – but he seems even more frightened of Pasco, who he believes is probably insane. Pasco served as a cavalryman. If the armourer at the army barracks in Bodmin is correct and the shots that killed the three men were from a pistol of the type issued to cavalrymen, then he has to be our prime suspect.'

'I agree,' Carpenter said, 'but at the moment it is mere conjecture. Even their involvement in smuggling has not been proved – although I don't doubt it is so. You have put together a very good circumstantial case based on probabilities, but we need to obtain proof – and that is not going to be easy.'

'True,' Amos agreed, 'although we know for certain smuggling *is* taking place along this part of the coast – and if Pasco is involved, he will most likely go out armed. If we are fortunate enough to catch the gang red-handed and he has the gun in his possession, then, provided the evidence against them all is strong enough, I think we might persuade one or more of the smugglers to turn Queen's evidence and have him convicted.'

'First we need to catch them in the act,' Carpenter said. 'That means having precise information about a time and a place. It would also seem that a great many men are likely to be involved. We would have to call upon the army or the militia for help. It's a task the army doesn't relish and the militia are local men who couldn't be relied upon to keep their part in it a secret.'

'There is also the possibility that with so many ranged against them the smugglers will realise they have no chance of escape and Pasco will get rid of the gun,' Amos mused. 'Without it we would have little chance of getting him convicted of murder – and that is what we are in Cornwall for, not to catch smugglers.'

'Exactly!' Carpenter agreed. 'But I agree with you that smuggling and the murders are almost certainly connected. I will make urgent inquiries about the two Davey brothers, while you try to learn as much about these smugglers as possible without endangering yourself. We still need to find a link between the murder of the two Excise men and the schoolteacher. Have you learned anything from the Kernow women that might help us?'

'Nothing,' Amos replied, 'but I haven't spent a great deal of time in the cottage since I moved in. I will see what I can find out before our next meeting.'

'Good! How are you getting along with the widow and her daughter?'

'I get along well with the widow,' Amos replied, 'but am finding the daughter more than a little difficult.' He told Carpenter about his first meeting with Talwyn and the more recent misunderstanding about his visit to Chinatown.

Much to his chagrin, Detective Inspector Carpenter reacted to his story in exactly the same manner as had Andrew Elkins. He laughed.

'You will need to practise your charm on her, Amos,' he said when his humour subsided. 'Or perhaps not. I believe she is an attractive young woman and this case is complicated enough without your becoming involved with the daughter of your landlady.'

'There is very little fear of that,' Amos replied wryly. 'She seems to view all men with suspicion . . . although she appears to get along well enough with the new teacher she has taken on at the school.'

'Perhaps she prefers brains to beauty, Amos, so keep your mind on the job in hand. Find the killer of her father and all will be forgiven.'

At the entrance to the Penrice estate Amos parted company with his superior officer. He was reluctant to go straight back to the cottage because he knew Maisie and Talwyn would not yet have gone to bed. Not wishing to endure Talwyn's hostility for the rest of the evening, he decided to ride on to look at the ships in Charlestown harbour, and perhaps spend an hour in the Rashleigh Arms. He thought it worthwhile to maintain the rapport he had with the inn's landlord. Even though he might gain no more useful information there, it would suit his purposes to become accepted as a regular customer whose presence no longer attracted attention.

He was approaching the inn when he was startled by a sudden commotion close at hand. Recovering quickly, he realised it was nothing more serious than the sound of boys leaving school at the end of their evening lessons. Acting on an impulse, he turned his horse and made for the school. He tied the animal outside the building and went inside.

Andrew was tidying the classroom and was surprised to see Amos, but he seemed pleased, and when asked how he was getting on he said, 'The lessons are going well . . . so well that tonight I overran by half an hour without noticing it – and without anyone in the class telling me. That is very good indeed. It means the boys are here because they are keen to learn.'

'It also means that they find your teaching of interest,' Amos commented.

'I hope so.' Andrew began packing schoolbooks into a satchel. 'I tried to make my lessons interesting when I was in Bristol, but most children at the ragged school were attending only in order to receive the soup and bread that was given out free at midday. At the private school, too many boys attended merely because their parents wanted to show friends and acquaintances they were wealthy enough to send them there.' The last book safely stowed inside the satchel, Andrew secured it and explained, 'I am taking the books with me so that I can go through them at home and give myself an idea of each boy's ability and aptitude.'

Impressed by the dedication Andrew was already showing towards his new appointment, Amos asked, 'Does that mean you will not have time to call in at the Rashleigh Arms for an ale before you go on your way?'

'An ale is exactly what my throat needs right now. I have talked for longer this evening than for many months.' Giving Amos a shrewd and rather impish look, Andrew added, 'Are you inviting me to the Rashleigh Arms because you crave my company . . . or are you filled with trepidation at the thought of spending an evening with the sharp-tongued Talwyn?'

'Let's say it's a little of both.'

Hitching the strap of the satchel over his shoulder, Andrew checked the windows were closed, then, snuffing out the lamps in the schoolroom, he followed Amos from the building, locking the door behind him while Amos untethered his horse.

As they were walking the horse to the Rashleigh Arms stable, Andrew said, 'You should not take Talwyn too seriously, you know. She is really a very nice girl – and recognised by the Cornish teaching fraternity as a quite brilliant teacher. Charlestown is lucky to have her. With her skills she could find a position in any school in the country.'

'I believe her father was well thought of too,' Amos said, hoping to draw some information on the murdered man from his companion.

'He was indeed. He taught me for some years . . . in fact, were it not for him I would probably not be a schoolteacher today.'

The statement took Amos by surprise. 'I hadn't realised you had attended Charlestown school. Neither Maisie nor Talwyn thought to mention it.'

'I doubt if they even knew I had been Edward Kernow's pupil until I told them . . . but it wasn't here, at Charlestown. My father is a Wesleyan minister and for a long time he was on a circuit in mining country. That's where Edward Kernow had his school for a while, teaching the sons of mine and shift captains – and me – together with a few miners' sons, whether or not their parents always had money to pay for their tuition. He was very well liked. He only came to Charlestown when mines began closing and running a school on the moor was no longer profitable.'

Amos picked up on Andrew's words excitedly. 'Edward Kernow taught on the moor? You mean . . . Bodmin Moor? Where, exactly?'

'His school was held in the chapel of a little village you have probably never even heard of, Amos. The village is called . . . Henwood.'

16

For a long while after Amos had stabled his horse and entered the Rashleigh Arms with Andrew, he hardly heard what was being said to him. In just a couple of sentences describing his schooling, Amos believed his companion had given him an important clue to something that had puzzled both Detective Inspector Carpenter and himself. A piece of information that could tie schoolteacher Edward Kernow in with the men who Amos believed had murdered him – and he was convinced were also responsible for the murder of two Excise officers.

There were still a great many unanswered questions to resolve and much detective work to be done, but Amos was greatly encouraged by what he had learned from his companion.

He was still mulling over his thoughts when Thomas Stephens came to the table and busied himself wielding his ever-present damp cloth on the tabletop, at the same time asking how Amos was enjoying the company of the late schoolteacher's widow and her young daughter.

Despite the landlord's statement that he did not ask questions of his customers and kept out of other people's business, Amos knew that the innkeeper was intrigued to know the identity of his companion. After commenting on the weather, the number and nationalities of the few ships in the harbour, and the prospects for that season's harvest, Amos decided to satisfy the landlord's transparent curiosity.

'Landlord, I would like you to meet Andrew Elkins, Charlestown's new schoolteacher. He is convinced that his pupils are all very bright boys. I believe your son is one of them?'

'He is indeed!' Thomas Stephens suddenly became effusive and, beaming at Andrew, said, 'I am *very* pleased to meet you, sir. I hope this might be the first of many such occasions. As for young Nicholas, my son, I think you will find him as bright as anyone else in your class.'

Thomas Stephens was more garrulous than Amos had ever seen him. His unnecessary cleaning of the table forgotten, he leaned closer to Amos and Andrew. 'This is a most unexpected pleasure and something to be celebrated in an appropriate fashion. I have something very special I will bring out to you . . . and, in view of the occasion, I will join you.'

When the landlord had disappeared through a door that Amos believed led to the cellar, Andrew said with genuine bewilderment, 'What is he talking about . . . something special? Do you know?'

'I suspect he has some high quality brandy to offer us,' Amos replied. 'Brandy from casks that have never been contaminated by the chalk mark of an Excise officer.'

'You mean ... *smuggled* brandy?' The schoolteacher seemed genuinely alarmed. 'Do you think we ought to ... ?'

'Stephens will be very upset if we were to refuse it,' Amos said. 'Accept it in the spirit in which it is being offered – and that is not a pun. He is delighted to be able to do something he hopes will please his son's teacher. As for the brandy ... I have no doubt it will be excellent, but much stronger than you are used to drinking, so, if you value your reputation, treat it with great respect.'

Andrew Elkins had a very engaging smile and it put in an appearance now. 'Thank you for the warning, Amos. Neither my father nor Talwyn would be in the least amused were I to become the worse for drink so early in my teaching days at Charlestown school. My father practises total abstinence – and I believe Edward Kernow drank only in moderation.'

'What sort of man was Edward Kernow?' Amos decided this was a good opportunity to learn something about the man whose murder he was investigating.

'He was a good man, in every sense of the word,' Andrew replied. 'Firm but kindly. As well as being an excellent teacher, he was an outstanding member of the community outside his work. Talwyn quite obviously adored him and there was never a hint of scandal in his private life.'

'Why would anyone want to murder such a man?'

Andrew shook his head. 'That is a question that has been asked by anyone who ever knew him.'

At that moment Thomas Stephens returned to the table carefully carrying three pewter tankards. As he placed them on the table Amos caught the heady whiff of brandy, of a much higher proof than that found in a legally acquired ardent spirit.

Raising one of the tankards, the landlord of the Rashleigh Arms proposed a toast. 'To a long, happy and successful career at Charlestown school, Mr Elkins,' he said.

Andrew and Amos joined Stephens in the toast and, while the young teacher fought to regain his breath as the fiery spirit passed down his throat, Amos said, 'Perhaps it's not the strength of your brandy but the spirit of Edward Kernow that is causing him to choke, landlord. Andrew was just telling me that he was almost a teetotaller.'

'And so he was,' the landlord agreed, 'but I never held that against him. He was a good man.'

'So I believe. In fact, Andrew and I were just wondering who would want to murder such a man . . . and for what reason?'

'I wouldn't know the answer to either of those questions, Mr Hawke . . . and I don't think I want to. Sometimes such matters are best forgotten. Now, I'll be leaving you to enjoy your drinks while I get on about my business.'

It was quite evident the landlord was not at ease talking of the murdered schoolteacher and he appeared

suddenly uncomfortable to be talking to them at all . . .
but why? Amos had believed Stephens to be happy
enough when he was introduced to the new Charlestown
schoolteacher.

As the landlord hurried away to the bar, Amos looked
about him and saw a man dressed in the clothes of a
miner about to seat himself at a nearby table. He immediately recognised him as one of those who had been
in the company of Hannibal Davey on the night the
smugglers had delivered their contraband to the
Rashleigh Arms . . . possibly the brandy they were
drinking at that very moment!

He was confident that the man – and his association
with Hannibal Davey – was the reason the landlord had
broken off their conversation so abruptly. Thomas
Stephens was clearly far more closely involved in the
smugglers' activities than he would wish to be known.

It was yet another disjointed piece of the puzzle he
and Detective Inspector Carpenter had come to Cornwall
to solve.

17

On Saturday evening, Amos was in his room reading when Maisie called up that they had a visitor and would he care to come down and have a cup of tea with them?

He accepted the offer and, going downstairs, was delighted to find that the visitor was Andrew. Seated in the kitchen – a sure indication that he had been accepted as a friend of the family – he was talking to Talwyn, and Amos could not help noticing that she was displaying an animation that was invariably absent when she was in conversation with *him*.

However, Andrew greeted him warmly enough and, as Amos sat down at the table and Maisie placed a cup of tea in front of him, the recently appointed Charlestown schoolteacher said, 'It is really you I have come to speak to, Amos. You remember that when we were talking of Henwood last night you said that the last positive information of your father's whereabouts was when he was working at the Wheal Notter there?'

When Amos nodded, Andrew continued, 'Although I wasn't aware of it then, my father told me when I went home that he has been to Henwood twice this week, standing in for the local circuit minister who isn't too well. Whilst there he renewed the acquaintance of Humphrey Penrose, a man to whom he gave spiritual comfort when his wife died, leaving him to bring up their two young children, a boy and a girl. The boy left home some years ago, going to America with a relative's family, and soon afterwards his father married again, to a widow with two young daughters of her own. Unfortunately, a great deal of friction has developed between Laura, the daughter of his first marriage, and the new family.'

It was a situation that mirrored Amos's own, and he could sympathise with Laura. He wondered about Andrew's purpose in telling him of the girl's problems . . . but the schoolteacher was speaking once more.

'Young Laura is a bright girl . . . very bright. Unfortunately, Henwood has no school now. Even if it had it is doubtful whether her stepmother would allow money to be spent on educating her. As a result, Laura has been allowed to run wild, but my father has been talking to her this week and he is convinced there is a great deal of good in the girl. It seems she has been inspired by stories of Florence Nightingale in the Crimea and would like to become a nurse. Indeed, there is an old woman in the village who treats more sick people than the local doctor and she often calls on Laura to help her. My father has asked me to go to Henwood and speak to Laura to assess whether I believe she has the potential to achieve her goal. I thought you might like to accompany me to the village tomorrow.'

'I would very much like to come with you.' Amos thought it an excellent opportunity to have another look at the area in which he believed the smuggling gang to be based. 'As for the young girl . . . It is an admirable ambition to have, but thanks to Florence Nightingale the whole concept of nursing has undergone a remarkable change. She will certainly need an education – and a good one – if she is to become one of the new breed of nurses.'

Talwyn turned on him scornfully. 'Are you claiming to be an expert on nursing now?'

'No,' Amos replied quietly. 'I am not an expert, but when I was slightly wounded in the Crimea I spent some days in Florence Nightingale's hospital at Scutari. I had been in other hospitals before, but found she had given an entirely new meaning – and status – to the work of the nurse.'

He spoke with a total lack of rancour in response to Talwyn's scorn, and she felt unexpectedly ashamed of her unwarranted derision.

'I am sorry . . . I wasn't aware you had been wounded . . .'

It was the first time she had ever made a genuine apology to Amos, and it surprised her as much as it did Amos and her mother, but he tried to pass it off lightly, saying, 'There is no reason why you should have known.'

Andrew headed off the awkward silence that followed

by saying, 'I think Laura is aware of the need for an education if she is to achieve her ambition, which is why my father has asked me to go and see her.'

'If you decide she *is* clever enough ... what will happen then? As you say, there is no school in Henwood now,' Amos asked.

'I think my father will try to find someone in the Wesleyan church prepared to sponsor her to attend our school at Charlestown ... but a bigger problem will be finding somewhere for her to live round here. We would take her into our house, in St Austell, but my grandmother is living with us and she is not too well right now. My mother could not cope with a young girl too.'

'How old is this girl?' Talwyn asked.

'I am not quite certain,' Andrew replied, 'but she must be about thirteen or fourteen, I suppose. I know she was working at the Wheal Notter as a young bal maiden before the mine closed. I believe she helps out in the dairy of a local farm now but earns little more than her keep plus a little butter and milk for the family.'

'Has she ever been to school?' Talwyn queried.

'She must have received some tuition because I know she can read a little,' Andrew said, 'but I don't know where she picked that up. Your father's school in Henwood was only for boys.'

'Then she is going to have to work very hard indeed, both in and out of school hours, if she is to have a realistic chance of a nursing career,' Talwyn pointed out. 'But that still doesn't solve the problem of accommodation – or school fees. Much as I would like an opportunity to help the girl, we are working to an extremely tight budget at the moment.'

'We might be able to do something about accommodation, Talwyn,' Maisie said hesitantly. 'We have the back room upstairs, next to Amos's room. I know it's small and the slope of the roof in there makes it seem even smaller, but it's clean and watertight – and if all the old bits and pieces we've put in there were removed it would make a very pleasant little room for a young girl. I doubt whether she would have had her own room in a moorland cottage.'

'That would be wonderful for her,' Andrew said enthusiastically, then, suddenly realistic, he pointed out, 'We would still need to find the rent for her.'

Maisie shrugged. 'I am not as young as I once was. Nothing is coming easier for me and Talwyn is kept busy now with all the problems of the school, so I could do with a little help around the house and in the garden. I would like to have a few chickens if I had help with them. The only extra would be her food – and I doubt if she would eat enough to make a serious difference to what I spend now.'

'I can't believe this is happening,' declared a delighted Andrew. 'However, there is still the question of her school fees. I could not – and *would* not – ask you to accept her as a non-fee-paying pupil, Talwyn. Quite apart from the loss of income an extra pupil should provide, it would lead to resentment among other parents who are working hard to pay the fees for their own children.'

'I'll pay her fees,' Amos said unexpectedly. 'At least,

until your father can find a sponsor in his church who is willing to take it on.'

'Why?' Talwyn asked suspiciously. 'Why should you do such a thing for someone you have never even met?'

'Because I realise exactly how she must feel about life,' Amos replied. 'I know what it is to lose a parent and suddenly have stepsisters or stepbrothers moving in and taking precedence over you. I was able to join the Royal Marines; her escape would be to take up nursing. I think she deserves to have that chance and I would like to help her achieve it.'

Talwyn did not question Amos further, and Maisie thought that as a result of all that had been said in the cottage that evening her daughter might be seeing Amos in a new light – and she was delighted.

18

The following day, Amos accompanied Andrew to Henwood village to pay a visit upon Laura's family, Andrew mounted on his father's horse. The animal was ageing and somewhat tired, but they succeeded in reaching Henwood by noon and Andrew led the way to the cottage where Laura was living with her father and his new wife and family.

The home was neither tidy nor particularly clean, and its state reflected the woman who lived there. Amos took an instant and irrational dislike to her, but he told himself it was due more to the similarity of the situation he had experienced as a child than to the condition of the house, or the thin-faced, tight-lipped woman who met them at the door.

When Andrew said he had come to speak to her and her husband about Laura, the woman said, 'Oh? What has she been up to now? Whatever it is, I am taking no responsibility for her – and neither is her father.'

Taken aback by the woman's reaction, Andrew said, 'As far as I am aware she has done nothing wrong, Mrs Penrose. My father is Thomas Elkins, who was minister here some years ago, and has been standing in for William Truscott this last week. But you mentioned your husband just now. Is he in the house at the moment? My father has discussed Laura with him and he asked me to come here and have a word with her – I am a teacher.'

'Has she been on about that again? That girl has ideas way above her station in life, as I've told her many times – and told her father too. It's high time she took a steady job in one of the mines and settled down to bring some money into the house before she sets about finding herself a husband, same as most girls of her age.'

'Your husband,' Andrew reminded her firmly. 'We have ridden a long way to speak to him. Is he here?'

'He's out back, working in the garden . . . but if you ask me—'

'Shall we go out to the garden and speak to him there?' Losing patience with the garrulous woman, Amos cut across her diatribe and put the question to Andrew.

The woman glared at him for a moment before addressing one of the two young girls who had been listening but saying nothing. 'Go and find your pa. Tell him there's someone to speak to him . . . about Laura.'

Humphrey Penrose entered the house after kicking the worst of the mud off his boots against the granite wall of the cottage, outside the back door. Looking from Andrew to Amos, he settled his gaze upon the former,

115

saying, 'You'll be Andrew Elkins. You favour your father. I won't shake hands with you – mine are covered in mud from the garden. I try to grow most of the vegetables we eat in the house. With little or no work on the mines every penny counts.'

After sympathising with Penrose about the lack of work to be had in the area, Andrew introduced Amos, adding, 'He came with me because he's been trying to find out something about his father, who used to work at the Wheal Notter, just up the hill from here.'

While they had been talking, the miner's wife had left the room and Penrose said, 'I never had much to do with they who worked up at Notter, although Mary might have known him. Her first husband was working up there when he was killed . . . but I believe you've come to speak to me about Laura.'

'That's right. I was hoping I might be able to have a talk with her. Is she around?'

Looking apologetic, Penrose said, 'She'd usually be at the dairy, up at Sterrett's farm, but there was a bit of an argument with Mrs Sterrett yesterday and Laura's no longer working there.'

Andrew had come to Henwood in order to learn something of Laura's character, and at mention of an argument he showed immediate interest. 'What was the argument about . . . was Laura at fault?'

'Well . . . not exactly . . . although Mary would say she was. The Sterretts were putting more and more work on Laura and for the past two days she'd come home with her frock so muddied it needed to be washed. Mary said she couldn't afford to waste soap like that every

116

day and that the Sterretts should supply it. Yesterday she met Mrs Sterrett in the village and there was an argument about it. The result was that Mrs Sterrett went straight back to the farm and told our Laura she didn't want her working there any more.'

Humphrey Penrose hurried his story because his wife was coming back into the room, but he was not quick enough to prevent her from hearing the final part of it.

'Are you telling them about Laura coming back here so muddy that she needed to wash her clothes? If she'd had the gumption to tell the Sterretts that she was a dairymaid and not a farm labourer, she'd never have got herself in that state in the first place. If they'd wanted her to do such work they should have paid her for it as well as paying for her clothes to be washed – and I told Harriet Sterrett so, too.'

'Laura was helping the Sterretts out because their farmhand was off sick,' Humphrey Penrose said, with the air of a man who knew that whatever he said would not be accepted. 'The Sterretts are not a lot better off than we are. They were paying Laura the best they could – with what they produced on their small farm. Milk, butter, eggs and the occasional loaf and cake. We were pleased enough to have it.'

'I'd have been happier to have had money to spend on things *I* felt we needed,' Mary Penrose retorted. 'But doing *proper* work doesn't suit Miss High-and-Mighty, so I won't put up with any complaints from her if she goes hungry ... and, unless I'm mistaken, this is her coming in now, so you can just tell her so.'

Laura opened the door and came inside the cottage

hurriedly, as though expecting to find someone she knew inside. When she saw Andrew and Amos, she stopped in her tracks and the eagerness left her expression. 'Oh, I thought it was Mr Elkins's horse outside. I'm sorry . . . I'll leave you.'

'No . . . wait!' Her father's voice brought her to a halt. 'Minister Elkins's son came here on his father's horse to speak to you. He's a schoolteacher and his father has asked him to come here and have a few words with you.'

Laura was older than Andrew had suggested she would be. Amos thought she was probably about fifteen, or even more. Dark-haired and dark-eyed, she was tall for her age, but she was still a young girl and, aware of how important this interview could be for her, she looked from Amos to Andrew and back again with increasing concern.

In a bid to put her at her ease, Amos smiled and said, 'It's Andrew who will be speaking to you. I just came to keep him company . . . and to wish you luck.'

'Luck! There's little enough of that in the life of a mining family – and the sort of life that girl is looking for will take more than luck. It needs a miracle, so don't go raising her hopes. When you've gone it'll be me who is left to put up with her – and I've got enough to do as it is, what with a husband out of work and no money coming into the house.'

'It can't be easy for you, Mrs Penrose,' Amos said appeasingly, 'but if Laura is as intelligent as Minister Elkins obviously believes her to be she will be able to work at something that brings in more money than working as a bal maiden – even when there *is* work available on a mine. At the very worst, you will have

118

one fewer mouth to feed. Now, while Andrew takes Laura outside, I would like to ask you if you ever came across my father, who once worked at Wheal Notter. He seems to have disappeared off the face of the earth . . .'

The teacher took the hint and left the house, accompanied by Laura. Addressing Mary, Amos said, 'Did you ever hear of a Doniert Hawke up at the Wheal Notter? I haven't seen him since I left Cornwall to join the Royal Marines, many years ago.'

'Doniert Hawke? Yes, I knew him. He worked with my first husband for a while, but I never saw much of him after that.'

'That would no doubt be before the Wheal Notter shut down. I don't seem to be able to find anyone who knows where he might have gone after that.'

'Oh, I think some of the men saw him once or twice after that,' Mary said surprisingly. 'So he couldn't have gone very far away.'

'They saw him after he stopped working at the Wheal Notter?' Amos looked at Mary Penrose with interest. 'Very long after?'

'Some time after, I believe,' came the reply. 'In fact, the last time anyone mentioned him couldn't have been much more than a few months since. It was after Cap'n Billy Arthur had that big to-do with Hannibal Davey – now that's the man you ought to speak to. He and your father were both going around with the Davey crowd at one time. If you want to learn any more you could always speak to Hannibal – but for your own sake try to catch him when he's in a good mood. He's not partial to anyone who asks too many questions about him or his doings.'

119

19

Riding back to Charlestown from Henwood village, Amos mulled over what Mary Penrose had said about his father being seen after the Wheal Notter closed, and of his close involvement with Hannibal Davey – and Captain Billy. It meant that the latter had not told him the full truth of what he knew about his father. He would try to find the elusive ex-miner again – and this time draw the whole story from him.

Unfortunately, Amos was not able to devote the whole of his attention to the matter, being very aware of the two arms about his waist, and an intermittent barrage of questions from Laura, who was riding behind him on the horse.

When it became clear that Laura's stepmother was beginning to have second thoughts about allowing a potential source of revenue to leave the house despite the friction that existed between them, Amos and

Andrew had decided to waste no time in taking the young girl back to Charlestown with them. Humphrey Penrose had given his permission, and while he and his second wife were still arguing about the matter Laura had gathered her pitifully sparse belongings into a bundle and departed from the house with the two visitors.

The Methodist preacher's horse was too old and infirm to carry two riders, and, with Laura's belongings safely stowed in his saddlebags, Amos suggested he should carry her with him on his horse. While the two men were discussing the best method of carrying a young woman behind the rider, Laura solved the problem by clambering on to the horse behind Amos and, much to the disapproval of her stepmother, making herself comfortable astride the animal in an admittedly most unladylike manner.

Now, as they rode along, Laura would occasionally tighten her arms about Amos's waist in an involuntary display of excitement and put a question to him about the huge change of lifestyle she was about to make. One of her first questions was put with a degree of trepidation.

'Andrew said that you will be paying for me to have lessons at Miss Kernow's school?'

'That's right . . . at least, I will be until Minister Elkins can make some arrangements for his church to help.' Amos dragged his thoughts back from his father's connection with Hannibal Davey.

'Why? What do you expect from me in return?'

Recognising that the blunt question resulted from the

121

puzzlement of a young girl who had been brought up in the belief that nobody did anything without wanting something in exchange, Amos replied, 'I don't expect anything from you . . . unless it's that you will take full advantage of the opportunity you are being given to make something of yourself.'

'I will,' she said fervently, 'I *really* will . . . but why should you spend money on someone you have never met before? Are you rich?'

Amused, Amos replied, 'No, I'm not rich, but I can afford to spend a few pence to give someone a chance to change their life for the better – as I did when I was able to join the Royal Marines when I was a couple of years younger than you are now. Besides, I feel I owe a debt to Florence Nightingale and her nurses who treated me at Scutari. They were all well trained and a far cry from any nurses I had met before then. We can never have too many such wonderful women.'

'You were in Scutari? Did you ever meet Miss Nightingale?' There was both disbelief and awe in Laura's voice.

'I met her on a number of occasions. She was a very busy woman, but rarely too busy to have a word with a wounded soldier . . . or marine.'

For much of the remainder of the ride, Amos was obliged to answer a whole barrage of questions from Laura about her heroine and the work carried out by her nurses at the Turkish hospital at Scutari. It soon became apparent to him that the ambition to become a 'Nightingale nurse' was no sudden whim, but had been burning within Laura for a very long time.

He was convinced that the few pence he would be spending on her each week would not be wasted.

When Amos and Andrew arrived at Penrice with Laura, Talwyn was at home in the cottage. She was seated at a table in the window of the living room, writing out a syllabus for the next few weeks' lessons, when she saw the little party arrive.

She registered instant disapproval at her first sight of Laura with her arms about Amos's waist, riding behind him astride the horse, her dress up about her knees. She was older than Talwyn had been led to believe and the schoolmistress felt she should have shown a modesty befitting her age and sex. However, she did not allow her displeasure to show when she left the cottage with her mother to greet the new arrival.

The introductions were made by Andrew, who said, 'Laura, this is Mrs Kernow and Miss Kernow – your new teacher. Talwyn, and Mrs Kernow, I would like you to meet Laura, who has come to stay with you and attend the school.'

'Well, this *is* a surprise,' Talwyn said to Laura. 'We were expecting you – but not quite so soon.'

Alarmed, Laura said, 'It doesn't mean . . . I have to go back to Henwood?'

'Her father gave his permission for Laura to come here and attend the school, but her stepmother did not entirely approve, so we thought it best to bring her along with us right away,' Andrew explained. 'I think Laura is afraid that if she is made to return, her stepmother might persuade her father to change his mind.'

'There is no question of her returning.' Maisie had observed Laura's consternation and now she added, 'She is very welcome here and we have been looking forward to her arrival. Talwyn, why don't you show Laura to her room, while I make a cup of tea and prepare us all a meal. I don't suppose anyone has had anything to eat along the way.'

'Do I have my own room ... a *proper* room?' Laura queried. 'I don't have to share it with anyone?'

At Laura's barely contained excitement as she asked the questions, Talwyn's heart went out to her. 'It is your very own room – you don't have to share it with anyone and nobody is allowed inside without your express permission,' she said. 'Come along and I will show you. I think you are going to like it ... I hope you will enjoy school too.'

'I'm a bit scared of that,' Laura confessed. Then, remembering she was talking to the woman who would be teaching her, she added hurriedly, 'What I mean is ... I know I'm going to enjoy it, but I'll be so far behind everyone else of my age.'

'If you are as bright as Minister Elkins – and Andrew – seem to think you are, you'll catch up with everyone in no time at all,' Talwyn said. 'And you will have the added advantage of having me here to answer any questions you may have about your work. By the way, I will expect you to call me Miss Kernow when we are in school, but at home I am Talwyn.'

They were on the staircase to the back bedrooms now and when the landing was reached, Talwyn opened one of the two doors leading off it to reveal a neat and newly cleaned room. Inside was a single bed, a diminutive wardrobe and a chest of drawers, with a vase of recently cut and fragrant flowers placed upon the window shelf.

'Here you are. This is your room.'

Laura squealed with delight and clambered on the bed in order to look out of the window to see the same view as that enjoyed by Amos from the adjacent room.

'It's *lovely* . . . and my very own!'

'That's right, it is your very own – and I hope you are going to be very happy here.'

'I am, I just *know* I am, but . . . is that your room next to mine?'

'No.' Talwyn's enthusiasm faded a little. 'That is Mr Hawke's room.'

Laura did not notice the change in the tone of Talwyn's voice, or the fact that she had called Andrew by his first name, yet had used Amos's surname. She said, animatedly, 'He is nice . . . do you know that he has met Florence Nightingale? He was telling me about her on the way here.'

'Yes, I do know . . . but I don't suppose you will see very much of him while you are here. He comes and goes at all hours.'

Remembering the manner in which Laura had arrived at the cottage, Talwyn felt unease that Laura should speak with such enthusiasm about Amos, and about the fact that they would be sharing the same landing without supervision. She decided she should warn Laura about becoming unduly familiar with him – but she would

125

leave it for now. This young and unsophisticated moorland girl was so obviously delighted with all that had come into her young life that day, Talwyn had no wish to spoil it in any way.

20

For the next few days Amos visited the coastal villages around Charlestown, frequenting the inns during the evening hours, hoping to see Captain Billy once more, but he seemed to have left the area. Amos met a couple of men who claimed to know the ex-miner, but neither had seen anything of him recently.

Then, one evening, when Amos was drinking in the Rashleigh Arms, he saw two men he recognised as having been with Hannibal on the night when smugglers had been active in the area.

He hoped they might be joined, as before, by Hannibal and the other men, but after he had waited and watched them until very late, the men parted company and left, and Amos was forced to admit it had probably been no more than a social visit to the Charlestown inn by the pair.

It was midnight before he arrived home, and as he

made his way to the rear of the cottage he was surprised to see a light still burning in the room now occupied by Laura. Quietly letting himself into the house, he crept up the stairs and stopped on the landing. The door to Laura's room was closed, but light was showing from a gap beneath the door.

Amos listened at the door for a while but could hear no sound from within. He hesitated for a few moments, wondering what to do. It was very late to be knocking on the door of Laura's room but if she had fallen asleep and left a candle burning . . .

He knocked softly and in reply a startled voice said, 'What . . . ? Who is it?'

'It's only me . . . Amos,' he called softly. 'I have just come in and saw a light in your room. I was afraid you might have fallen asleep and left a candle burning. I'm sorry to have disturbed you. Good night!'

Instead of a reply, there was the sound of Laura hurrying across the room, then the door opened and she appeared in the doorway. Much to Amos's relief, she was fully dressed.

'I'm sorry if I worried you,' she said, adding, 'What time is it?'

'It's after midnight. I'm surprised you are not in bed. You'll be tired for school in the morning.'

'It's school work that has been keeping me awake. Miss Kernow – Talwyn – gave us some sums to do this morning and I couldn't do very many of them, so I brought them home with me. I've been trying to do them here, but I'm still not very good, especially with the fractions. Can you do arithmetic?'

128

'Well, I wouldn't say it's my best subject, but yes, I can work out fractions. Do you want me to help you . . . now? It is very late.'

'If you can help me to understand them a little better I'll go straight to bed afterwards.'

'All right.' Aware there was only room for one chair in Laura's room and that if he went in there they would need to sit upon the bed together to work on the sums, he said, 'Bring them out here and we'll sit on the top stair and see if we can sort them out.'

A few minutes later they were sitting together on the top stair, the candle from Laura's room balanced on the top support of the wooden balustrade. After a cursory glance at the work that was causing her problems, Amos realised, to his relief, that the sums were of a very elementary nature and he began to explain them.

Laura had a very quick brain and she soon grasped the essentials of adding, subtracting, dividing and multiplying fractions. As she worked out the last few remaining sums, Laura suddenly looked up and asked, 'Was my stepmother able to tell you anything about your father when he was working at the Wheal Notter?'

'Not really . . . she suggested I should ask Hannibal Davey about him.'

Laura looked up in alarm. 'You must stay away from him. He and his brother are scary.'

'What do you mean by "scary"? Have they ever done anything to frighten you?'

'They didn't have to *do* anything. They only had to look at me and it was enough to make my skin creep. Especially after what happened when Hannibal and the

129

men working on his pare broke through into the Wheal Phoenix workings.'

'Oh! What *did* happen?'

Laura shuddered. 'There was a fight. One of the Wheal Phoenix men was killed and another died later. Everyone knew that Hannibal and his brother had killed them, but nobody dared say anything. At the inquest it was said the men died as a result of a roof fall – but the captain of the Wheal Notter knew different. It was him who persuaded the mine owner to have it closed down.'

Laura had just confirmed the sketchy information that Captain Billy had given to Amos about the Daveys and the incident that had occurred at Wheal Notter. It was something he hoped he might be able to use in the future. He had a sudden thought, and aired it aloud. 'I wonder whether the hole connecting the two mines is still there?'

He did not expect Laura to have the answer to his question, but she surprised him by saying, 'Yes, it's still there, but Wheal Phoenix had that part of their mine shut off. The men wouldn't go down there because they said it was haunted – and all the ore had been taken out anyway, so Wheal Phoenix expanded to the south and east instead.'

'What an interesting story,' Amos mused. He had one further question. 'Is the same captain still in charge of the Wheal Phoenix?'

'Yes, Captain Woodcock. He lives in the big house just up the valley towards Minions.'

'Well, thank you for filling me in on the history of the Wheal Notter ... but now we had better finish off those sums, or you will be so tired you won't be able to do your schoolwork in the morning.'

'That's all right. Now you've shown me how to do them it will only take me a few minutes in the morning to finish them off when I get to school. Thank you. You are very kind to me.'

They were sitting close to each other and suddenly, without warning, Laura leaned across the space between them and kissed him quickly on the cheek. Then, as though aware of the presumptuousness of her action, she scrambled to her feet, her cheeks scarlet ... and at that moment Talwyn appeared at the bottom of the stairs, an expression of stern disapproval upon her face.

'I *thought* I heard voices while I was in bed, but felt I must be imagining things. What on earth are you two doing together at this time of night? No, don't tell me, I have no wish to listen to any excuses now, it is far too late. Laura, go to your room this instant. We will talk more of this in the morning ... *Go!*'

Suddenly tearful, Laura snatched up the candle, turned and fled inside her room, leaving the hall in darkness. From the gloom at the foot of the stairs, Talwyn said contemptuously, 'I shouldn't be surprised at your conduct, Mr Hawke ... but I am. You too will go to your room now and I will wait here until I hear the door close before I return to my own part of the house. I will have more to say to you in the morning.'

'No you will not!' Amos declared fiercely, descending the stairs as quickly as he dared in the darkness. 'You will listen to what I have to say first, and then *you* can go to *your* room and think about it.'

131

Taken completely by surprise, Talwyn could only splutter in protest as Amos took a firm grip of her arm and propelled her into the kitchen. There was just enough light from the dying fire for him to see sufficiently to guide her to a chair and seat her upon it.

'What do you think you are doing?' Talwyn demanded when she had recovered somewhat from being so roughly manhandled.

'I'm doing what I should have done much sooner,' Amos declared, 'putting you very firmly in your place. I have endured your behaviour because it really doesn't matter very much to me – but I have no intention of standing back and saying nothing when I see your narrow-minded bigotry destroying the future of a young girl who probably has far more to offer the world than you ever will.'

Talwyn began to protest, but she got no further than 'How dare you . . . !' before Amos said very firmly, 'Shut up! You have said quite enough over the last week or two . . . now it's my turn. I really don't give a damn what you think of me – I am old enough and big enough to take your rudeness and insinuations. Laura is not. She is a sensitive young girl who has had a very difficult time but who is working hard – working *very* hard – to make something of herself. I am not going to stand by and say nothing when I see an insensitive and twisted spinster schoolteacher destroy all that girl is working for.'

Talwyn was so taken aback by the sheer forcefulness of Amos's tone of voice that she could not find the words she wanted, and so said nothing. He continued, 'I came home tonight and saw a light on in Laura's room. I thought twice about knocking on her door at such a late hour, but there was a possibility that she might have gone to sleep and left a candle burning. That would have put everyone in the house in danger, so I did knock. She was not asleep – and was not even dressed for bed. Instead, aware of how much she has to learn in order to catch up with the others in your school, she was working on the sums you had given to the class this morning. She had mastered most of them, but was having difficulty with fractions and asked me if I could explain them to her. I did, and was very impressed with her quick mind. Laura is more eager to learn than anyone I have ever met and I would be more than happy to help her reach her goal. However, I realise that with you prepared to think the very worst of me, whatever I do, my presence in the house can only prove a hindrance to her. Your bias against me might even prevent her from achieving all she is so desperate to accomplish. As I said just now, I am old enough to sort out my own problems . . . she is not. I won't leave the house immediately because she would believe that she had caused my departure and would take it very much to heart. I don't want that to happen, so I will give you notice here and now that I shall go as soon as I have found alternative accommodation. That should give you time to find another lodger and give Laura time to forget what has happened tonight. Now, if you have a conscience and any finer feelings, you will go upstairs and apologise to Laura for upsetting her, and ensure she doesn't feel guilty about staying up until all hours of the night in order to meet the standards *you* set in *your* school. I really don't expect you to do that, because I don't think you have a generous enough spirit ... but your conscience is your business, not mine. Now, I am going to bed – and you can do exactly what you wish. I really don't care.'

With this, Amos left the kitchen and climbed the stairs to his room, heavy-hearted, but feeling justified in the action he had just taken.

Behind him, in the kitchen, Talwyn was left stunned by the berating she had just received and with the certain knowledge that she would have a lot to think about before sleep came to her that night ... if, in fact, it came at all.

Amos did not share Talwyn's prospective battle with sleeplessness. He went to bed in the belief that the events of the night would keep him awake – but they had quite the opposite effect. Within minutes of laying his head upon the pillow, he had fallen into a very deep sleep.

He did not hear the gentle knock on the door of the room next to his, or the soft-voiced conversation that continued long after Talwyn and Laura had crept quietly downstairs to the kitchen.

Amos slept so soundly that by the time he woke in the morning both Talwyn and Laura had left for school, and when he came down from his bedroom it was quite apparent that Maisie Kernow was unaware of anything that had occurred during the night.

21

Amos said nothing to Maisie about his intentions, but as soon as he had washed and had breakfast, he set off for Penrice manor, to call on Sir Joseph Sawle. His story to the butler was that he had a question to put to the baronet about his missing father. In reality, he wanted Sir Joseph to ask Detective Inspector Carpenter to meet him later that morning in a small, disused quarry workings on the edge of the Penrice estate.

Marcus Carpenter arrived at the rendezvous on foot soon after Amos and they held their discussions seated on a gigantic slab of rock which had been dislodged from the quarry face many years before. Here they were hidden from the view of anyone passing the quarry entrance by a huge pile of waste earth and stones.

'You wanted to see me,' the detective inspector said. 'Have you learned something of importance?'

'I have learned a great many things in recent days,'

Amos replied. 'Unfortunately, most only tend to confirm what we already suspect. I've been given nothing that might be used as evidence against our suspects. However, one of the most important things I've discovered is a link between schoolteacher Kernow and the ex-Notter Tor miners who we believe are heavily involved in smuggling. It provides a possible motive for his murder. Most of the miners – including Hannibal and Pasco Davey – are from the Henwood area and Edward Kernow ran a school there until the mine ceased working. It means he would have recognised the Daveys and others involved in smuggling had he come across them when they were engaged in their activities. Everyone I have met who knew Kernow declares that he was an honest and law-abiding man. Had he accidentally come across any of the men in the act of breaking the law he would have reported them . . . probably to Sir Joseph Sawle. The Davey brothers would have been aware of this – and if all that is said about them is true, they would have had no compunction about killing him in order to avoid arrest. They are both very violent men.'

Amos told Carpenter about the deaths of the two miners on the occasion when the Notter Tor miners broke through into the Wheal Phoenix workings, adding, 'Because the other miners were so terrified of the Davey brothers, they gave false evidence at the coroner's court and the deaths were recorded as being the result of a roof fall.'

'You are certain of this?'

'Yes. The Daveys are very dangerous men to fall foul of. Have you been able to learn anything about their army service?'

'Not yet,' Carpenter replied, 'although I sent a telegraph message to London and said it was urgent. I will send another message stressing that the information is vital to a murder investigation.'

'There is something else that came about as a result of what I learned of the incident involving the Davey brothers,' Amos said. 'The breakthrough from one mine to the other means that somewhere below ground access may be gained to the Wheal Notter from Wheal Phoenix. It's in a section of the workings that is now deserted. Not only is the ore exhausted there, but the miners are convinced it is haunted by the two men who died . . . and miners are very superstitious men. The same works captain who was running the Phoenix when the incident occurred is still in charge there and lives near the mine. His name is Woodcock. If you can speak to him, swear him to secrecy and obtain the plans of the mine's underground workings, I will go down and try to confirm my suspicions about the Wheal Notter adit's being used to store contraband. If Woodcock could make a rough plan to give us some idea of the Wheal Notter underground workings that would be doubly helpful. Once the mine's connection with smuggling is confirmed we can keep a closer watch on the Daveys and their accomplices and catch them when a landing is made – calling in the military to help us if you think it advisable.'

'That would no doubt put all the men, including the Daveys, away for a very long time,' Marcus Carpenter agreed, 'and it would undoubtedly please Sir Joseph Sawle; but, as I told him, we are in Cornwall to solve murders, not catch smugglers.'

'You told him that?' Amos was surprised. Sir Joseph Sawle not only was an important man in the county, but had many friends in Parliament – and it was well known among members of the Metropolitan Police that the inspector in command of London's detectives was a very ambitious man and careful not to say anything that might upset men of influence. Besides, it was rumoured that Cornwall would soon have its own constabulary – and it would need a chief constable. Carpenter might consider himself as a possible candidate.

'Perhaps I did not put it quite so bluntly,' Carpenter admitted, 'but as a result of the information I gave him, he had the officer in command of Cornwall's Excise services call on him to discuss what he sees as an unacceptable increase in smuggling activities along the Cornish coast. The Excise officer conceded, albeit reluctantly, that with so many Royal Navy ships deployed in trouble spots around the world, smugglers carrying contraband between France and the southern coast of our country are enjoying a freedom they have not experienced since the latter years of the last century. It seems that only this week a Royal Navy warship arriving at Plymouth from Roscoff reported that a well-known Cornish smuggling vessel had been in the French port, openly taking on board a considerable cargo of brandy. It will doubtless soon be on its way to the midnight beaches of Cornwall. Unfortunately, although the combined coastguard and Excise services are having some success in rooting out corrupt officers, he admitted that there are still many within the service who are unwilling to make themselves unpopular in their communities by arresting offenders.'

'That has always been a problem,' Amos conceded, 'and although ordinary folk – even the smugglers themselves – have little sympathy with those who are ready to kill in order to protect their trade, they are terrified of the Daveys. There can be no doubting that a great many of them know enough to have the Daveys convicted of murder, but are too scared to say so.'

'Quite probably,' Carpenter agreed, 'and I do think we should learn as much as possible about their smuggling activities, but when I take action I want to be absolutely certain we are going to be able to convict someone for murder.'

'Then I suggest we try to secure the arrest of Captain Billy ... the woman in Henwood called him Captain Billy Arthur. He can be taken in on a vagrancy charge, if necessary. He knows far more than he has told me so far, but he too is terrified of Hannibal Davey. That could well be because he knows more about the murders than is good for him.' After a moment's hesitation, Amos added, 'I also have reason to believe that my father had a close association with both Captain Billy and the Daveys at one time.'

Detective Inspector Carpenter looked inquiringly at Amos. 'How do you feel about that? Would you prefer to be removed from this investigation?'

'Most certainly not,' Amos said emphatically. 'Should it turn out that he is implicated in some way and is still alive, who better than me to persuade him to turn Queen's evidence against the Daveys?'

Carpenter nodded, apparently satisfied with Amos's reply. 'Very well ... but if I can obtain plans of the underground workings from the captain of Wheal Phoenix I will not allow you to go down there alone. I will come too.'

Amos doubted whether his superior officer had ever experienced the conditions they were likely to encounter underground in an abandoned mine working, but he did not express the thought. Instead, he said, 'That makes a lot of sense, sir, and I think we should do it as soon as possible.'

'I will pay a call on this mine captain in the next day or two. Is there anything else you wish to discuss with me?'

Amos hesitated before saying, 'Yes, sir, but it's of a more personal nature. I really don't think I can learn anything more from the Kernow family and the daughter is far from happy to have me living in the family house. I would like to change my lodgings as soon as I can find suitable alternative accommodation.'

Detective Inspector Carpenter gave Amos a searching look, aware that there was probably more behind Amos's statement than he had disclosed. 'Do you really believe there is nothing more to be learned from them?'

'Nothing, sir.'

'Very well. Where you lodge doesn't matter, just as long as solving the murders of the Excise men and Edward Kernow remains in the forefront of your thinking. The present arrangement seems quite satisfactory to me, but I am not the one living with the Kernows. Do whatever you think is best – but keep me fully informed of what is happening.'

22

When Amos left Detective Inspector Carpenter, he walked back to the Kernow cottage with the intention of collecting his horse and riding along the coastline to see if he could see any signs of mules having been brought down from the moor in readiness for the arrival of the smugglers' vessel reported to have been loading contraband at Roscoff.

Although not impossible, it would be expecting a great deal of the pack animals to be brought from Bodmin Moor to the coast and led back the same night heavily laden with contraband. It was far more likely they would be brought to the area in advance and grazed in a quiet spot for some hours before performing their nocturnal task.

He intended telling Maisie he would not be at the cottage for dinner when Talwyn returned home with Laura at the end of the morning's lessons at Charlestown

school. He did not relish the thought of yet another alter-
cation with Talwyn, although he realised he would need
to tell Maisie of his decision to move out of the cottage
in the near future. However, that could wait until he
had found suitable accommodation elsewhere – it would
be a shame to unsettle her before it was absolutely necessary. If another reason for his reluctance to commit
himself to a leaving date occurred to him, he was resolute
in banishing it. Talwyn disliked and despised him – it
would be best for them both if he went.

If, as seemed highly probable, there was to be a raid
on the Wheal Notter adit, it might be helpful if he found
lodgings in the moorland border town of Liskeard. The
town was close enough to the moor to enable him to
stay in contact with all that was going on there, yet large
enough for his presence not to create too much interest.

When he arrived at the Kernows' house, Amos
checked his horse then saddled up before going inside.
There was no sign of Maisie in either the kitchen or the
lounge, so he called upstairs.

There was no reply, but he thought he heard someone
calling from outside, possibly from the back garden.
Surprised he had not noticed Maisie there when he had
arrived, he went outside and called, 'Maisie . . . are you
out here?'

The reply was immediate. 'I'm here . . . by the cherry
tree . . . Please help me.' Her voice sounded strained, as
though she was in pain, and Amos hurried to the
orchard.

He saw her long before he reached the gate. She was
lying beneath a branch that was bowed down with the

weight of fruit, one of her legs inexplicably caught up in the woodwork of a sawhorse that was partly lying across her.

There was also a great deal of blood staining her leg and the dress she was wearing.

'Maisie . . . ! What on earth have you been doing?' He called out the question before reaching her.

'I wanted to pick some cherries . . . to make a pie. I couldn't quite reach one of the branches and didn't know where the ladder was . . . so, foolishly, I dragged the sawhorse here thinking I could reach the branch by standing on one of the supports. Then, when I tried to climb a bit higher, my foot slipped and the sawhorse fell over on me. I can't free myself. I think there must have been a nail poking through the wood . . . it's gone deep into my leg . . .'

While she was talking, Amos had been examining the wooden sawhorse in which Maisie's leg was trapped. Home-made of rough-cut timber, it had a number of pieces of wood tacked on to the original framework to provide additional rigidity and strength. It was a primitive structure, put together using whatever material was to hand. As a result, many of the nails were much too long and protruded far beyond the pieces of wood they were holding together. It was one of these that was impaling Maisie's leg at a point midway between her left knee and the narrow band of lace around the bottom of her drawers.

The drawers themselves were soaked in Maisie's blood and Amos realised she must have been trapped for a long time. There was no way of knowing how deeply the nail was embedded in her flesh and it would be dangerous to risk trying to pull her leg free.

'Do you have a saw anywhere, Maisie?' he asked.

'There should be one in the empty pig house, beside the stable where you keep your horse, but—'

Interrupting her, Amos said, 'Try to stay as still as you can. Once I get the saw I'll have you out of there in no time.' Without giving her any further explanation, Amos set off at a run from the orchard.

There were in fact three saws in the disused pigsty. Choosing one with a coarse blade, Amos hurried back to Maisie.

Cutting her free was not the simplest of tasks and at one stage he needed to turn her on to her side, moving what remained of the sawhorse with her. It caused her a great deal of pain, but a few moments later she was attached to only a small section of the piece of wood from which the offending nail protruded.

After a quick inspection of the wound, and without giving Maisie any prior warning, Amos tugged nail and wood free from her leg.

Maisie gave a shriek of pain and Amos quickly took a clean handkerchief from his pocket. Folding it to make a pad, he placed it on the wound and instructed Maisie to hold it in place. Then, gathering her up in his arms, he headed for the house.

Once inside the kitchen, he sat her down in the most comfortable chair and said, 'Do you have any clean cloths, Maisie? I want to clean up that wound and put on another pad. When that's done I'll go to the manor and have someone come and sit with you while I go off

144

to fetch a doctor. You've lost a lot of blood and that wound is a deep one. It needs more expert treatment than I can give you.'

Despite the pain she was in, Maisie said, 'You have been wonderful, Amos. I don't know what would have happened to me had you not come along when you did. I had been lying there for a long time ... and had swooned off a couple of times.'

'You have been very brave, Maisie ... but some cloths ... ?'

He found clean linen cloths in a drawer of the kitchen dresser, and also a number of fresh towels. A kettle was simmering gently on the side of the kitchen range and, pouring some of the water into a bowl, Amos began to clean up the area around the wound, apologising as he did so.

'This must be very embarrassing for you, Maisie, but there is so much blood, both fresh and dried, that I can't see what needs to be done. Fortunately, the nail that entered your leg seems to be fairly new and hasn't had time to rust ... but it caused a nasty gash even before it went in.'

'Edward ... my husband repaired the sawhorse only a week or so before he died,' Maisie explained, and became suddenly tearful. 'He would have been so cross at my foolishness, but I've never had to pick fruit from the orchard before. He always did it for me.'

She was still tearful when they heard a sound from outside and a moment later Laura entered the house through the kitchen doorway and stopped, open-mouthed at the scene before her.

'You are the very person I was wishing was here,' Amos said with genuine relief. 'This is a wonderful opportunity for you to learn what being a nurse is about. Mrs Kernow had an accident in the garden and has a very nasty wound caused by a nail. I was going to clean as much of it as I could before going to Penrice manor and asking one of the servants to come here and stay with her while I went for a doctor. Now you are here you can carry on with what needs doing.'

While he was talking, Maisie had glanced at the clock and now she said, 'What are you doing home so early, child . . . and where is Talwyn?'

'One of the girls at school had convulsions and was sick,' Laura explained. 'Her father is one of Sir Joseph Sawle's gardeners, and they live in a cottage just the other side of the manor. Talwyn asked me to bring her home and said I didn't need to go back to school. She said she would help me to catch up with anything I had missed when she came home.'

'Oh dear!' Maisie exclaimed. 'Whatever am I going to do about getting something to eat for everyone?'

'You are going to do nothing,' Amos replied firmly. 'In fact, now Laura is here I will carry you up to your bedroom and you can stay there and let her clean you up and change your clothes ready for the doctor.'

'When I've done that, you can tell me what we are to have and I'll cook for us,' Laura said eagerly. 'I *like* cooking. Before my pa married again he used to say I took after my ma who everyone says was the best cook in Henwood.'

'There you are, Maisie,' Amos said, 'I am leaving you

in very good hands . . . but you won't need to cook for me, Laura. There are some things I need to attend to after I have made certain the doctor is on his way. First I will get Mrs Kernow upstairs to her bedroom, while you gather all the clean towels and cloths that you can find and bring them up to her room. Glancing at Maisie's leg, he added, 'Mrs Kernow's leg is still bleeding badly, so you'll need to make certain you put a pad on it and tie it tightly.'

As Amos carried Maisie upstairs, he was unaware of Laura's disappointment that he would not be eating the meal she was to cook. She had been excited at the prospect of impressing him with her skill in the kitchen.

23

When Amos had left the cottage, Laura busied herself with Maisie. After dressing the wound on her leg and securing a pad as instructed by Amos, she found clean drawers for her patient and helped her change into a nightdress and nightcap. As she worked she chatted to the older woman, learning exactly what had happened in the garden.

'What a good thing that Amos came home when he did,' she remarked, when she had the full story.

'It certainly was,' Maisie agreed. 'Had he not found me when he did I could have bled to death. There was no way I could have freed myself.'

'Not only did he come along in time, but he knew exactly what to do when he found you,' Laura said worshipfully. It was quite evident to Maisie that Laura thought Amos was wonderful, but she was unprepared for the question that followed. 'Why doesn't Talwyn like him?'

Startled, Maisie replied, 'I don't think her attitude towards him has anything to do with liking or not liking. Talwyn took the loss of her father very badly and resents the need to have a paying guest in the house. She would behave the same towards anyone, no matter who it was.'

'I don't think Amos believes that.'

'Why do you say that, Laura? Has he said something to you?'

'No,' Laura said hurriedly. She had no wish to discuss the events of the previous night. 'It's just the way she speaks to him sometimes. But, as you say, after what happened to poor Mr Kernow she would probably behave exactly the same towards anyone whom you *had* to have in the house.'

'Yes, but after this morning she has reason to be very grateful to Amos. Had it not been for him she would probably have lost a mother as well as a father . . . Now, would you have a bit of a tidy round the bedroom before the doctor arrives? Then you can go and prepare something for dinner when Talwyn arrives home. You'll find potatoes in the scullery and can pick a few peas from the garden . . . and cut some meat off the ham that's in the meat safe – but don't forget to close the door tight when you're finished; I don't want any blowflies getting in there. I had intended to make a cherry pie too . . . but we won't talk about that.'

* * *

Talwyn arrived home just as Dr Cheadle was leaving. The sight of him alarmed her. 'What is it, doctor? Why are you here? Has something happened to my mother . . . or is it Laura?'

Quick to reassure her, Dr Cheadle said, 'Your mother has had an accident, as a result of which she has a nasty wound in her leg, but she is going to be all right. She just needs to rest and build up her strength. Lots of meat broth and that sort of thing. You have a good little helper in there who is taking care of her at the moment and, fortunately, she was found by someone who had sense enough not to try to pull her free immediately. Had that happened it would probably have severed an artery . . . and I would be making a very different prognosis . . .'

The doctor's remarks made very little sense until Talwyn hurried inside the house and went upstairs to her mother's bedroom. Here she heard from her the full story of what had happened.

Biting back criticism of her mother's part in causing the accident, Talwyn cuddled her instead, tearfully remembering the doctor's words about what would have happened had she been found by someone who tried to pull her free of the sawhorse before he could see what he was doing.

Mother and daughter were interrupted by Laura, who appeared in the bedroom carrying a tray on which was a meal for Maisie. She announced that Talwyn's dinner was ready, with her own, in the kitchen. When Maisie was propped up in her bed supported by pillows and able to tackle her meal comfortably, Talwyn and Laura went downstairs. The table was laid for only two and

Talwyn asked, 'Will Mr Hawke not be joining us for dinner?'

'No, he said he had things to attend to.' Laura put hot vegetables on to their two plates as she spoke.

'What sort of things?'

Laura shrugged. 'I don't know. Looking for people who might have known his father, I suppose.'

Talwyn wondered whether Amos really did have things to do, or whether he was trying to avoid her because of their confrontation the previous night. She was also confused about her feelings towards him. She still believed that her anger at finding him with Laura at such an hour had been justified, even though after talking to Laura she accepted his version of events, but she had to admit that his response had taken her completely by surprise. In her heart she realised that it had been fully deserved, but what she did not expect were her confused feelings because he had not taken her to task for her manner towards *him*, but in defence of Laura and the disastrous effect it was likely to have upon *her* future.

Talwyn was a just woman as well as an intelligent one, and she was able to admit to herself that Amos had been a convenient scapegoat on whom to vent the anger and sorrow she felt at losing her father in such a tragic manner. She had behaved appallingly towards him, and by taking Laura's part in such a decisive manner last night he had shaken her severely and forced her to face the facts. What he had done for her mother this morning took her thinking much further. She now had cause to be truly grateful to him. Had she lost her mother so soon after the death of her father . . . Talwyn shuddered. It did not bear thinking about.

Laura, unaware of her teacher's thoughts, looked dismayed. 'Don't you like your dinner, Talwyn? Have I done something wrong?'

'Dinner . . . ? No, I'm sorry, Laura, your dinner is delicious. My mind had wandered away for a moment. I was thinking of what might have happened had Mr Hawke not come back to the cottage when he did. My mother and Dr Cheadle were full of praise for the way he coped.'

'And so they should be. When you've finished eating you can see Mrs Kernow's clothes that I've put in the scullery. They are absolutely soaked in her blood. But Amos knew exactly what needed to be done.'

'Mother told me that you did very well too, Laura. She believes you have chosen to take up the right profession. She said that Florence Nightingale will be proud to have you as one of her nurses when you are ready.'

Laura was delighted with such praise . . . and pleased that Talwyn seemed to enjoy the meal she had prepared. When the plates were empty, she said shyly, 'I've made a cherry pie, too . . . although Mrs Kernow had already prepared the pastry before she went outside to pick the cherries. You will have some?'

When the pie had been cut in pieces and placed on plates for the three women there was still almost half left, and Laura said, 'I shall save this piece for Amos. I think he deserves it. I hope he likes it.'

Although she was convinced nothing untoward had happened the previous night, Talwyn was aware that

Laura was infatuated with Amos – and the events of the day would have done nothing to lessen the girl's feelings for him. Then she had a sudden thought. She already suspected Amos might have deliberately gone out in order to avoid her, but now she remembered that the last thing he had said to her last night was that he would look for other lodgings. Could that be the reason why he was not here with them now ... ?

Looking up, she saw Laura watching her anxiously. It was a moment before she realised why. Laura had cooked the dinner ... the first meal she had made for them since coming to the cottage. The cherry pie, in particular, would have a special significance.

Spooning some of the pie into her mouth, she beamed at the young girl. 'I am sorry, Laura, I seem to have such a lot to think about today ... but this pie is absolutely delicious. I have no doubt at all that Mr Hawke will think so too.'

24

Dr Cheadle had been a friend of Edward Kernow, and when Amos called on him at his St Austell home and explained what had happened to Maisie, the physician declared he would go to her immediately. By the time Amos left the house the doctor was already calling for a servant to have the pony and trap made ready and brought to the front door for him.

Satisfied the doctor would waste no time in making his way to the Kernow cottage, Amos mounted his own horse and headed westward through the small town.

As he approached the magistrates' court a number of officials were leaving the building. Among them was Sir Joseph Sawle. The magistrate recognised him and called out a greeting. Making apologies to his companions, he broke away from them and hurried to meet him.

When he reached Amos, he said, 'I am so glad I have met you, Hawke. Inspector Carpenter told me you were anxious to speak to a certain William Arthur . . . otherwise known as "Captain Billy". He suggested that if he was located I should have him arrested as a vagrant, in order that you might question him with regard to matters connected with the murders you are investigating. It seems the magistrate at Looe has pre-empted me. He arrested Arthur for vagrancy two days ago and sentenced him to a month's imprisonment with hard labour. He has been sent to Bodmin gaol.'

'Will I be able to visit him there?' Amos asked eagerly.

'Perhaps not in the normal run of things,' the magistrate replied, 'but in view of your inquiries it can be arranged. When would you like it to be?'

'As soon as possible,' Amos replied. 'Today?'

'I did not expect it to be quite *so* soon,' Sir Joseph Sawle said, 'but come back to the court with me and I will write a note to the warden of the gaol.'

Amos dismounted, and as the two men walked towards the courtroom building Sir Joseph said, 'Inspector Carpenter tells me you are finding Mrs Kernow's young daughter a little too temperamental for your liking and are considering seeking new lodgings?'

'That's right,' Amos agreed, 'but I won't be doing anything immediately . . .' He recounted the events of the day and explained that the reason he was in St Austell was to ask Dr Cheadle to go to the cottage and examine Maisie's injury.

'The poor woman!' Sir Joseph sympathised. 'I will ask Lady Sawle to call on her and see if anything might be done to help her. The Kernow family is not having the best of luck at the moment. I am glad you will be at the cottage for a while longer, at least. It sounds as though they have need of a man about the place.'

Sir Joseph Sawle was an important man in Cornwall and one of the county's most senior magistrates. His name on the note that Amos produced for the Bodmin gaolers was sufficient to have a heavily perspiring Captain Billy brought from the treadmill where he had been employed for the last hour.

Manacled at wrists and ankles with heavy chains, Captain Billy shuffled into the room where Amos was waiting, but showed little gratitude for the respite the visit was giving him from the physical exertions of his 'hard labour'. He greeted Amos with: 'What do you want of me ... and how did you know I was here?'

'Magistrate Sir Joseph Sawle told me you'd been arrested for vagrancy. I had been to see him to ask if my father had been convicted of anything that might explain his disappearance.' Amos spoke firmly, having prepared his story in advance. 'I told him I was looking for you because I believed you knew far more about my father's disappearance than you had admitted to me.'

'You told him that? Why? Why was there need to mention my name to a magistrate at all? I told you everything I know about your pa ... and I'm beginning to wish I'd minded my own business.'

'You came to see me of your own accord because you thought you might get something out of it for yourself,' Amos retorted, 'and told me as little as you thought you could get away with. Unfortunately for you, I have met a woman in Henwood who knows both you and my father. She told me that not only did you work together at the Wheal Notter, but you and he were seen together *after* that . . . and I don't think what you were doing then had anything to do with mining. You told me nothing about that, did you . . . Billy Arthur?'

Captain Billy shrugged with apparent nonchalance. 'There's no reason why I should have told you anything at all.'

'That's quite true,' Amos agreed, 'and I have no doubt Hannibal Davey will say the same when I tell him I've come to see him as a result of what you've told me about my father . . . that he seems to be one of the last people to have seen him before he disappeared.'

'I never said anything of the sort!' Captain Billy protested angrily.

'Didn't you? Oh well, someone did . . . and I might as well say it was you. It shouldn't make any difference; I doubt if Hannibal Davey has friends in Bodmin gaol.'

'The Davey brothers have friends *everywhere*,' Captain Billy declared, 'and on both sides of the law. There are one or two prisoners in this gaol who are enjoying an easier life than me, thanks to Hannibal Davey.'

'Well, that shouldn't worry you too much,' Amos said easily. 'You'll be out of here in a few weeks . . . unless I suggest to Sir Joseph Sawle that he looks into some of the things you've been doing since you left Wheal Notter. Things that, sadly, probably involved my father. If I do that you're likely to be here for a lot longer than a month. You will certainly have plenty of time to get to know Hannibal Davey's friends a lot better.'

For the first time since Captain Billy had been brought

157

into Amos's presence he appeared seriously concerned. 'Why would you want to do such a thing? I've never done anything to harm you.'

'You've never done anything to help me, either,' Amos retorted. 'Even though you were closer to my father than anyone else I have spoken to. I believe there is a great deal more you *could* tell me – if I give you reason enough.' Wishing to make it appear as if he accepted that Captain Billy was going to tell him nothing new, Amos went on without a pause, 'Anyway, I have wasted enough of your time . . . and mine too. I'll be on my way now and let you get back to the treadmill. I doubt if I'll be speaking to you again before I tackle Hannibal Davey, but Sir Joseph Sawle will have a few questions to put to you. After that you shouldn't be short of company. Those friends of Hannibal you mentioned will be interested to find out what you and Sir Joseph had to talk about . . .'

'Wait!'

Captain Billy's call rang out as Amos reached the door, and the prisoner's perspiration now owed nothing to the treadmill. 'If Sir Joseph Sawle comes in here to speak to me you'll be signing my death warrant as surely as any judge.'

'Why?' Amos swung round to face the frightened man. 'What is it you know about Hannibal Davey that is serious enough to have him want you dead . . . and what does it have to do with my father?'

When Captain Billy did not answer immediately, Amos turned to go once more, and the convicted man said hurriedly, 'All right, I'll tell you . . . but I beg you not to let anyone know that you've learned it from me.'

'There's no reason why I should go out of my way to make trouble for you, Cap'n Billy. I just want to find out about my father.'

'Well, you're not going to like what I have to tell you,' said the frightened man, 'but I don't think your pa is still alive.'

It was a possibility that Amos had already forced himself to face, yet Captain Billy's words came as a shock nevertheless. 'What makes you think that?' he demanded.

'For the same reason I try to keep out of Hannibal's way . . . because he knew too much about Hannibal and Pasco and didn't like what they were doing. Also, like me, he was fool enough to let them know he didn't like it.'

'What *were* they doing?'

Captain Billy's manacles rattled as he sat wearily down upon a bench in the room before beginning his story. 'It all started a long time ago, when we were at Wheal Notter together. Me and your pa were on the pare with Hannibal, Pasco and two others when we broke through into the Wheal Phoenix workings. We *did* see the fight between the Daveys and the Phoenix men.'

'The one in which the Wheal Phoenix men were killed?' Amos wanted to confirm the situation beyond all possible doubt.

'That's right . . . but your pa and me said we were farther back in the workings and saw nothing. The other two Wheal Notter men gave evidence to the coroner that our breaking through into the Phoenix had caused a roof fall which killed the Phoenix men . . . your pa and me weren't asked to give evidence to anyone.'

'The two miners who gave evidence to the coroner . . . where are they now?'

'That's just it . . . one was still working with the Daveys until he disappeared for no apparent reason. The other was like your pa and me – he wanted to break his tie with them, but one morning he was found dead at the Cheesewring quarry, just up beyond Henwood village. It was decided that he'd fallen over the edge during the night . . . although no one bothered to ask what he'd been doing up there in the first place.'

'You think the Daveys had something to do with his death?' Amos asked.

'I think they had *everything* to do with it,' Captain Billy declared fiercely.

'So this dead man – and you and my father – were tied in with the Davey brothers . . . working at what? Mining?'

'Not all the time.' Captain Billy was holding nothing back now. 'When we were mining together and things weren't going too well, we'd go down Mevagissey way. Your pa knew one or two men there who made a bit of money freetrading – smuggling – and we would help them out. It wasn't too much at first, just enough to put a bit of money into our pockets, but when the Wheal Notter finally closed down, Hannibal got the idea of making a living out of it, and it was then we began to make some real money. For a while it was fine – we were doing well and were earning enough to keep the top Excise men happy too . . . but then they began getting new men drafted into the service at Fowey and Falmouth. Men who weren't prepared to take money to look the other way when freetrading was going on. Your pa and me, and Toby Martin – him who died up at the Cheesewring quarry – decided we wanted no more to do with the Daveys and their way of doing things.'

'So my father was still around then,' Amos said. 'What makes you think something might have happened to him?'

'Word went around that Pasco Davey wanted to speak to Toby, your pa and me. He had a "business proposition" to put to us, we were told. I smelled a rat right away, because Pasco Davey isn't bright enough to even know what a "business proposition" means – he leaves any thinking that's to be done to his brother. I made certain that I never went anywhere near either Pasco or Hannibal, but I heard that your pa was working for the Daveys and had been seen on a boat that came from France bringing in contraband. I haven't heard anything of your pa since then – and we know what happened to Toby Martin . . . Now do you see why I'm frightened of Hannibal and Pasco Davey?'

'But why should they be so anxious to do away with you after all this time? There were two Excise officers killed a little while ago, I believe. Do you know anything about it? Could that be why they want you out of the way?' Amos decided not to mention the killing of Edward Kernow at this juncture. He was deeply disturbed by what Captain Billy had disclosed about the possible fate of his father . . . but he was still a detective sergeant investigating what was now apparently more than three murders.

'You came here to ask me about your pa and I've told you all I know,' Captain Billy replied. 'It's probably far more than is good for you, but if you take heed of what I've said to you about asking questions of the Davey brothers, I might well have saved your life. It wouldn't be worth very much once you spoke to Hannibal or Pasco and showed them how determined you are to learn what's happened to your pa. Now, I'd be happy if you'd leave me alone to serve out my sentence and not come here again. When I'm let out I intend getting as far away from Cornwall and the Davey brothers as I can.'

Amos left Bodmin gaol aware that he had not managed to secure firm evidence of murder against Hannibal and Pasco Davey, but he was increasingly convinced that if he succeeded in putting the two men behind bars with little chance of ever being released, Captain Billy might be persuaded to give evidence against them. However, the ex-miner had been sentenced to only a month in prison. Before that time was up Amos needed to find evidence that would convince a court of their implication in murder.

25

By the time Amos reached the Kernow cottage it was
close to midnight and he was feeling weary . . . very
weary. It had been a full and eventful day and he was
looking forward to slipping indoors quietly and unnoticed and going straight upstairs to his room – and
to bed.

His spirits sank when he led his horse to the stables
at the back of the cottage and saw that lights were still
burning in the kitchen and also in Laura's bedroom. He
believed it meant that Laura had left the lamp burning
for him in the kitchen and was waiting in her room for
his return. If Talwyn was aware of the situation, she
would be listening for him too, and the last thing he
wanted right now was to have a further confrontation
with the sharp-tongued young teacher.

Entering the cottage, he drove home the bolt on the
scullery door, entered the kitchen – and came to a

startled halt. Talwyn was seated in one of the armchairs that were placed either side of the kitchen range.

Thinking immediately of the events of the previous night, he said, 'If you want to make certain I go straight to my own room and have nothing to do with Laura, you had better follow me upstairs and stand guard on the landing until you hear me snoring. I can assure you, you won't need to wait for very long. I am dog tired.'

Talwyn flushed. 'I jumped to the wrong conclusions last night, Mr Hawke, and I am sorry . . . and before you say that I should be making my apologies to Laura, I have already done so. I have also praised her determination to catch up with other pupils of her age, and told her I am impressed with her work on fractions – which you so ably explained to her.'

Acting on the advice of the adage that declared attack to be the best form of defence, Amos had said what he did in anticipation of yet another acrimonious exchange with the fiery-tempered schoolteacher. Now he felt like a balloon that had been jabbed with a sharp object . . . but Talwyn was speaking again, in the same tone of voice.

'My reason for waiting up for you is to thank you for your actions this morning when my mother was injured.'

Maisie's accident had momentarily slipped his mind, so certain had he been of being the object of Talwyn's censure. 'How is she?' he asked. 'Did the doctor arrive in good time?'

'He did, and he was unstinting in his praise for you. In fact, I am given to understand that had it not been for your prompt and positive actions I might well have lost her. I . . . I don't think I could have taken another such blow . . .'

Her voice broke with the emotion she was feeling, leaving Amos uncertain whether he found her present mood harder to cope with than her more usual ill-humour. Suppressing an urge to reach out and comfort her, which he was sure would be met with disdain, he decided to beat a hasty retreat while he was still in favour with her. 'I am glad she is on the road to recovery,' he said. 'I'll go to my room now. It has been an eventful day.'

'Oh, you can't go just yet,' Talwyn said hurriedly. 'Laura would never forgive me. She cooked dinner for everyone today and her delicious *pièce de résistance* was a cherry pie. We have all had some, but she insisted on saving a large portion for you. She would be very hurt if you did not at least try it.'

Still wary of her, Amos said, 'Well, if it's as good as you say it is, I can probably manage it all. I have eaten nothing since breakfast.'

Taken aback, Talwyn said, 'Then you need more than a piece of cherry pie, however good it may be. I will find you some ham and cheese to have first. There might even be a drop of cider to help it go down . . .'

Amos found such uncharacteristic concern for him unnerving and, although he realised it would probably be more sensible to accept her present attitude as a purely temporary respite from the norm and say nothing, he found it impossible to remain silent.

'I was very happy to be able to help your mother this

165

morning, because I have grown fond of her, and I am delighted the doctor was pleased with what I was able to do, but I would have done the same for anyone I found in a similar situation, so please don't feel you owe me anything. It doesn't change who I am – or who you are. You have made it perfectly clear you don't like me, and I have accepted that. I told you last night I would find new lodgings, and nothing has changed since then. However, I don't want to add to your mother's problems, so, if you agree, I will remain here until she is on her feet again and feeling better. Now, you have stayed up late to thank me, and I appreciate your civility, but you need to be up in the morning to teach at school. There is no need to find food for me. Laura's cherry pie will be enough to take the edge off my hunger. I will take it up to my room and eat it there.'

Talwyn took a deep breath and Amos tensed himself in anticipation of a sharp response from her. Instead, she said, 'Your rebuff is fully justified, Mr Hawke. My behaviour towards you since our first unfortunate meeting has been inexcusable. My mother has taken me to task over it and, more recently, both Andrew and Laura have suggested I was being most unfair to you. In my more reflective moments, I know they are right, so I have tried to analyse why I have been behaving in such a manner towards you. I eventually came to the conclusion that I had been so terribly hurt by my father's death – and, in particular, the manner in which he died – that I desperately needed to find a scapegoat. In view of the manner of our first meeting, you fitted the role perfectly . . . at least, you did in the beginning. As time went by I found it increasingly difficult to justify my attitude towards you – but I still needed someone to hate for what had happened and, no matter how irrationally I realised I was behaving, I tried not to weaken. Then, last night, your reaction to my unfair criticism of you and Laura brought me to my senses. Believe me, I am deeply ashamed of my behaviour, Mr Hawke. If you refuse to accept my sincere apology I will fully understand, but I do realise that you are in no way to blame for my unhappiness, and in my right-thinking moments I realise that without you life would be even more difficult for both me and my mother. It would be a great relief to me if you could find it in your heart to forgive me and let me try to make amends by making a new start.'

It was some moments before Amos could think of an adequate reply. When he eventually spoke, he said, 'I do understand the pressure you have been under and I have tried to make allowances for that. I was angered last night only because I felt your dislike of me was spilling over to include Laura, who in no way deserved to be spoken to in such a manner. However, as you have made your peace with her and she has accepted your apology, I can hardly do less. If you really want us to make a new start, I can assure you that nothing would give me greater pleasure.' Extending a hand to her, he gave her a rather weary smile and said, 'Shall we shake hands on a new understanding and a new beginning?'

26

'I'm glad you and Amos have decided to be friends,'
Laura said happily as she and Talwyn walked together
from the cottage to the schoolhouse next morning.

'I am pleased to hear that,' Talwyn replied. Giving
Laura a mischievous sidelong glance, she added, 'I was
a little concerned that you might be just a tiny bit jealous.'
The expression of dismay that came to Laura's face
caused Talwyn to place a hand affectionately on the
young girl's arm and say, with a smile, 'I am only teasing
you, Laura . . . although I do believe you find our Mr
Hawke attractive.'

Laura was silent for such a long time that Talwyn was
beginning to think that, despite her attempt to be jocular,
she had offended her young companion, then Laura said
seriously, 'Yes, I do find Amos very attractive. He's . . .
oh, I don't know, somehow much more *interesting* than
any of the men and boys I knew up on the moor. He has

done so many things and seen so many places that no one else I know has done or seen. Yet I don't want to enjoy them through knowing someone like Amos. I want to see and do them for *myself*, and if I am to become one of Miss Nightingale's nurses there won't be any time for men in my life . . . and I think I want to be one of her nurses more than I want anything else in the world.'

Talwyn looked at Laura approvingly. 'You are a very special and determined young woman, Laura. I realise that and so too does Mr Hawke . . . and Andrew too. They are both prepared to do everything within their power to see you achieve your ambition.'

'I know,' Laura said, 'and I am grateful to both of them.' Hesitating, she looked at Talwyn uncertainly for a few moments before saying, 'Are you and Amos really friends now?'

Talwyn nodded, slowly at first, then with more conviction. 'Yes, I think we each respect the other – and that is a very good basis for friendship.'

'If that's the case, why do you still call him Mr Hawke, and not Amos?'

Taken aback, Talwyn said, 'Do I? I don't know . . . I suppose it's because that is how Sir Joseph Sawle and my mother first referred to him.'

'Yet that isn't what your mother calls him now. Ever since I first came to the cottage he's always been "Amos" to everyone except you.'

'Well, in that case I had better start calling him "Amos" too, hadn't I? Thank you for pointing it out to me, Laura.'

* * *

Amos too was greatly relieved that he and Talwyn seemed to have settled their differences. It would make life much more pleasant at the cottage and leave him free to concentrate on the investigation which had brought him to Cornwall, he told himself, refusing to dwell upon more personal implications.

He was still in the cottage, later that morning, when Maisie had a visitor. It was Andrew, who arrived carrying a bunch of flowers. Greeting Amos, he said, 'Dr Cheadle called at our house this morning to make a routine check on my mother and he told me about Maisie's unfortunate accident.' Holding up the flowers, he added, 'I thought these might help to cheer her up a little.'

'I am sure they will. I've taken her up a cup of tea, but the doctor said she needs to stay in bed for a few days and I think she is bored already. But if you chat to her for a while she won't have too long to wait before Talwyn comes home.'

'I can't stay for very long,' Andrew said. 'I have to go to Charlestown and speak to Talwyn. I thought I would catch her there when she completed her morning lessons.'

Andrew had suddenly become serious and Amos asked, 'Is there something wrong at the school?'

'No . . . at least, I don't think it is anything too serious, but I want to ask her advice. You see, this detective inspector from London who is staying up at the manor has been to the school during the past few days, questioning the boys about anything they might have seen on the night Talwyn's father was murdered. Last night one of the fathers was waiting for me when school ended.

He expressed disapproval of, as he put it, "having a stranger who does not understand Cornish ways" questioning his son about things he knew nothing about . . . and that he'd be best keeping to himself, even if he did.'

'What sort of "things" do you think he was talking about, Andrew?'

'I think you know as well as I do, Amos. Smuggling.'

'Yet everyone I talk to keeps trying to tell me that smuggling is a thing of the past,' Amos commented innocently.

'Having stayed at the Rashleigh Arms you must be well aware that it isn't,' Andrew said. 'Thanks to the Royal Navy it *had* almost died away before we became involved in the war against the Russians, but when the navy could no longer provide ships to patrol the coast it started up again, and if rumour is to be believed there are some extremely ruthless men involved.'

'Ruthless enough to kill a schoolteacher, if he somehow got in their way.'

'Possibly,' Andrew said, 'and if that is so they are hardly likely to draw the line at doing the same to anyone else, whatever his age, if they believed he could implicate them in smuggling – and murder.'

'Then, if anyone *does* knows something they should tell this London policeman about it so that these murderers – and that is what they are – can be arrested and brought to justice, before another innocent and honest man is killed.'

'That would be so in an ideal world, Amos, but someone has to be the first to step out of line in order for that to happen. You are a Cornishman, you know they would never turn in one of their own to a "foreigner" – and that's what this London detective is in this part of the world.'

'So why is it necessary for you to speak to Talwyn about it? You have already spoken to the boy's father who came to see you. Talking about her father's death will only upset her.'

'I know that, Amos, but the man who came to see me said he wasn't the only one who was upset at having his son interviewed by the London detective. He said others are talking about taking their children out of school – not in protest, but for their safety should word get around that some of them have been giving the policeman information. He said they intend tackling Talwyn about it, she being the one in charge of the school.'

Amos realised that as he had been chosen to accompany the senior detective to help with the investigation because of his knowledge of the Cornish and their ways, he should have warned Detective Inspector Carpenter against just such an eventuality as this.

'Is this London policeman likely to come to the school again to speak to the boys?'

'He said he would come back today ... and if he learns nothing from them he might have a chat to the girls, in case they know anything.'

'Then you do need to speak to Talwyn,' Amos agreed. 'Suggest that she speaks to Sir Joseph Sawle about the problem. He has a great interest in the school and wouldn't want to see anything happen that might result in it being closed. He could speak to the policeman and ask him to call off his questioning of the schoolchildren – but try not to worry her too much.'

27

Persuading Detective Inspector Carpenter to bring his questioning of Charlestown school pupils to an end proved easier than Amos had anticipated.

Walking to Penrice manor, he had decided he would use his usual subterfuge of wanting to speak to Sir Joseph Sawle about his father in order to arrange a rendezvous with Carpenter in the nearby quarry. Once there he would repeat the details of his conversation with Andrew.

However, before he arrived at the big house he saw the detective riding towards him and it was Carpenter who spoke first.

'Ah . . . Amos! This is a fortunate meeting. I was on my way to the cottage to leave a note for you. I have some exciting news. I have received the information I requested about the Davey brothers and it confirms everything you have heard about them. They are as bad as they come.'

Dismounting from his horse, Carpenter walked beside

Amos along a path that wound through the trees beside the manor driveway, continuing to talk as they went.

'Hannibal was in trouble almost from the day he joined the army. He committed nearly every crime in the book and the number of floggings he was given during his service would have killed a man of lesser strength and constitution. He was finally dishonourably discharged a few years ago. His brother, Pasco, suffered similar punishment only twice – but the man who carried out the first flogging was later found murdered. Pasco was strongly suspected of the crime but the murdered man had flogged so many other convicted soldiers during his service life that Pasco's guilt could never be proved. He also served various prison sentences for acts of violence and was suspected of killing two prisoners taken during a skirmish in one of the African campaigns, but by then he had built up such a reputation for himself that no one dared give evidence against him. For the same reason he seems to have led a charmed life here, in Cornwall. Finally – and this is highly significant in view of what has happened here – when his regiment was ordered to give up the pistols with which they had been issued, Pasco reported that his had been "lost". It was the final straw as far as the army was concerned. He received his second flogging, spent a time in a military prison and was dishonourably discharged from the army.'

Looking triumphantly at Amos, Detective Inspector Carpenter added, 'I don't think we can have any doubts that either man is capable of murder – and the missing cavalry pistol is highly significant.'

'No doubt about it,' Amos agreed. 'The case against the Daveys grows stronger with every piece of information we are given on them. It *is* still largely circumstantial, but if we can arrest them on a serious enough charge, and they are found in possession of the pistol, I think we can be confident of securing a conviction against them.'

'I entirely agree,' Carpenter said, 'and that brings me to my second piece of news. Yesterday evening Sir Joseph had a few of his magistrate friends to dinner at the manor. It so happened that one of them is a major shareholder in the Wheal Phoenix, the mine alongside the one in which we are particularly interested. I think Sir Joseph referred to him as an "adventurer". I told him I had heard that two miners had been killed there when miners from Wheal Notter broke through into their workings and said I was interested in seeing where it had occurred. He said he would send word to the mine captain to take me below ground and show me the exact spot. When I suggested that my visit be kept secret, he thought my interest was as a result of the controversy surrounding the verdict of accidental death recorded at the inquest. When I also told him I had only a limited time in Cornwall, he agreed to arrange for Captain Woodcock to take me – us – to the mine tomorrow. We are to go to the mine captain's house at dusk and he will escort us to the mine after dark, when there are fewer surface workers about. He says there are a number of shafts leading to the older workings that are of particular interest to us, and once underground it will make no difference whether it is day or night.'

'That's perfectly true,' Amos agreed. He wondered

whether the senior detective was aware of just how much climbing up and down ladders was likely to be involved in the visit to the two mines, but all he said was, 'I suggest you choose footwear suitable for clambering up and down narrow and probably rickety ladders, sir. They can be dangerous, especially if there has been rain in recent days.'

The two men made their arrangements for a rendezvous the next afternoon to the north of St Austell, where they were less likely to meet anyone who might recognise them. They would then ride on together to the Wheal Phoenix.

Amos also mentioned the reaction of the boys' fathers to the inspector's questioning. Brushing his carefully worded arguments aside, Carpenter said, 'It doesn't matter very much now. In view of the latest developments I am not going to have time to talk to any more of them anyway, and if we succeed in arresting the Daveys no one need fear retribution.'

It was not until Carpenter had mounted his horse and was about to ride away that he asked, 'By the way, do you still intend to leave the Kernows' cottage at the first opportunity?'

'No,' Amos replied. 'Talwyn and I had a serious talk about everything and I think we understand each other a little better now.'

Satisfied, the detective inspector nodded. 'I am pleased to hear it, Amos ... but don't get *too* friendly with the girl. We are here on a murder investigation. When it is done we will be returning to London and I want no complications to interfere with any of our plans.'

28

Amos left the cottage in Penrice after dinner the next day, having told Talwyn he would probably be going to North Cornwall and was unlikely to be home until the following day. He was glad she did not question him about his destination. He felt that after their recent frank talk he would not find it easy to lie to her about his movements.

The two London detectives met as arranged, in the sprawling village of Bugle, which had been built at the heart of the china clay mining industry. It was dominated on all sides by the white, man-made mountains of clay waste, which over the years had grown ever closer to the houses and now actually spilled over into some of their gardens. It was a busy industrial area and two horsemen excited no interest as they rode together through the village.

Not wishing to arrive at the home of the Wheal

Phoenix mine captain before dark, they stopped to eat and drink in Bodmin, the town that was the capital of Cornwall in all but name. The inn where they ate was close to the brooding grey-stone prison which housed Captain Billy Arthur, who Amos had suggested might be persuaded to make a hasty decision to turn Queen's evidence rather than share his temporary abode with the Davey brothers, should they be arrested while he was still in custody.

'Do you believe his evidence would be of significant value?' the senior policeman queried.

'I am convinced that Cap'n Billy knows enough about the Davey brothers to hang both of them if the incentive to talk is great enough – and he could give us the names of others who possess similar knowledge. That's why he is so terrified of meeting up with them. For the same reason, he would never give evidence against them if there were the slightest possibility of their ever being released from custody.'

'If we can arrest the whole of the gang on charges of large-scale smuggling the penalties involved will be so severe that those arrested will be clamouring to turn Queen's evidence against the Davey brothers,' Inspector Carpenter declared. 'However much the men who are working with them fear the Daveys, the certainty of transportation for life should prove a more frightening prospect than the vengeance of two doomed men.'

'I hope you are right. But Hannibal and Pasco have terrorised the area for so long it will be hard to convince those who know them that their control of the lives of the men and women about them has finally come to an end.'

'Don't worry, we will succeed,' Carpenter said, with a confidence that Amos wished he could share in such a wholehearted fashion.

Captain Sidney Woodcock, manager of the huge Wheal Phoenix mine complex, greeted the two London detectives effusively . . . *too* effusively. He exuded a heavy aroma of alcohol that alarmed Amos, who was aware that his life, and that of Inspector Carpenter, might very well depend upon the actions of this man, who would need a clear head should things go seriously wrong.

It was already dark, and after the two policemen had refused the offer of a drink, Captain Woodcock said he would escort them to the shaft he had singled out as giving them the best chance of going underground without being observed.

'Are you coming down with us?' Amos asked.

'No, I don't think there's any need for that. I have been suffering from a bit of rheumatism of late and find the ladders hard going. I've prepared a plan of the underground workings of both Wheal Phoenix and Wheal Notter and will supply you with hard hats, candles and a key to the gate I've had put up to separate the two underground workings. You'll be all right down there by yourselves. I've marked the spot on the plan where the breakthrough from Wheal Notter occurred, and where my miners were killed by the roof fall. There will be no one down there to bother you: all my men are working on the other side of the Phoenix. When you come to grass again, put your

179

helmets and the key in the porch, then I'll know you have come up safely. If they're not there I'll need to send men down looking for you . . . and I don't think you'll want that.'

'I hope it will not prove necessary,' Carpenter said, 'but shall we make our way to the shaft now? I would like to be back at Penrice by dawn.'

The unsteady gait of the Wheal Phoenix mine captain as he led the way to the mine workings made Amos feel relieved he would not be coming underground with them. When the two men began their descent with lighted candles affixed to the brim of their hard miner's safety helmets, he knew his apprehension had been justified.

The distance from grass to the bottom of the shaft was in the region of three hundred fathoms and it took the two men almost an hour to complete the descent, the intervals between rests decreasing dramatically as they neared the bottom of the narrow shaft. When Detective Inspector Carpenter stood on solid ground once more, he slumped against the rough rock of the tunnel side and complained that his aching legs felt as though they had run a five mile race.

Instead of sympathising, Amos pointed out that when this section of the mine had been producing ore, miners arriving at the bottom of the ladder would have been faced with the prospect of working an eight or ten hour shift of hard physical labour before climbing back up to grass with tools strapped to their backs to walk perhaps a mile or more back to their homes.

'What a way to earn a living!' Carpenter commented,

then, straightening up and pushing himself away from the side of the tunnel, he said, 'Right, let's go and find the Wheal Notter workings. You will be able to make more sense of the plans than me, Amos, so you can lead the way.'

As darkness fell round the cottage in Penrice, Laura announced to Talwyn that she was going to her room. She had a book she wished to read before turning in for the night. She had spent much of the evening cleaning and dusting downstairs while Talwyn remained in the kitchen, ironing.

'Will you take these clothes of Mr Hawke's up with you and put them in his room?' Talwyn said. Then, aware of Laura's expression of disapproval, she amended her request. 'I am sorry, Laura . . . will you please take *Amos's* clothes upstairs with you when you go?'

'Of course.' Laura beamed. 'You'll soon get used to calling him by his first name – and he'll be so pleased that you'll wish you had done it from the very beginning.'

'Our first meeting was not exactly conducive to exchanging first names.' Talwyn explained about the unfortunate incident that had occurred at the entrance to the Penrice estate. It produced the same reaction Amos had met with whenever he told the story. Laura giggled.

She put a hand to her mouth immediately and looked apprehensively at Talwyn, but the older woman gave her an embarrassed smile. 'It's all right, Laura. I can laugh at it too . . . now! However, I was very angry at the time . . . angry about so many things, and I am afraid that Mr Hawke – Amos – bore the full brunt of my appalling behaviour. If I am honest, he behaved with admirable restraint. In fact, the only time he has really lost his temper with me was the night I vented my anger upon you.'

'That's because he's nice,' Laura declared. 'I like him very much . . . and I know you will too when you know him better.'

Still happy in the knowledge that she had been instrumental in improving relations between Amos and Talwyn, she carried Amos's newly ironed clothes upstairs from the kitchen, balancing them carefully in the crook of one arm while she held a lighted candle in a holder in her other hand. When she opened the door to Amos's room she looked around for somewhere to lay down the clothes. After placing them on the chest of drawers, she decided she would put them away for him.

She tucked socks and underwear in a top drawer which held similar items before searching for a drawer that would take the shirts. She found clean shirts in the bottom drawer, and shifting the items that were already there to make room for the newly ironed items she uncovered a box. When she pushed it to one side she found it extremely heavy – and it was then she noticed the outline of a handgun etched into the box's cover.

Curious, yet aware that she was being unforgivably inquisitive, she lifted the lid of the box. There, nestling in a shaped, cloth-lined compartment, and surrounded by divisions containing bullets, percussion caps, a small powder flask and the many other accoutrements that were necessary for the use and upkeep of such a weapon, Amos Hawke's revolver lay exposed to her horrified gaze.

29

While they were climbing down the shaft of the Wheal Phoenix, Detective Inspector Carpenter and Amos had relied upon the uncertain illumination provided by the candles affixed to their helmets to guide them down ladders that had not been inspected for many years. Now, having arrived at the level which would connect with the Wheal Notter workings, Amos lit the bull's-eye lantern which he had carried in a knapsack slung over his shoulder during the descent.

Due to the rough nature and irregularities of the walls and roof of the workings, the lantern cast many shadows. The two men instinctively spoke in whispers as they made their way along a tunnel carved out of solid rock and earth by men who had worked – and died – far beneath the ground in pursuit of ore which had made fortunes for men who had probably never set foot on the first rung of a mine shaft ladder.

At times, the tunnel was high and wide enough to have allowed a horse and wagon to pass through in comfort. Elsewhere, both men needed to stoop as they eased their bodies through spaces that would have barely allowed the passage of a child in comfort. A miner would spare no more time or effort than was absolutely necessary in pursuing an often elusive lode of ore.

'By God! The men who worked here certainly earned their money,' exclaimed a breathless and perspiring detective inspector after the two men had negotiated a difficult part of the level which involved scrambling over heaps of waste rocks in a particularly narrow section of tunnel.

'We should reach the gate between the two mines in a few minutes,' Amos said reassuringly. 'Once in the Wheal Notter workings we will need to go up a level in order to reach the adit. From that point we must remain as quiet as we possibly can. Sound travels a long way in an empty mine.'

It was another ten minutes before they reached the gate which marked the boundary between the two mines. Set in a stout timber frame, it was an impressive affair, constructed of heavy wooden slats joined together by forged iron bars and secured by a heavy chain and a large padlock. Using the key given to them by Captain Woodcock, Amos swiftly unfastened the padlock and swung the door open. He lifted the bull's-eye lantern to inspect the tunnel on the Wheal Notter side of the gate before stepping through the opening, closely followed by Detective Inspector Carpenter.

Securing the padlock behind them, Amos turned his

attention to the tunnel ahead. The light from the lantern disclosed a well-worn path from the gate leading into the Wheal Notter workings.

'There was no similar track on the other side of the gate,' he pointed out quietly. 'It means that the smugglers inspect it regularly to ensure that no one is coming through from the Wheal Phoenix.'

'They obviously leave nothing to chance,' Carpenter agreed. 'We can expect them to have guards on the store of contraband – and they will probably be armed. We will try not to let them know we are here but, should we fail, are you carrying your revolver?'

'No,' Amos admitted. 'I didn't even think of it.'

'You should have brought it,' Carpenter said disapprovingly. 'This is just the sort of operation it was intended for. Fortunately, I have mine, but we must hope it will not prove necessary to use it.'

'We will need to be careful with the lantern,' Amos said, 'especially once we reach the adit we believe is being used by the smugglers. It's there for drainage so is likely to be straighter and less cluttered than the levels we've been along so far. If there is anyone on guard they will be able to spot a light from a fair distance. I'll close the lantern shutter as far as possible, but we'll still need to see our way.'

'Let's find the adit before we worry too much about that,' Carpenter said. 'We don't need to make an inventory of what they have in there, merely satisfy ourselves beyond any doubt that it is where they store their contraband – and without making them aware that we know.'

Amos thought he would be more confident of maintaining such secrecy had the Wheal Phoenix mine captain been a more sober and less garrulous man, but he kept his thoughts to himself and tried to concentrate on the task in hand.

The plan of the underground workings of the Wheal Notter provided by Captain Woodcock proved less accurate than it might have been. After climbing the ladder which took them some ten fathoms to the level from which the adit had been driven, the two men found secondary tunnels that were not shown on the plan, going off from the one they were in. However, despite such discrepancies, the two detectives had no difficulty finding the opening from which the adit sloped gently downwards to emerge on the slopes of Notter Tor.

Now they needed to proceed with extreme caution, the shutter of the lantern closed almost entirely, allowing only the merest sliver of light to escape. Their progress was accordingly slow and, suddenly, Amos stopped. In a whisper he said to his companion, 'Can you smell anything?'

'No . . . yes I can! It's brandy!' Despite the need to whisper, Carpenter could not keep the excitement from his voice.

'Are you satisfied now that this is where the smugglers are storing their contraband?' Amos whispered. 'Shall we go back?'

'No, we will see if we can learn anything more,' came the reply.

Amos felt they had discovered all they had come for . . . but Carpenter was the man in charge.

The heady tang of brandy grew stronger as they advanced farther along the adit, and now it was mixed with the aroma of tobacco smoke and they could see a light which was much closer than was comfortable. Amos realised it was a candle, or candles, burning on the far side of a barrier formed by lines of small barrels, the outlines of which could be seen stacked in staggered tiers between the two detectives and the mouth of the adit, some hundred yards or so farther on.

They could hear voices now, two men talking with the uninhibited certainty of men whose tongues had been loosened by drink.

'Have you seen enough now?' Amos whispered the question to his companion, but before Carpenter could reply there was a commotion beyond the brandy barrel barriers.

Loud voices were heard and it seemed that more men had entered the adit from the outside. One man in particular was angry. His booming voice carried clearly to Amos and Carpenter as he berated the men who had been taken by surprise.

'Is this how you spend your time when you are supposed to be on guard? By the look of both of you, you'd have been in a drunken stupor before the night was out. When did you last check the gate to the Phoenix workings?'

One of the men to whom he was talking made a reply that was inaudible to Amos and Carpenter, but it did not please the previous speaker. Raising his voice even more, he shouted, 'Hannibal and me are the ones who give the orders. You're here to do as you're told

'– and you have been told to check that gate every hour.'

There was an inaudible reply which fuelled the ire of the new arrivals at the smugglers' cache, and another angry voice immediately confirmed the identity of the newcomers to their unseen listeners.

'You're not paid to think . . . which is just as well for you. If you were, you'd starve. Pasco and me have just come from the Cheesewring inn, up at Minions, where Cap'n Woodcock's son is drinking with some of his mates. They were talking about that detective from London. He is coming to the Wheal Phoenix to have a look at the spot where the two miners were killed. It seems he's not satisfied with the coroner's finding and is poking his nose into places where it's not wanted – and where it could land a great many of us in trouble. Have you heard anyone down there today?'

Once again the reply to his question was lost to the two unseen listeners, but it brought an immediate response from the man Amos believed to be Pasco Davey. 'How would *we* know when he is due at the mine? Do you think we should have gone up to Woodcock and asked him? You can both get down there now and check that the padlock is still on the gate. Tomorrow, Hannibal and me are going to get our own padlock to put on it to make certain no one comes through – but that doesn't mean you won't need to check on it. Now, get down there and report back to us. Hang on – before you go you can top those mugs up with brandy, and we'll take them with us when we leave. You've both had quite enough for one night.'

189

By this time, Amos and Detective Inspector Carpenter were already beating a hasty retreat back the way they had come. However, before they arrived at the ladder by which they would descend to the level where the gate was situated, Amos whispered, 'We'll never make it to the bottom before the two smugglers get to the top.'

'Then what do we do? We can hardly arrest them here.'

They had reached the entrance to one of the side tunnels that had not been shown on Captain Woodcock's plan. 'We'll hide in here,' Amos said. 'But let me go first. It's not on our map and we don't know what we might find along there.'

The two men made their way cautiously along the tunnel, which had obviously been cut to follow a lode of ore, although it had evidently not been a major seam because the tunnel was at times so low that the two men needed to crouch almost double in order to negotiate it.

They soon came to a spot where there had been a minor rock fall. After clambering over the rubble they decided to stop on the far side and wait for the two smugglers to complete their examination of the gate between the two workings and return to where the contraband was stored.

They heard the men pass by the entrance to the tunnel, grumbling about the task they had been ordered to carry out, and when they had passed out of the hearing the two detectives discussed what they had heard earlier.

'There can be no doubt now about both the Davey brothers being leaders of a smuggling gang,' Amos said and Carpenter agreed with him.

'You are quite right, Amos. We have learned enough tonight to have arrested them on the spot . . . for smuggling. Now we need to catch them in the act, together with the men who are working for them, and put pressure on the gang members to turn Queen's evidence against the Daveys in respect of the murders.'

After a while, Carpenter said, 'How long do you think the two smugglers will remain in the vicinity of the gate to the Phoenix workings?'

'Long enough to convince the Davey brothers that they have thoroughly checked everything in the area . . . although not so long that they might be accused of taking too much time over it,' Amos replied. 'Rather than both of us sitting here doing nothing, why don't you wait here and listen for the two men coming back – even if you don't hear them you should see the light from their lantern as they pass by the entrance – while I go and see if this tunnel leads anywhere. We need to know as much about the Wheal Notter workings as possible if we are to raid it at some time in the future.'

'With luck we will capture most of the smugglers on a beach somewhere,' Carpenter replied. 'I wouldn't fancy mounting an assault on this place, especially if more than one of them is armed . . .'

Making his way along the tunnel, the light from his bull's-eye lantern partially shielded, Amos thought of what Carpenter had said. An assault on the adit was likely to cost a great many lives unless the smugglers were taken completely by surprise. However, the manner in which the Davey brothers had learned of Carpenter's visit to the mine was an indication of how difficult it would be to mount a secret operation on the scale that would be required to take the smugglers.

While he was engrossed in his thoughts, the light from his partially shielded lantern fell upon a few pieces of heavy timber. Aware that there was now no possibility of being seen from the level along which the two smugglers would pass, he swung the lantern shutter fully open to take full advantage of the light it gave.

It was well he did so. The timber was left over from pit-work round the mouth of a shaft in the floor of the workings that left only a narrow shelf on which a man might make his way around it.

Using his lantern, Amos discovered that the tunnel came to an end no more than a dozen or so paces beyond the gaping hole in front of him. The dimensions of the shaft were quite small and now he saw it extended upwards through the roof of the working.

He realised that this was a ventilation shaft, also known as a 'winze', of which there would be a number on most mines. Advancing to the edge of the winze, he shone the beam of his lantern into the narrow opening.

The shaft went down a long way to a lower level, perhaps fifteen or twenty fathoms below. It was so far that the beam from Amos's lantern barely touched it . . . but he could just make out something at the bottom of the winze that sent a chill through him.

In the frustratingly feeble beam it appeared to be a body, but he could not be certain. He told himself it could equally have been a bundle of cast-off mining clothes, thrown down the narrow shaft from any level . . . or perhaps from above ground when the Wheal

Notter closed and some disgusted miner discarded the clothes which were symbolic of a way of life that had come to an end.

Amos worked his way precariously around the narrow shelf at the edge of the opening in a bid to find a better viewpoint, but he quickly discovered that his view of whatever was at the bottom of the shaft required not an advantageous angle but a more powerful lantern.

Returning along the tunnel to where he had left Carpenter, he found the senior detective waiting impatiently for him.

'The two smugglers returned minutes ago,' Carpenter said. 'We need to get out of the mine before the Daveys either send one of their men back down here to keep guard on the gate, or decide to go to the Wheal Phoenix to try to find out when we came down here. They could even find our horses and wait for us to go and collect them . . .'

They had left their horses with a generous helping of hay in a disused building beside the mine captain's house and Amos felt there was little chance of their being discovered, but he appreciated the detective inspector's concern.

As the two men made their way out of the narrow tunnel, he told Carpenter what he had seen, or thought he had seen, at the foot of the winze. It caused the detective inspector to pause for a moment, but when Amos admitted he could not be certain it was a body, he shrugged it off.

'We can't risk jeopardising our whole investigation because of something you think you might have seen,' he said. 'We would look extremely stupid if we sacrificed weeks of work and the chance to catch two murderers for the sake of something that turned out to be no more than a bundle of rags!'

Not until they had safely made their way through the gate between the two mine workings, climbed the endless ladders, retrieved their horses and ridden well clear of the mining area did Carpenter broach the subject again.

Less fraught and inclined to be more sympathetic now, he said, 'I am aware of what you must have been thinking when you saw what you believed to be a body at the bottom of the shaft in the Wheal Notter, Amos. In view of what we have learned about the Davey brothers, and the information given to you by your informant in Bodmin gaol, it is a painful possibility that, if it is indeed a body, it might be that of your father. If it is, then you have an additional reason for ensuring that these two villains are brought to justice and receive the punishment they deserve. That can best be done by pursuing our present course. Once we have them safely behind bars you can return to the Wheal Notter and I will ensure that you are given all the assistance you require in order to put your mind at rest, one way or the other.'

Amos knew he would have no peace of mind until he discovered what – or who – was at the bottom of the Wheal Notter winze, but he was equally aware that Detective Inspector Carpenter was right.

It made him even more determined to bring Hannibal and Pasco Davey to justice as swiftly as possible.

30

The discovery of a revolver in Amos's room had left Laura in an agony of indecision. Although aware that she ought to say something about her find to Talwyn, she had very strong feelings for Amos and knew she owed him a great deal. In fact, she felt disloyal to him even thinking about telling anyone of her find.

On the other hand, she owed even more to Talwyn and her mother – and her very future depended upon the goodwill of the teacher.

Foremost in her mind was the mysterious shooting of Edward Kernow. What if his death and the gun in the drawer in Amos's room were somehow connected?

Laura quickly dismissed such thoughts. She refused to believe Amos had anything to do with such a terrible occurrence. No, she told herself, there had to be a perfectly logical explanation for the gun being where it was. If that was so, any action she took would be unnecessary – and what would he think of her for nosing among his belongings in the first place?

It was the latter argument that convinced her to neither say nor do anything. Had curiosity not got the better of her, the presence of a gun in Amos's room would never have come to light.

She would say nothing and try to forget she had ever seen it. That would be the easiest solution to the problem . . . but the decision did not leave her feeling at all comfortable.

Talwyn went downstairs the following morning to find a note from Amos on the kitchen table. It said he had ridden through the night and not arrived home until after dawn. He asked her to allow him to sleep on, promising to be up and about by the time she and Laura returned from school.

Amos was true to his promise. When Talwyn and Laura arrived home, they found a still drowsy Amos in the kitchen. He had a kettle boiling on the hob and had already taken a cup of tea upstairs to Maisie.

In answer to Talwyn's question about the success of the journey he had supposedly made to the north coast in search of his father, Amos replied that until further inquiries had been made it was impossible to say quite how successful it had been. He added that he was not even certain he wanted this particular line of inquiry to arrive at a conclusion because there was a possibility it would confirm that his father was no longer alive.

Amos felt his story was close enough to the truth to satisfy his own conscience. At the same time, it hinted of an unexplained situation that was sensitive enough to preclude further questioning.

However, it created an atmosphere that made their meal a somewhat subdued and contemplative affair. Laura, in particular, was exceptionally quiet, but it was not until dinner was over and Talwyn had gone upstairs to make her mother comfortable that Amos tackled her about her lack of conversation.

He spoke to her in the kitchen where she was washing up the dishes, saying, 'You were very quiet at the dinner table, Laura. Is something worrying you?'

'No, why should there be?' Her reply was too swift, and too abrupt.

'I don't know,' Amos said, 'but you are usually the one who is able to brighten up our mealtimes. Are you sure there is nothing troubling you?'

There was a great deal troubling Laura, and Amos was its source, but she, in common with Amos at the dinner table, was careful to avoid telling the truth. 'I'm perfectly all right, but each day at school I realise more and more just how far behind everyone else I am. I expect that's what I was thinking about.'

Amos was immediately sympathetic. 'I know how you must feel, Laura, but I am convinced you have nothing at all to worry about. You'll not only catch up with everyone else, but forge ahead of them so fast that they will be the ones left wondering if they will ever be able to catch you.'

Laura looked up from the dishes she was washing and once again felt a deep guilt at not being able to tell him what was really bothering her. She was saved from

197

having to continue to make further innocuous conversation by the arrival of Talwyn, carrying a tray on which were Maisie's dinner plates.

'Hello, you two. What are you looking so serious about?'

'We were discussing Laura's lessons,' Amos replied. 'She is concerned that she has so much to learn in order to catch up with the other girls of her own age. I told her she has nothing to worry about – that she will not only catch up with them but one day leave them all far behind.'

'And so she will,' Talwyn said positively. 'Even though some of the brighter girls have realised just how clever she is and are working twice as hard in an effort to remain ahead of her. Laura is the best thing to happen at Charlestown school since I began teaching there. One day I am going to be very proud of having been her tutor.'

31

It rained heavily for the next few days and Amos spent the time quietly. He did not venture far from the Penrice cottage. Meanwhile, Maisie was recovering from her injury well and was no longer confined to bed.

On the day the rain ceased, although heavy, threatening clouds were still scudding in off the sea, Amos walked to Charlestown in the late morning. His main reason for the excursion was to shake off the feeling of claustrophobia engendered by the days spent in the small cottage. He took with him a small shopping list from Maisie, and needed to buy a few things from the village shop for himself as well.

When he had completed his shopping he went to the harbour and watched the activity there for a while. On one side sailing vessels from ports in South Wales were unloading Welsh coal, while on the opposite quay lines of horse-drawn wagons were loading similar vessels with pure white china clay, refined in the numerous works a few miles to the north. It was possible to tell on which side of the docks a man was working by the colour of the dust that begrimed face, hands and clothes.

After watching the busy scene for a while, Amos took out his pocket watch. It showed a quarter past midday and he decided to have a drink at the Rashleigh Arms before meeting Talwyn and Laura when school came out and accompanying them back to the cottage.

Walking up the hill from the harbour towards the inn, he was surprised to see Andrew coming towards him, carrying a heavily laden satchel slung over his shoulder.

After the two men had exchanged mutually cordial greetings, Amos indicated the satchel and said, 'It looks as though you might have some bulky cargo for one of the ships down in the harbour.'

Smiling, Andrew replied, 'It's nothing more exciting than a number of items for the school that Talwyn asked me to pick up in St Austell. I didn't realise it was going to be such a heavy package, but I've been promised a meal with you all at the cottage as a reward when I've made the delivery. Unfortunately, I'm a little early. School won't be out for more than half an hour and I don't want to go in and disrupt Talwyn's lessons.'

'Then why don't I give you an additional reward by buying you a drink at the Rashleigh Arms while we wait for school to end?'

'That sounds a good idea to me,' Andrew said gratefully. 'I've worked up quite a thirst carrying this from St Austell.'

'I would give you a hand with it,' Amos said, 'but, as you can see, I've been shopping too. Some of it is for me, but most is for Maisie.'

As the two men made their way to the village inn, Andrew said, 'I believe you and Talwyn are getting along much better now?'

'I think we understand each other a little better than we did, thanks to Laura,' Amos agreed. 'She was indirectly responsible for our improved relations ... was it she who told you about it?'

'No, it was actually Talwyn herself. She said you pointed out her lack of good manners in what she called "a very vigorous manner". I think she quite admired you for taking her to task in such a forthright fashion.'

'It certainly helped to clear—'

Amos never completed his sentence as Andrew brought him to a sudden halt. Reaching out and clasping his arm, the schoolteacher said, 'Wait! Let those men coming from the Rashleigh Arms go on their way before we get there.'

Looking towards the inn, Amos was startled to see Hannibal Davey leaving the premises accompanied by a number of men, among whom he recognised some who had been with the bearded ex-miner on the night when contraband had been landed at Crinnis beach. The group made its way up the hill and turned into a lane only a short distance away.

Releasing his grip on Amos's arm, Andrew explained, 'There were a couple of men amongst that group whom I never expected to see in Charlestown. In fact, I had hoped I would never meet them again! I wonder what they are doing here? Whatever it is, it will be to the benefit of no one except Hannibal and Pasco Davey . . . and it will undoubtedly be something outside the law!'

Amos realised that Andrew must have known the big miner from his schooldays in Henwood. 'That was Hannibal Davey with the black beard, I believe?' he said.

'That's right . . . but how do you know him?'

'It was Hannibal who frightened away the man I went to visit in Chinatown. Both he and Laura's mother told me that my father had once worked with Hannibal. I thought I would ask him if he knows anything about my father's present whereabouts.'

'I doubt very much if he would tell you, even if he knew,' Andrew commented, 'and I suggest you keep well clear of him. The Daveys are trouble – serious trouble.'

'Which one of the group was his brother?' Fishing for information, Amos added, 'Is Pasco as bad as Hannibal?'

'Worse! Both brothers scorn the guidelines by which civilised folk live, but Pasco also has a sadistic streak. He likes to cause suffering to both people and animals. Their father ended his days in the asylum in Bodmin and there is no doubt that Pasco has inherited his insanity . . . but I have never met anyone who would dare even hint of it within his hearing. He is much smaller than his brother and does not sport a beard, but he has the same dark countenance and hair colouring as Hannibal and has an angry red scar extending from cheekbone to chin, which he likes people to believe he acquired in battle, when he was a cavalryman. I suppose it *could* be the truth, but

Pasco has never impressed me as a man who would risk his life for Queen and country. He is more likely to have been wounded in some fracas of his own making.'

By now they had arrived at the Rashleigh Arms. Going inside, they made their way to the taproom. It was quiet in there and Thomas Stephens hurried to greet them, being particularly servile in his manner towards Andrew.

'Good day to you, gentlemen . . . and it is an especial honour to see you again, Mr Elkins. My son Nicholas has taken a new interest in his lessons since you came to the school. He says you make them not only easier to understand, but fun too. What will you both have to drink . . . and they come with my compliments?'

Both men ordered ale, but before the effusive landlord hurried away to draw it from the giant barrel that rested on wooden blocks behind the bar, Andrew said, 'I trust you do not allow Nicholas to mix with your customers, Mr Stephens. I just saw a couple of men leaving your inn whom I knew when I lived on Bodmin Moor and whose reputation is unenviable, to say the least. He is a bright boy and I would be very upset to see him led into evil ways by such men.'

Suddenly ill at ease, Thomas Stephens said, 'I keep my business separate from my private life, Mr Elkins. As for my customers . . . as long as they pay their way and make no trouble while they are in the Rashleigh Arms I ask no questions of them and make one man as welcome as the next. But I thank you for your comments about my Nicholas. I hope to see him make something of his life when he goes out into the world.'

When Stephens left to draw the ale, Amos said quietly, 'Our landlord is obviously very proud of his son, but it's my belief that he knows far more about the Davey brothers and their business than he would have us believe. I have seen Hannibal in here before . . .'

At that moment Thomas Stephens returned to the table with two tankards of ale. Thanking him, Amos raised his tankard in a toast to Nicholas, and the landlord left the table with his good humour restored.

Waiting with Andrew outside the school gate, Amos smiled to himself as the released pupils walked sedately out through the doorway, aware that their teacher was watching them from inside the classroom, only to erupt in a babble of sound as soon as they reached the gate and the 'young ladies' became noisy young girls once more . . . although there was nothing very childish about the bold looks that were directed at himself and Andrew by some of the more mature students.

In the schoolroom, the two young women seemed pleased to see them . . . even Laura, who Amos felt had rather distanced herself from him during the past few days. Her attitude troubled him, but he had put it down to the fact that she was working so hard at school, and so had said nothing to her. The four set off together to walk to the Penrice cottage, but soon Andrew and Laura became engaged in an animated conversation about some of the subjects she had been learning that morning, and Amos found himself walking with Talwyn while the other two fell behind.

Pleased to be walking with Talwyn, out of the others'

hearing, Amos said, 'Despite her own misgivings Laura seems to have come on amazingly well in the short time she has been at your school.'

'Yes,' Talwyn agreed. 'She is an exceptionally intelligent girl and very quick to learn. I have never come across a brighter pupil from any walk of life in all the years I have been teaching.'

'So she should have no difficulty in becoming one of the new breed of nurses when the time comes?'

'Not if that is what she still wants when I have taught her all I can,' was the surprising reply.

'Do you think that she might not still want it, then?' Amos queried. 'She is so passionate about nursing.'

'Much of the passion came from wanting to find a way out of the situation she found herself in at her home in Henwood,' Talwyn said, '. . . that and an awareness of a more glamorous world beyond the bounds of a small moorland village. I believe she would make an exceptional teacher – and Andrew might just possibly be the one to convince her of that.'

Looking over his shoulder, Amos saw Andrew and Laura sharing a joke together. 'I'm not sure Laura would settle for a teacher's life,' he said. 'Yes, she *is* aware there is an exciting world beyond a mining village . . . beyond Cornwall too. She wants to see some of that world and she won't achieve that as a teacher.'

'Why not?' Talwyn queried. 'My first teaching post was not in a school. I became governess in the household of a relative of Sir Joseph Sawle who had married a Frenchwoman and moved to France with his young family. I went with them and lived there for two years.

Once I had learned the language and customs of the land I had a wonderful time. Laura could do something similar if she so wished.'

Talwyn's revelation took Amos by surprise. He wondered what other undisclosed experiences had helped to shape the woman she was today. There had been no evidence of a man in her life during the time Amos had been at the Penrice cottage, but Talwyn was an intelligent and attractive young woman. He doubted whether she had gone through life without *some* romantic involvement.

32

When Amos reached the cottage with the others Maisie told him that a servant from Penrice manor had come seeking him with a message that Sir Joseph Sawle wished to see him as early as was convenient. The servant had told her the baronet had received information that might prove helpful in Amos's search for his father.

Aware the message probably originated with Carpenter and that, if so, it meant the detective inspector wished to speak to him urgently, Amos said he would go to the manor house immediately.

Maisie protested that the information would wait until they had all eaten dinner, but Amos pointed out that Sir Joseph was a very busy man and was liable to be absent from Penrice if he did not catch him now.

Reluctantly, Maisie agreed and said she would keep

Amos's meal warm for him if he had not returned by the time it was served.

Escorted to the study of Penrice manor by Mrs Button, Sir Joseph Sawle's housekeeper, Amos found Carpenter there with the baronet.

When the housekeeper had closed the door behind her, Sir Joseph explained to Amos that he had told her the detective inspector had discovered something during his inquiries that might be of help to Amos, adding, 'I have learned over the years that telling something to Mrs Button is the most efficient means of ensuring the household servants know what is going on in the shortest possible time. It means that no one need speculate on the presence of Mr Carpenter at our meeting.'

'Has there been a new development in the case, sir?'

'Yes,' the detective inspector replied. 'Sir Joseph has received information that there is to be a large quantity of contraband brandy and tobacco brought ashore tonight at Crinnis Bay – the very place where you found evidence of such activity while you were staying at the Rashleigh Arms.'

'Do we know whether the Davey brothers are involved?'

His question was answered by Sir Joseph. 'No, but I am assured this is a large consignment, and although no names have been mentioned I am informed by the Excise men that they do not believe more than one band of smugglers is operating on the south Cornish coast.'

Amos did not doubt it. The Davey brothers would not tolerate other gangs working in their area, but he had other concerns about what Sir Joseph had said. 'Does this mean that Excise officers are aware that a landing at Crinnis is planned?'

'Yes indeed. As a matter of fact the details have been received through their own sources and they intend to mount a major operation against the smugglers.'

'But ... the army will be involved too?' Amos persisted.

'Calling in the army will not be necessary,' the baronet declared. 'I am assured by the senior Excise officer involved that he is able to provide all the resources needed to apprehend both the smugglers on shore and those delivering the merchandise to them.'

'They will possibly succeed in capturing the contraband, and arresting *most* of the smugglers involved ... but only if luck is with them.' Concerned that the planned operation was to be carried out by Excise officers only, Amos explained his misgivings to Sir Joseph. 'For the Excise officers involved, taking possession of the contraband would constitute a success, but Detective Inspector Carpenter and I have come from Scotland Yard to catch a man – or men – who has murdered at least three times. Unless this operation is carefully planned with that end in mind, *our* mission is likely to fail – and Scotland Yard has built its reputation on success, not failure.'

Amos's blunt and impassioned appeal somewhat dampened Sir Joseph's enthusiasm for the planned Excise operation, but it did not quench it. Turning to the detective inspector, he said, 'You are the senior officer, Carpenter. What are your views?'

The London detective threw a quick glance in the direction of his subordinate, and Amos remembered that less than a week before Carpenter himself had reminded Amos of their reason for being in Cornwall.

'Amos is quite right, of course,' he said. 'We *are* here to catch a murderer . . . but we are here at *your* request and if you believe that by putting a stop to the activities of the smugglers we will be preventing further murders, we will abide by your wishes.'

The detective inspector's reply was purely political. He was aware that collecting evidence to secure the arrest of either of the Davey brothers for murder was going to be more difficult than he had anticipated. It would take time and a conviction was by no means certain. Failure to bring a murderer to justice would not be viewed favourably by the Metropolitan Police commissioner. If the operation planned by Sir Joseph Sawle and the Excise officials failed to provide evidence that could convict the Daveys of murder, he could return to London and report that the actions of the very magistrate who had requested the assistance of Scotland Yard's detective force had prevented him from bringing the investigation to a successful conclusion – despite the fact that both detectives had warned Sir Joseph of the possible consequences of his actions. At the same time, Carpenter had avoided incurring the displeasure of the Cornish magistrate by objecting outright to his plan. He had deliberately left that to Amos, knowing how the latter felt about bringing the Davey brothers to justice.

Amos had just been given a valuable lesson in self-preservation by a master of the art.

Sir Joseph Sawle was aware that Carpenter had cleverly shifted responsibility for the outcome of the murder investigation to him, but he was philosophical about it. 'Oh well, if the operation puts to an end the spate of killing we have suffered in Cornwall, it will be most welcome. And if the courts carry out their duty and transport the men we arrest it will hopefully free Cornwall from the scourge of large-scale smuggling once and for all. Now, shall we discuss the details of tonight's little adventure? I will, of course, be in nominal command, although I will leave the senior Excise officer to lead his men against the smugglers. However, I feel we should all go armed, just in case we are caught up in the mêlée and need to defend ourselves. I suggest that when we have discussed our strategy we go our separate ways and meet again when darkness falls, somewhere on the far side of Charlestown, so as not to excite undue speculation . . .'

33

During the week that followed Laura's finding of the revolver in the drawer in Amos's room, she had come to accept that there must be a perfectly logical explanation for his possession of such a weapon.

She knew he had been an officer in the Royal Marines and had served in the war in the Crimea. No doubt it was a souvenir he had collected there . . . or perhaps it had saved his life on a number of occasions. There might be so many reasons why he should have the gun.

Laura had studied Amos's behaviour carefully since making her find and had convinced herself that there was nothing sinister in his manner. He was no more and no less than the generous man who was paying for her education, without demanding anything in return. She decided she would say nothing to anyone and forget she had ever seen the weapon.

On the day she walked with Talwyn, Andrew and

Amos from Charlestown, she was as sympathetic as anyone else when he answered the summons from Sir Joseph Sawle and returned to say he would be going out that night and did not expect to return to the cottage until the early hours of the following day.

In answer to their questions, Amos was particularly vague, saying only that he needed to follow up something Sir Joseph had told him, but was not optimistic that it would produce any results. No one pursued the matter further and Amos was relieved that he had once more been able to avoid telling an outright lie.

He did not leave the cottage until dusk and it must have been an hour later when the three women made their separate candlelit ways to bed. On the landing Laura shared with Amos, she was about to go into her room when she suddenly decided she would like to have another look at the boxed weapon, to satisfy herself that she really *had* seen a handgun and had not, somehow, made a mistake.

Aware she was being unforgivably intrusive and would find it very difficult to explain her presence in the room to anyone who found her there, Laura opened the door quietly, her heart beating fast, and tiptoed to the chest of drawers in which she had found the gun.

Placing the candle in its holder on the floor, she opened the drawer slowly and quietly, then pushed aside the same shirts she had found there before to uncover the box with the tracing of a handgun etched on the lid.

Her heart beating even faster now, she lifted the lid – and let out a gasp of surprise. A few of the accessories she had seen before were still in the box, together with oil and cleaning materials, but the handgun had gone. So too had the powder flask, percussion caps and lead bullets . . .

Riding to the rendezvous with Sir Joseph and Carpenter, Amos was unhappy about the forthcoming encounter with the smugglers. He felt very strongly that the detective inspector should have tried to dissuade Sir Joseph from supporting a purely Excise service operation against them.

Unless the Davey brothers faced murder charges which could be substantiated, no smuggler would dare turn Queen's evidence against them and so risk reprisals at a later date. As a result, the two men would be charged only with smuggling. And although times were changing, men involved in smuggling could still expect to be dealt with far more leniently by judges and juries in Cornwall than those convicted of other crimes.

Amos had very strong personal reasons for wishing to see the Davey brothers convicted of murder. Although convinced that they held the answer to the fate of his father, he knew he was unlikely to learn anything from them unless they had nothing more to lose by telling him.

He was also uneasy about the source of Sir Joseph Sawle's information. Captain Billy had said that there were Excise officers – senior men – who were in the pay of the Davey brothers. If this were so it could mean that the Excise men were deliberately being lured to Crinnis Bay while the smugglers made their rendezvous elsewhere! In that case, not only would the efforts of Sir

Joseph and the London detectives have proved to be futile, but Amos's pretence of being in Cornwall for no other reason than to find his father might be seriously compromised as a result of his presence at the scene.

It was for this latter reason that, when he met Sir Joseph and Detective Inspector Carpenter, he suggested he should stay back when they joined the Excise men. Although he would be within hailing distance and try to keep them in view as far as was possible in the darkness, he would not form part of the main ambush party, but would remain in the background until any action took place.

'In other words,' said Sir Joseph, 'you will act the part of a long stop, eh? It is a good idea, just in case any of the smugglers slip past us. I don't want a single one of these people to escape. Now, I said I would meet the chief Excise officer just past the entrance to the mine, up ahead. Do you want to come and be introduced before you disappear into the darkness, Sergeant Hawke?'

'No, thank you, Sir Joseph, I'll stay back and follow on when you and the Excise men move off. When we see the signals from the boat bringing in the contraband I'll choose the best spot to take up my own position.'

'Splendid. Well, good luck. This should be a night for us all to remember and one, I trust, that every smuggler will wish to forget.'

'I am sure we all share the same sentiments, Sir Joseph,' Carpenter said. 'But while you ride on and let the chief Excise officer know we are here, I have a few last minute details to discuss with Amos. I will join you in a few moments.'

When Sir Joseph had ridden out of hearing, Carpenter said, 'You are not happy with what we are doing tonight, are you, Amos? Is it because you believe your father may be one of the smugglers?'

'I almost wish we would find him among their number tonight,' Amos replied truthfully. 'If we did I might be able to persuade him to give evidence against the Daveys. No, to be honest, I have a bad feeling about this whole business. I am not at all convinced of the honesty of the Excise men involved, or the accuracy of their information. It all seems far too easy. The very fact that the smugglers' earlier operations have remained undetected for so long means we are dealing with men who are both experienced and well organised. If they have realised that time is running out for them they are likely to have planned something big – and planned it very carefully. My feeling is that while we are all gathered here, they could be landing a huge cargo of contraband somewhere else along the coast. Alternatively, knowing the military is not involved, they could have enough men to strike such a blow against the Excise service that it will be rendered incapable of cohesive action for months to come – during which time they will increase their activities to an unprecedented level.'

Marcus Carpenter was silent for a minute before saying, 'I share a great many of your misgivings, Amos, and I have already sent a report of your earlier comments to London, but let us hope our doubts are misplaced and that tonight will prove successful for all of us. Now, tell me where you mean to take up your position in case I need to find you in a hurry.'

When Carpenter had ridden after Sir Joseph, Amos realised that the detective inspector had once again revealed his political skills. If the Excise ambush proved to be a failure, he could refer to Amos's misgivings, forwarded to London by himself, as proof that the two detectives had not been in full agreement with the action taken.

On the other hand, should it prove successful, he would point to his good judgement in going along with the ambush, *despite* the lack of enthusiasm from his second-in-command.

34

It was a long and frustrating night for the men waiting on Crinnis beach. The Excise officers were being held back beyond the sand, awaiting the arrival of the free-traders, who were expected to signal from the nearby cliffs to the smuggling vessel which should be waiting in the bay. They would take no action until the boat from the ship had grounded on the gently sloping beach and was being unloaded. The plan was for them then to move in *en masse* and silently surround the smug-glers. Meanwhile, boats manned by armed coastguards, waiting in the lee of cliffs on either side of the long beach, would move in to cut off any attempt at escape out to sea.

It was a simple plan ... far too simple, in Amos's opinion. It did not take into consideration the extreme violence which could be expected from men faced with a lengthy period in gaol, or, even worse, transportation to Western Australia, the latest of the penal settlements in that far distant land to strike fear into the hearts of generations of felons.

The spot where Amos had chosen to wait for the arrival of the smugglers was close to the path used by them during the time he had been staying at the Rashleigh Arms. It was well above the long sandy beach of Crinnis and from here he could see the lights of vessels passing along the English Channel, far out beyond the bay . . . but that was not the direction on which he was concentrating his attention.

Sir Joseph Sawle's information was that this would be a major delivery of contraband. If so, the smugglers would need every one of the mules Amos had seen grazing close to Notter Tor, on Bodmin Moor. If his theory was correct, the animals should already have been brought from the moor and put to graze somewhere in the vicinity of Crinnis.

However, as far as Amos was aware, no one had checked for their presence anywhere in the area, and, as the night hours passed without any sign of either smugglers or their pack animals, his belief that Sir Joseph Sawle and the Excise officers had been deliberately fed with false information strengthened.

A ship delivering contraband to the waiting smugglers might have been expected to be cruising just off the coast, ready to come inshore as soon as darkness permitted and the signal that all was clear had been received. It was now close to midnight and there was no sign of either the ship or the smugglers who should have been on the beach ready to take delivery of its cargo. Something was quite obviously wrong, and as more hours passed without any sign of clandestine movement it became increasingly apparent there would be no delivery of contraband this night.

It came as no surprise to Amos when Detective Inspector Carpenter left the beach and came back to find him, saying, 'Have you seen or heard anything from back here, Amos?'

'Nothing at all,' Amos replied, 'and it's far too late for anything to happen now. The smugglers would want to reach the safety of the moor by daybreak. We have been completely hoodwinked by Hannibal and his men.'

'I fear you are right,' Carpenter agreed, 'and although Sir Joseph is reluctant to admit it, I believe he feels the same way. He has told the senior Excise officer that he will remain here at the beach for another hour, then return home – and we will go with him, leaving the Excise men to maintain their watch until daybreak. He has also ordered their senior officer to report to him at the magistrates' office in St Austell in the morning – *this* morning now – with a full report on how the information about the supposed landing was obtained.'

'I don't think I would care to be in his shoes,' Amos commented. 'Sir Joseph has a reputation for not suffering fools gladly, especially when they make *him* appear foolish.'

'Well, he has only himself to blame for the fiasco this has turned out to be. After all, we did warn him.'

Amos smiled to himself in the darkness, remembering that it was he and not Carpenter who had cast doubt on the operation when it was first mooted. He realised that the detective inspector was already mentally working on the report he would be sending to the Metropolitan Police commissioner.

'I'll be getting back to Sir Joseph,' Carpenter said. 'He said an hour but I doubt if his patience will last that long.'

When the senior detective had left him, Amos tried to work out exactly what the Davey brothers had hoped to gain by luring Sir Joseph and the Excise officers to Crinnis beach in such a manner. He was in no doubt that they were responsible for providing the false information about smuggling activities.

It was highly probable that a delivery *had* been made, perhaps somewhere far away from Crinnis, but Amos had a niggling suspicion that there was more to the plot than that. He was convinced their smuggling had been successful in the past because a number of corrupt Excise officers had kept them informed of the service's movements, letting them know the safest spots and times at which to bring contraband ashore.

It was a system that had worked well for them in the past, so why do something different now? Why call attention to themselves by even suggesting that a large-scale smuggling operation was about to take place – and why do it in a way that virtually ensured the involvement of magistrate Sir Joseph Sawle?

It was while he was pondering this question that a sudden and disturbing thought came to him. Hannibal Davey was a cunning man and quite capable of deceiving Excise officials into believing a delivery of contraband was being made tonight at Crinnis . . . but what if the true objective of the deception was neither to lure Excise men and coastguards away from the true landing place, nor an attempt to humiliate magistrate Sir Joseph Sawle?

What if the target was in fact Detective Inspector Carpenter?

Amos believed that both the detective inspector and Sir Joseph would probably dismiss such a theory as preposterous, but neither man had experienced the fear that Hannibal succeeded in instilling in those who felt they had upset him, or witnessed the lengths to which Hannibal was prepared to go in order to safeguard himself – as was instanced by the placing of a man to check whether Amos followed him from the Rashleigh Arms on the night they had both been drinking at the Charlestown inn.

It was possible too that neither man entirely shared Amos's certainty that the Davey brothers were responsible for the murders of Edward Kernow and the two Customs men . . . among others!

In common with the people of Charlestown, Hannibal would be aware of the reason for Carpenter's presence in Cornwall, and he also knew that the London detective's investigations had led him to the mine where two other men had died at the hands of him and his brother . . . and where their contraband was stored. He would also know that Carpenter had been questioning the Charlestown schoolchildren about anything unusual they might have seen on the night of Edward Kernow's murder. Questions that meant Carpenter had somehow connected the murder with Hannibal's smuggling activities.

As a suspicious, cautious and ruthless criminal, Hannibal would be prepared to go to extreme lengths to prevent the detective inspector's investigation from moving any closer to him.

The more Amos thought about it, the more convinced he was that his theory made sense. However, as he had anticipated, neither Carpenter nor Sir Joseph was inclined to take such misgivings seriously when they met to make the return journey to Penrice.

'It will be obvious to anyone that the murder of the two Excise men was probably the work of smugglers,' Carpenter agreed, 'but Sir Joseph brought me to Cornwall specifically to investigate the death of the schoolteacher. Nothing has been said to make the Daveys aware that we connect the murders, or that I believe they are involved.'

'That is not so,' Amos pointed out. 'They must know that your questioning of the pupils at Charlestown school was clearly an attempt to learn if any of them knew anything about smuggling activity in the area. We also know that Hannibal was aware that you went to the Wheal Phoenix workings with the apparent intention of looking at the spot where two miners died at the Daveys' hands – even though they had managed to persuade the coroner that they died from other causes. It also took you too close to the place where their contraband is stored. You have become a threat to him.'

Before Carpenter could reply, Sir Joseph, who had been listening impatiently to the conversation, said, 'This Davey has made us look damned foolish, and when word gets out about our wasted night we are going to be the laughing stock of the county. That's what the man intended – and he has succeeded – but I can't see him being devious enough to make his plan more complicated than that. I have ordered the chief Excise officer to have some answers on my desk by noon tomorrow. Heads will roll over this – with his most likely to be the first. Now, let's get home. I have had enough of smugglers and their work for one night.'

35

In spite of Sir Joseph Sawle's dismissive remarks, Amos was on edge for the whole of the short ride back to Penrice, and he kept his coat unbuttoned in order to give him quick access to the revolver tucked in his waistband, should it be needed along the way.

He did not relax until they arrived at the gateway to the Penrice estate. Then, just as the three horsemen turned off the lane, Amos thought he detected a faint glimmer of light to one side of the gateway. Before he could bring it to the attention of the other two men, who were riding just ahead of him, a voice called out urgently, 'Mr Carpenter . . . Mr Carpenter, sir!'

'Yes . . . what is it?' Carpenter replied in surprise, at the same time reining in his horse.

No sooner had he spoken than the shutter was thrown back on a lantern and the beam fell upon the London detective. A voice called 'Shoot him!' and there was an immediate loud report, followed by a cry of pain from Inspector Carpenter.

Amos had pulled his revolver free from his waistband when the unseen man called out Carpenter's name and now he fired, aiming above and to the right of the lantern.

There was a shouted curse, and as the lantern fell to the ground and went out he fired again . . . and then a third time.

Now there was the sound of men running away through the trees to one side of the driveway and Amos sent a fourth shot after them.

He would have fired yet again, but the round misfired and now the horses, frightened by the noise of the shots, were milling about, making further shots dangerous.

Sir Joseph had moved alongside the detective inspector. 'Are you hurt, Carpenter? Did their shot hit you?'

'Yes.' The London detective spoke through his teeth and sounded to be in great pain. 'In my right side . . . I seem to be bleeding badly . . .'

'Hawke . . . you know where Dr Cheadle lives. Go and get him out of bed and tell him to come here as quickly as he can. I will help Carpenter to the house and see what can be done for him.' Now there was a need for urgent action Sir Joseph was at his authoritative best. He added, 'Come to the manor when you return. I'll tell the servants you had the windows of your bedroom open in the cottage and I sent you off to fetch the doctor when the sound of shots brought you running.'

226

Pushing the revolver back inside the waistband of his trousers, Amos turned his horse and set off towards St Austell.

It took a great many pulls of the bell-cord at the door of the doctor's house before the nightcapped head of Dr Cheadle appeared at an upstairs window. He was cross at being woken at such an hour, but when Amos identified himself and said he had been sent by Sir Joseph Sawle because the London detective inspector had been shot and badly wounded, he realised it was a very real emergency.

Promising to be down as quickly as he could dress, he asked Amos to go to the rear of the house and wake the groom who lived above the stable and tell him to saddle up his horse.

Amos and Dr Cheadle set off for Penrice after Amos had given only a sketchy description of the manner in which Detective Inspector Carpenter had sustained his wound. He did not feel it necessary to explain his own part in the incident and there was little conversation between the two men as they rode as fast as was possible in the darkness.

Once at Penrice manor the doctor was immediately taken up to the room occupied by the wounded man, while Amos remained anxiously pacing the hallway until Sir Joseph came downstairs about twenty minutes later.

'How is he?' Amos asked apprehensively.

'He has lost a great deal of blood,' Sir Joseph replied, looking weary. 'Fortunately, it seems, the bullet passed right through his body. Dr Cheadle says that is a good

227

thing because it means he has no need to probe around to find it. Unfortunately, he has no way of telling what damage it might have done on the way. It certainly passed close to the liver, even if it never actually damaged it. Cheadle's main concern is the amount of blood that Carpenter has lost. However, I would say he has been fortunate. Had you not been there he would certainly have been finished off by those villains . . . me too, most probably. Did you hear a second shot from one of them?' Seeing Amos's expression of surprise, he added, 'I thought I did, but could not be certain.'

'No. I fired immediately after the first shot and got off three more before my revolver misfired.'

'You did well, dear boy, and judging by the way the lantern was dropped to the ground I would say it was with some success. You won't have had time to search the area yet, of course?'

'No,' Amos confessed. 'I was so concerned for Inspector Carpenter that I came straight here with the doctor.'

'Of course.' Sir Joseph nodded his head vigorously. 'Thinking about it somewhat belatedly in view of what has happened, both Carpenter and I should have taken your views far more seriously. They were quite obviously lying in wait for Carpenter . . . can you think why?'

'Yes, I think I have a very clear idea why . . . but can we leave the discussion until later, Sir Joseph? There is nothing more I can do here for Inspector Carpenter and I would like to return to the scene of the ambush as soon as possible and see what I can find. As you said, I probably hit at least one of them, and if he is seriously hurt he might not have been able to get away. I will come back here in the morning to report what I have learned, and to check on the condition of Inspector Carpenter. One thing more . . . I would like to borrow a lantern, if I may.'

'Certainly! Most of the servants seem to be up and about. I will send one to find a lantern . . . and may I commend you for your conduct throughout the whole of this sorry affair. You can be quite certain it will receive fulsome praise in the report I shall be submitting to your commissioner in London. But there is little more I can do tonight. Dr Cheadle says he will remain with Carpenter so I will go to my bed for a couple of hours. I feel the day ahead is going to be a very busy one.'

Amos returned to the scene of the shooting and soon found the lantern dropped by one of the waylayers. Examining it, he saw that something had been scratched into the base but had been painted over. Neverthless – and significantly – he thought he could make out the word *Notter* beneath the paint, indicating it had probably once belonged to the now defunct Bodmin Moor mine. He would be able to be more certain in the morning, but now he wanted to make a more detailed search of the area.

It was apparent from the disturbed state of the ground that the men who had attacked Amos and his companions had been lying in wait for a considerable time, but it was not until he widened his search that he found what he was seeking.

Where the branches of a bush were broken it seemed

someone had fallen – and there was evidence that whoever it was had been bleeding badly. It appeared too that he needed support when he was moved away. There were marks on the softer patches of earth indicating that his feet had been dragging along the ground.

Following the trail, Amos found a place where horses had been tethered, and was able to deduce there had been four men involved in the ambush. The footsteps ended here, but a continuing search disclosed a heavily bloodstained neckcloth, which might have been used to pad a wound. Then, of much more interest, he discovered a bone-handled hunting knife with a folding blade, on the handle of which was a silver shield crudely engraved with the initials *JCL.*

It was clear that Amos had succeeded in wounding at least one of the four men, probably seriously. If it turned out to be the owner of the hunting knife and he could be identified, there was certainly enough evidence to have magistrate Sir Joseph Sawle issue a warrant for his arrest.

Amos was able to follow the tracks of the horses to a gate which opened on to a field behind the manor. He expected all four horses to head northwards, towards St Austell and Bodmin Moor, but, much to his surprise, only two horses went in that direction. The other two turned south.

It was the tracks of the latter that he followed, and he observed that the horses had been travelling side by side, very close to each other, as though the rider of one might be supporting his companion.

As he bypassed a darkened farmhouse on a lane

which led to the small village of Pentewan, the lantern carried by Amos suddenly failed. A few more minutes would have brought him to the lane where he would have lost the trail anyway. Amos decided to abandon his tracking and make his way home to the cottage.

36

Dawn had begun to give shadowy form to the trees around the cottage by the time Amos made his way to his bedroom. At first he found sleep elusive, but he woke with a start to hear sounds in the kitchen and, dressing blearily, made his way downstairs to collect hot water with which to shave.

Maisie was in the kitchen. Seeing the state of him, she said, 'It doesn't look as though you had much sleep last night.'

'No. I didn't get in until shortly before dawn, but I need to be out again early.'

She made sounds of disapproval. 'An active young man like yourself needs his sleep. There's plenty of hot water in the kettle; take it and go and wash and shave. By the time you get back down I'll have a cup of tea and breakfast ready on the table for you. I doubt if the girls will be down just yet – they were both still busy with schoolwork when I went up to bed. That Laura is a glutton for learning, and no mistake. If she keeps on the way she's going there will come a day when our Talwyn has no more she can teach her. Mind you, there's no fault in that. I can think of a whole lot of mothers who'd be mightily relieved if their own daughters spent the evenings learning, instead of getting up to other things they shouldn't.'

When he had washed and shaved Amos returned to the kitchen and, smelling the aroma of frying bacon and eggs, realised he was hungry. Taking a seat at the kitchen table, he said, 'I don't think Laura will be very long. I heard her moving about in her room while I was shaving.'

'Then I had better go upstairs and make certain our Talwyn is awake once I've given you your breakfast,' Maisie said, busying herself with the food in the frying pan on the hob. 'She's not the easiest of persons to get up in the morning.'

Maisie had just left the kitchen when Laura appeared. She looked tired, and when Amos commented on her appearance she said, 'Yes, Talwyn and me were working late – and I was woken up very early this morning. I heard you come in.'

'That would have been just before dawn,' Amos said. 'I'm sorry if I disturbed you.'

'I don't think it was you who woke me up. I heard something a long time before you came in. I don't know what it was, but I didn't get back to sleep again until it was light.'

'You should try to get to bed earlier,' Amos

commented. 'Maisie said you are working very hard until all hours of the night.'

'I could say the same about you,' Laura pointed out. 'You can have had hardly any sleep at all, yet here you are having breakfast and looking as though you are ready to go out again as soon as you've eaten.'

'I have things to do,' Amos replied. He was saved from needing to amplify his brief explanation by the return of Maisie, who set about cooking breakfast for Laura, chatting non-stop all the while. By the time the food was transferred to a plate and set on the table before Laura – and long before Talwyn had found her way to the kitchen – Amos had left the house and was making his way, on foot, to Penrice manor.

Sir Joseph Sawle was also at breakfast and he invited Amos to join him. Explaining that he had just eaten, Amos declined the offer, but accepted a cup of coffee, at the same time asking after Detective Inspector Carpenter.

'Dr Cheadle was with him for a long while. Before he left he gave him something to make him sleep and I have instructed one of the maids to stay in the room in case there should be any change in his condition. Cheadle says he is very weak – he is most concerned about him. He'll be back to see him later this morning. I have sent a footman off with a telegraph for Scotland Yard and said I will forward a detailed report later today. No doubt you will be doing the same?'

When Amos nodded, the magistrate asked him what he had discovered at the scene of the previous night's incident. Hearing that the wounded man appeared to be heading in the direction of Pentewan, Sir Joseph said, 'There is an excellent parish constable named Mitchell who lives not very far from there. I will call him in and ask him to make discreet inquiries as to whether anyone knows anything of a wounded man who might live there, or could have passed through the village shortly before dawn.'

Swallowing the last of his bacon, he then asked Amos whether he was prepared to continue his investigations without the detective inspector's supervision after the latest serious turn of events. Amos replied that he was more determined than ever to see the killers – and would-be killers – brought to justice.

'Splendid,' the baronet said. 'In my letter to the Metropolitan Police commissioner I will say that in view of the considerable progress you have already made – progress that has so alarmed these criminals that they attempted to dispose of Carpenter – I want you to take charge of the investigation on my behalf. Would you like me to request that they send another detective to assist you?'

'Not at the moment,' Amos replied. 'If your constable at Pentewan is thoroughly trustworthy I would prefer to work with him – secretly at first – and have the Davey brothers believe that with the detective inspector out of action there is no Scotland Yard presence in Cornwall. It might make them over-confident, or perhaps give them an incentive to bring in an extra large delivery before someone else comes to Cornwall to continue the inspector's investigation. In the meantime I will try to find out who shot him.'

'It will not only be Scotland Yard our suspects need to be concerned about,' Sir Joseph said. 'Now that all counties in the country have been ordered to establish paid police forces we will be having urgent meetings here, in Cornwall, with a view to setting up such a body along the lines of the Metropolitan Police. For that reason alone I would like you to achieve success in your hunt for the killers of Edward Kernow and the Excise men. It will make our task a great deal easier in view of the opposition we have already received to the idea of a police force paid for from county funds.'

'You can be assured that I will do my utmost to succeed,' Amos promised, as sounds in the rest of the house betokened the return of Dr Cheadle.

After spending some time with the wounded detective inspector, the doctor was shown to the study and he looked grave when Amos asked about his patient's condition.

'It is not easy to form an opinion just yet. He has lost a great deal of blood and I need to keep him opiated in order to alleviate the considerable pain he would otherwise be suffering.'

'But . . . he *is* going to make a full recovery?'

The doctor shrugged apologetically. 'All I can say is that I am doing as much as any doctor with a long lifetime of experience *can* do. I am afraid that no guarantees can be offered when one is dealing with an internal bullet wound.'

Obliged to accept the non-committal prognosis, Amos asked, 'When will I be able to speak to him?'

'Certainly not today,' was Dr Cheadle's firm reply,

'and probably not tomorrow either. After that I might try to reduce his laudanum and he will be more aware of what is going on around him. Now, if you have no more questions . . .'

'I have just one,' Amos said, 'and the answer might prove important in finding out who shot Detective Inspector Carpenter. If a Pentewan or Mevagissey man was seriously hurt, but didn't want it generally known, who would he turn to?'

'Had you put that question to me three months ago there would have been only one answer,' Dr Cheadle replied. 'Dr Vincent was Mevagissey's physician for more than fifty years – and he was as happy to take his fee in kind as in cash. As well as having a never failing supply of fish, I have heard it said there was more contraband drink in his cellar than in the Customs bond at Falmouth. But Vincent retired three months ago and moved to a cottage up by Corran Farm, just the other side of Heligan House. A young doctor from Plymouth way moved in to take his place but it hasn't been long enough for the villagers to take to him. If something needs to kept quiet and the injured party is from Mevagissey, or Pentewan, then Dr Vincent is still the man he will go to – and I don't doubt he would receive the treatment he required.

'Now I will be on my way. I think it would be beneficial to keep a servant girl in attendance upon Mr Carpenter, Sir Joseph, and if you have any concerns about him, please do not hesitate to call me out immediately.'

Shortly after the doctor was shown out of the study

a servant announced the arrival of Cornwall's chief Excise officer, who was accompanied by the official who had been in charge of the previous night's fiasco. Slipping out of a side door so as not to meet with the Excise men, Amos once more followed the path taken by the smugglers during the dark hours of that morning. He learned nothing new and, looking at his watch and seeing it was now well past one o'clock, he made his way to the Kernow cottage.

When Laura finished her breakfast she rose from the table saying she was going upstairs to fetch the things she needed for school. Maisie said, 'While you are upstairs will you put your head into Amos's room and see if he has left any dirty clothes in his basket? You'll find it in the corner, beside the wardrobe. I am washing this morning. My leg is a bit painful and I don't want to go up and down stairs any more than I need to. If you have anything to be laundered you can bring it down at the same time, too.'

Having collected her books and a couple of items of her own clothing that required washing, Laura went into Amos's room. Crossing the floor, she was startled to become aware of a smell that had once been quite familiar to her, but one she had not experienced for some years.

It was the odour given off after an explosion of black powder – gunpowder. Extensively deployed as it was in tin and copper mines, Laura had always known when it had been used by her miner father because it permeated his clothing and clung to his hair, irritating her nose

238

when he gave her a cuddle on his return from a shift in the Wheal Notter.

The smell was quite strong in Amos's room now, albeit not as pungent as she remembered it from her childhood, and for a moment she was puzzled ... then she remembered the boxed handgun ...

Passing the chest of drawers where she had seen the weapon, Laura hesitated. Finding the gun in the first place had been unintentional and she had wished many times that she had not made the discovery in the first place. She still felt uncomfortable about last night's surreptitious examination, but to check the gun again would be something very different, especially if her sense of smell had not betrayed her and she discovered that it had been fired ... She knew she would never be able to rest if she did not pursue the matter.

Placing her books on the bed, she stood in front of the drawers, still uncertain. Then, as she hesitated, Talwyn called up the stairs, 'Hurry up, Laura, or we will be late.'

'Coming!' she called in return, but instead of obeying Talwyn's call immediately she pulled open the bottom drawer and, pushing aside some of the clothes there, exposed the box.

As she lifted the lid the pungent odour of burned gunpowder assailed her nostrils with an almost physical violence.

37

'Is something troubling you, Laura?'

Lost in her thoughts, Laura started guiltily at Talwyn's question and said defensively, 'No, why should there be?'

The two young women were returning to the cottage after lessons and Talwyn had been watching the younger girl closely ever since they had left the schoolhouse.

'You haven't seemed yourself all morning,' she said. 'You are usually the first to put up your hand when I ask a question, but there were times this morning when I doubted whether you had even heard me speaking.'

'I think I must be a bit tired,' Laura lied. 'I didn't sleep very well.'

'That is probably my fault,' Talwyn said apologetically. 'We stayed up so late last night that I didn't find it at all easy getting out of bed this morning. It is very satisfying to have such an able and intelligent pupil, but you need to get your sleep. I must remember not to keep you up so late . . . for both our sakes!'

For the remainder of the walk home Laura tried to behave normally, but she felt miserably guilty at not telling Talwyn of the discovery she had made in Amos's room.

She felt even worse when she and Talwyn reached the cottage. Maisie was agog with excitement and could hardly wait for them to step inside the house before regaling them with her news.

'You'll never guess what was going on around us while we were all asleep last night,' she said dramatically. 'It's a wonder we weren't all murdered in our beds. Such goings on! I don't know what things are coming to, I really don't. First your poor, dear father – and now this!'

'What are you talking about, Mother?' Talwyn demanded. 'What is "this"?'

'Why, it's that policeman from London who is staying up at the manor with Sir Joseph. He was shot during the night . . . and not a stone's throw from this cottage! He and Sir Joseph were coming home from somewhere in the early hours of the morning when someone jumped out of the bushes down by the lane and shot him. They say he's at death's door.'

'Are you sure you haven't got hold of some exaggerated story, Mother? Where did you hear about it?'

'Mr Woods, Sir Joseph's gardener, came along this morning with some greens for us from the kitchen garden up at the manor. He said there wasn't one servant still in bed by the time dawn broke. Dr Cheadle spent half the night at the manor and came back again this morning.'

'Do they have any idea who is responsible?' Talwyn asked. 'Could it have been a poacher?'

'Not according to Mr Woods. He says there's nothing in these woods to make it worth a poacher's while to risk his freedom for it. No, Talwyn, there's a madman on the loose around these parts. A madman with a gun. First your poor, dear father, and now this London policeman.'

Neither of the two women noticed Laura standing pale and shaking inside the kitchen doorway listening to their conversation. Suddenly, without saying a word, she rushed past them and fled upstairs to her room.

Breaking off the conversation she was having with her daughter, Maisie would have hurried after her but Talwyn put out a hand to restrain her. 'No, leave her alone, Mother.'

'Why, what's wrong with the girl?' Maisie demanded. 'Is she sickening for something?'

'No, but she was working until very late last night and has got herself overtired.'

'I knew it,' Maisie said. 'I was saying so to Amos only this morning. I like to see a young girl trying her hardest at whatever she's doing, but there's no sense making herself ill because of it.'

'She will be all right,' Talwyn said reassuringly. Then, changing the subject, she asked, 'Where is Amos? Is he coming home for dinner?'

'He went out early but said he'd be home as soon after one as he could . . . that means any time now and dinner is nowhere near ready!'

'I'll give you a hand,' Talwyn said. 'We'll leave Laura up in her room for a while to sort herself out.'

'Have you heard about Sir Joseph Sawle and that policeman from London being caught up in a shooting last night at the entrance to the manor drive?'

Maisie greeted Amos with the question as he stepped through the doorway into the kitchen of the Penrice cottage and he realised he should have known that news of the shooting would be the main topic of conversation in every household for miles around. He had no desire to be drawn into conversation about it and wished he had possessed the forethought to have his meals out for the next couple of days, or until the immediate excitement had died down.

'Yes, it's a bad business,' he replied. 'I believe the policeman is very badly hurt . . . Do you mind if I take a jug of water upstairs with me and freshen myself up before we eat? I seem to have got myself a bit hot and sticky this morning. I think it must be the hottest day of the year.'

Taking a spelter jug from a kitchen shelf, Amos carried it outside to fill it from the well at the back of the house. As he returned with it to the cottage he was unaware of Laura watching him from her bedroom window, a tortured expression on her face.

He passed through the kitchen and went on his way upstairs, while, behind him, a disappointed Maisie said, 'I would have thought he would have been a bit more excited about what happened last night, instead of going on about the weather!'

Talwyn smiled at her mother's indignation. 'You forget that Amos has fought in wars, Mother. People being shot are nothing new to him.'

'I suppose you are right,' Maisie admitted grudgingly, 'but he could have *pretended* to be interested. He must know how upset *we* are at such a thing happening ... again.'

Upstairs, Amos had stripped off his shirt and was flannelling his upper body with the cold water when there was a knock on the door of his room. It was so soft that he felt he might have been mistaken, but then it was repeated, louder this time.

Towelling himself off, he went to the door and opened it to reveal Laura standing outside, gaunt-faced and trying with only a modicum of success to control the shaking that threatened to take over her body.

Concerned, he said, 'Laura ... what's the matter? Has something happened?'

As though she had not heard his question, Laura's lips framed words three times before they escaped as sound. 'Why, Amos ... ? How could you ... ?'

Once again words failed her and suddenly tears flooded her eyes.

Alarmed, Amos pulled her gently into the room. For a moment it seemed she would resist, but then she stepped inside and, guiding her to the bed, he sat her down before saying, 'What is it, Laura? What is it you think I have done?'

He was at a total loss to know what he might have done to upset her in such a way.

'You know, Amos ... You *must* know. The gun in your

drawer . . .' Suddenly it all came out in a rush, how she had first brought the ironed shirts to his room and discovered the revolver, had smelled burned gunpowder and known the gun had been fired that morning, and returned from school to learn that Detective Inspector Carpenter had been shot.

Tearfully, she added, 'I know you were out there when he was shot, Amos – I heard you come in later. Why did you do it? And . . . was it you who shot Talwyn's father too?'

Shocked, Amos said, 'You believe I shot Detective Inspector Carpenter . . . and might have killed Talwyn's father?'

'I don't *want* to believe it, Amos . . . truly I don't. I haven't said anything to anyone else about the gun, but . . . I'm so confused I don't know what to think . . .'

She was crying uncontrollably now and, feeling desperately sorry for her, Amos sat down on the bed beside her and pulled her to him. After only a token show of resistance, she leaned against him, sobbing bitterly.

Neither of them heard Talwyn come up the stairs until, framed in the doorway, she looked at them in disbelief and exclaimed, 'What on earth . . . ? What do you think you are doing, Laura? Does this have something to do with the way you have been behaving today?' Looking from Laura to Amos and back to Laura again, she said, in a clipped voice, 'Is there something I ought to know about?'

Making a desperate effort to gain control of herself, Laura pulled away from Amos and said, disjointedly,

'No . . . It's just me . . . I'm being silly . . . I'll go to my room . . .'

'No you won't.' Aware of Laura's desperately confused state, Amos had reached a sudden decision. Preventing Laura from rising from the bed, he stood up and said to Talwyn, 'Yes, I am the cause of Laura being so upset, but it isn't what I think you believe it to be. Laura has discovered something that has resulted in such a conflict of loyalties that she just doesn't know what to do . . . doesn't even know what to think any more. Please sit down and let Laura tell you herself what she's discovered – and why she doesn't know what to believe.'

Wide-eyed now, Laura looked at Amos in dismay. 'But . . .'

'No buts.' Amos cut her short. 'Just tell Talwyn exactly what you have told me and why you are so upset.'

Her emotions in confusion, Talwyn's initial inclination was to dispute Amos's command of the situation, but curiosity got the better of her and she sat down on the room's only chair to hear what Laura had to say.

After a difficult and distraught beginning, Laura gradually gained control of herself as she told how she had found the boxed gun in the drawer in Amos's room and decided she had to keep the discovery to herself because she knew she had no right to look inside the box in the first place. Then she described how she had recognised the smell of burned gunpowder in the room that morning when asked by Maisie to fetch Amos's washing and had once more checked the gun and discovered that it had been recently fired. She said she had still been wondering what she should do when she and Talwyn returned from school and learned of the shooting of the London detective.

As Laura's story unfolded she looked fearfully in Amos's direction, as though she expected him to contest what she was saying, but he said nothing. When the tale came to an end, a pale-faced Talwyn looked at Amos in horrified disbelief, and when she spoke it was in a voice that none of her pupils at the Charlestown school would have recognised.

'Is all this true, Amos? Did you shoot the London detective? If so, who else have you shot ... and why?'

Aware that foremost in Talwyn's mind now must be the shooting of her father, Amos said, 'All that Laura has said about her discoveries is perfectly true, but – and I quite understand why – she has arrived at the wrong conclusions. I *was* at the scene of the shooting last night ... but I did not shoot Carpenter.'

'You *admit* to being there when he was shot ... ?' Talwyn looked at him in horror. 'I am sorry, Amos, but I am going to have to report this to Sir Joseph Sawle. Perhaps he will be able to find out who you really are and what you are doing here.'

'Sir Joseph already knows ... and he is the only man in Cornwall who does. But in view of what Laura has learned and the distress it has caused her, I think it's time you were both let into the secret. First, I must apologise to you, Talwyn, for gaining admission to your home under false pretences.'

'You mean ... you are not in Cornwall to search for a missing father? You are here for some other reason?'

'In fact, I *am* searching for my father, but that is being used as the cover story to hide my real reason for being here. You see, I too am a Scotland Yard detective, brought to Cornwall to try to find the killer of your father. Justification for such subterfuge was clearly shown last night when Detective Inspector Carpenter was shot and seriously wounded, because of who he is.'

Startled, but still sceptical, Talwyn said, 'If your story is true, what were you doing out last night – and why did you fire *your* gun?'

Acknowledging the validity of her questions, Amos replied, 'Sir Joseph, Carpenter and myself were lured out by some false information received by Sir Joseph. When we discovered it to be false we returned to Penrice and were waylaid by four men. When they shot Carpenter I fired back and hit at least one of them ... possibly two.'

'Does that mean these men now know who you are?'

'No. I was riding behind Sir Joseph and Carpenter, and before a lantern could pick me out I had shot the man holding it and he dropped it. Nevertheless, although I hope my identity will remain secret for a few more days, it looks as though I shall now be placed in charge of the investigation and won't be able to stay undercover for very much longer. For that reason it will probably be best if I move from the cottage. We are dealing with utterly ruthless men and I don't want to put any of you at risk.'

Still struggling to come to grips with all she had learned in the last few minutes, Talwyn said, 'Let me be quite certain I have all the facts straight ... you are here in Cornwall at Sir Joseph's request to investigate the murder of my father?'

'Yes.'

'Have you discovered anything yet?'

Choosing his words carefully, Amos said, 'I have learned a great deal. In fact, I am satisfied I know the identity of his murderer, but before I make an arrest I need to know I can prove his guilt in a court of law.'

'But the murderer must know that you – or your inspector – are getting close to him or he would not have tried to kill him last night. Won't he try to do the same to you once he knows who you are?' Talwyn sounded concerned.

'Most probably,' Amos agreed. 'That's why I feel it would be better for me to move elsewhere, to avoid putting anyone else in the house in danger.'

Shaking her head vigorously, Talwyn said, 'There is no question of your going anywhere else. You are putting your life at risk to find my father's killer. Mother and I will do everything in our power to help you. No risk will be too great if it helps bring my father's murderer to justice.'

'Thank you,' Amos said, 'but it might be better if we said nothing to your mother just yet.' Looking at the younger girl, who still sat on the bed, wide-eyed at the unexpected turn of events, he added, 'But what about Laura? There is no reason for her to be involved in this.'

Rather more perceptive of Laura's feelings for Amos than he was himself, Talwyn asked, 'What do you think, Laura? Would you prefer to live somewhere else while all this is going on?'

Looking from Talwyn to Amos, Laura said, 'Would you rather I left? I mean . . . after the way I've behaved . . .'

'If it hadn't been for you this would not have come out in the open the way it has,' Amos declared, 'and I am grateful to you for that. It hasn't been easy pretending to so many people that I am someone I am not.'

'It cannot have been easy for Laura either,' Talwyn said sympathetically. The drama of Laura's story and Amos's revelations had overtaken more personal considerations, and she was herself again. 'Finding that a man you both liked and respected was hiding a gun in his room . . . especially after the events of last night.'

'Well, she has proved she can keep a secret,' Amos said, 'but I really don't want to put anyone at risk unnecessarily.'

'I don't *want* to go away anywhere,' Laura declared emphatically, 'but I will if you would rather I did.'

Once again Talwyn felt she understood Laura's feelings and she said, 'I certainly don't want you to go anywhere, Laura. I feel you belong here and I enjoy your company. So, unless Amos has any objections . . . ?'

Aware from Laura's expression that his reply would be important to her, Amos said, 'I too enjoy having Laura around and she has proved her loyalty to her friends by tackling me about the gun and giving me an opportunity to explain before she dashed off to tell all and sundry what she had found. That would have made things very difficult for me – and for the investigation I am involved in. My only concern is that I put anyone in danger by remaining here.'

'I expect Miss Nightingale's nurses faced far more

danger without even thinking about it,' Laura said, 'and I'm happier here than I have ever been anywhere else. I don't want to leave.'

'Then that's settled,' Talwyn said in her best school-teacher voice, just as they heard Maisie calling from the bottom of the stairs.

'Talwyn? I thought I sent you up there to fetch everyone down to dinner. Another few minutes and it won't be worth eating.'

'Coming!' Talwyn called. Then, turning to Amos, she said, 'We will talk later about any problems that might be caused when it becomes known who you really are, but now you had better put your shirt back on and we will all go down to dinner. For the time being we will say nothing to Mother about what has been discussed up here.'

38

That evening Amos accompanied Talwyn to the manor. They had agreed they would tell the servants at the big house that Talwyn was there to consult Sir Joseph about the school, while Amos was accompanying her in view of what had happened in the grounds of the manor the previous night.

In reality, Amos wished to learn how Detective Inspector Carpenter was progressing, and also to inform Sir Joseph of the day's events at the Kernows' cottage.

There was no apparent change in the condition of Carpenter, but the magistrate's main concern appeared to be that Laura was now included among those who were aware that Amos was in fact a Scotland Yard detective.

'Are you confident she will be able to keep it to herself?' he asked. 'After all, she is still only a school-girl, and if my memory serves me correctly she comes from a village that features prominently in our inquiries.'

'After the way she has conducted herself during this past week I would be happy to trust her with any of my secrets, Sir Joseph. Besides, her knowledge of Henwood and the area might well prove very useful to us,' Amos replied.

'I agree with Amos's assessment of her character,' Talwyn said. 'She is a quite exceptional girl and, at the risk of embarrassing Amos, I would add that she idolises him and would do or say nothing likely to cause him harm.'

Sir Joseph was momentarily amused, but his gravity swiftly returned and he said to Amos, 'Have you pointed out to Miss Kernow that we are dealing with callous and evil men and that it might be safer for her, her mother and this young girl if you were to leave their cottage now we seem to moving closer to arresting them?'

'You mean . . . there is more than one man involved in the murder of my father?'

Aware that he had disclosed more than he had intended, Sir Joseph cast a swift, apologetic glance in Amos's direction before replying, 'It is highly probable there are a number of men involved, my dear, but when we make an arrest we need to be certain we have the man who actually fired the shot that killed your father.'

'Then Amos will need all the support Mother and I can give him,' Talwyn declared firmly. 'Especia7lly now his colleague has been wounded. I would like to think I am doing something to help. I know Mother will feel the same – and if there is likely to be any danger I believe we must let her into the secret about Amos and warn

253

her of what might happen. As for Laura . . . she hopes one day to become one of Florence Nightingale's nurses and is not lacking in the courage she will require for such a career . . . especially if she feels she is doing something to help Amos.'

'Thank you. I hope we shall soon put these men behind bars and so remove any danger that might be posed to your household,' Sir Joseph said. 'What do you think, Mr Hawke?'

'We certainly can't allow Mrs Kernow to remain in ignorance of the danger my presence in the cottage might pose to her.'

'Very well.' Sir Joseph was satisfied. Addressing Talwyn once more, he said, 'May I suggest you kennel that large dog of yours in your garden at night? I know he is a friendly enough creature to all and sundry, but he would no doubt make a fuss if someone came prowling around in the darkness. Now, there is someone else who needs to be let into the secret: Parish Constable Mitchell, who lives near Pentewan. He has asked to be considered for a post in the force we shall be forming in the county and I am confident he can be trusted to keep your true identity secret for as long as is necessary, Hawke. I sent a message to him today, asking him to make inquiries to ascertain whether anyone in the village has suddenly become mysteriously incapacitated during the night—'

He came to an abrupt halt when Talwyn's head suddenly jerked up in surprise. 'Is there something in what I have just said, that strikes a chord with you, Miss Kernow? You see, when Detective Inspector Carpenter was shot, Mr Hawke returned the fire and we know he wounded at least one of the assailants. He followed his trail as far as he could and it appeared to be leading to Pentewan. The wounded man would have required the services of a doctor, but, for obvious reasons, would not have wanted it known that he had been shot. Have you heard of someone who fits the bill?'

'Possibly, although it may be no more than a coincidence. One of the girls I teach at Charlestown lives at Pentewan, although the family is originally from somewhere on Bodmin Moor. Laura knew her there. She did not come to school this morning and another girl from the same village said her father had been taken ill during the night and that Charlotte – that is the name of the girl in question – needed to stay home to help her mother.'

'What is this girl's surname?' Sir Joseph asked, as he wrote some details in a notebook open on the desk before him.

'Lightfoot,' Talwyn replied. 'I believe the father was a miner on the moor, but came down to work on one of the mines at Crinnis. He was dismissed a few months ago, but can still afford to send Charlotte to my school and she is fond of occasionally appearing at school flaunting a silk handkerchief, or perhaps a Breton lace shawl. She is not very popular with the other girls.'

'Lightfoot?' Remembering the initials JCL on the hunting knife he had found, Amos was instantly interested. 'You say Laura knew her on the moor?'

'That's right. In fact I think Charlotte's father worked on the same mine as Laura's.'

Amos and Sir Joseph exchanged knowing glances and Amos said, 'I think we should ask Constable Mitchell to make a few discreet inquiries about Mr Lightfoot and his sudden illness – and try to discover his Christian names. When he has learned something perhaps he could come along to the cottage – also discreetly – and introduce himself.'

'Of course.' Sir Joseph added something to his notes then closed the book, saying, 'I think we are moving ahead, albeit slowly, Hawke. Hopefully Mr Carpenter will soon begin to make progress towards a recovery, but I will keep you informed – and also make certain you are aware of any correspondence I receive from Scotland Yard.'

Walking back to the cottage, Talwyn said very little, and eventually Amos commented on her silence. 'You are very quiet, Talwyn. Are you beginning to wish you hadn't got yourself involved in all that's going on at the moment?'

'I have been involved since the day someone killed my father,' Talwyn replied. 'No, I want to become even more closely involved, but I was remembering how I behaved towards you when we first met. I showed such poor judgement that you probably won't welcome my wanting to help you.'

'We didn't exactly get off to the best of starts,' Amos admitted, 'but it's not easy to be enthusiastic about meeting someone for the first time when their horse has just dumped you on your backside on wet grass with your shopping strewn all around you.'

256

'True,' Talwyn said wryly, 'but I carried things too far.' Giving him a sidelong glance, she added, 'For what it's worth, I find it difficult to think about it now without wanting to laugh at myself. I must have looked ridiculous.'

'*I* never laughed,' Amos declared. 'I don't think I would have dared. You were absolutely furious.'

They both laughed now, but neither was laughing at the other and Talwyn said, 'Thank goodness it's behind us now. I hope you will let me feel that I am doing something useful in the search for my father's killer.'

39

Two days after the shooting of Detective Inspector Carpenter, Parish Constable Mitchell called on Amos at the Penrice cottage while Talwyn and Laura were at school. Maisie Kernow had not yet been enlightened about Amos's true role and, believing the constable had come to visit him in connection with his missing father, she continued with her cooking while the two men walked together in the garden. There the village constable told Amos the results of the inquiries he had made about the man named Lightfoot who lived in Pentewan.

'I believe your suspicions are probably fully justified,' said Mitchell, 'and that the hunting knife could well be his. He is known in the village as "Jimmy" Lightfoot, although I have been unable to find out his middle name – and his family are being particularly close-mouthed about the nature of his mysterious "illness". I do know that the new doctor from Mevagissey hasn't been called in, but old Dr Vincent, who retired some time back, has been to Lightfoot's house every day since he took to his bed. Not only that, but old Auntie Harriet from the village is calling at the house a couple of times each day with her medicine basket.'

Feeling he should explain Auntie Harriet a little more fully, he said, 'She's called in to help out when a woman is in labour, or, I believe, in a great many cases to ensure that an unmarried woman never arrives at that stage.'

'You mean . . . she's an abortionist?' Amos asked. 'Do you have proof of that, or is it no more than village gossip?'

'If I had proof I would have brought her before a magistrate before now,' Mitchell declared, 'but, as you'll appreciate, there are very few women willing to come forward and make a complaint once Auntie Harriet has got them out of trouble.'

'How well do you know her?' Amos asked. 'Do you think you could persuade her to tell you exactly what is wrong with Lightfoot? Whether or not he has been shot and, if so, how serious is the wound?'

Mitchell shook his head. 'No. The reason folk call on her services so often is because they know she can keep her mouth shut. Mind you, there was a man down at Mevagissey who was very unhappy because he said she had aborted his wife of their sixth child. She'd had five daughters in as many years and was determined not to have any more, but rumour has it that the aborted baby turned out to be a boy. He could perhaps prove helpful, although if he made an official complaint about her he

259

would be very unpopular with a great many people. He would know that.'

Thoughtfully, Amos said, 'All the same, you could have a word with this Auntie Harriet and tell her you know about that particular woman. Point out that if she refuses to tell you whether or not Lightfoot is suffering from a gunshot wound and he is subsequently arrested and charged with attempted murder, she will be brought to court charged with aiding and abetting him and as a result spend the rest of her life in prison.'

'Would that really happen . . . or is it no more than a bluff?' Mitchell asked.

'It's no bluff,' Amos replied. 'But if she co-operates we could conveniently forget she has been treating him.'

After some moments of contemplative silence, Mitchell asked, 'Why is it so important to have Auntie Harriet confirm what there can be little doubt about? Lightfoot was almost certainly one of those who waylaid the detective inspector.'

'*Almost* just isn't enough,' Amos replied, 'as you will need to learn if you ever become an officer in an official police force – especially here, in Cornwall, where I believe there is even more resistance to such a force than there was in London. You will need to have every case you take to court tied up so tightly that it cannot be unravelled. We *almost* have enough evidence to arrest someone for the murders of Edward Kernow and the two Excise men – but Detective Inspector Carpenter and I have had to hold back because there is still a small gap between certainty and the probability of being convicted by a jury of fellow Cornishmen. If we *know* that Lightfoot is suffering from a gunshot wound then that, combined with the finding of the initialled hunting knife at the scene, will be sufficient to have him arrested for attempted murder. Faced with the prospect of transportation for life, he might be willing to give us the evidence we need to fill that gap. So find out what is wrong with him and we might be able to take the first positive step to bringing our murderers to justice.'

'I can see there is going to be far more to being a policeman than there is to carrying out the duties of a parish constable,' Mitchell said ruefully.

'You will learn,' Amos replied. 'At least, you will if it is what you really want to do.'

'It is,' Mitchell said eagerly, 'and with the years of experience I have had as a parish constable, Sir Joseph thinks I might be able to join the new Cornwall police as a sergeant, at least.'

'Find out the truth of Lightfoot's "illness" then, and, if he has a bullet wound, whether he is well enough to be brought before Sir Joseph. I'll go visit him in prison and if he comes up with the evidence we need to convict the murderer of Edward Kernow, I'll add my recommendation to that of Sir Joseph.'

Parish Constable Mitchell walked away from the Penrice cottage elated with thoughts of what the future might have in store for him.

That evening, sitting in the kitchen in the presence of Talwyn and Laura, Amos told Maisie the real reason why he was in Cornwall and how Laura and Talwyn had discovered his secret. He apologised for deceiving her for so long, adding that he would undoubtedly need to reveal his true role very soon, now that Carpenter had been shot and he had been placed in charge of the investigation.

Much to his surprise, instead of being shocked by his disclosure, Maisie gave him a hug and kissed him warmly on the cheek, saying, 'Bless you, Amos, for what you are doing. You have renewed my belief that Edward's killer will be brought to justice. I was beginning to believe he would never be found.'

'Thank you for your faith in me,' Amos replied, much relieved by her reaction to his disclosure, 'but, as I have told Talwyn and Laura, I could be putting you all at risk by remaining here after what they did to Detective Inspector Carpenter.'

'That is a risk that Talwyn and I will accept willingly,' Maisie said firmly, 'but there is another consideration that might prove serious for us.'

'What is that?'

'The school,' Maisie replied. 'You saw the reaction of the parents when the London policeman questioned the pupils about the night of poor Edward's murder. What do you think they will do when they learn who you are and that you are staying at the cottage with us?'

40

For the next few days Amos was unable to discuss Maisie's concerns with Sir Joseph Sawle because the magistrate was kept busy with his duties. They included meetings with Excise and coastguard chiefs in an effort to discover how the smugglers had been able to make fools of them all and set such a successful ambush for the London detective inspector.

The source was eventually traced to a senior Excise official in the port of Fowey, who insisted that details of the proposed landing of smuggled goods had been passed to him by a mysterious informant. The unknown man had apparently not wished to claim a reward for his information, but had felt it his 'public duty' to pass on the details to the authorities.

Predictably, this informant had never been seen again and Sir Joseph was furious that the abortive operation on Crinnis beach should have been mounted on the strength – or weakness – of such uncorroborated evidence. He believed that the anti-smuggling operation could not have been instigated without the collusion of someone in authority in the service and he was writing to London to demand that a full inquiry be launched by the minister responsible.

When his anger at what he referred to as 'the incompetence of the whole Cornish Excise service' had subsided, Sir Joseph reported to Amos, who had called at the manor to check on the condition of the detective inspector, that although Carpenter was regaining strength, everyone was still concerned about him. The magistrate had sent a telegraph to Scotland Yard stating that there was little more that could be done in Cornwall to hasten the senior detective's recovery. He suggested that the wounded man should be moved to London as soon as was practicable, in order that he might be treated by surgeons with experience of gunshot wounds.

A reply had been received only a couple of hours prior to Amos's visit to the manor house. The Metropolitan Police were sending a police surgeon to Cornwall to assess Carpenter's condition and arrange for his repatriation to London, probably on one of the passenger vessels from foreign ports which frequently put in at Falmouth to land mail and passengers before setting off on the final leg of their voyage to London.

While Amos was digesting the implications of this information, Sir Joseph added, 'The telegraph is not entirely about Inspector Carpenter. The Metropolitan Police commissioner has approved my request that you be allowed to remain in Cornwall and take over the murder investigation. In view of your increased responsibilities you are to assume the rank of acting detective inspector. They also express full confidence in you and authorise you to use whatever means you deem necessary to capture those responsible for the cowardly attack on Inspector Carpenter – and you are to pursue this end regardless of expense.'

'I am grateful to the commissioner – and to you, Sir Joseph, for your support. And, rather than wait for our killers to plan their next move, I hope to be able to take action against *them*. Does Bodmin gaol have its own hospital?'

'Yes, and it is considered quite adequate,' Sir Joseph replied, 'although I would not care to place myself in the hands of those who tend the prisoners there. Why do you ask?'

'Because if Constable Mitchell learns that this man Lightfoot, from Pentewan, is suffering from a bullet wound we will have enough evidence to implicate him in the attempted murder of Detective Inspector Carpenter. If Lightfoot is not actually dying, I want Mitchell to arrest him on a warrant issued by yourself and convey him to Bodmin gaol immediately. If his accommodation and care in the Bodmin gaol hospital is less comfortable and caring than he would like, then he might be more inclined to tell us who was with him. If, as seems highly probable, it was the Davey brothers, you will have sufficient justification to issue a warrant for their arrest too – but in their case we will choose the right moment to execute it, when we can be certain of finding the weapon that murdered Edward Kernow and the two Excise officers.'

Sir Joseph gave Amos a quizzical look. 'You are wasting no time exercising your new authority, Hawke. Do you think Inspector Carpenter would approve?'

'In his present state I doubt very much whether he is capable of coherent thought,' Amos replied. 'His shooting and the elaborate plan that made it possible is evidence that the men we are after will stop at nothing to avoid detection and arrest. At the moment they are unaware who I really am, but I am very soon going to have to come out and declare myself. As soon as I do, everyone in the Kernow household will be at risk. I would like to put the Davey brothers on the defensive before then – and perhaps make some of their accomplices think twice before risking the hangman's rope on their behalf. It is those men I am really hoping to put pressure upon. If I can somehow make them fear Scotland Yard more than they fear the Daveys, we will be well on the way to a murder conviction . . . but we do have another problem.'

'Only one?' Sir Joseph queried sardonically. 'What is it?'

'It is to do with the Charlestown school . . .'

Amos told the magistrate of the threats made by the fathers of some of the pupils to take them out of the school after they had been questioned by Carpenter, adding, 'When they learn that a detective has been lodging in the home of the schoolteacher I think many of them will remove their children in protest. By no means all of them are actually engaged in smuggling themselves, but there is hardly a family in the district who has not had someone involved in the past. There will be a great deal of resentment at having a man from London come down here making arrests – even though I myself am a Cornishman. I know Maisie Kernow is particularly concerned about such a problem's arising.'

'Then you can tell widow Kernow to put her mind at rest right away,' Sir Joseph replied firmly. 'I own a great many of the houses in and around Charlestown, and have influence with the owners of others. Anyone removing a child from Charlestown school without a genuine reason can look for work and accommodation elsewhere. Cornwall will soon have a full-time constabulary and they will need to accept that law and order will be paramount in this area for as long as I am a Justice of the Peace. We will not be dictated to by a band of criminals.'

Sir Joseph rose to his feet. 'Now, I will write a letter giving you unlimited access to any prisoner held in Bodmin gaol, and then we will go and see whether Inspector Carpenter is awake.'

41

James Colan Lightfoot was taken into custody at dawn thirty-six hours after Amos's conversation with Sir Joseph Sawle, and the arrested man was taken to Bodmin gaol escorted by Parish Constable Mitchell and a number of special constables sworn in for the occasion by the St Austell magistrate. They left behind them a village with the characteristics of a disturbed beehive, its residents brought from their beds by the shrieks and wails of Lightfoot's wife and daughter, who had tried unsuccessfully to prevent the arrest of the wounded head of the household.

The previous evening John Mitchell had spent a very long time interviewing Auntie Harriet and had eventually succeeded in eliciting the information that Lightfoot was indeed suffering from not one but two bullet wounds, one in his neck, the other in his thigh. The retired Dr Vincent had needed to probe for the latter, causing his patient much pain and loss of blood.

Of the two wounds the one in the neck was the more serious, but Auntie Harriet confirmed that with continuing medical attention Lightfoot would make a full recovery, and in her opinion was already out of immediate danger.

The news of Lightfoot's arrest was brought to the Penrice cottage by Constable Mitchell the same afternoon, and Amos was saddling his horse with the intention of riding to Bodmin gaol to interview him when a servant came summoning him to the manor.

When Amos arrived there he was shown into the study, where Sir Joseph held out a telegraph that had just been received from Scotland Yard. A police surgeon would be arriving from London that evening and the magistrate had already sent a message to the senior coastguard at Fowey, asking him to make one of his steam launches available to convey Detective Inspector Carpenter and the surgeon from Charlestown to Falmouth on the following day. Sir Joseph had ascertained from that major Cornish port that there were currently no fewer than five London-bound ships at anchor in the sheltered harbour there, one a hospital ship from India, which had put in for minor repairs caused during a storm in the Bay of Biscay.

It was on this ship, with its extensive medical and surgical facilities, that Sir Joseph was hoping to arrange passage to London for the wounded detective inspector and the Metropolitan Police surgeon.

As a result of receiving this information, Amos put

off his visit to Bodmin gaol and later that evening returned to Penrice manor to meet the surgeon and discuss the arrangements for returning him and Carpenter to London. There were signs that the current spell of good weather was likely to come to an end in the not too distant future, and the surgeon decided he would risk moving his patient late the following morning.

Amos was at Penrice manor the next day to bid farewell to his senior officer, but it was no more than a courtesy gesture. He had visited Carpenter on a number of occasions since the latter had been wounded, but each time had found him so stupefied by the pain-killing opiates being given to him that it had been impossible to hold an intelligent conversation.

As the carriage taking Carpenter and the surgeon to the harbour at Charlestown disappeared along the drive, Amos had begun walking back to the cottage when he was brought to a halt by a hail from Sir Joseph's butler, who told him that the baronet wished to speak to him.

Believing that Sir Joseph would probably have something to say about the departure of Carpenter from the manor, Amos made his way through the great house to the study. Here, as expected, the baronet's first words concerned the wounded policeman. 'Poor Carpenter does not appear to have made much progress while he has been at Penrice. I do hope they will be able to do something for him in London.'

'I hope so too,' Amos said. 'He will certainly be assured of receiving treatment from surgeons who have a great deal of experience of treating bullet wounds. The police surgeon himself served with the army in the Crimea and he has arranged for the detective inspector to be taken to a military hospital.'

Sir Joseph nodded his approval before saying, 'By the way, another man arrived from London no more than half an hour ago. I believe he has been travelling all night. He came to the manor asking for you.'

Amos was startled. 'From London? No one there outside the commissioner's office is supposed to know my whereabouts. Who is he ... and where is he now?'

'I have not met him myself,' Sir Joseph replied, 'but the butler tells me he is a giant of a man with an Irish-sounding name. He apparently said that you were his commanding officer in the Crimea.'

Amos looked at Sir Joseph in disbelief. 'It sounds like Harvey Halloran! He was a Royal Marine colour sergeant and second-in-command of my small police force in the Crimea. He is a first class man to have around ... but how on earth has he found me here?'

'You had better ask him yourself. I had him taken to the servants' hall until I was able to speak to you. I am aware that your presence here is meant to be a secret and had he not been known to you I would have had him arrested – although if the description of him is correct, I doubt if I would have been able to find sufficient servants to secure him! I am told he is an extremely powerful-looking man.'

'He is also an ex-prizefighter,' Amos said, 'and has always proved thoroughly loyal to me – but I want to know how he learned where I was to be found.'

'Then I will send for him and we will discover his secret together.' As he was speaking Sir Joseph tugged at the bell-pull which hung down from the ceiling alongside the fireplace. When a maid appeared in answer to his call he sent her off to fetch the unexpected visitor.

The maid returned a few minutes later accompanied by Harvey. When he saw Amos, the big man sprang smartly to attention, his expression registering delight as he said, 'I am relieved to see you, sir. When word went around that Detective Inspector Carpenter had been shot, I feared the worst – especially when no one could tell me anything about you – so I thought I had better come and find out for myself.'

Introducing Harvey to Sir Joseph, Amos said, 'I appreciate your concern, Harvey, but how on earth did you find me? My presence here is supposed to be a close secret – at least, the fact that I am a detective is. As far as I am aware, my whereabouts is not known to anyone at Scotland Yard.'

'That is so, sir,' Harvey said, still standing stiffly to attention, 'but you told me you were going off somewhere with Inspector Carpenter, and when I heard that he was shot and seriously wounded I knew you were involved in something dangerous and might need some help . . . so here I am.'

'That still doesn't explain how you found out where I was,' Amos pointed out.

'It wasn't too difficult,' Harvey explained. 'When it was said that Surgeon McIntyre was being sent to fetch the inspector back to London, it was quite easy to find out where he lived. All I needed to do then was to hang

272

around his street for less than twenty-four hours before a hackney carriage drew up outside the house to take him to the railway station. I hurried forward and handed the surgeon's pieces of luggage up to the carriage driver from the servant and read the address on the labels fixed to them. They said "Penrice Manor, St Austell, Cornwall" ... and so I knew where I might find you.' Giving Amos a broad smile, the big man added, 'The surgeon even gave me twopence towards my fare for helping with his luggage!'

'You showed considerable initiative,' Sir Joseph said. 'You ought to be a policeman yourself!'

'Thank you, sir,' Harvey replied. 'As Mr Hawke knows, it is something I would like very much.'

'Would you, now?' Looking speculatively at the big man, Sir Joseph asked, 'Did you ever instruct men in drill during your service in the Royal Marines?'

It was Amos who replied to the baronet's question. 'Before becoming a colour sergeant at the outbreak of the Crimean war, Harvey was drill sergeant in the Royal Marines barracks at Gosport, Sir Joseph – and a formidable figure he was too!'

'I can well believe it,' Sir Joseph said. Then, addressing Harvey, he said, 'In a few days' time the magistrates are meeting to appoint a chief constable. He will be responsible for forming a Cornwall County Constabulary. The favourite candidate for the post is Colonel Gilbert, currently of the Royal Artillery. When I spoke to him informally after his interview, he told me that, in his opinion, one of the most important appointments he would be making if he became chief constable would be that of a police sergeant major, to teach drill and discipline to new recruits. His belief is that this would be the foundation stone on which the new force should be built. You could be just the man he is looking for. If Colonel Gilbert is appointed I will suggest he has a word with you – if Mr Hawke is willing to endorse your suitability for such a post?'

'I will do that with no reservations whatsoever,' Amos said. 'Having been Harvey's commanding officer in the most difficult circumstances, I would be happy to recommend him for a post that would seem to be made for him.'

'Excellent!' Sir Joseph said. 'Now I will leave you two to decide how you might work together now he is here – and I have no doubt you will find some way for Halloran to assist you, Hawke. By the way, where are you staying, Halloran?'

'I haven't been in Cornwall long enough to look round,' Harvey replied, 'but I am sure I will find somewhere.'

'There is a very comfortable room attached to the stables,' Sir Joseph said. 'It is kept to accommodate the servants of any visitors to Penrice, but I am not expecting anyone in the foreseeable future. Speak to my head groom and move in there until you have seen Colonel Gilbert and decided your future.'

42

Harvey accompanied Amos to the Penrice cottage and was introduced to Maisie. Explaining who the big man was and his reason for coming to Cornwall, Amos said, 'When we were in the Crimea together Harvey was always around to take care of me when we ran into serious trouble. I think it became a habit that he is reluctant to break.'

Maisie was genuinely relieved. She had been very concerned at the thought of Amos working on his own to catch the men who had murdered her husband. 'You need someone to look after you with all that's going on around here at the moment,' she said, 'and I must say he looks more capable than most men I have met.' She turned to Harvey. 'My daughter and a pupil who stays with us here will be home for dinner soon. You must stay and have some with us, although I hope your appetite doesn't match your size.'

Harvey protested that he had not expected to eat with them and did not want to deprive the others of their food.

'You'll be depriving no one,' Maisie declared. 'I haven't yet got used to my husband not being around and am cooking as though he is still here.'

Harvey had been told by Amos that he was lodging with the widow of the murdered schoolteacher and, after expressing his sympathy, Harvey said, 'It was a terrible thing to happen, Mrs Kernow, but now Mr Hawke is in charge of everything those who did it will soon be behind bars, you mark my words. I've probably known Mr Hawke longer than anyone else and I could tell you some tales about the things I've seen him do. I never served with a better officer and now he's a detective he's respected in London by those on both sides of the law. Hardened villains tremble in their boots if they know Mr Hawke is after them.'

Amos grinned. 'Harvey tends to exaggerate about some things, Maisie, but I don't know another man I would rather have with me if ever I run into serious trouble.'

'I am not surprised,' Maisie said. 'It would be a brave man – or a foolish one – who deliberately upset him.'

Amos thought she had unwittingly raised an interesting possibility. Harvey *was* a very big man – and a tough one – but so too was Hannibal Davey. He wondered what would be the outcome if ever the two met in combat . . .

His thoughts were interrupted by Maisie, who said, 'I think I can hear our Talwyn and Laura coming. They will enjoy having someone new to talk to at the dinner table, especially someone who can tell us about Amos. He has succeeded in saying very little about himself during the time he has been with us.'

They were seated around the kitchen table, eating, when Talwyn asked in apparent innocence, 'Did you and Amos see much of each other when you were both in London, Mr Halloran?'

'Oh yes, we would often meet up and talk about old times – it was him who got me a pension when I had to leave the Royal Marines because I had been wounded. He also got me work in the garden of the house where he was lodging – and that reminds me of a piece of news I think will be of great interest to you, Mr Hawke, sir. Mrs Pemble has a new lodger in your old room. He's one of the civilian clerks at Scotland Yard – and unmarried. You'll be delighted to know that Joyce has transferred her affections to him. I don't think he's got the gumption to escape from her . . . so it will be quite safe for you to return to London in due course.'

Unaware of the effect his words had made upon the women around the table, Harvey beamed at Amos, whose scarlet cheeks might have been the result of choking on his food as Talwyn asked brightly, 'Who is Joyce? You have never mentioned her to us, Amos.'

Belatedly aware that everyone had momentarily ceased eating and was looking at him with interest, Harvey realised he might have been guilty of an unthinking indiscretion. He tried to talk his way out of it.

'Of course, I'm not saying there was ever anything between you two. It was just that . . . well, Joyce is

277

determined to find a husband, and you were available . . . at least, that's what she thought . . .'

Harvey was floundering and Talwyn said provocatively, 'This is a part of Amos's life we have heard nothing about. Tell us more, Mr Halloran.'

'There is nothing more to tell,' Amos said firmly, 'and Harvey has far more interesting things to talk about.' Giving the big man a stern look, he said, 'Laura's ambition is to become a Nightingale nurse. Tell her about the time you spent in Miss Nightingale's care – and how she came to rely upon you to keep order in her wards.'

Laura had kept out of the potentially volatile conversation until now, but the mention of Florence Nightingale and Amos's disclosure that Harvey had not only met the world's most famous nurse but had actually helped her in her work whilst recuperating in her hospital animated her as nothing else could have done. She immediately bombarded him with a series of questions that dominated the talk at the table for the remainder of the meal.

However, Talwyn had no intention of allowing the subject of 'Joyce' to be forgotten. Later, when Laura and Harvey were still talking of Florence Nightingale and Maisie was listening enthralled, Amos helped Talwyn clear the plates and dishes from the table. When they were together in the kitchen, Talwyn asked, 'You have never mentioned Joyce to us before, Amos. Were you very fond of her?'

'No,' Amos replied honestly. 'She is a nice girl and will make someone a good wife, but I always knew that someone was not going to be me.'

Taking from him the plates that he had just scraped clean of scraps, she said, 'Has there ever been anyone that you felt you would like to marry?'

Amos was silent for a while before saying, 'There *was* a girl – a Turkish girl. I met her in the Crimea. I thought we had a great deal in common – in fact, just about everything but language. Her father was a provincial governor, but he was also a very shrewd businessman. When I refused to give him the sole concession to supply the British garrison with meat and local produce there was a sudden cooling of his daughter's ardour. There has been no one since and little opportunity as a London policeman . . . How about you?'

His directness was intended to take the initiative from her and it succeeded. Already flustered by the realisation that her interest in his answer had been rather keener than he supposed, Talwyn put on what Amos had come to regard as her 'schoolteacher face'. She was about to tell him that her private life was none of his business when she recognised that she had invited such a question by her own inquisitiveness. Instead, she said with what dignity she could muster, 'As a teacher, and a full-time governess before that, I have had no more time to form romantic attachments than a policeman. Even if I had, I have met no one worth the huge disruption it would cause in my life.'

Maisie had entered the kitchen quietly in time to hear her daughter's words. She made no comment, but smiled quietly to herself.

43

Early the following day Amos set off for Bodmin gaol accompanied by Harvey, who was mounted on one of Sir Joseph Sawle's horses that had been put at the big man's disposal.

Harvey had never before been to Cornwall and he was particularly impressed with the conical man-made mountains of china clay waste inland from St Austell, and also with the spectacular views of the English Channel to be seen from the high ground in the same area.

'If I am taken on as drill sergeant in the new Cornwall constabulary I think I could come to like this place,' he said, adding anxiously, 'Do you believe this new chief constable will take me on?'

'With Sir Joseph's recommendation, there can be little doubt about it,' Amos replied, 'especially if you are able to help me arrest the men who murdered Edward Kernow and the others.'

Amos had told Harvey that the Davey brothers were prime suspects for all three murders, and, after remaining quiet for a while, Harvey said, 'This Hannibal that everyone seems to be so frightened of . . . is he as big as me?'

'He is probably not quite so tall, but he's heavier and he and his brother have a vicious streak. It seems they actually enjoy hurting people.'

Still thoughtful, Harvey said, 'From what you've told me men are frightened of Hannibal because he is big and enjoys violence and that it's only because of this that his brother hasn't been locked away in an asylum, is that right?'

'I'd say that's a fair assessment of the situation,' Amos replied, 'but Pasco is not only mad, he's also a killer . . . and, remember, he has a gun.'

Harvey nodded acknowledgement of what his companion had said. 'And you need to find this gun in his possession when the time comes to arrest him?'

'That's correct,' Amos agreed, 'but before that I need to persuade a member of the Daveys' gang – preferably more than one – to give evidence against them, and that isn't going to be easy.'

'It would probably be easier if someone was to show that this Hannibal isn't as tough as he wants everyone to believe,' Harvey said. 'If someone was to cut him down to size.'

'I don't know where this conversation is going – but forget it!' Amos said in sudden alarm. 'Hannibal and his brother are very dangerous men and I would like you to still be around when I have gathered enough

281

evidence to arrest them. Whatever you do, don't precipitate anything!'

The letter written by Sir Joseph Sawle authorised only Amos to visit Bodmin gaol. While he was visiting Lightfoot, Harvey said he would take their horses on to the stable of the inn nearest to the gaol and meet Amos there when his business with Lightfoot was at an end.

Aware that the wounded prisoner would not recognise him as the man who had shot him, Amos had already decided he had nothing to lose by identifying himself as a Scotland Yard detective when they met. Lightfoot would be receiving no other visitors to whom he could pass on the information.

The gaol's hospital comprised two cells on the top floor, and when Amos was shown into one of them he found the wounded man lying beneath a rough grey blanket with only a wafer-thin, straw-filled mattress between his body and the rough wooden boards of the bed.

'Hello, Lightfoot, and how are you today?'

Thinking that Amos was one of the gaol's medical staff, the wounded man replied, 'I was better before I was brought in here. I was beginning to believe I would recover, but now . . . ? Anyway, what do you care?'

'I care a great deal,' Amos said cheerfully. 'You see, I am a friend of the London detective who was shot by you and your companions. I would hate you to cheat justice by dying before the judge makes an example of you.'

Lightfoot gasped. 'Who are you? What are you doing in here? I haven't done anything wrong.'

'You don't get two bullet holes for doing nothing,' Amos pointed out. 'Besides, your hunting knife was found at the scene of the shooting with your blood on it and the trail of you and your friend led me to Pentewan. You are guilty enough to spend a year or two enjoying life on a prison hulk before you are transported . . . for life. Who is the man who helped you home, by the way? As he cares so much for you he might like to keep you company on the journey to Australia.'

'I'm saying nothing,' Lightfoot said, 'and you'll not make me, so you might as well save your breath and go away.'

'Mind you, there are a couple of ways you can escape transportation,' Amos continued as if Lightfoot had not spoken. 'The first is that if the man you waylaid dies, then you'll be hanged instead. The second is to turn Queen's evidence and tell magistrate Sir Joseph Sawle what you know about the men whose idea it was to shoot the London detective.'

'I've already told you, I'm saying nothing, so you're wasting your time here. You might as well go and leave me alone.'

'I have plenty of time to waste . . . but you haven't. However uncomfortable you might be here, you'll probably survive, but the life you have known and no doubt enjoyed is over. Imagine never being able to finish a day's work and look forward to going home to your wife and family. In fact, the only time you might possibly see them again is if they're sitting in court while you stand in the dock waiting to hear the judge pronounce the sentence that is going to take you away from them for ever. If you are a caring man – and I think you might be – that is going to be very hard ... not only for you, but for them. It's a great pity, because you have a good wife, and a daughter who is bright enough to make something of herself, given the support of her father. But what future is there for a girl, however bright, whose father has been transported for life for attempted murder?'

'She'll get by,' Lightfoot declared in a voice that lacked conviction. 'I've got friends who'll look after her – and my wife too.'

'If you're talking of who I think you are, these friends in whom you have so much faith will be able to help no one. They will have ended their lives dangling at the end of a hangman's rope long before you've even settled in on the prison hulk. You would be well advised to think seriously about what I am saying to you. These men are guilty of murder and, anyway, the day of the large-scale smuggler is over. The recruits who are coming into today's Excise service are honest men.'

'Better men than you have thought they could come here and change the way Cornishmen have lived for centuries,' Lightfoot retorted defiantly. 'Your friend from London was one of them – and look what's happened to him!'

'You would be well advised to think rather of what's happening to *you*,' Amos replied. 'These friends you are protecting – and in whom you have so much misplaced faith – have murdered two Excise men already. They

284

have also killed schoolteacher Edward Kernow; two miners from Wheal Phoenix; a man you probably knew, named Toby Martin, who could have told the truth about what happened when Notter miners broke through into Wheal Phoenix workings – and they probably also killed a man who is lying at the bottom of a ventilation shaft at Notter. The men you have so much trust in are also trying to have Cap'n Billy Arthur and Doniert Hawke put out of the way because they know enough to have them both hanged – and now you are in the same position. You know too much. These so-called "friends" of yours will be greatly relieved when you're either transported or, if the London detective dies, hanged for your part in his murder.'

When Amos paused, Lightfoot said nothing. Encouraged by his silence, Amos continued, 'You see, I know a great deal about these men and can promise you it won't be long before they are arrested . . . and hanged. There are a lot of men like you who have worked for them – and are still working for them. The sensible ones are those who realise there is no longer a place for men like them in Cornwall. They are the ones who will turn Queen's evidence and help speed the Daveys' conviction. Those who hold on to a misplaced loyalty to these so-called "friends" will either suffer their fate, or be transported, as you will be.'

Preparing to leave the hospital cell, Amos said, 'Think of what I have said, Lightfoot – and think what your decision will mean for your family. But don't spend too long in thought. Once your colleagues realise that the power of the pair you look up to is broken for ever, there will be a rush of men hoping to save their own skins – and to save *their* families. When that happens no one is going to give priority to a man who helped to shoot a London detective, and the courts will only grant pardons to one or two men who give evidence against the Daveys.'

Amos banged on the door to alert the gaoler standing guard in the passageway outside that he wished to be released, but Lightfoot called, 'Wait! Who are you? I'm not saying I will tell you anything ... I'm not saying that, but if ever I want to speak to you, how can I contact you?'

'Get a message to magistrate Sir Joseph Sawle that you want to speak to the detective from London. It will reach me.'

Amos left the gaol hospital in the firm belief that he had been able to make an impression upon the Pentewan man – but he would not be leaving the prison immediately. First he wanted to speak to Captain Billy Arthur once again.

When Captain Billy was brought to the empty cell where he was to be interviewed by Amos he was limping badly and his fingers were cut and bleeding.

When Amos expressed concern, the prisoner made a gesture of resignation and explained, 'I fell when I was on the treadmill and injured a knee. The surgeon said I wasn't fit enough for the treadmill any more, so I've been put to picking oakum.' He held out his hands to show the cuts and sores to Amos. 'I don't know which is worse, the treadmill or oakum picking. It's done these no good. Still, it won't be many days now before I'm out of here.'

'Don't pin too many hopes on that, Billy. While you've been in here things have been happening outside that have made magistrate Sir Joseph Sawle very angry. He was returning to Penrice manor with the London detective in the early hours of the morning, after being out looking for smugglers, when some men jumped out of hiding and shot the detective.'

The news startled Captain Billy. 'Was he killed?'

'Well, he's not dead yet, but Sir Joseph knows it was the work of the Davey brothers and he's determined to see them hang – for this and the other things they've been involved with.' Taking a gamble, Amos added, 'He's already arrested two of the men who were involved in the ambush and made them aware that if the detective dies they will both hang. Even if he lives, the best they can hope for is transportation for life. As a result they are beginning to talk and mention the names of others who have been involved with the Davey brothers. Yours is one of those he's been given; that's why I doubt whether you'll be getting out of here as quickly as you expect.'

Captain Billy was both angry and fearful. 'Why should I be drawn into this? All my dealings with the Davey brothers ended a long while ago – and I have more reason to be frightened of them than anyone. Who are the two who have mentioned my name to Sir Joseph?'

'One I believe is called Lightfoot . . . Jimmy Lightfoot. I think the other lives close to him, but I've forgotten his name for the moment.'

'It'll be his brother-in-law, Sam Rodda from Mill cottage. One rarely goes anywhere without the other . . . and if you want to learn anything about your father, they are the ones you ought to be speaking to, not me. Rodda and Lightfoot were both close to him.'

'Why didn't you tell me this before, Billy? Why leave it until now? What else do you know about him that you haven't told me?'

Captain Billy shrugged. 'Why should I tell you anything? Apart from a drink and a few pence – which you can obviously afford – you've done nothing for me.'

Walking to the door and banging on it to attract the attention of the warder, Amos said, 'I'll do something for you now, Billy . . . something that might well save your life.' As the sound of jangling keys could be heard from beyond the cell door, Amos went on, 'Send a message to Sir Joseph that you're prepared to give evidence against the Daveys – and do it now, before it's too late. The Daveys are doomed men and as soon as they're in custody those who have worked with them will be clamouring to give evidence against them in order to save their own skins. Only those first in line will get the chance.'

Amos went to meet Harvey well pleased with his visit to Bodmin gaol. Not only had he probably identified the man who had helped Lightfoot escape from the scene of the ambush at Penrice, but he believed he might have frightened both Lightfoot and Captain Billy enough for them to give serious consideration to telling Sir Joseph what they knew about the Daveys. In so doing he had also learned the names of another two men who had known his father well.

'This Hannibal Davey ... is he a big, black-bearded scowling man who likes to be surrounded by men who laugh at his jokes and treat him the way staff officers treat a commander-in-chief?'

Startled, but amused by Harvey's simile, Amos replied, 'It certainly sounds like him. Why do you ask? Do you think you might have seen him?'

Harvey nodded. 'I stopped in for a drink in an alehouse at the other end of town and he was in there with half a dozen others. The landlord was treating him as though he was royalty.'

'He would,' Amos commented. 'No doubt Hannibal keeps him well supplied with smuggled brandy. What do you make of the man now you've seen him?'

'He carries a lot of weight,' Harvey replied, 'but too much of it is on his belly. I've beaten bigger men in the prize ring.'

'Don't get any ideas, Harvey,' Amos said, amusement changing to alarm. 'Remember that you'll be joining the Cornwall police soon.'

'I'll remember, Mr Hawke, sir, but when you're ready to arrest Hannibal Davey, you make certain you have me there with you.'

44

In the evening of his return from Bodmin gaol, Amos called on Sir Joseph Sawle at Penrice manor and told him what he had learned from Lightfoot and Captain Billy. As a result, Sir Joseph agreed to issue a warrant for the arrest of Sam Rodda and have Constable Mitchell execute it the following day. Amos would accompany him.

The magistrate expressed satisfaction at the manner in which the investigation was being carried out, but queried whether or not Amos felt he was any closer to obtaining the evidence needed to arrest and convict the Davey brothers for the murders of Edward Kernow and the Excise officers.

After a few moments of contemplation, Amos said, 'I am far more confident than I was a few days ago. I also believe that Captain Billy knows enough to give us the evidence we need, but he is a convicted vagrant and a drunkard. Even if we could persuade him to stand up in court and tell what he knows about the Daveys, he would hardly impress a jury. His evidence would need to be corroborated – and apart from any other consideration he has no incentive to tell what he knows about them. No family to think about. All the same, I would like him to be kept in custody for a while longer if it is at all possible. He knows a great deal about the activities of the Daveys and his knowledge could prove vital to us if corroborated.'

'Holding him in custody is not quite as simple as it sounds,' Sir Joseph replied. 'He will have to be released on time, but I will have him brought before me again and order him to report to the court on a daily basis while inquiries are made about his means of support. If he fails to meet these conditions I will have him rearrested.'

Amos returned to the Penrice cottage to complete a report on the progress he was making in his investigation, for forwarding to Scotland Yard. It was one of the tasks he had inherited from Detective Inspector Carpenter. Meanwhile, Harvey had gone off with Parish Constable Mitchell, to be shown around the area for which Mitchell had responsibilities.

Amos found only Talwyn in the house. Andrew's father was preaching in the Wesleyan chapel at Charlestown and Maisie had expressed a wish to go to the service to hear him speak. It would be the furthest she had ventured from the cottage since her accident, and, as her leg had not yet completely healed, Laura had volunteered to accompany her in case she found she needed help.

Making a pot of tea for Amos and herself from the kettle that was gently steaming on the kitchen range, Talwyn asked him whether he had made any progress in the hunt for her father's killers.

'We've moved a little further forward today,' Amos replied. 'I've been to visit Lightfoot in gaol, and, although he wasn't particularly forthcoming, while I was there I learned the name of one of the men who was most probably with him on the night he was shot. He'll be arrested tomorrow.'

'Is he someone I would know?' Talwyn asked.

'Possibly. He's another Pentewan man ... Sam Rodda.'

'Oh no!' Talwyn cried, obviously distressed. 'He is married to Kitty Rodda and they live at Mill cottage. I know them both and have been friends with Kitty for as long as I can remember. She is a lovely girl who has been dogged with the most awful luck for the last few years. She and Sam have two adorable children, but both have suffered from fits since birth and doctors doubt whether either will survive childhood. Sam dotes on them both ... and on Kitty too. If he's mixed up in anything wrong it will only be because he is desperate to get money for them all. His father owned his own fishing boat and he, Sam, and Sam's brother used to earn a good living from it until one day they were caught in a sudden storm and driven on to rocks, a little way along the coast. Sam was the only survivor and by the time he was rescued he'd been in the water for so long it took him quite a while to recover. When he did, he and Kitty had nothing. Oh, poor, poor Kitty! She works so hard for her family, yet fate keeps slapping her down. She's been through so much already . . . and now this. It's a tragedy.'

Talwyn was close to tears, showing a tenderness and vulnerability that was far removed from the emotion displayed by the woman he had first known.

'Yes, it's sad, Talwyn, but there is little doubt that he was involved in the shooting of Detective Inspector Carpenter . . . and he might even have been involved in the murder of your father.'

'No, I can't believe that. I don't *want* to believe it. As for the inspector . . . perhaps there is some mistake there too. Could it have been anyone else?'

'I would like to say there was some doubt, Talwyn, but at this stage I am afraid I can't.'

'What will happen to him,' she asked. 'I mean . . . if he is taken to court and found guilty? What punishment can he expect to be given?'

'He'll be transported, probably for life. If someone spoke up for him and was able to convince the court there was some good in him, the sentence might be reduced to, perhaps, fourteen years. I don't think it will be any less than that, but when he's arrested I will speak to him. If he decides to co-operate it *could* be less, but I can't promise anything.'

'Don't you ever feel sorry for some of the men and women you arrest, Amos? Do you ever wonder whether you are doing the right thing?'

'Very often, but I also feel sorry for the victims of such people . . . and the families of the victims. Women like you and your mother – and the families of men like Detective Inspector Carpenter.'

293

There was silence between them while Talwyn digested this, and then she said, 'I know you are right. You see the whole canvas, while I am looking at just one tiny detail. It's just . . . I *know* Kitty. Why should one person have so much pain to bear?'

Such a question was unanswerable and Amos replied, 'Thank you for giving me the background to the Rodda family, Talwyn. It won't make what I have to do any easier, but if there is anything I can do for Rodda that will help his family, I will do it.'

Still with a tortured expression, Talwyn looked at him and said, 'I am sorry, Amos. It is unfair of me to burden you with the troubles of the Rodda family. Put it down to the outburst of a silly and emotional woman.'

'I prefer to look upon it as the reaction of a warm and caring person,' Amos replied. 'I can find no fault with that.'

Amos was aware that he felt closer to Talwyn at this moment than to any woman he had ever known. The realisation disturbed him. It could only complicate an already difficult investigation – and he felt Detective Inspector Carpenter would not approve.

45

Amos was never to know whether Detective Inspector Carpenter would have approved or disapproved of the improving relationship with Talwyn Kernow.

Parish Constable Mitchell came to the cottage late the next morning. He had received an urgent message to report to the magistrate, and bring Amos with him. The two men arrived at Penrice manor to be given grim news. Carpenter had arrived in London on board the hospital ship, only to suffer a massive and unexpected haemorrhage while waiting to be taken ashore. He had died within minutes.

The inquiry into his shooting had now become yet another murder investigation. Amos decided it was time to cast off the cloak of subterfuge beneath which he had been hiding since his arrival in Cornwall, and go all out to bring the Daveys to justice as swiftly as possible. Sir Joseph agreed with him and Amos and Mitchell left the manor with a warrant for the arrest of Sam Rodda tucked safely inside a pocket of the parish constable's coat.

On the way to Mill cottage, Amos discussed the circumstances of Rodda's family with his companion.

'I know about them, of course,' Mitchell said, 'even though I have never done more than pass the time of day with either Sam Rodda or his wife. There is no one in the Pentewan area who doesn't feel desperately sorry for the whole family.'

'That's the impression I was given by Talwyn,' Amos said. 'She has known the Roddas for many years and describes them as a close and loving family. Unfortunately, he is involved in murder now – and it's the murder of a senior policeman. There can be no room for sentiment.'

'True,' John Mitchell agreed. 'All the same, I am glad the Roddas' cottage is a little way out of the village. They are a well-liked young couple. If they had friends and neighbours around them an arrest wouldn't be easy.'

'Then we had better get it over with as quickly as possible,' Amos said, 'before anyone gets wind of what is going on.'

Mill cottage nestled in a recess carved out of the hill-side at the side of a road that followed the course of a narrow, fast-flowing river, coloured milky white by the waste from the clay workings beyond St Austell.

The door of the cottage was opened by a young woman whose tired expression could not hide the fact that she was extremely pretty. Behind her, somewhere in the cottage, a child was crying.

Amos was the first to speak. 'Mrs Rodda? Is your husband in, please?'

Suddenly apprehensive, Kitty Rodda said, 'He's out the back, making a seesaw for the children. The piece of wood was washed ashore on Pentewan beach . . . but he asked the coastguard and he said it was all right for him to bring it home . . .'

'We haven't come to speak to him about anything that has been washed up on the beach . . . but we do need to have a word with him.' This time it was Constable Mitchell who spoke.

The child's crying had increased in volume and now a man's voice called, 'Kitty . . . are you there? What's the matter with Matthew?' A few moments later there were the sounds of footsteps and a young man appeared behind Kitty Rodda.

He stopped when he saw the two men in the doorway and his face paled as his glance shifted from one to the other.

The woman turned and Amos stepped past her. Coming face to face with her husband, he said, 'Samuel Rodda, I am Detective Inspector Hawke from Scotland Yard, in London. I believe you know Parish Constable Mitchell. He has in his possession a warrant issued this morning by Sir Joseph Sawle for your arrest on suspicion of murdering Detective Inspector Marcus Carpenter.'

There was a heart-rending scream from Kitty and she cried, 'No! There must be some mistake. Tell them, Sam . . . tell them you've done nothing wrong.'

Ashen-faced, her husband said, 'I've killed no one . . . and that's the truth.'

'But you are not denying you were with James Lightfoot and others when Sir Joseph Sawle and Detective Inspector Carpenter were waylaid and shots were fired?' Amos put to him.

'I was told we were only going to warn off someone who was interfering with . . . with a business venture. I had no idea Sir Joseph Sawle would be involved, or that anyone was carrying a gun.'

Sam Rodda had already said far more than his friend Lightfoot, and Amos said, 'You will come with Constable Mitchell and me and we will discuss the matter further at St Austell magistrates' court before you are taken to Bodmin gaol.'

While he was speaking, Kitty had been sobbing with a clenched fist held up to her mouth. Now she pleaded, 'No! Please don't take him away. I need him here . . . we *all* need him.'

'I am sorry,' Amos said, 'but Constable Mitchell will keep you informed of what is happening to your husband.'

In the background the child's crying had become louder and increasingly distressed and Sam Rodda spoke gently to his wife. 'Go to Matthew, Kitty – and fetch Sally in from out the back. I'll speak to Sir Joseph and see if we can't sort this out, somehow.'

Mitchell handcuffed Rodda and led him away from the house. Amos followed them. When they reached the lane, he looked back and saw a deeply distressed Kitty standing in the cottage doorway with her son held up to her shoulder and her free hand clutching that of her tearful daughter.

Amos and John Mitchell set off on horseback, with the arrested man walking between them. After a few minutes he asked, 'Am I going to walk through St Austell handcuffed like this?'

'You are certainly going to St Austell, where Sir Joseph will be waiting at the magistrates' court to commit you to Bodmin gaol to await trial.'

'But . . . I was telling you the truth. I *didn't* know that anyone was going to be shot.'

'I am afraid that will make no difference to the charge – or the outcome of your trial,' Amos pointed out. 'You were in the party that waylaid Sir Joseph and Detective Inspector Carpenter. Carpenter was shot and has died as a result of the wounds he received. All four of you who were there are equally guilty of his murder.'

'That means . . . I might possibly hang?' Sam Rodda put the question in fearful disbelief.

'It means you will most certainly hang.'

It was only because Amos had keen hearing that he heard Sam Rodda's whispered 'Poor Kitty . . . poor Kitty!'

46

By the time Amos and Mitchell reached the St Austell magistrates' court with their prisoner, the morning's business was over, the only cases to have occupied Sir Joseph's time and patience being two separate findings of 'drunk and disorderly'. Both defendants pleaded guilty and were given fines of two pounds each, the amounts being immediately paid into court.

Upon the arrival of the trio from Pentewan the court was hurriedly reconvened. When the charge against Rodda was read out and he acknowledged that he understood it, he was ordered to be taken to Bodmin gaol to await a preliminary hearing.

Amos was in the magistrates' office discussing the case with Sir Joseph and the parish constable when there was a knock at the door and one of the court officials appeared to say that Rodda had said he would like to speak to 'the London detective'.

When Amos entered the cell, Rodda was seated on the solidly built wooden bench seat, his head in his hands. When he looked up at his visitor, his expression was that of a man who had forsaken hope.

'You wanted to speak to me?' Amos asked.

'I am in serious trouble, aren't I?' Rodda's words were as much a statement as a question.

'Just about as serious as it gets.'

'I really didn't know they intended shooting anyone,' Rodda insisted. 'Nobody is going to believe me, but it's the truth, I swear it is.'

'By "they", I presume you are talking of Hannibal and Pasco Davey?'

After only the briefest hesitation, Rodda nodded and Amos felt a thrill of excitement. The arrested man had tied the Daveys firmly into the killing of Carpenter. This could be the break which he and Carpenter had been working towards. The tragedy was that it had been brought about by the senior detective's own death.

It had been Amos's intention not to visit Rodda until he had sampled a few days of prison life, but if he could be persuaded to incriminate the Daveys here and now, it would mean that Sir Joseph could issue a warrant for their arrest immediately.

'Who was it who actually fired the shot that hit Detective Inspector Carpenter?' he asked.

'Pasco,' Rodda replied. 'I think he would have shot Sir Joseph Sawle too, had there not been someone else there who shot him first. Was that you?'

Ignoring the question, Amos said eagerly, 'Pasco was

301

shot? Are you quite sure? You are not talking of Lightfoot?'

'No, it was Pasco. He said it was little more than a scratch – but it was enough to prevent him from using his gun arm after firing. I don't know any more than that. I was too busy trying to help – to help someone else.'

'Don't start playing games, Sam. You were helping Lightfoot and it's far too late to attempt to protect him now. You know he's already in custody?'

Rodda nodded. 'But he didn't know there was going to be any shooting, either.'

'You shouldn't have been surprised,' Amos said. 'You must have known that Pasco had a gun – and had used it before?'

When Rodda made no reply, Amos persisted, 'Well, did you know?'

'I didn't even know that Pasco was going to be with us. It was Hannibal who asked me and Jimmy to go with him. I thought it would just be the three of us and that Hannibal would probably give this London detective a beating and warn him off for coming to Cornwall and interfering in the way we do things.'

'Interfering?' Amos spoke angrily. 'We were asked to come here because an innocent man – a schoolteacher – had been callously murdered. Is that what you call "the way you do things" in Cornwall?'

'I told you, it was Hannibal who asked us to go with him. He said he would pay us well and I was desperate for money for Kitty and the kids. I would never have gone had I known Pasco was going to be involved, and

302

neither would Jimmy. Pasco frightens both of us. He's not sane.'

'Were either of you with Pasco when he shot and killed Edward Kernow on the cliffs near Charlestown?' The unexpected question paid off.

'I wasn't – but Jimmy saw it happen. Fortunately, Pasco didn't see *him* – but Kernow wasn't shot on the cliffs. He was carried there and thrown over. At least, that's what Jimmy said.'

Startled, Amos asked, 'If he wasn't actually killed on the cliffs, where was he shot – and why?'

'I don't know any details; you'll need to ask Jimmy. He didn't want to talk about it. He said that if Pasco knew that he'd seen anything, his own life wouldn't be worth a candle – and he's right. The Daveys make certain that whenever they do something particularly serious they always cover their own backs. You'll need to ask Jimmy what he knows – but don't be surprised if he won't tell you.'

The information that Edward Kernow had been shot elsewhere and dumped over the cliff came as a surprise to Amos. He needed to speak to Lightfoot and try to persuade him to tell all he knew. It would not be easy.

However, that was a problem he would face later. Sam Rodda's unsolicited description of what happened and who had been present on the night Carpenter had been shot had told Amos far more than he had expected to learn, and he needed to take the fullest advantage of the arrested man's readiness to talk.

Leaning closer to Rodda, he said, 'I want you to listen very carefully to what I have to say to you now, Sam.

303

Then you will need to make a decision about it – and it will be the most important decision you have ever made in your life . . . or will ever make.' Confident that he had Rodda's full attention, he continued, 'Before Constable Mitchell and I arrested you, I was told all about you: the tragedy of the boat accident; you and Kitty and the heartache of having two invalid children. I felt very sorry for you, but the way I felt had nothing to do with whether I should arrest you or not. I had to do my duty. And I told you the truth when I said that by being one of the four men who waylaid and shot Detective Inspector Carpenter you are as guilty as the rest and so will hang with the others . . .'

Rodda's body shuddered violently for many moments. Then he shook his head repeatedly, an expression of anguish on his face, and said, 'I *didn't* know . . . I *really* didn't.'

'That doesn't change your guilt under the law . . . but I believe you, and I think I can offer a way out for you, if you are prepared to accept it.'

'I'll do *anything*,' Rodda declared. 'I know I got myself into this mess, but I don't want Kitty and the kids to suffer for what I've done. What do you want me to do?'

'You've just told me what happened on the night Inspector Carpenter was shot – and also what you know about the shooting of Edward Kernow. I would like you to repeat your story in as much detail as you can, to magistrate Sir Joseph Sawle. It will be written down and signed by you . . . and then you must be prepared to stand up and repeat it before a judge and jury at the Assizes. I will also need you to give me a list of all the men you know who are involved in smuggling with the Daveys, especially those who might have witnessed other killings that we know have been committed by Pasco or Hannibal. Many are no doubt as horrified as you are by what the Daveys have done. You have my promise that I won't use the list to bring anyone to court for smuggling. I haven't come to Cornwall for that ... but I am determined to see the Daveys hanged for murder, and I believe a great many people will breathe sighs of relief when that day comes.'

Sam Rodda had displayed a variety of emotions as Amos was speaking and now he said, 'I would like to help you to bring the Daveys to justice ... I really would, but what *I* want – or even what *you* want – doesn't matter to me any more. All I care about are Kitty and the kids. The Daveys are all-powerful. Even if you arrest them they can still pose such a threat to the families of anyone who gives evidence against them that you are never going to get anywhere.'

'That might have been the situation before this,' Amos said firmly, 'but now they have murdered a Scotland Yard detective – and that changes everything. No one – and I do mean *no one* – does that and gets away with it. I have told you that we already have enough evidence to hang both you and Lightfoot and, unless you help us, you *will* both hang. I am giving you a chance to save your life – and Lightfoot too if he is willing to help me. I can understand your concern for your wife and children, but I promise that if you are willing to give evidence against the two Davey brothers I will have them sent somewhere safe – unless you have a family

305

who would be willing to take them in until after the trial?'

'I have no one . . . at least, no one who is far enough away to be safe from the Daveys.'

'Then we will speak to Sir Joseph Sawle and ask for his help,' Amos promised. 'If he can offer them a place where the Daveys will not find them, will you tell all you know in return for a pardon?'

As the moments passed without a reply, Amos began to think he had failed after all. Then Rodda said, 'If you can take Kitty and the kids somewhere where they will be protected and the friends of the Daveys can't find them, I will tell you everything you want to know . . . but can I speak to Kitty first and explain to her what is happening?'

Elated, Amos said, 'If you come up to Sir Joseph Sawle's office and make your statement, I have no doubt that he will arrange for someone to go out to your cottage and bring Kitty here to see you. You are doing the right thing, Sam. The evil power that Hannibal and Pasco seem to have over people needs to be brought to an end. You will be doing something that no one else has had the courage to do.'

47

When Amos apprised Sir Joseph Sawle of his conversation with Sam Rodda, the magistrate was jubilant.

'We have them at last, Hawke. Well done! Well done indeed!'

'We certainly have enough evidence to arrest them for shooting Inspector Carpenter,' Amos agreed, 'and we will, but I will need to question Lightfoot again. If I feel he knows enough about Edward Kernow's murder to incriminate the Daveys I will try to persuade him to give evidence too. Then, if Captain Billy can be persuaded to tell his story of the Wheal Phoenix murders, we will have so much against the Daveys that they will have nothing to lose by admitting they killed the Excise officers. But we must capture Pasco's handgun when we arrest him and call on the armourer at Bodmin barracks to give us his expert opinion that the bullets which killed Edward Kernow and the Excise officers were fired from it – and that it was an ex-cavalry-issue pistol. The judge might or might not agree that the armourer's evidence is admissible, but the jury will have heard what he has to say – and the fact that Pasco was found to be in possession of a stolen cavalry pistol will help them make up their own minds.'

'I am in full agreement, Hawke, so bring Rodda up to my office right away and we will commit his statement to paper.'

When Sam Rodda was brought up from the magistrates' court cells, his first question was about the arrangements that would be made for Kitty and their two children's safety.

Sir Joseph assured him that Kitty and the children would be taken to Penrice immediately – and Kitty brought to St Austell to see her husband. Tomorrow they would be sent by carriage to a small estate in Devon owned by Sir Joseph and occupied by his brother, who was a fellow Justice of the Peace. There, they would be perfectly safe.

Satisfied with this arrangement, Rodda made a long and detailed statement. Although it incriminated himself, he was assured by Sir Joseph that all charges against him would be dropped upon the conviction of the Davey brothers.

In his statement, Rodda had Hannibal calling out 'Shoot him!' when the light from the bull's-eye lantern fell upon Carpenter. This was something Amos was able to verify, having heard the cry, even though he did not know at the time who had made it. Rodda then confirmed that the shot was fired from a pistol held by Pasco.

The arrested man reiterated that he had believed that the ambush would result in nothing more than a warning – albeit a physical one – to the London detective by Hannibal Davey against trying to prevent Cornishmen from pursuing an occupation, namely smuggling, which had been carried on for hundreds of years, often with the approval of landowners, many of whom also served as magistrates.

When the statement had been signed, and counter-signed by Sir Joseph, Amos led the arrested man back down the stairs to the cell. On the way, Rodda said, unexpectedly, 'I believe you have been asking round for news of Doniert Hawke?'

Captain Billy had told Amos that Sam Rodda had known his father, but Amos had deliberately refrained from asking him questions about the association until Rodda had made his statement about the Davey brothers. With that now behind them, he replied, 'That's right. He's my father, but I haven't seen him for a great many years. What do you know about him?' Somewhat hesitantly, he added, 'Do you know if he is still alive?'

'He was alive when I last heard ... although he wouldn't have survived had he stayed around here; Hannibal and Pasco would have seen to that. He knew far too much about them – and knows even more now. He was with Jimmy Lightfoot when Edward Kernow was shot.'

His words brought Amos to a startled halt. Turning to Rodda in disbelief, he said, 'My father was in Charlestown only a few weeks ago? Everyone I have spoken to says he hasn't been seen for months – or even years.'

'Well, Jimmy and I both saw him.'

'But what was he doing in Charlestown – and how did he come to witness the murder of Kernow?'

'I can't tell you how he came to see Kernow killed . . . but did you know that he married again after your stepmother died?'

'No, I didn't. Who did he marry . . . and where is he now?'

'He did very well for himself, marrying a French-woman who was the widow of a man who owned three or four ships trading out of Roscoff. Doniert – your father – is living over there now and seems to have discov-ered a talent for finding cargoes to fill the ships that belong to his new wife. He often sails with the various ships and, as I understand it, most of his cargoes are honest and above board – but he also makes money supplying contraband goods to Hannibal Davey. Mind you, there's nothing illegal in that, not in the way he does it. He pays for it legally in France and sells it to Hannibal here, transferring the goods at sea outside the three mile limit, to boats sent out by Hannibal who is the brains behind smuggling in this area. He's the one who breaks the law by bringing brandy and tobacco ashore without declaring it. It suits Doniert well, because he makes money from Hannibal without having to come in contact with either him or his brother, and he's wise to do so. Doniert is important to the Daveys now, but he's not indispensable, and he knows far too much about them. Anyway, after he'd made a particular delivery in the usual way, he brought his ship into Charlestown to deliver a legitimate cargo. It wouldn't have excited any interest because I doubt whether Hannibal and Pasco even know the names of the ships they are dealing with, and Doniert wasn't in for more than a few hours. But it was long enough for Jimmy and me to see him. I needed to get home early, but Doniert went off with Jimmy and they both saw what happened to the school-teacher . . . but Jimmy will be able to fill you in on the details. The trouble is, I think he might have told others of what he saw and if the Daveys have found out . . .'

Sam Rodda had no need to complete the remainder of his sentence. When the cell door had slammed shut behind him, Amos's thoughts were in a whirl.

Not only was his father alive and well in France, but he had also been a witness to the murder that Amos had been sent to Cornwall to investigate. Fortunately, there was another witness closer to hand and Amos intended to question him again at the earliest opportunity.

48

When Amos returned to the Penrice cottage that evening and led his horse to the stable, Laura was in her room working and she waved to him from her window. Talwyn had also seen his arrival. Leaving her mother preparing supper in the kitchen, she entered the stable as he was filling a tub with water from the cottage well for his horse.

Her first words were about Sam Rodda, and Amos said, 'He has been charged with the murder of Detective Inspector Carpenter and is now on his way to Bodmin gaol where he'll be held until a date is set for his trial.'

He was upset to see tears well up in Talwyn's eyes as she said, 'Poor Kitty. I wonder what will happen to her now?'

On the ride back to the cottage from St Austell, Amos had been wondering whether he should tell Talwyn what had been arranged for the Rodda family. Now, her obvious distress helped him to reach a decision.

'Kitty was allowed to visit Sam in the cells at the magistrates' court after his arrest and she and the children are sleeping at Penrice manor tonight.'

Startled by his news, Talwyn asked, 'Why? What's going on? Why aren't they staying in their own cottage?'

'I'll explain, Talwyn ... but it must remain a secret between the two of us. You must never so much as breathe a word to anyone or it might put their lives in jeopardy.'

'I don't understand ... ?'

'I had a talk with Sam and then spoke to Sir Joseph,' Amos explained. 'Sam has agreed to tell the court all he knows about the shooting of Inspector Carpenter: who actually fired the shot – and what led up to it. There is no doubt at all that his evidence will be enough to hang at least two of the men involved – and I don't think I have ever come across men who deserve such a punishment more. However, they are both very dangerous and wield a great deal of influence among their own kind. Kitty and the children are to be taken somewhere where they will be safe until the trial is over. The actual place to which they are going is a secret and I think it best if it remains so. To tell you the truth, *I* don't know exactly where they will be.'

'What of Sam ... will he still hang?'

Amos shook his head. 'No. He is being allowed to turn Queen's evidence. It means that in return for ensuring the principals in this tragic affair are convicted, he will be pardoned.'

313

When the full import of Amos's words registered with her, Talwyn's face registered relieved disbelief. 'You mean . . . Kitty, Sam and the children will be able to put this nightmare behind them and pick up their lives again?'

'They can . . . if the community will let them. Unfortunately, my experience is that men or women who help the police in such a way are often ostracised by those they have always regarded as their friends. Mind you, it's my opinion that the men Sam will have helped to get convicted are so utterly evil that anyone who has a hand in ridding the world of them should be regarded as a hero.'

'Are those he will be giving evidence against local men?'

'No. They are from Bodmin Moor, although I believe they originate from the far west of Cornwall.'

'Then Sam and Kitty will be all right,' Talwyn declared. 'Detectives and the like from outside may not be popular, but neither are lawbreakers who come here and stir up trouble. Sam and Kitty are well liked by everyone who knows them.'

Amos was not quite as convinced as Talwyn . . . but she was talking once more. 'Do you think Sir Joseph would mind if I went to the manor to see Kitty this evening? She will be feeling very lonely and vulnerable. I would like to reassure her that she has friends who *will* stand by her, whatever happens in the future.'

'I think that would be a very kind thing to do,' he said. 'I'll walk up to the manor with you. There are a number of people out there who have a lot to lose, and

I'd rather you didn't walk alone at night. I will have a word with Harvey and ask him to keep an eye on the cottage. Detective Inspector Carpenter's gun will still be up at the manor. I'll ask Sir Joseph if he'll allow Harvey to carry it with him when he's on his night patrols.'

Amos took Talwyn to Penrice where, after initial hesitation, Sir Joseph allowed the schoolteacher to visit her friend. While the two young women were talking in the room Kitty was occupying with her children, Sir Joseph entertained Amos in his study and they discussed the astonishing news that his father had been a witness with Lightfoot to the murder of Edward Kernow, although neither man had been implicated in the crime.

'I intend to visit Bodmin gaol tomorrow and get the full story out of Lightfoot,' Amos said. 'It would seem he is in a position to tell us exactly what happened and who was involved. It should clinch the case against the Daveys.'

'It should indeed,' Sir Joseph agreed, 'but would you mind putting off your visit to Bodmin until tomorrow afternoon? It is now certain that Colonel Gilbert has the support of a considerable majority of my fellow magistrates and in the next few days will be appointed as the first chief constable of the Cornwall constabulary. I have had a number of meetings with him during which we have considered the force he will command. We have also discussed the murder investigation carried out by yourself and the late Detective Inspector Carpenter, and the part in the proposed constabulary that might be played by Halloran. Colonel Gilbert has expressed a wish to meet you both and I have tentatively suggested that tomorrow morning would be a suitable time.'

Amos had wanted to interview Lightfoot at the earliest opportunity ... but a few hours would make little difference to his investigation. He agreed to the meeting.

Talwyn spent almost an hour with Kitty Rodda, and when she had said goodbye to her friend she and Amos set off together to make their way back to the cottage in the darkness.

'How is Kitty bearing up?' Amos asked.

'She is understandably apprehensive about the future,' Talwyn replied, 'and is aware that whatever has been agreed with Sir Joseph, Sam is still in prison with a charge of murder hanging over him.'

'If he doesn't change his mind about giving evidence against the Daveys there is nothing to worry about,' Amos assured her. 'What do the children make of it all?'

'It is a very close family and so they are missing their father, but they think that staying in a manor house is a great adventure.'

After walking for a few minutes in silence, Talwyn said, 'Although Kitty is very worried about Sam, she is grateful to you for what you are doing for him. She says that losing Sam would have been the final straw for her. I mentioned what you said about folk around Pentewan not forgiving him for giving evidence against the Daveys but, like me, she doesn't think that will happen. If it does, she says she won't care as long as she, Sam and the children have each other, because they can always go off and make a new life together.' Looking in his direction in the darkness, she asked, 'Did what I told you about the long period of bad luck the Roddas have suffered influence what you have done for them, Amos?'

'To be perfectly honest, I desperately needed Sam to turn Queen's evidence. The knowledge you gave me of his background helped me to persuade him. Had I *not* known what I did, I would probably have offered him a lighter sentence and not insisted that Sir Joseph arrange a full pardon in return for his evidence. I am sometimes angry when I see a man escape the justice he deserves by giving evidence against an accomplice when I know that the former is probably more deserving of punishment . . . but I don't feel like that in this case. Although it was naïve of Sam not to anticipate what actually happened, I believe his story. In view of how it turned out, he would have been hunted down by the Daveys because he knew who had shot Inspector Carpenter. As it is, they are probably convinced he won't dare to say anything for fear of incriminating himself.'

'I am glad you feel that way about it, Amos, and happy I have been able to help Kitty, if only in a small way.' Hesitantly, she added, 'Kitty swears that Sam had nothing to do with the death of my father and was at home for the whole of the day and night he was killed.'

'Sam told me he wasn't involved,' Amos said, 'but he did know about the killing. You see, it was witnessed by Lightfoot and . . . and by another man who was with him at the time. Although they were not involved, and were apparently in no position to do anything to prevent it, they *did* see who killed him. I intend to speak to Lightfoot about it tomorrow.'

Bewildered and upset by his revelation, Talwyn said, 'But . . . why did Lightfoot not tell anyone about it at the time?'

'Because he was too frightened of the men involved . . . just as Sam is frightened of them.'

'You mean it's the same men?' Talwyn was more confused than ever. 'But what could my father possibly have had to do with such people?'

'That's what I want Lightfoot to tell me when I see him, although Sam said he wouldn't even talk to *him* about it.'

For the remainder of the walk to the Penrice cottage, at Talwyn's insistence, Amos told her what little he knew about her father's death, and the man responsible, as told to him by Sam Rodda.

It upset her to be reminded of what had occurred on that night, and although she tried to compose herself before entering the cottage it was apparent to Maisie that her daughter had been crying and she wanted to know the reason. Fortunately, perhaps, she accepted Talwyn's explanation that she had been upset by the plight of Kitty and her two children. Although she made no comment and was not aware of the true reason for Talwyn's unhappiness, she found comfort in the fact that Talwyn was no longer ashamed to show such emotion before Amos.

Later that night, as Amos lay in bed in the darkness of his room, he wondered why he had not followed his instinct and taken Talwyn in his arms to comfort her when she was so upset.

He could not know that Talwyn was lying awake too, wondering the same thing.

49

The following morning, when Amos arrived at Penrice manor where he and Harvey were to meet Colonel Gilbert, prospective chief constable of the proposed Cornwall constabulary, he found the ex-Royal Marine nervously pacing back and forth in front of the house. He had gone to great lengths with his appearance.

His boots were polished to a standard that would have gained the approbation of a commanding officer had Harvey been on a ceremonial parade. His coat and trousers too were immaculate, having been carefully pressed and brushed by an understanding Penrice manor housemaid. He had also managed to obtain a brand new grey billycock hat to complete the ensemble.

Observing Amos's incredulous expression, Harvey asked anxiously, 'Do I look all right, Mr Hawke, sir? I'm not too overdressed to meet Colonel Gilbert?'

'Harvey, you are absolutely immaculate – exactly as

a prospective drill sergeant should be! If I were chief constable I would recruit you on the spot!'

Beaming, Harvey said, 'I wish you *were* to be the chief constable. It would be just like old times.'

Amos gave the ex-Marine sergeant a wry smile. 'You're quite right, Harvey; we even have people wanting to shoot at us.'

'Don't you worry about that, Mr Hawke, sir. We'll soon have those Daveys behind bars ... at least, we will if this Colonel Gilbert will let me join his police force.'

'Well, we will never find out by waiting out here. Let's go in and meet the man, Harvey, and see how we both get on with him.'

Colonel Gilbert was a man in his forties, of upright, military bearing. He wore long sideburns which linked up with a heavy moustache, giving him a somewhat fierce appearance. He first shook hands with Amos, saying, 'I believe you are making excellent progress in your investigation into the cowardly assassination of Detective Inspector Carpenter, Hawke?'

'We expect to be making the final arrests very soon, sir,' Amos replied, 'and by so doing we should be putting an end to a reign of terror enjoyed by the perpetrators for far too long.'

'Splendid! Sadly, I understand they are both ex-soldiers ...' Suddenly shifting his attention to Harvey, he said, 'Now, *this* is how I like to see an ex-military man. You will be Mr Halloran, who I understand was a colour sergeant in the Royal Marines?'

'That is correct, sir,' Harvey replied, adopting the

clipped tones used by non-commissioned officers when speaking to a senior officer. 'Second-in-command to Mr Hawke when he was in charge of a Royal Marine police force in the Crimea.'

Colonel Gilbert glanced briefly at Amos before returning his attention to Harvey once more. 'I believe you were badly wounded during the Crimean war and invalided from the Marines. Are you now fully recovered?'

It was Harvey who cast a glance at Amos now, with a hint of despair in his eyes, but, replying to Colonel Gilbert, he said, 'Fully recovered, sir. So much so that I have discussed with Mr Hawke the possibility of returning to the Royal Marines ... but I so enjoyed working with Mr Hawke on police duties that I feel I would like to give such work a try ... sir.'

Amos said, 'I can attest to Halloran's state of health, sir. He is every bit as fit as he was in the Crimea, where he was renowned for his strength and stamina.'

Colonel Gilbert acknowledged Amos's endorsement with a nod of his head without shifting his glance from Harvey. 'You have also performed duties as a drill sergeant, I believe?'

'Yes, sir, drill sergeant in the Royal Marine barracks at Gosport before the war and commended for my work by the commandant.'

'You would appear to be just the man I am looking for, Halloran. I think Sir Joseph has told you that I am only one of six candidates for the post of chief constable of what is to be the Cornwall Constabulary. However, Mr Coode, Clerk of the Peace, has informed me of the

322

results of the poll taken among the county magistrates. It seems my appointment has been approved by a majority of twenty-three votes and is to be officially endorsed next week. If you agree, I would like you to be my first recruit to the new force as drill instructor, with the rank of sergeant major and a salary of sixty pounds per annum. It will be no sinecure, I can assure you. The authorised strength for the constabulary below the rank of inspector is sixteen sergeants and a hundred and forty-four constables. I will expect them to be drilled to the standard of guardsmen – or Royal Marines – and that would be your responsibility. Do you think you are up to such a challenge?'

'If you recruit the right calibre of man, sir, I will give you the smartest constabulary in the country,' Harvey said jubilantly.

'Good man! I know you are helping Inspector Hawke at the moment – and from what Sir Joseph tells me of the villains you are after, he has need of men he can rely upon. When he has finished with you come and see me at my home in Bodmin. Until we begin recruiting in earnest you can practise your drill on my young daughters. I fear they are in sore need of discipline.'

The meeting between the four men broke up in an atmosphere of unexpected geniality and Amos and a delighted Harvey were leaving Penrice manor when a man whom Amos recognised as one of the clerks in the St Austell magistrates' court came cantering along the driveway on a lathered horse.

When he saw Amos, he pulled the horse to a flank-heaving halt and asked, 'Aren't you the detective from

London who has had two men arrested and sent to Bodmin for the murder of your inspector?'

'That's right. Is something wrong?'

'Yes,' said the breathless clerk. 'A message arrived at the court for Sir Joseph not half an hour ago. You had better come back to the manor with me. One of the prisoners committed suicide during the night.'

Both Amos and Harvey returned to the manor with the clerk and were present in the study when he broke the news of the suicide to Sir Joseph and Colonel Gilbert – who remained a silent but deeply interested observer.

'Is this likely to affect our case against the Davey brothers?' Sir Joseph asked Amos anxiously.

Amos looked at the clerk. 'You haven't told us which of the prisoners has died.'

'It was Lightfoot,' the man replied and Amos breathed a huge sigh of relief before replying to Sir Joseph's question.

'Had it been Rodda, the case against the Daveys for killing Inspector Carpenter could have collapsed,' he said. He knew it would also have caused great distress to Kitty Rodda – and to Talwyn.

'What about the case against the Davey brothers for the murder of Edward Kernow?'

'Lightfoot's death *does* create a problem there,' Amos admitted, 'and I feel we need to be able to prove at least two murders against them if we are to be certain of gaining a conviction. But the only other man who it seems could give evidence against the Daveys on that count is my father – and he is living in France.'

'Is there any likelihood of the Daveys admitting to the murder of Kernow – and others – if we are able to show them they have no chance of escaping justice for Carpenter's murder?' Sir Joseph asked.

Amos shook his head. 'I doubt it. We need to be in a position to prove every charge we make against them.'

'That is what I thought,' Sir Joseph said despondently. 'Nevertheless, I think it is important to show the public that the Davey brothers are subject to the same laws as everybody else. I will issue arrest warrants for them, on the charge of murdering Detective Inspector Carpenter, and we will discuss additional charges when we have them in custody.'

'Very well, Sir Joseph. In the meantime I would like Constable Mitchell to go to Bodmin gaol and make inquiries into the circumstances of Lightfoot's suicide – in particular, whether anyone other than the medical staff visited the prison's hospital for any reason whatsoever. If he finds that another prisoner might have spoken to him, that man should be immediately transferred to Launceston gaol. I would also like Mitchell to check the names and addresses of all prisoners in the gaol, including those recently admitted on remand. If he recognises any of them as having any possible connection with the Davey brothers, they too must be immediately transferred. We can't risk losing our other witness. For the same reason, when the Davey brothers are arrested, they too should be lodged in Launceston gaol – and allowed to speak to no one.'

50

When Amos passed on the information about the suicide of Lightfoot, Talwyn found it difficult to come to terms with the tragedy. Although his daughter was not popular with many of the girls in Charlestown school, she was still one of her pupils and part of Talwyn's school life.

'How could such a thing happen?' she asked. 'I thought that men shut up in prison were closely supervised.'

It was dinnertime in the cottage and Amos was seated at the kitchen table with Maisie, Talwyn and Laura.

'It's impossible to watch all the men all the time,' Amos replied. 'My experience, and that of colleagues at Scotland Yard, is that if a man is really determined to commit suicide he will find a way, even if he's wounded and supposed to be bedridden, as Lightfoot was. But when I spoke to him he was defiant, not suicidal. I am convinced that someone in league with the Davey brothers got to him. Captain Billy says they have friends everywhere . . . even in prison. Hopefully, Hannibal and Pasco will soon be joining them – I have warrants for their arrest in my pocket – but first I need to find out exactly where to find them. I presume they must live somewhere on Bodmin Moor, but I don't know where.'

'I do,' Laura declared unexpectedly. 'They live in an old cottage not far from Notter Tor, about a half-mile out of Henwood, on the lane to Kingbeare. It's a spooky place, with broken windows and torn and dirty curtains. I used to be frightened of going past it when I was smaller and would run with my head down, trying not to look at it.'

Surprised but grateful for her information, Amos asked, 'Do you know whether anyone else lives there with them?'

'I think they sometimes have women there, but nobody seems to know who they are, where they come from, or where they go to. If anyone is curious, I have never heard them asking questions.'

Maisie shuddered. 'It sounds the sort of place that decent folk should keep well clear of. Do you think you'll need to go there, Amos?'

'If he does, I hope he has a great many men with him,' Talwyn commented. 'The Daveys are very dangerous men.'

'I will be taking Harvey with me,' Amos said. 'He's as good as a whole platoon.'

'That's as may be,' Maisie said seriously, 'but you be sure to let us know before you go off after these men, so we can worry about you.'

Amos was still laughing at Maisie's remark when there came an urgent hammering on the kitchen door. Laura was the first on her feet and she opened the door to reveal a hot and bothered Constable Mitchell standing there.

Stepping inside the doorway, he addressed himself to Amos, wasting no time on formalities. 'Hannibal Davey is in the Rashleigh Arms at Charlestown. Harvey is keeping watch on the place to make certain he doesn't go off anywhere. He said that Sir Joseph gave you the warrant for his arrest.'

'He did,' Amos confirmed, as he pushed back his chair and rose to his feet hurriedly. 'Is Pasco with him?'

'No . . . at least, he wasn't when I came away, but two men who look as though they might be miners are drinking with him.'

'Then let's go. I would have liked to take Pasco at the same time, but this is too good an opportunity to miss.'

'Amos! Take care!'

It was not Maisie who expressed concern as the two men hurried from the cottage, but Talwyn.

When Amos and Constable Mitchell turned the corner into the lane where the Rashleigh Arms was situated, they saw Harvey lounging casually against the wall of the china-stone yard adjacent to the inn, apparently disinterestedly watching the comings and goings between harbour and village.

Easing himself away from the wall when they reached him, he said, in answer to Amos's questioning look,

328

'He's still inside. I've walked past two or three times and glanced through the window, just to make certain. There are three men with him now and the landlord has spent more time talking to them than attending to his own business.'

Acknowledging Harvey's information, Amos asked Mitchell, 'Have you brought handcuffs with you?'

When Mitchell, looking decidedly nervous, confirmed that he had, Amos said, 'Right, let's go inside and arrest him.'

He led the way into the bar room of the Rashleigh Arms, followed closely by Harvey, with Constable Mitchell bringing up the rear. Apart from Hannibal and his three companions there were few customers in the room, but they all looked up when the three men entered and strode purposefully towards the table where their quarry sat.

Hannibal's eyes narrowed when he recognised Amos, but he did not move, even when Amos stopped at the table.

Taking up a position beside the big man, Amos said, 'Hannibal Davey, I have in my possession a warrant for your arrest for the murder of Detective Inspector Carpenter.'

Scornfully, and confidently, Hannibal said, 'You know what you can do with your warrant – and I suggest you go back to London and do it there.'

His suggestion provoked raucous laughter from his companions and one of them said, 'That's right, Hannibal, you tell him. We'll not put up with foreigners coming here and laying down the law to us.'

Ignoring the speaker, Amos said evenly, 'I am taking you into custody, Davey, and either you will come quietly or I will need to subdue you.'

'He won't be taking you anywhere, Hannibal, we'll see to that.'

It was the same speaker as before, but, taking no more notice of him than had Amos, Hannibal placed his hands on the table in front of him and levered himself to his feet. Glaring malevolently at the detective, he said, 'You're not taking me anywhere and I'll not need help from anyone, but I promise that *you* won't be leaving the Rashleigh on your own two feet. Not that you'll know very much about it . . . or anything else, by that time.'

Suddenly, Thomas Stephens, who had been listening with growing concern in the background, stepped forward and said nervously, 'I don't want any trouble in here, Hannibal. I know Mr Hawke and he's a reasonable man. Come into the back room and talk about this . . . this *misunderstanding*. I'm sure we can come to some arrangement and settle it amicably . . .'

'Take no notice of Stephens, Hannibal.' It was the mouthy man again. 'Show this jumped-up Londoner how we deal with them who come here full of their own importance . . .'

Suddenly, Amos found himself pushed to one side, and now it was Harvey who confronted the giant Cornishman. Bringing his face close to the other man's, he said, 'No, Hannibal, show *me* how you would like to deal with your betters. Forget what Mr Hawke said to you, *I* am arresting you for the murder of Detective

330

Inspector Carpenter, and I would advise you to come quietly.'

'Come *quietly*!' Hannibal roared angrily. Then, without any warning, he lunged across the table at Harvey . . . and grabbed only air.

Sidestepping with a speed that was remarkable in such a big man, Harvey jabbed two quick punches into his face, both of which caused Hannibal's head to jerk back alarmingly.

Hannibal roared again, but there was pain as well as anger in the sound now. Scrambling clear of the bench on which he had been seated when the policemen entered the room, he knocked one of his companions to the floor in the process. Then, spreading his arms wide with the intention of encompassing Harvey in them, he rushed at the ex-marine . . . but, once again, Harvey was not there.

This time, he ducked as well as sidestepping but straightened to launch a two-fisted attack on his would-be assailant that sent him staggering backwards over his companions seated on the nearside of the table and falling backwards on to the board, scattering tankards and plates.

He momentarily regained his balance, but his feet had hardly touched the floor before Harvey landed a right-handed punch on his bearded chin that caused the big Cornishman to perform a backward somersault over the table and land spreadeagled, face down on the bar-room floor amidst broken plates, spilled ale and misshapen pewter tankards.

The fight, if the brief, one-sided encounter came into

such a category, had lasted less than a minute and the unexpected outcome left Hannibal's companions stunned.

Leaning across the table to look down upon his unconscious adversary, Harvey shook his head in apparent disappointment and said, 'That's a pity. I was told he could fight.' Turning his attention to the shaken men who had been drinking with Hannibal, he went on, 'How about you? Would any of you like to see if you can do any better? If not, I suggest you leave . . . *now!*'

The three men made an immediate dash to the door, each eager to be the first to reach the street outside.

Addressing the stunned landlord of the Rashleigh Arms, Amos said, 'I remember warning you once before about the type of men you encourage in here, Mr Stephens. I have a feeling I shall be back to speak to you again before very long.' Shifting his attention to Constable Mitchell, he said, 'Handcuff Davey with his hands behind his back. When you've done that, Mr Stephens can produce a pail of water to throw over him to bring him round. Then we'll take him through St Austell on his way to the magistrates' court and let folk see him in custody. It will prove he is not as invincible as he would have them believe. It will also show them that *nobody* is above the law. It might serve to make your life easier when the Cornwall constabulary comes into being.'

51

When Sir Joseph Sawle was informed of the arrest, he set out post-haste to St Austell and, convening the magistrates' court, had Hannibal brought before him and remanded him in custody, to await trial on the charge of murdering Detective Inspector Carpenter.

In view of the seriousness of the charge and the possibility of a rescue attempt by miners – or smugglers – Sir Joseph sent to Bodmin barracks requesting a military escort for the enclosed van conveying Hannibal to Launceston gaol.

When the magistrate congratulated the three men on their arrest of the wanted man, Amos said, 'It could not have taken place without Halloran. The speed at which he despatched the man who was feared throughout Cornwall for his strength and prowess will greatly enhance the image of the new Cornwall constabulary when it is formed.'

'Splendid!' beamed the delighted magistrate. 'I will ensure that Halloran's part in the arrest is made known to Colonel Gilbert . . . but what about the other Davey brother?'

'I am concerned about him,' Amos admitted. 'I had hoped to be able to arrest both brothers together, but when Constable Mitchell told me that Hannibal was at the Rashleigh Arms at Charlestown, the opportunity to take him there and then was too good to be missed. Unfortunately, it means that Pasco will have been warned and we may have difficulty locating him, but I have learned where he lives and would like to raid his home at dusk tomorrow, if you could swear in a number of special constables to assist me. Also – and I realise this is extremely short notice for such a large operation – I think the Excise service should raid the Wheal Notter adit at the same time, entering the mine both from the adit and also from the Wheal Phoenix workings. They will need bolt cutters because Detective Inspector Carpenter and I overheard Hannibal say he was going to attach his own padlock to the gate between the mines to supplement the one placed there by Captain Woodcock of the Wheal Phoenix. With luck the Excise officers will discover a large amount of contraband and should also capture a couple of smugglers who might well implicate the Davey brothers in their activities.'

Waiting until Sir Joseph had completed making notes of all that he had said, he continued, 'While the Excise officers are in the Wheal Notter I would like them to check what I believe to be a body lying at the bottom of a ventilation shaft. I will draw a map to show them where to find it.'

Initially taken aback by the scope of Amos's proposed operations for the following day, Sir Joseph recovered swiftly. 'I will send a message to the officer commanding the Excise service in Cornwall, telling him to organise his men for the raid tomorrow. As you say, it is short notice, but he is aware of my displeasure at his short-comings and my lack of faith in his department. It will be his belief that I am deliberately giving him such a short time to organise the raid because I have no confidence in the loyalty of his men. He will be at great pains to ensure my distrust is unfounded.'

When Amos returned to the Penrice cottage accompanied by Harvey, he was greeted with great relief by the three women, all demanding to know what had occurred.

'I had no need to do a thing,' Amos said. 'Harvey told Hannibal he was arresting him – and that's exactly what he did.'

'But ... didn't he put up a fight?' Talwyn queried. 'Everyone is so terrified of him that no one dares even say anything to upset him, far less try to arrest him.'

'Well, he did have some notion that he wasn't going to be arrested,' Amos said, glancing at his companion, 'but Harvey showed Hannibal Davey and his friends that he wasn't as tough as they all thought him to be. He was lying face down and unconscious when Constable Mitchell put the handcuffs on him.'

'You knocked out Hannibal Davey?' Laura looked at

the embarrassed ex-marine in awe. '*Nobody* has ever done that before. You . . . you'll be *famous!*'

'He will certainly be respected,' Amos agreed, 'and that won't be a bad thing because Cornwall is recruiting its own county police force and Harvey has been invited to become its sergeant major, turning recruits into policemen.'

'We will all sleep more soundly in our beds knowing there are men like Mr Halloran out there to protect us,' Maisie declared. 'Had there been something like it earlier, Talwyn's poor, dear father might still be here with us.'

Both Amos and Harvey murmured suitable expressions of sympathy which satisfied Maisie . . . but Talwyn's thoughts had travelled in a different direction. Addressing Amos, she said, 'Does that mean you will be returning to London when Cornwall has its own police force?'

The unexpected question was of interest to everyone in the room and they all looked to Amos for an answer.

'I am a Metropolitan Police officer,' he replied, 'and so my place of duty is in London, but I won't be required to return there until I have seen the killers of your father and Detective Inspector Carpenter convicted in the courts.'

'But that is likely to be very soon now,' Talwyn persisted. 'You could be gone in a week or so . . . perhaps even sooner than that.'

'It's possible, of course,' Amos conceded, 'but I haven't arrested Pasco yet. Even when I have I still need to present a case to the court that will ensure the conviction of the Davey brothers. I believe I will be here for weeks rather than days.'

He had spent little time thinking about his return to London. Now, as he looked at Talwyn, he found that, much as he had always enjoyed his work as a London detective, the thought of leaving Cornwall and resuming his work in the country's capital did not appeal to him quite as much as it might once have done.

52

That evening, when Maisie was already in bed and Talwyn was helping Laura with her schoolwork in the kitchen of the cottage, Amos was in his room writing a report on the day's happening for the police commissioner in London when the peace of the household was rudely broken by a heavy pounding on the kitchen door.

A youthful, albeit breathless, voice called out urgently, 'Miss Kernow! Miss Kernow . . . come quickly!'

Hurrying to the kitchen door, Talwyn flung it open to reveal a young boy fighting to regain his breath. 'What is it? What's the matter?'

'It's the school, Miss . . . It's on fire!'

'How . . .'

Talwyn had hardly begun to ask her question when the breathless boy said, 'I don't know nothing more than that, Miss. We could see the flames from our cottage and when we went down Mr Elkins was there with some men, trying to get water to put the fire out – but the schoolhouse was well alight, Miss. Mr Elkins told me to come here and tell you. I ran all the way.'

'Good boy. I'll come down right away.'

Amos had come downstairs when he heard the boy at the door, thinking the caller might be seeking him. Now he said to Talwyn, 'I'll come with you.'

'And me,' said Laura.

Maisie could be heard calling from the bedroom, demanding to know what was happening, and as Talwyn struggled into her coat, which was hanging behind the kitchen door, she said to Laura, 'Stay and tell Mother what is happening first.'

As she and Amos hurried from the cottage, half walking, half running along the drive towards the gate, Talwyn fretted, 'How could the school catch fire? Andrew is always meticulous about checking all the lamps before he leaves, but the boy said he was fighting the fire, so he must have still been there when it began, even though school should have finished more than half an hour ago.'

'He sometimes extends his lessons until past nine o'clock,' Amos pointed out, 'and he will occasionally go for a quick drink in the Rashleigh Arms before going home. Either eventuality would explain why he was still around so late.'

'Well, we will soon find out,' Talwyn said grimly, breaking into a trot.

The flames from the burning schoolhouse were visible through the trees long before they reached Charlestown and Talwyn was plainly upset by the sight. As they drew closer it was possible to see that the building was well alight, even though the horse-drawn fire engine from St Austell was on the scene and water was being drawn through leather hosepipes from the pond used to top up and flush the water in the inner harbour.

Men from the village and sailors from ships in the harbour were forming human chains along which to pass buckets of water to throw on the burning building, but with little noticeable effect.

When they arrived, Andrew Elkins left the chain of men, one of the many bystanders moving in to take his place. As he came towards them it could be seen by the light from the burning schoolhouse that his face was blackened by smoke and his eyes were reddened. He was wearing no coat and one sleeve of his shirt was badly scorched, part of the cuff actually burned away.

Addressing his fellow schoolteacher, he said, 'I am *so* sorry, Talwyn. I tried to put it out, but it took hold so very quickly.'

'How did it happen?' Talwyn demanded, trying unsuccessfully not to sound too censorious, aware that Andrew had probably worked harder than anyone else in an effort to contain the blaze. 'Did you knock over one of the lamps?'

'No,' Andrew replied grimly. 'It was no accident. I was seated at my desk when there was the crash of breaking glass and a large earthenware jar was thrown through the window. It was stuffed with straw and topped up with fish oil that someone had set fire to before throwing it through the window. Unfortunately, it landed by the open cupboard where we keep the books and papers. Burning straw and oil went everywhere. I might have been able to put it out had not the cupboard and everything in it caught fire. I did try, using everything – including my coat – but the fire took hold too quickly. As it was I burned one of my hands rather badly and I was lucky to escape with my life.'

Aghast, Talwyn cried, 'Andrew, you poor dear! Thank the Lord you *did* succeed in escaping . . .'

She glanced towards the schoolhouse, which was already little more than a blackened shell, with flames licking up through the partially collapsed roof, before looking where the scorched cuff of Andrew's shirt flapped about his wrist. 'Let me have a look at that hand . . .'

Before he could reply, the voice of the newly arrived Laura said, 'No, I'll do that. You go and check the things that have been salvaged from the fire and see if there's anything that can be put somewhere safe.' Pre-empting a reply from Talwyn she reached out and took Andrew's arm, wincing as she saw the burned skin.

'That looks very nasty,' Amos commented. 'Take him down to the harbourmaster's office, Laura. They will have something there to put on it . . . but before you go, Andrew, were you able to catch a glimpse of whoever it was who threw the jar into the schoolroom?'

Andrew shook his head apologetically. 'No. I was busy writing when it crashed through the window.'

'But whoever threw it would have known you were inside the building?'

'Well, the lamps were still burning and anyone

looking through the window would have seen me,' Andrew replied. 'It obviously never troubled their conscience.'

'Who would have done such a thing?' Talwyn demanded angrily. 'First my father ... and now this! The Kernow family have done nothing but help the people of Charlestown by educating their children. Why, Amos?'

Her pleas were heard by some of those standing nearby and some of the men, shamefaced, turned away from the distraught schoolteacher.

'I have yet to discover *why* your father was murdered, Talwyn,' Amos said in a voice that was deliberately loud enough for the same bystanders to hear, 'but it is clear why your school has been burned down. It's because you have provided lodgings for the man who is here to catch those who killed your father. They have proved they care neither for human life, nor for the well-being of the community that has misguidedly protected them for so long. Well, the guilty parties will soon receive their just deserts. I only wish the problem of providing a new school could be solved as quickly.'

53

It was after midnight before the school fire was finally extinguished, leaving the night air heavy with the pungent odour of smoke and water-soaked embers. Everything salvageable had been safely locked in a store-room at the rear of a carpenter's shop.

Andrew had not returned to the scene after being taken off by Laura, and when she had treated his burns and seen him safely on his way home, accompanied by his neighbours, who had been attracted to Charlestown by the fire, Laura returned to the Penrice cottage with Talwyn. In the meantime, Amos remained at the scene questioning anyone who would speak to him, in the hope that someone might have seen the arsonist. It came as no surprise to him that he learned nothing. Eventually, when only two small groups of men were left chatting nearby, Amos decided that he too would go home.

He had no sooner left Charlestown behind than he

thought he heard footsteps following him along the lane. In view of all that had happened that night, Amos was taking no chances. Stepping on to the grass verge of the lane, he waited in the shadow of an elm tree until the unknown follower drew level with him.

Stepping out into the lane, he thrust out his arm to bring the shadowy figure to a halt. 'Who are you?' he demanded. 'Why are you following me?'

'It's me, Cap'n Billy,' came the hoarse reply, 'and I wasn't following you, I was trying to catch up with you.'

Recovering from his surprise, Amos asked, 'Why did you want to catch up with me? I thought you had decided you had no wish ever to speak to me again?'

'That was before I knew who you were,' Captain Billy replied, 'although I always suspected you were more than someone just looking for the father he hadn't seen for years. You wanted to know far more of my business than I was prepared to tell to a complete stranger. Knowing you are a detective from Scotland Yard after Hannibal and Pasco makes it different. Nobody in his right senses would want to upset you ... as I believe Hannibal Davey has already learned.'

'You told me you couldn't say anything to me because Hannibal has friends. Nothing has changed.'

'Oh yes it has,' Captain Billy said. 'Word is going around about the way Hannibal was arrested. It's being said that he is no longer the man he once was and that the man from London who was with you only needed to hit him a couple of times and he was finished. But it's not Hannibal I came to talk to you about – it's Pasco. He's the one who set fire to the school.'

Immediately attentive, Amos demanded, 'How do you know? Did you see him do it?'

'No, but he's been staying in Charlestown for a few nights with a woman who used to live with him up on the moor. She knows what he's been up to.'

'Is he still with her, or has he gone back to the moor?'

'Neither. He timed the firing of the school well. Within half an hour of the alarm's being raised he was on a ship leaving Charlestown harbour.'

Startled, Amos said, 'Pasco has gone? Where . . . ?'

'According to his woman he's gone to France. He told her that if he likes it there, he'll send for her. If he doesn't, he'll move on.'

'Where in France was the ship bound?' Amos was deeply concerned that Pasco would escape justice.

'I don't know. I don't even know the name of the ship,' Captain Billy replied, 'but the harbourmaster will be able to tell you.'

Angrily, Amos said, 'We could have had both Hannibal and Pasco behind bars had you decided to co-operate earlier and agreed to stand up in court against the Daveys. Now . . .' He shrugged in a gesture of frustration.

'Had you told me you were from Scotland Yard I might have been inclined to tell you more than I did,' Captain Billy countered, 'but you'll still not find me saying anything official against either Hannibal or Pasco until it's absolutely certain that they'll never be free to take their revenge on me.'

'Well, with the Daveys both well away from this area you will have no reason to leave, so I will be seeing you again. When it's certain they are never going to trouble ordinary people again I'll be back to clear up one or two little matters that they have been involved with in the past. In the meantime, keep out of trouble or you might find yourself sharing a cell with them. Now, where will I find the harbourmaster at this time of night?'

Captain Billy walked beside Amos in silence until Charlestown was reached and then, as the two men parted company, Amos to make his way to the harbour and Captain Billy heading up the hill towards Chinatown, the ex-miner called out, 'If you decide to go after Pasco you had better go armed. His woman said he's gone off carrying a pistol.'

The harbourmaster's office was closed, but the watchman at the harbour had been on duty since dusk, before the fire started in the school. He was able to tell Amos that three ships had sailed on the tide that night. One, a coal carrier, was returning to Wales. The second had left with a cargo of china clay, bound for Holland.

The third was a ship named *L'Hirondelle*, leaving on a return voyage to the French port of Roscoff, laden with a general cargo.

Amos knew this had to be the vessel on which Pasco had fled the country. Unfortunately, there was nothing he could do about it tonight. Any further action would need to wait until he was able to discuss the situation with Sir Joseph Sawle in the morning.

54

When Amos reached the Penrice cottage and saw a candle burning in the kitchen window, he thought that Talwyn had probably left it alight for him, expecting him to return home earlier than he had. Much to his surprise, he found she was in the kitchen, seated in one of the wooden armchairs beside the fire, on the far side of the room from the single candle on the window ledge.

A kettle was steaming gently on the side of the hob and, hurriedly rising to her feet, Talwyn asked softly, 'Would you like a cup of tea? Everything is ready.'

He was about to decline and say he intended going straight to bed when the coals on the fire shifted, allowing a tongue of flame to escape. In its light he saw her face. She had been crying.

Changing his mind about going to bed right away, he said, 'I would love a cup of tea if you will join me, but it's very late for you to still be up.'

'Why? I have nothing to get up early for in the morning.' There was bitterness in her voice as she added, 'In fact, I can think of very little left in my life that is important now. All that my father worked so hard for over the years has gone . . . Probably destroyed by the very people he put his heart and soul into helping.'

'That isn't true, Talwyn,' Amos said gently. 'In fact, it is probably my fault that your school was burned down. I was aware I posed a danger to you by staying in your cottage, and I warned Sir Joseph about it, but I never imagined the whole community would suffer as a result.'

Pausing in the act of adding boiling water to the tea leaves in the pot, Talwyn said, 'What do you mean? Do you *know* who started the fire?'

'Yes, it was Pasco Davey. I was given the information when I was on my way home. That's why I am so late. I needed to return to Charlestown to check on some of the things I was told.'

'Pasco Davey shot my father . . . and now he's done this! Why, Amos? What has the Kernow family ever done to make him so determined to destroy us?'

'It's no good trying to apply logic to anything Pasco does, Talwyn. One of the reasons he is so feared is because he is so unpredictable. There is a streak of sadistic madness in him that makes him dangerous to everyone around him. Although I still don't know why your father became a victim, the school was probably burned down because it is considered to be yours – and you and Maisie are giving lodging to the man who arrested his brother and who is after him. I feared something like this might

348

happen when my true identity became known. I should have moved out of your cottage as soon as Inspector Carpenter was shot.'

'If Pasco Davey is unbalanced – as he undoubtedly is – it would probably have made no difference,' Talwyn reasoned. 'He would still have attacked the school. Oh, I don't know what Mother and I are going to do, Amos, I really don't. We had such a happy and contented life only a few months ago, but now . . .'

She choked upon the words and turned away from him, but not before he had seen tears well up in her eyes. 'I'm sorry. I'll go to bed now . . .'

'You won't go anywhere . . . at least, not yet.' Amos had regretted his lack of action on a previous occasion when Talwyn was upset, and he was determined it was not going to happen again.

Stepping towards her, he gathered her to him. He sensed a momentary resistance, but then she leaned her face against his shoulder and he held her tight as sobs racked her body and suddenly she was clinging to him as though her life depended upon it.

He desperately wanted to find words to give her some comfort, but he found himself repeating inanely, 'It's all right, Talwyn, it's going to be all right . . .'

Talwyn was in no hurry to break free from Amos's comforting embrace but, eventually, she raised her head from his shoulder and, looking up at him with a brave attempt at a smile, said, 'I am sorry, Amos . . . you never got your cup of tea, did you?'

With his arms still about her he replied, 'I'm not complaining, Talwyn.'

349

'Would you like me to make it now?'

'Only if you want one yourself.'

'I think I do. It has been a harrowing night, although I feel much better now . . . Thank you.'

Reluctantly he released his hold on her and she moved to the fireplace and began making the tea. He waited until it was poured and placed on the table for both of them before he said, 'I am glad I was here to help you a little, Talwyn. Very glad.'

'So am I,' Talwyn replied, 'and you comforted me more than a little. You have managed to put me together. I feel able to face the world again . . . at least, I will in the morning. Just now I feel absolutely drained, physically and emotionally.'

As they sat down in the dim light of the dying fire and the single candle, she asked, 'When do you expect to be able to arrest Pasco Davey?'

'I was hoping we might be able to arrest him at his home tomorrow,' Amos replied, 'but he is not going to be there. It seems that almost immediately after setting fire to the school he fled the country, taking passage on a ship from Charlestown bound for Roscoff, in France.'

'You mean . . . he has escaped and will never be brought to justice for killing my father?' Talwyn was visibly distressed once more and Amos hurriedly reassured her.

'No, I don't mean that, although he has made arresting him a little more difficult. First thing in the morning I will ask Sir Joseph to write an official letter for me, setting out the crimes that Pasco is known to have committed, and for which a warrant has been issued for his arrest, here in Cornwall. Armed with this I too will go to France. There are two ships in Charlestown sailing to Roscoff tomorrow. I intend to be on one of them.'

'Do you speak any French?' Talwyn asked.

'Regrettably, no,' Amos replied, 'but I doubt whether Pasco does, either.'

Draining her cup and standing up abruptly, Talwyn said, 'Dawn is not too far away and you are going to have a very busy day, so you must try to have at least a couple of hours' sleep.'

'Yes.' Although he recognised the logic of what Talwyn was saying, Amos felt a sense of deep disappointment that the intimacy they had enjoyed for such a brief while was coming to an end.

'Thank you again for being so kind and understanding tonight, Amos.'

'As I said before, I am glad I was here.'

Then, taking him off guard, Talwyn took a step forward and kissed him briefly on the lips, before turning away and hurrying from the kitchen.

Lying in bed before he fell asleep, Amos wondered whether her kiss had lingered just a little longer than gratitude demanded. He hoped it had, but he wasn't sure . . .

In her own bedroom, Talwyn could have given him a definitive answer, but she was fast asleep.

55

When Amos awoke and reached out to take his watch from the bedside table, it showed the time to be 7.30. He felt he had hardly enjoyed any sleep at all, but there were a great many things to be done and he could hear sounds from the kitchen.

He rose from his bed and washed and shaved in cold water, then, still bleary-eyed, made his way downstairs to the kitchen where Maisie, Laura and, to his surprise, Talwyn, were all gathered.

Speaking to Talwyn, who was dressed for outdoors, he said, 'You couldn't have had much sleep. I thought you might have enjoyed a lie-in this morning.'

'It would have been very easy to have remained there for another hour or two,' she agreed, 'but, like you, I have things to do.'

'I thought *you* should have stayed in bed longer too,' Maisie commented to Amos, 'but I heard you moving about upstairs and have your breakfast ready for you. A ham omelette should set you up for whatever the day demands.'

'I am grateful to you, Maisie,' Amos said, seating himself at the place set for him at the kitchen table. As his breakfast was transferred from frying pan to plate, he spoke to Laura, seated across the table from him. 'Were you able to do something for Andrew's burns?'

'Yes. The captain of one of the ships – I think he was Norwegian – was in the harbourmaster's office and he went off and brought what I needed from his ship. Andrew's hands were quite badly burned, but I was able to cover them with lint soaked in a mixture of linseed oil and limewater, then wrap them in bandages to keep the air out. It will help, but I told Andrew he must see a doctor this morning. After I have helped Mrs Kernow in the kitchen I'll go into St Austell and make certain he has had the burns looked at properly.'

'It sounds as though you have already done everything that needed to be done right away,' Amos said approvingly. 'Andrew is very lucky you were around. Where did you learn to treat burns so competently?'

'Miners up at the Wheal Notter often suffered burns when they were careless setting explosives,' she said. 'I once saw the mine doctor treating one of the men and asked what he was using.' Aware that Talwyn might think she was putting Andrew's problems ahead of the disaster that had befallen her, she went on quickly, 'If you would rather I came to the school with you instead, Talwyn, I can always go to visit Andrew later.'

'There is very little I could do about anything, even

if I went to Charlestown,' Talwyn replied. 'No, Laura, you go to see how Andrew is and wish him well from all of us. I believe Amos is going to the manor. I will go with him and discuss with Sir Joseph what we are going to do about the school.'

Amos immediately expressed his pleasure at having Talwyn's company on the way to the manor house and, busying herself about the kitchen, Maisie was pleased that Talwyn and Amos would be spending at least some of the morning together. She felt it would prevent Talwyn from brooding too much on what had happened, but she wondered what Sir Joseph would have to say about the events of the night. She and Talwyn had depended for their income on the success of the school. Now it was no more and she had great concerns for the future.

Sir Joseph had been told of the fire by the maidservant who brought the early morning tea tray to his bedroom, but she had been unaware of the cause of the blaze. His initial belief – as Talwyn's had been – was that it must have been the result of carelessness on Andrew's part. However, when he began criticising 'such irresponsible behaviour' to Talwyn and Amos when they arrived at the manor later in the morning, Amos cut his tirade very short.

'The fire had nothing to do with Andrew Elkins, Sir Joseph. He was lucky to escape with his life and actually suffered rather nasty burns to his hands trying to extinguish the flames. The fire was deliberately started when a primitive fireball was thrown through a school window . . . by Pasco Davey.'

'That villain! Was he seen to carry out the arson attack?'

'No, but he told a woman friend in Charlestown what he was going to do. I learned of it from Billy Arthur.'

'This man has become a danger to the whole community, Hawke. You *must* arrest him when you raid his home today. I have arranged for a number of special constables to be sworn in to assist you—'

'I am afraid they are not going to be needed.' Amos interrupted the magistrate for a second time, explaining, 'It seems that Davey left the country soon after causing the fire. He took passage on a ship bound for Roscoff.'

Sir Joseph looked at Amos in dismay. 'You mean . . . he has escaped us?'

'Not if I can do anything about it, Sir Joseph. I intend to follow him to France, if you will give me a letter setting out the reasons why Pasco is wanted on warrant here, in Cornwall – and if I can obtain the necessary passport.'

'I can do all that for you,' Sir Joseph declared. 'But my letter will be in English. Do you have any knowledge of French?'

'None at all,' Amos confessed, 'but if I can locate my father in Roscoff I will enlist his help – and also ask him what he knows about the death of Miss Kernow's father. But I need to get there quickly. It is possible, according to something Rodda told me, that Pasco knows my father witnessed the murder. If so, his life is in danger – and I am sure I don't need to remind you that he is our only witness now.'

'It is also possible that by the time you find your

355

father, Davey could have learned that you are in France searching for him and have moved on.'

The comment came from Talwyn, and she continued, 'If Sir Joseph writes his letter, explaining why you are seeking Pasco Davey, I will translate it into French for him to sign and put his official magisterial stamp on. The French are very impressed with official documents – but only if they are written in their own language.'

'That would help a great deal,' Amos said gratefully.

'Yes, it will *help*,' Talwyn agreed, 'but it will not compensate for your ignorance of the French language. I have a much better idea. If Scotland Yard will pay for my fare to France, and my accommodation for the time we are there, I will accompany you . . . No, hear me out, Amos.' She cut short his protest before it was uttered. 'You could waste a tremendous amount of time looking for someone with enough knowledge of English to help you find Pasco Davey – let alone help you arrest him for an alleged crime that has been committed in England. On the other hand, if a French-speaking woman asks a Frenchman for assistance he is likely to help her in any way he can. I know things should not work that way, but, realistically, they do in France.'

'It could be placing you at great risk,' Amos pointed out. 'We know Pasco is armed and he would not hesitate to shoot a woman if he thought it was going to save his skin.'

'If he shoots at someone it will be at you,' Talwyn said bluntly. 'Anyway, I have more reason than anyone else to want to see Pasco Davey brought to justice. I

356

want it so much that if I had the money, I would pay my own fare to go to France and seek him out – even if it meant going there on my own.'

Sir Joseph had been listening in silence as Talwyn made her passionate speech, and his gaze had not left her face. Now, after a few moments of silence, he shifted his attention to Amos and said, 'Miss Kernow is talking a great deal of sense, Hawke. Having someone with you who is fluent in the language would cut a great many corners for you, and having spent some time in France with my brother I agree with her that a pretty face is worth more than a dozen official documents. So, what do you say?'

Amos was not convinced. 'I can see a lot of sense in what you are both saying, Sir Joseph, but I am concerned for Miss Kernow's safety. Pasco is a desperate and dangerous man. Quite apart from that, Scotland Yard will spare almost no expense to catch the killer of Detective Inspector Carpenter, but I think they would draw the line at paying for a young woman to accompany me to France! Besides, Miss Kernow needs to make plans for her own future here in Cornwall, now her school has been destroyed.'

'There is no reason why Scotland Yard needs to be consulted on the question of finance – or propriety,' Sir Joseph said airily. 'You are here at my request and Cornwall will pay whatever bills I consider reasonable in order to capture and convict this very dangerous man. As for Miss Kernow's future . . . I will ensure that neither she nor her mother suffers further from the actions of this madman! Now, are you going to take Miss Kernow along with you, or are you going to go to France alone and risk having Davey make good his escape?'

Amos tried to weigh the danger of a possible confrontation with an armed man whose sanity was in question against the undoubted help Talwyn could give to him in the pursuit of Pasco Davey, but his thinking was complicated by an awareness of the pleasure he would derive from being in Talwyn's company, and he was still not certain which consideration had taken precedence when he found himself saying, 'I will go to Charlestown right away and see if I can arrange a passage for two in the fastest ship leaving for Roscoff today.'

56

'At what time do you think we will arrive at Roscoff?' Talwyn put the question to Amos as they stood together on the heaving deck of the schooner *Puffin*, bound for Roscoff with a cargo of items produced in the Charlestown foundry.

'According to the master, if the wind stays in the same quarter we should have a Roscoff pilot on board by the time we wake in the morning.'

'As quickly as that?' Talwyn expressed her surprise.

'A smuggling vessel would probably knock a couple of hours off that time,' Amos said. 'They can usually outrun any other vessel to be found in the English Channel.'

The mention of smuggling vessels made Talwyn shudder. 'Pasco Davey and his brother sound absolutely evil. It would have been reassuring to have Harvey with us.'

'It certainly would,' Amos agreed, 'but he was off somewhere with Constable Mitchell and there was no time to find him and have him join us. I will just have to put my trust in my revolver – if it becomes necessary.'

'I sincerely hope it will not,' Talwyn said fervently.

Amos and Talwyn had found little time to talk prior to joining the *Puffin* because of all that needed to be done before they set out on the hurriedly arranged voyage, and now Amos said, 'When I left you with Sir Joseph this morning you were going to ask him about the school. Could he offer you any hope for the future?'

'Yes. He was quite positive and extremely generous. He said that as the school was burned down as a direct consequence of his suggestion that Mother and I should take you in as a lodger, he would see to it that we should not suffer as a result. He has promised to have a disused store he owns in Charlestown fitted out as a temporary school. I believe it is where we put everything that was salvaged from the old school. Until it is ready to take pupils he is going to give me a weekly sum equal to what we were taking in school fees. It means I will be able to give something to Andrew in order to retain his services – and I know a certain young lady who will be delighted with that part of the arrangement.'

Puzzled for only a moment, Amos said, 'Are you talking of Laura? I wasn't aware anything was going on between her and Andrew.'

'I don't think it is . . . yet,' Talwyn replied, 'but she is quite besotted with him. She looks upon you as a hero because of what you do – the life you have had and, of course, your acquaintanceship with Florence Nightingale – but she has become increasingly fond of Andrew, admiring his academic mind. His vulnerability in the world in which we live also brings out the mothering instinct in her.'

'Hm! Unfortunately, she will need to make a choice between romance and nursing. Florence Nightingale's nurses are required to dedicate their whole lives to taking care of the sick and wounded – Miss Nightingale will accept nothing less.'

'Fortunately, she does not accept girls for nursing training until they are twenty-one,' Talwyn replied. 'That gives Laura four or five years to decide which is more important to her – and I have no doubt the choice will be hers for the taking. She is one of the most positive young ladies I have ever known – and Andrew admires her greatly. Personally speaking, I hope she chooses to make her future with him. She would make an exceptional teacher and one day they could jointly own and run a school as good as any in the country.'

'You could be right,' Amos agreed. 'My first thought was of the loss it would be to nursing, but that might very easily be offset by the gain to scholarship.'

'Well, that seems to have sorted out the future for me, my mother, Andrew and Laura . . . but how about you, Amos? Once Pasco has been arrested and he and Hannibal have been convicted, I know you will be returning to London, but what of your future career there? Will you always remain a detective?'

'That is a question I have been asking myself, Talwyn, and one to which I have no answer. I thoroughly enjoy my work and am currently an acting inspector, but an inspector's rank is the highest I could attain in the detective force – and it is quite possible I will revert to sergeant when I go back to Scotland Yard. If I am to reach a higher rank I would need to return to the uniform branch – and even then it would not be a foregone conclusion that I would gain promotion. There is a great deal of antipathy towards detectives from senior uniformed officers – and the power of promotion lies with them.' Giving Talwyn a wry smile, he said, 'But all that is in the future. At the moment I want to concentrate my efforts towards finding Pasco Davey and arresting him in a country where I have no jurisdiction, and with which we have no treaty of extradition. That should pose enough of a problem for the immediate future!'

Despite the movement of the ship during the night hours, Amos slept well, probably because the exhausting events of the previous night had caught up with him, but the next morning he was up early. Standing once more on the deck of the *Puffin* in a cool morning breeze, he watched the activity of the Roscoff pilot boats with a great deal of interest.

Emulating their Cornish counterparts, their crews were engaged in a race against each other to be the first to reach the *Puffin* and place their pilot on board to guide the ship into Roscoff. Amos watched as the oars dipped into the water at increasing speed, to emerge for a dripping moment as each oarsman put maximum effort into the contest.

When the successful boat bumped against the side of

the *Puffin* and a pilot clambered on board, the losing crews bowed over their oars, gathering the strength to return to the harbour entrance to await the next ship.

As the French pilot took up his position beside the helmsman, Talwyn emerged from a hatch which led to the cabins of the master and mate, the latter of which had been placed at her disposal for the voyage. Amos – and the mate – had been obliged to make do with a bunk on the crew's mess deck.

Amos smiled as she approached. 'Did you sleep well?'

'Like a log,' she replied. 'I think I must have been very tired. Is that the Roscoff pilot?'

When Amos confirmed that it was, she asked, 'What was the name of the ship that we believe Pasco took passage on from Charlestown?'

It took Amos a moment or two to think about it before he replied, 'It was a French boat ... I think it was *L'Hirondelle*. Why do you ask?'

Instead of replying, Talwyn made her way to where the French pilot stood beside the helmsman, and Amos followed.

The pilot saw them approaching and gave a brief, shallow bow to Talwyn. She addressed him in his own language, which brought forth a delighted smile of appreciation. For the next few minutes the two were engaged in animated discussion, during which Amos heard his own name mentioned. It brought a brief glance and nod of the head in his direction from the pilot before the conversation with Talwyn was resumed.

Eventually the helmsman called the pilot's attention to the task for which he had come on board and Talwyn returned to Amos. They walked together to the bow of the boat, and as they watched the French harbour buildings come closer Amos said, 'I heard you mention my name. Were you asking about my father?'

'Yes, but I didn't say you were his son, only that you were a relative. He says your father has been welcomed into the community and is fitting in well. He also told me where he lives and says he has an office on the harbour where his wife works most days. Her name is Gabrielle and she too is well respected in Roscoff.'

Looking at the harbour buildings as a tiny steam tug came alongside to take the *Puffin* into a berth, Amos felt a surge of excitement at the thought that he might be only minutes away from a reunion with the father he had not seen for so many years . . . but first there were other, far more serious problems to be addressed.

'Did you question him about Pasco Davey?'

'I asked him at what time *L'Hirondelle* came into port yesterday.' Pointing to a small ship two berths ahead of the *Puffin*, she said, 'That's it, there. The pilot thinks he saw it entered in the arrivals book as berthing soon after six o'clock yesterday evening, but he was not on duty then, so was unable to tell me any more. Perhaps we should speak to whoever is on board *L'Hirondelle* and ask if they have any idea of where Pasco might have gone . . . but shall we first see if your father is in his office?'

'No!'

Amos realised he had startled Talwyn and was swift to apologise. 'I'm sorry. I didn't mean to be so abrupt, but finally meeting my father after all this time might prove either very emotional or a great disappointment, either of which could distract me from my main reason for coming to Roscoff. We'll visit *L'Hirondelle* first – but we will need to be cautious. Pasco could still be on board.'

The examination of the *Puffin*'s passengers, crew and cargo was of a decidedly cursory nature and Amos realised that even without any documentation, Pasco would have had no difficulty in entering France.

Unfortunately, it would also make the task of finding him more difficult, as he would not have needed to provide any details to French officials of where he might be going.

The *Puffin* would be in Roscoff for at least twenty-four hours while the foundry goods were unloaded and a new general cargo taken on board. The ship's master said the small amount of luggage that Amos and Talwyn had brought to France with them could remain in the mate's cabin until they found somewhere to stay.

Before disembarking from the ship Amos felt it expedient to extract one item from his baggage, but he was very conscious of having the loaded revolver tucked in the waistband of his trousers, hidden by his jacket.

Cargo was still being unloaded from *L'Hirondelle*, and the harbourside around it was the scene of much noise and activity. However, Amos was relieved to find it would be unnecessary for him to make a decision about whether or not to take Talwyn on board the ship to act as interpreter for his inquiries. A sailor who appeared to be the captain of the vessel was on the quayside haranguing the dockside workers and exhorting them without noticeable effect to greater efforts.

When Amos approached him and addressed him in English, the Frenchman ignored him, but his attitude changed dramatically when Talwyn spoke to him in his own language. Suddenly the sea captain was all smiles and the dockers were able to enjoy a brief respite from his attentions.

After talking with the man for a while, Talwyn turned to Amos and said, 'Yes, he brought Pasco to France on his ship, and I don't think he was very happy with his passenger. He wants to know whether you are a friend of Pasco's . . . I wasn't quite certain how I should answer him.'

Amos was watching the captain's face as Talwyn spoke, and he received the distinct impression that the Frenchman understood everything that was being said. 'Tell him I am *not* one of Pasco's friends, but that there is some unfinished business that needs to be settled between us.'

He was correct about the captain's understanding of English. Long before Talwyn had translated Amos's words, he was replying to them – in French.

'He says he *thought* that Pasco was running away from something – or someone – and he did not feel comfortable having him on board, but he paid in advance – and he paid well.'

'Does he know where Pasco is staying in Roscoff?'

The captain's exaggerated shrug gave Amos his answer even before the man replied to Talwyn's translation of his question.

'He says he does not know, but as Pasco spoke no French at all he doubts whether he got very far from the docks last night.'

Thanking the captain, Amos turned to walk away with Talwyn. He would need to think about his next move. They had taken only a few paces when the Frenchman called after them and spoke rapidly to Talwyn.

When she turned back to Amos to translate, her concern was showing. 'He says that before Pasco left the ship, one of the crew spoke to him and told him of an Englishman living in Roscoff who might be able to help him. He gave Pasco the name of your father ... and told him where he could find him.'

57

The sign above the door of the shipping company still proclaimed that it was the office of '*B. Thiers, Compagnie Maritime*', even though B. Thiers had been dead for a number of years.

When Amos and Talwyn entered the outer office two middle-aged men were poring over documents while a much younger girl, seated at the desk nearest the door, was entering figures in a very large, cloth-bound ledger with a pen held in her right hand, while with her left she skilfully manipulated the coloured beads of an abacus.

The girl spoke to them first, asking in French how she could help them. Talwyn replied to her question at length and Amos caught the words 'M'sieur Hawke'.

The girl shook her head and gave an equally lengthy reply, which Amos correctly guessed was explaining that 'M'sieur Hawke' was not in the office.

The excitement with which he had entered died and he felt deeply disappointed, but the girl, smiling, was speaking again, and in a moment Talwyn was turning to Amos in deep concern.

'She says that your – that Mr Hawke would seem to have become suddenly very popular with his countrymen and women. She says another Englishman called no more than half an hour ago wanting to speak to him.'

'Pasco!' Amos exclaimed. 'Ask her if he left a name and where he is staying.'

In response to Talwyn's query another shake of the head accompanied the girl's reply and Talwyn explained, 'No. She says conversation was virtually impossible because he spoke no French and she speaks only a little English – but she thinks she managed to convey the information that Mr Hawke is away on one of the company's ships, but should be returning from Sweden some time tomorrow morning.'

'She actually told him that?' Amos expressed concern, but at that moment a door opened from an inner office and a slim and attractive woman, probably in her late forties, emerged carrying a single sheet of paper in her hands.

She gave a casual look at the two visitors before her glance returned abruptly to settle upon Amos. At the same time the office girl spoke to the woman in rapid French, among which he was able to pick out the words 'Madame Hawke', and he realised that this was the woman who was married to his father.

The girl must have explained that he and Talwyn were from England and wished to speak to her husband because the woman now said, in good English, 'Mr Hawke is not in the country until tomorrow, but may I help you?'

As she talked she was looking intently at Amos and now she spoke directly to him. 'You, m'sieur . . . what is your name?'

'My name is Amos.'

He hoped she might accept it without pressing him for a surname, but she immediately threw up her arms excitedly. 'I *thought* it must be! You are so like your father that I *knew* I could not be mistaken. You are Amos *Hawke*, the son of my husband!'

'He has told you of me?' Amos felt ridiculously pleased.

'But of course! Why should he not tell me of such a son? He will be so delighted . . . *I* am so delighted!' Dropping the paper she was holding on the desk where the girl was seated, she advanced upon Amos, embraced him warmly, and planted a kiss upon each of his cheeks. When she released him she turned to look at Talwyn, but it was to Amos she spoke. 'And this beautiful girl . . . she is your wife?'

Still recovering from Gabrielle's enthusiastic embrace, Amos said, 'No, Talwyn is a friend . . . a very good friend, who has accompanied me to France to help me with something I have to do here. She lived in France for a couple of years and speaks your language. Sadly, I do not.'

'It is of no importance. When I first met your father, *he* could speak no French. Now . . . he is not perfect, but he speaks enough to be successful in business. But where are you staying?'

370

Amos confessed that they had been in Roscoff for less than an hour and had not yet had time to find a place to stay.

'Good!' Gabrielle exclaimed. 'It means it will not be necessary to cancel any arrangements. You will stay at my house . . . the house of your father and myself. No, do not protest, we have far too many rooms that are never used. Where is your luggage? Someone will be sent to collect it. In the meantime I will take you to the house. You must treat it as your own. Your father will be overjoyed that you are here. So often he has spoken of you, wondering where you are and what you are doing. When we reach the house we will celebrate your arrival in France and you can tell me what has brought you here.'

Not until they had been conducted to the very impressive house that was occupied by Gabrielle and Doniert Hawke, and were seated on the balcony enjoying champagne and snacks produced by one of Gabrielle's servants, did Amos have an opportunity to reveal his profession to his newly found stepmother and tell her the reason he and Talwyn were in France.

Listening in shocked silence, Gabrielle eventually asked, 'This man . . . this Pasco Davey? He is known to Doniert . . . to your father?'

'Yes. They once worked together in Cornwall, but Pasco is undoubtedly insane and my father – and others – no longer wished to work with him. Unfortunately, my father knows enough about Pasco and his brother Hannibal to hang them both, and they want him out of the way. Hannibal is already in prison, awaiting trial for

371

murdering one of my colleagues, but Pasco made good his escape. If he can ensure that my father cannot give evidence against him, he might feel he will be able to escape justice. I am here to ensure he does not . . . but even if Pasco learns I am here it is unlikely to prevent him from trying to harm my father. He is not capable of rational thought.'

Mulling over what she had heard, Gabrielle finally said, 'Is it quite certain this Pasco is guilty of murder?'

The question was put to Amos, but it was Talwyn who replied. 'Amos was present when Pasco killed the detective who had come to Cornwall with him from London. In fact, I understand that Pasco is suffering from a bullet wound in his arm that was given to him by Amos. Pasco has also killed a number of other men. One of them was my father, and, although Amos's father was not involved, we believe he witnessed the killing. We are hoping he will return to England and give evidence for the prosecution once Pasco is captured.'

'It was your father who was murdered by this man?' Gabrielle reached out a hand to clasp Talwyn's arm. 'You poor child! Doniert returned very upset from a voyage to a port in Cornwall a few weeks ago. He said he had seen the murder of an innocent man. When I asked him if he had reported it, he said that had he done so his own life would have been in very great danger . . . but he said there was another witness who lived in England who he hoped would have told the authorities about it.'

'That other witness was unwittingly involved in the murder of my colleague,' Amos said grimly, 'and I was hoping he *would* give evidence against Pasco.

Unfortunately, he committed suicide in prison. The result, I believe, of a visit by one of Pasco's friends who threatened the man's family if he gave evidence against Pasco.'

'This man must not be allowed to remain in France,' Gabrielle declared. 'He must be caught and punished, but until he is, he poses a serious threat to Doniert. This afternoon we will call upon a friend. He is also the mayor, here in Roscoff. We will discuss with him what can be done about Pasco . . . but that is for this afternoon. For this morning this man can do no harm to anyone, so I would like to celebrate the arrival in my home of my stepson and his very charming companion . . .'

58

Gabrielle did all in her power to make Amos and Talwyn feel welcome in the house she shared with her second husband. They were given what must have been the two best guest rooms. Joined by a small shared balcony, both had extensive views over the approaches to Roscoff from the sea beyond a large and well-kept garden.

The house had been left to Gabrielle by her late husband. The marriage had been childless and she made it abundantly clear to Amos that she intended to look upon him as the son she had never produced for herself.

It soon became apparent that Gabrielle was highly regarded by the community in which she lived. As they walked to the building occupied by the town's mayor, M. Flourens, men and women greeted her respectfully.

The mayor too stood up from his seat behind a huge desk when they entered his office and greeted her as a close friend, with a kiss on each cheek. He did not speak

English, and when Gabrielle introduced her companions, using only their Christian names and explaining that they had just travelled together from England, he assumed they were man and wife.

When Talwyn was asked to explain the reason why they had come to France, she began by stating that Amos and she were not related in any way. The mayor raised a quizzical eyebrow, but his mild censure quickly changed to indignation when he learned that Amos was a Scotland Yard detective who had come to France seeking a man for whom he possessed an arrest warrant issued by a British court.

He told Talwyn bluntly that such a document carried no authority whatsoever in France and, furthermore, no extradition treaty existed between the two countries, so that even were Amos to find his man there was nothing that could be done about having him returned to England.

When she translated his words for Amos's benefit, he said, 'Please tell Mayor Flourens that I am fully aware I have no jurisdiction in France and would not dream of imposing upon his goodwill if this man were not probably the most desperate and dangerous killer I have ever had to deal with. Furthermore, he has not come to France merely in order to escape justice in England, but also, we fear, to continue his ways here.'

Talwyn translated what Amos had said, and when she had finished Gabrielle had something to add to her story, informing the mayor that her husband – the father of Amos – had unwittingly witnessed the killing of one of this man's victims when he was in England.

Amos was kept informed by Talwyn of what was being said by his stepmother to Mayor Flourens. When she paused in what was an excited and voluble explanation, he produced the letter written by Sir Joseph and translated by Talwyn and passed it across the desk to the French dignitary, with a request that he read it before listening to any more talk.

The mayor read the letter in silence and Amos gained nothing from his expression of what he might be thinking, but when he came to the end of the letter and placed it on the desk in front of him, Monsieur Flourens directed his attention to Talwyn and asked bluntly the reason for her presence in France with Amos.

Talwyn explained that she had felt that if Amos was going to be successful in his search for Pasco Davey he needed to have someone with him who spoke French. Then, with barely controlled emotion, she told him that she was also personally involved because of the murder of her father and the burning down of her school by the man they were seeking.

Her evident distress proved to be the turning point in what Amos had felt was becoming a losing battle in the bid to gain the co-operation of the senior politician in Roscoff. Pressing home his advantage when he heard Pasco described as a '*monstre*' Amos said, 'Tell M'sieur Flourens that in addition to killing your father and Inspector Carpenter, he almost certainly shot and killed two Excise officers and two other men.'

When this information was passed on, the mayor threw up his hands in an expression of horror and spoke in rapid French. Both women were visibly moved, and

Talwyn explained, 'M'sieur Flourens says that when he was on a visit to London last year he visited Scotland Yard and it was Inspector Carpenter who showed him round. He will provide you with all the assistance you need in order to capture Pasco, but asks whether you possess any information that might be of help to him and the *gendarmes* in finding him here in Roscoff?'

'Yes,' Amos said, 'but it is something I did not want to mention in front of Gabrielle for fear of frightening her too much.' Apologetically, he said to his stepmother, 'Many years ago my father worked with Pasco and his brother on the same mine in Cornwall. With others, he witnessed a fight involving both brothers in which two men were killed. False evidence was given in court which made it appear to be an accident. There were other witnesses who might have told the truth of what happened had they been asked, but all except one have since died in mysterious circumstances. The sole survivor is now living the life of a vagrant, terrified that Pasco will find him. It was he who told me that my father's life is likely to be in danger from Pasco. Now Pasco is here, in Roscoff, and has been given the address of my father's office. He actually called there this morning, asking for him. I must also add that Pasco is armed with a pistol that he stole before he was dishonourably discharged from the British Army.'

Gabrielle had been listening intently to what he was saying, while Mayor Flourens waited impatiently for Talwyn's interpretation, but Amos had not yet finished. 'Please tell the mayor that I too am in possession of a revolver. It was given to me by Inspector Carpenter and

I used it when Carpenter was waylaid and shot. I believe I wounded Pasco but, unfortunately, it was not serious enough to fully disable him. In view of Pasco's murderous nature and the fact that I am known to him, will the mayor give me permission to carry the gun here, in France?'

After the translation, the Frenchman took a few moments to think about all that he had been told before replying. Then Talwyn told Amos, 'You have the mayor's permission to retain the gun – and to use it if necessary, but only in self-defence – and when Pasco is arrested it will be by French *gendarmes*.'

'Please thank M'sieur Flourens,' Amos said, 'but I fear for my father's life. Will he arrange for *gendarmes* to meet his ship when it returns to Roscoff and remain as his escort until Pasco is in custody?'

When Talwyn had translated Amos's request, the mayor stood up from behind his desk and told Amos, via Talwyn, that the whole matter was now in his hands and he would do everything he considered necessary to protect everyone involved and have Pasco Davey arrested.

When they had left the town hall, Amos said to Gabrielle, 'M'sieur Flourens is a very pleasant man and most co-operative – but is he also efficient?'

'He is no better and no worse than any mayor we have had in Roscoff during my lifetime,' Gabrielle replied, 'but we will leave nothing to chance. I will arrange with my staff that as soon as Doniert's ship is sighted we are to be informed. When it docks we will be awaiting him on the quay. You and I will *both* be armed, Amos – and you can disregard what M'sieur Flourens said about only shooting in self-defence. This man you seek has already killed too many people. After many years of loneliness I have found great happiness with your father. I will not allow it to be taken from me by such a man as this Pasco.'

59

That evening brought a steady flow of visiting French relatives to Gabrielle's house, all of them curious to meet her previously unseen stepson.

Once again the presence of Talwyn was the subject of a great deal of speculation, but one or two of the more inquisitive – or hopeful – young girls quickly ascertained that Amos was in France 'on business' and that Talwyn had accompanied him in the role of interpreter. If some of the more worldly family members were sceptical, well, he was unmarried . . . and he was an Englishman.

It had been a busy day, followed by a very pleasant evening, but when Amos went to his room he knew he would not be able to sleep right away. A bottle of Armagnac had been thoughtfully placed on a side table in his room, together with a tumbler and a jug of drinking water. Pouring himself a generous measure, he took it to the balcony, made himself comfortable in a cushioned wicker armchair and gazed out over Roscoff's water-front, illuminated now by a multitude of lanterns casting a warm yellow glow over the quays. Beyond the harbour were more lights from small boats fishing in the approaches to the French port.

He had not been seated many minutes when he heard the sound of the glass-panelled door leading from Talwyn's room being opened. She came out on to the balcony and was startled to find Amos seated there.

'Oh! I am sorry. I did not realise you were out here.'

'There's no need to apologise,' he said. 'Come and sit down and enjoy the view. It's really rather special . . . would you like a drink? Gabrielle has had a bottle of fine Armagnac placed in my room.'

'No, thank you. I have drunk enough . . . far more than I am used to.'

'Yes, Gabrielle is a very generous hostess . . . but come and sit down anyway. You'll find it very relaxing – and I think you probably have need of it. You have been wonderful today. I really could not have managed without you.'

'Thank you, Amos. I *will* sit and relax for a while – and hope the night air helps to clear the effects of the drinks I have had.'

'You hold it very well,' Amos said, 'which is more than I can say for some of Gabrielle's relatives, although I don't think I heard anyone say a word out of place all evening – mind you, as they were all speaking French, I wouldn't have known anyway!'

'They were all extremely polite,' Talwyn agreed, 'although I think you might have been embarrassed had

381

you been able to understand what some of the young girls were saying about you. They are rather more forthright than English girls when it comes to expressing opinions about men – and you have taken the fancy of more than one of them.'

'Then perhaps it's as well that I *don't* understand French,' he declared. 'It means I can get on with the work I am here to do without being distracted by what is being said about me.'

'Admirable sentiments, Amos,' Talwyn said mischievously, 'but you do have to admit some of them are very attractive girls.'

'I don't think you were lacking when it came to admirers,' Amos pointed out. 'Had you not been tied to my apron strings as my interpreter, I would have seen very little of you during the course of the evening.'

'I doubt that,' Talwyn retorted. 'You are forgetting that I lived in France for a couple of years. I am not taken in by the flattery of Frenchmen, no matter how charming they may be.' Smiling at Amos, she appeared more relaxed than he had ever seen her, and she confirmed this impression by saying, 'Nevertheless, it was the most pleasant evening I have spent for a very long time. Even the knowledge that we have yet to tackle Pasco Davey did not spoil it. I think your father has married into a very nice family, Amos.'

'He has,' Amos agreed, 'and I like Gabrielle too. I think I could become very fond of her.'

'And she of you. I heard her telling many of her relatives how wonderful she thinks you are.'

'I seem to have acquired a new skill,' Amos said with

a wry smile. 'I haven't always been considered "wonderful" by women when we have met for the first time . . . especially younger women.'

'Dumping a woman on her backside on the wet ground is not the best way to make an impression upon her,' Talwyn replied with a smile. 'I doubt if such an introduction would enthuse even the most doting of French girls.'

'Well, I am glad we have succeeded in overcoming our initial misunderstanding,' Amos declared. He paused, and then repeated in a low voice, as if he was coming to terms with a new idea, 'Very glad.'

'Yes, I am too . . .'

Amos thought she was about to amplify her brief declaration. Instead, she rose to her feet and said, 'It *has* been a very full day, Amos . . . and I don't really want to think of what might happen tomorrow. But whatever it is I intend to be ready for it, so I am going to my room and hope I am able to sleep.'

'It won't be long before I follow suit,' Amos admitted, 'but I think I will stay out here for a few minutes longer and try to put my thoughts into some sort of order. It has turned out to be a very emotional day – and tomorrow is likely to follow the same course, if I am not careful. I need to remind myself that I am here to catch a murderer and not merely to enjoy finding the sort of family I have so often wished for.'

His words moved Talwyn deeply. Quietly she said, 'I am so happy that you *have* found them, after spending so many years without anyone. I was absolutely devastated when I lost my father . . . especially the manner in which it happened ... but in moments like this I realise how very lucky I was to grow up as part of a loving family. Pasco Davey will never know how much he destroyed when he killed my father, but he can never destroy my memories.'

Such thoughts had been building up inside Talwyn all evening, surrounded as she was by the many members of what was so obviously a close and happy extended family. She had told herself that she would be glad for Amos and not dwell upon her own loss, and she believed she had succeeded very well – until now. Feeling hot tears burning her eyes, she turned away and hurried to the door of her room – but when she reached it Amos was close behind her.

'Wait ... Talwyn!' His hands were upon her shoulders and he drew her round to face him. She made no resistance when he pulled her closer and said softly, 'I don't want you to go to your room feeling sad. This has been such an unexpectedly happy day for me, but it could not have happened without you, and it would not have meant so much had you not been here with me. I realised early on that the thing I probably enjoyed most of all this evening was having you here to share it with me.'

She was looking up at him as he spoke, but he was unable to read her expression. 'I'm sorry. This is probably coming out all wrong. I don't want to embarrass you ...'

'Shh!' She put a finger up to his lips. 'You are not embarrassing me – in fact you are saying all the right things. You and Gabrielle made me feel I was part of everything that was happening. It's just . . . oh, I don't know how to express it, Amos, but seeing such a happy family made me realise yet again what it is that Pasco has taken away from us . . . from me and Mother . . .'

With a conscious effort, she pulled herself together. 'I am sorry, Amos. You have quite enough to think about without having to cope with an over-emotional woman.'

'I find it much easier than dealing with an *un*emotional woman,' Amos said, 'and you have given *me* great support today. Thank you for that.'

'And thank *you*,' she said, 'especially for caring.'

Suddenly, she kissed him, for only the second time since they had known each other. Her lips lingered longer this time, but when his body responded to the nearness of her she broke away from him.

'Go and rest now, Amos – and whatever happens tomorrow, don't take any unnecessary risks. Pasco is a desperate man and has nothing to lose. You have.'

60

Amos's thoughts kept him awake for a long time, but when sleep did come he gave himself up to it completely. He was awakened by a violent pounding on the door of his room.

'Who is it?' Still befuddled by sleep, he only gradually became aware of where he was, and from the light coming through the window between the partly drawn curtains he could see it was barely dawn.

'Amos!' It was Gabrielle's voice, 'You must come quickly – your father's ship has arrived early. It is on its way in to dock now.'

'All right, I'm coming.' Looking round the room for his clothes, he located them on a chair in a corner. 'Are the *gendarmes* at the dock to meet the ship?' He called the question, not certain whether Gabrielle was still within hearing.

She was. 'No. The ship has arrived much earlier

than expected. M'sieur Flourens will have no one there yet.'

'I'll be down right away.' Amos hopped clumsily about the room in his hurry to pull on his trousers.

Talwyn had been woken by Gabrielle's urgent bid to wake Amos, and from the doorway of her room had heard the conversation between the two. She dressed hurriedly, and because Amos was halfway down the stairs before he remembered his revolver and returned to his room to collect it from his bag, she emerged from her room more or less fully dressed just as he reached the stairs once more.

'Wait for me. I'm coming too.'

Amos would have preferred Talwyn to remain in the safety of the house, but there was no time to argue. An agitated Gabrielle was waiting in the hallway. She was the only one of the trio who had successfully shaken off sleep, but the short journey to the harbour was made mostly at a trot and this, combined with morning air cooled by a breeze blowing off the sea, served to fully wake the others.

The docks were quiet. The only people in sight were a small group of French dockers chatting with a night watchman on the quayside where Doniert's ship would berth and, on the far side of the harbour, the four-man crew of a small coastal trading sloop preparing their vessel for an early sailing.

The trio waited on the quayside as the vessel for which they had so hurriedly abandoned their beds drew closer. The ship was a large, square-rigged barquentine, and as the crew busied themselves about the deck, preparing to berth, one man dressed in a heavy overcoat could be seen standing apart from the working sailors.

Gabrielle pointed him out excitedly. 'There he is, Amos. There is your father.' As she talked she waved energetically and the warmly clad man returned her greeting.

Despite the stomach-churning excitement Amos was feeling at the thought of the imminent reunion, he was fully conscious of the threat posed by Pasco Davey. 'You meet him when the ship berths, Gabrielle. Talwyn and I will go back to the office and wait for you there. We will be able to see Pasco if he comes anywhere near the ship, without his seeing us. That way *we* will have the element of surprise, and not him.'

Gabrielle could see the sense of this arrangement. 'I will bring your father to the office the moment he steps ashore – but will not tell him who is waiting for him. It will be such a wonderful surprise!'

Watching from the office window, Amos and Talwyn saw Doniert Hawke jump from ship to quay as soon as the vessel bumped alongside and give Gabrielle a warm kiss and hug. The only other people in sight were the French dockers who had been there when Amos and the two women had arrived at the docks and were now busy helping to moor the vessel. Amos was able to return his attention to his father.

He was not as tall as he remembered; there was little difference in their heights now. His hair was greying, too, but he appeared upright and fit and Amos realised he would have recognised him wherever the two men had met.

'You are very like your father,' Talwyn said, inter-rupting his thoughts. He could trust himself to do no more than nod in agreement, and, understanding the emotion he must be feeling, she reached out and squeezed his arm sympathetically, saying nothing more.

Gabrielle was speaking to her husband and telling him there was 'someone on business from England' in the office to see him. They had come close enough for Amos to see his father's perplexed expression when Gabrielle refused to give him any more details of the English 'visitor'.

Doniert and Gabrielle had almost reached the office door now and, after a final look through the window at the dockside area, Amos stepped into the centre of the office floor, facing the door, while Talwyn moved to one side, away from him.

The door opened. Gabrielle entered the office first and, seeing Amos, immediately stepped aside. Doniert had been close behind her and saw Amos immediately, but although it was daylight outside now, the sun had not yet struggled free from a bank of dark cloud which rose above the horizon to the east, and the interior of the office was in shadow.

Doniert stopped uncertainly, waiting for his eyes to adjust themselves, but Amos gave them no time. Without moving from the centre of the office, he said, 'Hello, Pa.'

Doniert's whole body convulsed, as though he was about to throw a fit; then, taking a hesitant pace forward, he said uncertainly, 'Amos . . . ?'

'That's right, Pa . . . it's been a long time.'

Doniert seemed rooted to the spot until Gabrielle said,

'It is your *son*, Doniert. What are you waiting for? Hug him . . . I did!'

As though he had only been awaiting such confirmation, Doniert ran forward, to be met halfway across the office floor by Amos. Father and son hugged each other, and Gabrielle and Talwyn looked on, trying not to cry.

Eventually, taking a step back, Doniert said, 'The last time I did that was when I said goodbye to you as you went off to join the Royal Marines. You don't know how much I have longed for this day.'

'I have spent a lot of time looking for you, Pa, since I came back from the Crimea and left the Marines.'

Doniert's face lost its expression of joy for a moment. 'There was a reason for not letting anyone know where I was, son, but you don't need to hear about that now.'

'I already know the reason, Pa . . . and we *do* need to discuss it. You see, I am a Scotland Yard detective now and have been in Cornwall investigating a series of murders that have occurred there . . . including the killing of Edward Kernow.'

Turning away for a moment, he called Talwyn forward and introduced her to his father, who seemed bewildered by Amos's revelation. He was even more stunned when Amos continued, 'I have established that the murders were committed by the Davey brothers. Hannibal is in Launceston gaol awaiting trial but unfortunately Pasco escaped – and he's in Roscoff now. So you see, we have a great many things to discuss.'

'They are not quite the sorts of things I thought we would be talking about when we met again,' Doniert said ruefully, 'although I realise that in my mind's eye

I have kept the memory of the thirteen-year-old boy I said goodbye to with such a heavy heart, all those years ago. Now you have come back into my life as a fully grown man.' Gabrielle had moved to her husband's side, and, putting an arm about her, he gave her a hug. 'We have often spoken of Amos, haven't we, Gabrielle, and wondered how he was and what he was doing? Well, here we are, having been reunited for only a few minutes, and, you know, I think I am proud of him already.'

61

The first thing Gabrielle did when they all arrived back at the house was to organise breakfast. Over the meal, by mutual but unspoken consent, talk centred around father and son and their activities during the years that had passed since they were last together. Talwyn welcomed the opportunity to learn a great deal more about Amos than he would ever have disclosed in conversation with anyone else.

It was not until breakfast was over that Doniert suggested he and Amos should take their coffee outside to the patio to discuss the more serious aspects of the latter's visit to Roscoff.

When they were settled in the sunshine of what promised to be a hot day, Amos said, 'I think the first thing we should discuss is your safety. You don't need me to tell you that your life is in danger for as long as Pasco is on the loose.'

Doniert nodded agreement. 'I am possibly more aware of that than you, but what do you think we should do about it?'

'Gabrielle and I have already done something about it,' Amos replied. 'We went to see Mayor Flourens yesterday. He promised to have *gendarmes* on the dock when your ship came in, but he obviously made no provision for the ship arriving early.'

Doniert gave his son a wry smile. 'Flourens is a good man – an honest man – but he is far too easy-going and I don't think he has ever come up against a man like Pasco Davey.'

'I doubt whether many men have,' Amos said, 'but, although I don't believe Pasco is aware of this address, I don't think we can take anything for granted. We have missed the opportunity of capturing him that we hoped to have when your ship came in, so I will ask Gabrielle to send a note to Flourens, asking for armed plain clothes guards to be placed here at the house. I am armed – and so is Gabrielle. I suggest you take to carrying a handgun too – even when you are home, or in the garden.'

'Do you seriously believe such extreme measures are necessary?'

'Yes, I do. Let me tell you why I and the detective inspector who was killed by Pasco were asked to go to Cornwall . . .'

Amos briefed his father on all he had learned during his time in Cornwall. Doniert interrupted frequently to ask questions, especially when the deaths of his former friends and fellow miners were mentioned.

'It is certainly a particularly gruesome record of

393

crime,' Doniert admitted when Amos paused in his narrative to allow a servant to replace the near-empty coffee pot on the table between them with a full one, 'and I know I am in danger because Pasco is so unstable, but why should he still want *me* out of the way? He doesn't know that I witnessed the killing of the school-teacher, and the other things happened a long while ago, when we were up on the moor. Besides, a coroner ruled that the deaths of the Wheal Phoenix miners were accidental.'

'That verdict satisfied very few people,' Amos said. 'I think Pasco knows that if he ever comes to court the coroner's verdict is likely to be challenged – especially if you and Billy are still around to give evidence against him and Hannibal – and I think he *does* know that you witnessed the killing of Talwyn's father. According to Sam Rodda, Lightfoot told a few people about it before he died – and now you are the only witness.'

'But, surely, from what you have told me, you already have enough evidence to convict Pasco and Hannibal of the murder of the policeman from London? They will hang for that.'

'They should,' Amos agreed, 'but, as you've just said, the man he shot was a policeman – a *London* policeman, who was on his way back from an abortive attempt to take *Cornish* smugglers. In your lifetime you will have seen trials for smuggling collapse – even trials for killing those whose duty it was to prevent smuggling. Could you guarantee a conviction by a Cornish jury against two Cornishmen accused of killing such a man? No, you couldn't, especially if friends of Pasco and Hannibal had managed to intimidate some of the jury and got rid of witnesses to other murders they had committed. I succeeded in shooting Lightfoot and wounding Pasco on the night they killed Detective Inspector Carpenter, so it's possible the Daveys would try to sow doubts in the minds of the jurors by saying I fired first and Pasco and the others feared for their lives. I didn't, as it happened – I only started shooting after Carpenter had been shot – but I have learned that quite often a jury believes only what it wants to believe. That is why you have become a danger to Pasco and Hannibal, Pa. Not only did you witness what happened between the Wheal Phoenix miners and the Daveys, but I believe that Pasco has in fact learned that you witnessed the killing of Talwyn's father.'

Doniert winced. 'I've always felt bad for saying nothing about that killing to anyone in authority . . . I felt worse this morning when you introduced me to the schoolteacher's daughter . . . but what could I do? My ship was only in Charlestown for a couple of hours and if I had missed it Pasco would have had me for certain.'

'Why *did* Pasco kill Edward Kernow?' Amos asked. 'And how did you come to witness it?'

'I met up with Jimmy Lightfoot by accident when the ship put in to Charlestown and we went up to the Rashleigh Arms for a quick drink together. Landlord Tom Stephens was horrified to see me there because the Daveys were around that night. I didn't want them to see me any more than Stephens did, so I was quite happy for Jimmy and me to take our ale to a back room overlooking the inn yard, with the only light coming from a lantern kept burning outside to deter thieves. That's where we were when we saw the schoolteacher murdered.'

Taken aback, Amos said, 'You mean . . . he was murdered in the back yard of the Rashleigh Arms? Why? What was he doing there?'

'I think he must have either realised something was going on, or been told, and came to see what was happening,' Doniert replied.

'What *was* going on?'

His father seemed uncomfortable at his question and Amos said, 'I know your ship had delivered a cargo of brandy to smugglers working for the Daveys, but you were outside the three mile limit, so there was nothing illegal in that. Surely Edward Kernow wasn't killed just because he saw brandy being delivered to Stephens?'

'No, there was more to it than that. Pasco was with the men delivering the brandy when someone else came into the yard. I recognised him straight away as the senior officer in charge of the Fowey Excise officers.'

Amos was not as shocked as he might have been. He remembered that the abortive trap set by Sir Joseph Sawle on the night Detective Inspector Carpenter had been shot and mortally wounded had been instigated as a result of information received from a senior Excise man stationed at Fowey. 'Can you remember the man's name?' he asked.

'Yes, Lieutenant "Paddy" Ireland. He's an ex-navy man.'

Making a mental note of the name, Amos asked, 'What happened next?'

'While Jimmy and I were watching, Pasco pulled out a leather bag hanging on a leather cord round his neck, inside his smock. He poured out a number of coins that looked like gold and was about to hand them to Ireland when Kernow appeared in the gateway leading from the lane that runs past the Rashleigh. I thought that when he saw what was going on he would turn round and lose himself as quickly as he could – but he didn't. He stepped inside the yard and asked Pasco, by name, what he thought he was doing. Instead of replying, Pasco reached inside his smock, pulled out a pistol and, without saying a word, shot him. Ireland stood there as though he couldn't believe what was happening, but the noise of the shot brought Stephens running from the bar room. When he saw Kernow lying in the yard, he kneeled down beside him, felt for a heartbeat and then, looking horrified at Pasco, said, "He's dead!" "Just as well for all of us," said Pasco as he reloaded his pistol. "He saw too much and would have been fool enough to report what he saw. Now you are here you can help me carry him to the cliff and throw him over. By morning the tide will have taken him out to sea and no one will ever know what happened." "Not me," Stephens said, shaking like a leaf, "I've got an inn to run and if I don't get back into the bar room right away, my customers will come looking for me." With that he scuttled away.'

'What did Pasco do then?'

'It looked as though he might go inside and order Stephens to come and help him, but at that moment Hannibal arrived. After sending the Excise officer away, Hannibal and Pasco carried Kernow's body out into the lane, where I think there were some mules. They must have used one to carry it away. Was the body ever found?'

'Yes,' said Amos. 'It was spotted early the next morning at the foot of the cliffs, before the tide reached it. The bullet that killed him was recovered and an experienced armourer from the army barracks at Bodmin is ready to go to court and swear that it was fired from the same gun that was used to kill two Excise officers some time before.'

'I don't doubt he's right,' Doniert said. 'I have heard rumours about it from some of the men collecting brandy from our ships.'

'You have just told me how Edward Kernow died,' Amos said. 'If we could convict Pasco of murdering him we could be certain of convicting both brothers for at least *some* of the other murders too – even with a Cornish jury. They would have sympathy with anyone involved in smuggling, but not with someone who shot an in-offensive man like Kernow in cold blood. He was well known and respected in Cornwall.' Looking specula-tively at his father, Amos said, 'Would you come back to Cornwall to give evidence at the trial of the Davey brothers, Pa?'

Before Doniert could reply, there were sounds from inside the house and Gabrielle ran into the garden crying, 'Amos . . . Amos . . . come quickly. They have found the man you are looking for!'

62

Events moved swiftly from the moment Gabrielle called Amos from the garden. One of the *gendarmes* detailed by Mayor Flourens had been sent to the house to inform him that Pasco had been located.

Questioned by Amos, with Talwyn interpreting, the *gendarme* said that Pasco was staying with a prostitute in a brothel in the dockland area of Roscoff. The information had been relayed to the *gendarme* by another occupant of the brothel.

Pasco's behaviour had perturbed some of the women, used as they were to dealing with the peculiarities of their clients, but his capricious mannerisms excited little undue alarm until the partner he had purchased for the night, making a routine search of his belongings while he slept, discovered a loaded pistol among his possessions.

She disclosed details of her find to a fellow prostitute

who had a regular client who was a *gendarme*. The information was duly passed on and reached the ears of Mayor Flourens, who immediately ordered a cordon of *gendarmes* to be thrown around the brothel, much to the embarrassment of the local priest who was stopped when leaving the premises only minutes after it had been placed under surveillance.

Doniert wanted to accompany his son to the place where Pasco had been located, but Amos insisted that he remain at the house, pointing out that he was known to be a prospective target for the man they were hunting. His presence would impede Amos and the *gendarmes* in their efforts to arrest Pasco, because of the need to protect *him*.

However, Amos would not be leaving the house alone. He found Talwyn in the hallway, waiting to go with him and the *gendarme*. She brushed aside his protest, saying, 'You are the only one who can identify Pasco Davey – but you do not speak French! How will you let the *gendarmes* know if you see him? No, Amos, you forget that I have a very strong personal interest in this. Nothing must be left to chance.'

Amos had been acquainted with Talwyn for long enough to know better than to argue with her when she had made up her mind about something. 'Very well, but keep out of harm's way, and stay where I can see you all the time . . .'

The brothel was a three-storey terraced house close to the docks and would appear to be a popular rendezvous. At least a dozen *gendarmes* were in the tiny front garden, mingling with a number of young – and not-so-young – women in various states of undress, all complaining loudly at being forced from their rooms.

Here too were their clients, mainly seamen, many still drunk from the excesses of the night before. They believed they were the unfortunate victims of a previously unheard of anti-vice swoop by the French police on an establishment that had enjoyed immunity from such attention for all the years of its existence.

Many other houses in the street were also brothels and their clientele were fleeing, together with dishevelled and hastily dressed 'ladies of the night', before they too became caught up in the unprecedented activities of the *gendarmerie*.

M'sieur Flourens was here and, in answer to Amos's translated questions, replied that, yes, he did have an equal number of *gendarmes* at the back of the house and, no, the whole house had not yet been evacuated. Pointing to a window with closed curtains on the very top floor he said that this was the room where Pasco had been closeted with a woman known among her many clients as *La Veuve Noire*, a name that Talwyn had difficulty in interpreting. The woman had since fled from the room and was being interrogated by the gendarmes. The mayor added that all the floors beneath this room had been cleared. Two armed *gendarmes* were guarding the only flight of stairs leading from that floor and two more *gendarmes* were on their way to join them now. When they reached their colleagues, all four would go to the top floor and evacuate the other rooms, leaving only the one occupied by Pasco.

Alarmed, Amos asked, 'What will you do then?'

'We will call on him to surrender,' was the reply. 'If he refuses we will break down the door and overpower him.'

'But I have explained that he is armed,' Amos protested, 'and he has murdered before. He will not hesitate to shoot again.'

'If he does he will learn that French courts also have the power to inflict the death penalty.'

'We do not want anyone else killed,' Amos declared. 'I want to take him back to England to be tried for the crimes he has committed there ... for murdering Talwyn's father. Let me go up there and talk to him through the door. I might be able to persuade him to give himself up.'

Instead of translating Amos's suggestion into French, Talwyn said, 'You cannot go up there, Amos. Pasco would delight in shooting you, whatever the consequences for himself, you know that.'

'Please translate what I have said, Talwyn,' Amos said firmly. 'I am not going to allow it to end like this.'

Reluctantly, Talwyn did as he wished, but even before she had finished talking the mayor was shaking his head vigorously. '*Non ... non ... non!*'

It was followed by a barrage of French. Talwyn said, 'M'sieur Flourens says you are absolutely forbidden to enter the house. He wishes to remind you that you are in France – and *he* is in command here. He wishes to co-operate with you in your bid to capture Pasco – but it will be done *his* way.'

'His way is *wrong*,' Amos insisted. 'No ... don't tell him that, but I am not happy with the way things are going. Come back out into the street with me, away from this madhouse. I want to be able to think.'

Talwyn followed him from the garden and he stood in the roadway, looking up at the window of the room occupied by Pasco for many minutes before saying, 'You have been looking up at that room for nearly as long as I have, Talwyn. Isn't there something about it that strikes you as unusual?'

Puzzled, Talwyn replied, 'No, it's exactly the same now as when I first looked at it.'

'That's exactly what's wrong,' Amos said. 'With all that's going on outside the house, don't you think that Pasco would be curious to know what's happening?'

'What are you trying to say, Amos?'

'I am saying that I don't believe Pasco is in there,' he said. 'In spite of all M'sieur Flourens's precautions, I believe he has escaped.'

'But . . . with all these *gendarmes* around the house, how could he get away?' Talwyn was not convinced.

'I don't know. Let's go round to the back of the house and see if we get any ideas from there.'

The terrace in which the brothel was situated was linked to a short row of houses set at right angles at one end of the road. This, in turn, was linked to a second terrace which extended on the opposite side of the road to the first, forming a cul-de-sac.

In order to reach the back of the brothel, Amos and Talwyn were obliged to retrace their steps to the cul-de-sac entrance, heading for a narrow lane which separated the back gardens of the terraced houses from those of an identical terrace backing on to them.

They had reached the last house in the cul-de-sac when suddenly screams and shouts erupted from inside, bringing them to a startled halt.

As they looked at the house, the front door was flung open and a man stumbled out through the doorway.

It was Pasco Davey!

63

The prostitutes and their clients did not leave the brothel quietly and their noisy protests woke Pasco. Leaping from the bed, he woke *La Veuve Noire*. Ignoring her sleepy protests, Pasco peered from behind the curtains at the window. The scene that met his eyes caused him to make for the chair where his clothes had been thrown the previous night.

'What is it? What are you doing?'

La Veuve Noire had been a dockland whore for many years and English was one of a number of languages she had acquired.

'The front garden is full of men who appear to be policemen.' Pasco was sitting on the bed, pulling on his trousers.

Now it was her turn to hurry to the window and look out at the chaotic scene at the front of the house. 'It is a police raid!' she exclaimed angrily. 'Someone must have forgotten to pay them.'

'Raid be damned,' Pasco exclaimed. 'They are after me.' Rummaging inside the bag containing his belongings, he was searching for his pistol when he heard the sound of the door opening as his recent bedmate fled the room, carrying with her what clothes she had been able to snatch up while Pasco had his back to her.

Cursing the woman, he crossed to the door and, closing it, turned the key in the lock. He now turned his attention to a trapdoor he had observed in the ceiling when he had entered the room the previous night. If only he could get up there it might be possible to remove some of the roof tiles and make a precarious escape across the rooftops . . . but first he had to open the trap-door, which was higher than he could reach. He also needed to barricade the door and he used the bed for this task.

While he was dragging the bed across the floor, the pain in his wounded arm reminded him that the bandage and dressing had not been changed for some days. The wound was probably infected, but that was the least of his problems now.

He manhandled a chest of drawers across the room to the end of the bed. It not only reinforced the barrier against the door but stood directly beneath the trapdoor in the ceiling. By standing on the chest of drawers he was able to reach the trapdoor and push it open – but the pain in his arm prevented him from pulling himself up into the roof space.

Swearing aloud, he picked up a chair and placed it

upon the chest. Balancing precariously on this makeshift stepladder he was able to put head and shoulders inside the roof space, but it was dark up there, and he could not risk falling through the ceiling.

Carefully climbing down again, he took the lamp that had been standing on the chest of drawers and lit it with a sulphur match from a nearby fusee box.

Gingerly climbing back on to the balancing chair he held the lamp up into the roof space – and could hardly believe his luck. The roughly mortared walls dividing the terraced houses did not extend all the way up to the roof. It would be possible to get far away from the house that was the object of the *gendarmes'* attention.

Despite his elation, climbing over what walls there were did not prove easy, hampered as he was by the lamp and hindered by his wounded arm. But escape was paramount and each painful obstacle took him closer to freedom.

Eventually, when it had become apparent that his exertions had caused his wound to break open, he reached the final house in the terrace and located a trap-door similar to the one through which he had gained access to the roof space.

Cautiously raising the trapdoor, he saw a bed beneath it. The fact that it was occupied did not deter him and, wasting no time, he dropped through the hatch.

A startled woman appeared from beneath the bedclothes, and on seeing Pasco she began to scream.

Ignoring the woman, Pasco drew the pistol from his waistband, opened the bedroom door and made his escape from the room. The woman's screams followed him down the stairs, but only one still sleepy man tried to stop him and a blow from Pasco's pistol sent him staggering backwards into the room from which he had emerged.

There seemed to be a great many people living in the house and as Pasco reached the ground floor he could smell breakfast being cooked, but by this time the house was in uproar. It took only a few more steps. Pulling open the front door, Pasco stumbled outside onto the front path.

When he saw Pasco emerge from the house, gun in hand, Amos's first concern was for Talwyn's safety. Pulling her to one side, he sprang out to intercept Pasco as he stepped from the front garden into the road.

Unfortunately, Amos had not noticed a low step, and as he tripped over it he was struck on the side of the head by Pasco's pistol and knocked to the ground. He was up again quickly, but it had been long enough for the hunted man to pass him by. Turning away from the cul-de-sac and the crowd of *gendarmes*, Pasco ignored Talwyn, but as he ran past her she stuck her foot out.

Pasco's bulk and the speed at which he was running spun her round and she fell to the ground – but Pasco fell heavily too. His finger was on the trigger of the pistol and as it hit the roadway it was discharged, the bullet ricocheting across the hard ground in the manner of a stone skimming across the surface of a pond.

Pasco made a frantic attempt to regain his feet, but Amos fell upon him, knocking him to the ground once more. The Cornish fugitive was a strong and desperate man and might still have made good his escape, but the pistol was in his right hand – and it was this wrist that Amos seized.

It was Pasco's wounded arm and he screamed in agony, pleading with Amos to release it. Instead, Amos applied additional pressure.

The sound of the shot had been heard by the *gendarmes* gathered in the garden of the brothel where Pasco had spent the night and they now came running. When they reached the spot where Amos had Pasco pinned to the ground Talwyn hurriedly explained what had happened and within moments, his handcuffed hands secure behind his back, Pasco was being held between two *gendarmes*.

Now that the wanted man had been captured, Mayor Flourens wanted Amos to give up the pistol that Pasco had been carrying. When Amos insisted that the weapon was vital to the murder trial in Cornwall, the mayor angrily declared that it would be a very long time before Pasco was returned there. The mayor intended him to be taken before a French court and no doubt to spend a long term in a French prison as a result.

When it seemed to Amos that his protests were falling upon deaf ears, he decided to try another tactic. He said that as the man who had restrained Pasco, he would need to be called to give evidence before a French magistrate. He and Talwyn would be obliged to explain to the court how Flourens had concentrated all his resources on the brothel, thus allowing Pasco to escape through the roof space – only to be apprehended by a single Scotland Yard detective with the assistance of an

Englishwoman, who had succeeded where Flourens and forty *gendarmes* had failed.

After giving the mayor sufficient time to reflect upon what he had said, Amos explained that if Pasco were simply to be given into his custody he would be returned to England that same day. The story would then be circulated that Flourens had played an essential part in Pasco's capture. Amos would ensure that a letter was sent from the commissioner of the Metropolitan Police to the minister responsible for French police praising Flourens and thanking him for his co-operation and assistance in returning a very dangerous criminal to face trial for murder in England.

When Flourens hesitated uncertainly, Amos added, 'After all, what crime has Pasco committed in France, apart from failing to have a passport? It is hardly an offence which justifies the use of forty *gendarmes* and the disruption caused to so many householders. On the other hand, Pasco has committed so many murders in England that his trial will create a sensation. The name of Monsieur Flourens will be known throughout Europe. It will no doubt deter other criminals from coming to Roscoff.'

Eventually, after giving the alternatives a great deal of thought, Mayor Flourens said, 'You present your case very well, M'sieur Hawke, and I am a reasonable man who believes the law must be respected – in both our countries. Therefore, in the greater interests of law and order, I will have this man kept in my cells, here in Roscoff, until you arrange for a boat to return him to England.'

Having reached his decision, Flourens turned his attention to Talwyn, who had suffered a cut and bruised knee. 'I thank you for the part you have played in arresting this man, mademoiselle. You are very brave.'

'You forget, I have a very personal interest in seeing him convicted,' Talwyn replied.

'Of course – and your father would be very proud of you.'

64

Amos had already explained to Gabrielle that if Pasco was captured quickly and returned to Cornwall straight away, he and his brother could be tried at the autumn Assizes, to be held at Bodmin in less than a fortnight.

As a result, a small but fast-sailing sloop belonging to Gabrielle and Doniert was ready to set sail with the prisoner soon after noon that same day. Escorted by six *gendarmes*, Pasco was taken to the ship heavily fettered at ankles and wrists, his ability to walk restricted to a laborious shuffle.

On the sloop he was taken below deck and a further chain added to his already weighty adornments. Passed around the footing of the mast, both ends of the addition were padlocked to the ankle chain.

Pasco attempted to persuade Amos to remove the fetters about his wrists, complaining that the weight of the chain was causing great pain in his wounded arm, and adding that he was likely to lose the limb unless it was properly cared for.

Amos was unsympathetic. 'I don't think you need worry too much about it, Pasco. You'll be hanged before you reach that stage.' Leaving the tethered man mouthing obscenities, Amos went up on deck.

As the crew prepared the ship for leaving harbour, Doniert came on board with Gabrielle. Amos thought they had come to see him and Talwyn off on their voyage, but much to his surprise – and delight – Doniert said he was coming to Cornwall with them to tell magistrate Sir Joseph Sawle all he knew about the murder of Edward Kernow and the deaths of the Wheal Phoenix miners.

'Thank you, Pa. It means that Hannibal and Pasco are going to get what they have deserved for very many years . . . but what eventually persuaded you to do it?'

'I really don't have any choice,' Doniert said. 'It is obviously very important to you and your career to see the Daveys convicted, and I realise the evidence I can give is crucial if Pasco is to be punished for the murder of Edward Kernow. Having met Talwyn I don't think I could live with myself if I didn't help to convict her father's killer. I spent a great deal of time discussing it with Gabrielle last night. She said she would not try to influence me either way, but trusted me to do what I know in my heart needs to be done.'

Talwyn had been listening, and now she came to Doniert and said a heartfelt 'Thank you', accompanying her words with a hug and a kiss. As she went off to repeat her actions with Gabrielle, Amos asked his father, 'Is Gabrielle coming to Cornwall with us?'

413

'No. I will return to her once I have given my statement to Sir Joseph, but Gabrielle will probably come to Cornwall with me for the trial.'

The Frenchwoman's farewell to Amos and Talwyn was an emotional one and she declared that meeting Amos had been one of the happiest moments of her life, adding that the occasion had been enhanced by the presence of Talwyn. She hoped they would all meet again very soon and declared she could not remember when she had experienced a more exciting two days.

Gabrielle remained on the quayside until the ship had passed from view – but the excitement was not over for those on board.

The sloop was making for the Cornish port of Fowey, where it was intended to anchor in the harbour and send word to Sir Joseph Sawle that they had Pasco on board and would keep him secured until an escort could be arranged to take him to the St Austell magistrates' court. There he would be remanded to Launceston gaol to await trial with his brother.

For the voyage, orders had been given that one of the crew was to remain with Pasco at all times and keep him under close supervision. Unfortunately, the French sailor carrying out this task during the dawn hours proved to be naïvely altruistic.

With the cliffs of Cornwall visible in the dawn light, Pasco succeeded in convincing his guard that he had a desperate need to visit the lavatory, which was situated on the upper deck, hanging over the stern.

In spite of the strict orders that had been given, the French sailor decided that no harm would be done by unfastening one side of the chain that secured Pasco to the foot of the mast and escorting him to the upper deck.

He went ahead of the prisoner up the ladder, but no sooner had they reached the deck than Pasco struck his kind-hearted escort a heavy blow with the weighty iron band around his wrist, knocking him back down the ladder. He then began shuffling and hopping his way to the sloop's gunwale with the intention of throwing himself overboard.

The sloop was entering St Austell bay and Amos, already on deck, was standing with his back to the hatchway, speaking to the helmsman, when he suddenly saw a look of consternation appear on the face of the other man. Swinging round, he saw Pasco attempting to lift his fettered legs on to the gunwale. Letting out a shout, Amos sprinted towards him.

He was still a few paces away when the chained man succeeded in his efforts and, clinging to the rigging to regain his balance, turned his head towards Amos, and gave a shout of triumph.

In a moment of anguish, Amos realised that if he jumped at Pasco in a bid to stop him, he would either only succeed in knocking him into the sea, or go over with him – but then he saw the chain which trailed across the deck from his fettered ankles.

At the very moment that Pasco released his hold and began falling forward into the sea, Amos pounced upon the chain. While Pasco was actually in mid-air between ship and sea, he succeeded in putting a quick turn of the chain about a brass cleat fitted to the gunwale to secure berthing ropes when the ship was docked.

The jerk when the chain tautened almost pulled Amos's arms from their sockets, but he succeeded in maintaining his grip and a moment later had taken a second turn around the cleat.

In the meantime, Pasco had crashed heavily against the sloop's side, but his cry of pain and frustration was cut off as the ship rolled in the slight swell coming off the English Channel and the top half of his body dipped under the water. For the next few minutes, as Amos shouted for help, at the same time ensuring that the chain did not slip, Pasco was alternately dipping into the sea and dangling in the air.

When help arrived from crew members, Amos was in no hurry to have the would-be escaper pulled back on board. Not until he believed the half-drowned man to be incapable of violence did he allow him to be hauled back over the gunwale and taken below decks to be secured to the mast once more and left to dry off and recover as best he could.

While the ship's captain berated the sailor who had so foolishly released Pasco, Doniert said to his son, 'Perhaps it might have been better for everyone had we simply left him to drown – to be tried by a court higher than any we have here on earth.'

'He will be tried by that court in due course,' Amos replied, 'but not until people in Cornwall have seen justice done – on earth. People like Talwyn and her mother.'

He added the last few words as Talwyn emerged from below deck and smiled to see the coast of Cornwall so close. Turning to share her smile with father and son, she said, 'Good morning! I hope you both slept as soundly as I did. It was good to know that all the excitement of the past few days had been left behind us.'

65

Pasco was taken ashore that afternoon and once more Sir Joseph Sawle had called upon the army to provide a mounted escort to take him to St Austell and set a guard around the court while he appeared before the magistrates.

In the event there was no trouble and the same soldiers escorted Pasco on his journey to Launceston castle gaol in a covered van. Meanwhile Talwyn was sent home to the Penrice cottage in Sir Joseph Sawle's carriage while Doniert prepared to make a statement to the magistrate about the incident that had occurred between the Wheal Phoenix miners and Hannibal and Pasco and another describing what he had witnessed on the night Edward Kernow was murdered.

Colonel Gilbert was in the office while the clerk was being found who would write down the statement. He had been confirmed as Cornwall's first chief constable and was now spending a few days with the senior magistrate, learning something of the processes of the law.

While they waited, Amos gave the two men details of the tracing and arrest of Pasco, and of his failed suicide attempt on the voyage back. Aware of the difficult situation in which Talwyn might find herself after the destruction of the Charlestown school, he made much of her part as translator in France – and told of her physical help in the arrest of Pasco when he escaped from the Roscoff house.

'She is quite an exceptional girl,' Sir Joseph commented. 'My brother and sister-in-law valued her highly – you are aware she learned French when she worked as a governess to their children in France?'

'Yes, and she learned well,' Amos said. 'She was invaluable. I couldn't have succeeded without her.'

'Oh, I am quite certain you would have found a way,' Colonel Gilbert put in, 'but would you say this has probably been the most difficult case you have ever investigated?'

Amos thought before replying. 'I don't think Scotland Yard has ever been asked to deal with a murder case on this scale before and it was made more difficult when Pasco Davey fled to France. Extradition would have been lengthy, frustrating – and by no means certain.' He bit back a smile, remembering the showdown between himself and Mayor Flourens. 'Fortunately, we were able to settle the matter at a purely local level when Pasco was captured, but I did promise the mayor of Roscoff that a letter would be sent at governmental level praising his co-operation in helping us to capture a very dangerous criminal.'

'I will ensure that is done,' Sir Joseph said.

Colonel Gilbert asked Amos what he would do now Pasco was in custody.

'My first task will be to write a full report on my actions during the past few days, then I will set about collating the evidence for prosecuting Hannibal and Pasco, ensuring we are able to prove every murder with which they are charged.'

'May I sit in on as much of your work as I can?' Colonel Gilbert asked. 'As chief constable of a force that is being built up from nothing, I feel such an experience would be invaluable.'

'Of course. I will be delighted to help in any way I can.' The court clerk entered the office at that moment and Amos added, 'I think we might begin with the statement from my father about the incident in the Bodmin Moor mines . . .'

After Doniert had made his statements, Amos asked Sir Joseph about the raid on the Wheal Notter adit.

'It was highly successful,' the magistrate replied. 'The Excise officers took possession of a huge quantity of contraband goods. It was taken to Looe and not to Fowey, and as the raid was carried out without the senior officer at Fowey being informed, he will no doubt be quivering in his shoes.' He was referring to Doniert's statement about the presence of that officer when Edward Kernow was murdered. 'The raiding party also climbed down the ventilation shaft where you saw what you thought might be a body.'

'Was it?'

Sir Joseph Sawle nodded. 'I am afraid so. It was identified as one of the four men working with the Davey brothers when they broke through into the Wheal Phoenix. A man named Tholly Hicks.' He turned to Doniert. 'You and William Arthur are the only two witnesses left alive.'

'We wouldn't have been had we agreed to meet Pasco when he wanted us to,' Doniert said grimly. 'Where is Cap'n Billy now?'

'I don't have an address for him, but he is due to report to the magistrates' court tomorrow if you wish to speak to him.'

'I hope to be back in Roscoff by then,' Doniert said. 'It's a pity, though – I would like to have had a word with him. I think I might have been able to persuade him to back up my evidence about the fight.'

'He has been too scared to say anything against the Daveys,' Amos said, 'and in view of the discovery of the body of Tholly Hicks he had very good reason, but he did tell me that it was Pasco who set fire to the school. When he knows that Hannibal and Pasco are being held in Launceston gaol and that there is a watertight case against them, he might be prepared to help us more. I am hoping that whoever witnessed the killing of the Excise officers might come forward too, especially if we can promise them immunity from prosecution for smuggling.'

'It is certainly worth a try,' agreed Sir Joseph, 'but where can we make a start on finding such witnesses?'

'I have one or two ideas on that,' Amos said, 'but first I will see my father safely back on board his ship.

I promised my stepmother I would send him home quickly – and he is going to be an important witness for us.'

As they left the magistrates' court, Doniert asked Amos, 'Do you really think you will be able to find men willing to tell you what they know about the killing of the Excise officers?'

'I intend to try,' came the reply, 'and I think I know just the man to spread the word about what will happen if they don't. I told Sir Joseph that I would take you straight back to your ship, but I think you and I will call in together and speak to him first. It shouldn't take more than a few minutes. First we will go to the livery stable at the White Hart and hire a couple of horses.'

The face of Thomas Stephens, landlord of the Rashleigh Arms, displayed sheer terror when Amos and his father walked through the door of the Charlestown inn.

Looking hurriedly around the bar room, he tried to usher them into the saloon at the back, but Amos resisted, saying, 'What's the matter, landlord? Are you frightened of being seen in the company of law-abiding men?'

'I'm not afraid for *me*,' the landlord replied, 'but if Pasco Davey gets to hear you're both here there will be far more trouble inside my inn than there was when you arrested Hannibal.'

'You have no need to concern yourself any more with what either of the Davey brothers thinks,' Amos said. 'Pasco is on his way to Launceston gaol to join his brother. The next time either of them sees daylight will be when he steps on to the scaffold in front of Bodmin gaol.'

'You've arrested Pasco?' Stephens's face registered disbelief. 'But he went to . . .'

Aware that he had been about to disclose more knowledge than he had a right to possess, the landlord ceased talking abruptly and Amos said, 'Perhaps we should go into the back after all . . . it might refresh that defective memory of yours.'

When they entered the back room, with its view of the yard cluttered with barrels and litter, Amos prompted the Rashleigh Arms landlord. 'Just now you were about to tell us that Pasco had gone to France – and you are quite right. So too did I, and I brought him back to Cornwall today, to be charged with a number of murders, including that of Edward Kernow, killed right here, in the back yard of the Rashleigh Arms, where you keep that "special" brandy to give to privileged customers. It's a murder you once told me you knew nothing about – and didn't want to know. I've no doubt that just now you are wishing more than ever that it was the truth – but it isn't, Mr Stephens, is it? In fact, I possess written evidence that you are an accessory after the fact to murder, a crime for which I could arrest you here and now with a promise that you would spend the next five years in prison – unless, of course, the judge, in his wisdom, decided to transport you for even longer.'

It was warm inside the small back room, but the perspiration that broke out on Thomas Stephens's forehead had nothing to do with the temperature. 'You wouldn't do that to me, Mr Hawke . . . I've always done

423

my best for you and looked after you well when you were staying here . . .'

'You have lied to me from the very first time I met you – about everything,' Amos retorted. 'You said you didn't know who Hannibal Davey was when I asked you about him; you never knew my father – or where he was; you knew nothing about the murder of Edward Kernow . . . Need I continue?'

'If I lied, it was because I was scared of the Davey brothers . . . I was frightened for you, too, of what they would have done if they'd heard you was asking too many questions . . . and that's the truth, I swear it.'

'I don't think your word is worth the breath you are wasting, Mr Stephens – and *that's* the truth.'

'What . . . what are you going to do? You're not going to arrest me? I've got a young family who depend on me . . .'

'More than one of the Daveys' victims left young families behind them,' Amos retorted, 'but that doesn't seem to have bothered your conscience too much.' He paused to look scornfully at the quivering landlord. 'However, I'm going to give you an opportunity to redeem yourself.'

'Anything, Mr Hawke . . . I'll do anything . . . I swear I will!'

'Good! The first thing you can do is write a list of all the smugglers you can name and give it to me next time I come this way. Then you can pass the word among them that I hold such a list and intend having the Davey brothers convicted of killing two Excise officers. I want the men who witnessed their killing to come forward.

You can tell them I am not interested in having anyone brought before a judge on smuggling charges; I am in Cornwall to solve murders. I will promise the men that, unless they were actually involved in the murder, anyone who comes forward will not be prosecuted for smuggling, and when the Daveys are convicted I will personally burn the list. However, if no one comes forward in time to have the Daveys charged with the murder of the Excise officers before the next Assizes, I will hand the list to Sir Joseph Sawle and the new chief constable of Cornwall and action *will* be taken against all of them. I don't need to remind you that your name will be on that list – not only for handling contraband goods, but also as an accessory to murder.'

'I'll do it,' Stephens said fervently, adding, 'I'll do everything you ask . . . no, I'll do more. I can give you the name right now of a man who saw one of the Excise men being killed. You know him too, Doniert. It's Tholly Hicks, who used to work with you up on the moor.'

Amos said grimly, 'You'll need to do better than that, Stephens. The body of Tholly Hicks has been recovered from a ventilation shaft up at Wheal Notter, the disused mine where the Daveys stored their contraband.'

66

After seeing his father safely on board the French sloop at Fowey, Amos waited until the vessel raised anchor and set sail before he rode back to St Austell, leading the horse that he had hired for his father. When the horses had been returned to the stables he set off to walk back to Penrice. He was longing to see Talwyn again.

However, when he reached the cottage it was Maisie and not her daughter who opened the door to welcome him – and she was effusive in her greeting. Throwing her arms about his neck, she cried, 'Amos! Welcome home. Talwyn has told me what went on in France and how you have captured the man who killed Edward. I am proud of you . . . so *very* proud of you.'

Embarrassed, Amos said, 'Thank you, but I was doing what I am paid to do. It is Talwyn you should be proud of – as I am. Had it not been for her Pasco Davey might have made good his escape and we would still be searching for him. Where is she now . . . is she all right?'

'She is fine, Amos – the happiest I have seen her since her father's death.'

'That's good,' said Amos. 'I think the part she played in capturing his killer has helped.'

'You could be right,' Maisie agreed, adding enigmatically, 'but I believe something more than that has happened to set her to rights once again.'

'Where is she now? I would have thought she would want to sit back and relax after the excitement of all that happened in France.'

'I think that is what she intended to do, but one of the servants from the manor called about half an hour ago to say that Sir Joseph would like her to call on him, so she got ready and went there straight away.'

'I wonder what he wanted?'

'I hoped you might be able to tell me. Never mind, we will know soon enough. In the meantime I will make you a cup of tea and call Laura down from her room. She has been working on her studies since returning from working on the new school. You can tell us all about your father, his French wife and his new life in France.'

Amos was out in the stable, grooming his horse, and Laura had returned to her room when, more than an hour later, Talwyn returned to the cottage in a happy mood. Leaving his task to be completed later, Amos entered the house to learn what Sir Joseph had wanted with her.

In reply to her mother's question, she said, 'Sir Joseph was with Colonel Gilbert, the man who has been appointed chief constable of Cornwall's new police force. Colonel Gilbert asked me a great many questions about France and what we did there. He seemed quite amused when I told him how Amos "persuaded" the Roscoff mayor to let us bring Pasco Davey back to stand trial in Cornwall. He said Amos showed considerable tact and initiative.'

'Amos and I were talking about Colonel Gilbert a while ago,' Maisie said. 'He says the colonel is new to police work and has a lot to learn but is aware of his lack of knowledge and anxious to remedy it. Amos believes he will prove an outstanding chief constable. What did Sir Joseph have to say about the school?'

It was a question that had been worrying Maisie greatly since the night of the fire.

'He visited the store that is to be the new school on his way back from the magistrates' court today,' Talwyn said. 'He says Andrew and Laura have been working so hard he believes it will be ready to take pupils in days, rather than weeks, but, whatever happens, he says we are not to worry ourselves about anything. He will ensure we do not lose any more than we already have as a result of the actions of a madman.'

'That's easy enough for him to say,' Maisie declared, 'but I won't be happy until the school is up and running and we have money coming into the house once more.'

'Well, if we aren't teaching pupils again very soon, it certainly won't be the fault of Andrew or Laura,' Talwyn said. 'I looked in on the old storeroom myself on my way home earlier today, and they have worked wonders.'

'They make a very good team,' Maisie said pointedly, 'and I am not talking only about getting a schoolroom ready, either.'

Talwyn looked disapproving. 'I know what you mean, Mother, but you really must be careful of what you say about them. Andrew is a teacher and Laura a pupil – and Amos thinks she is still no more than a child.'

Maisie looked pityingly at Amos. 'I would have expected you to know better than that, Amos. You should listen to Talwyn. As a schoolteacher she knows a little more about the ways of young women than you . . . and that is what Laura is. Did you know that it will soon be her seventeenth birthday?'

'No, I didn't know,' Amos confessed, 'but seventeen is no age.'

Maisie sniffed disdainfully. 'There you go, proving your lack of knowledge of the girls Talwyn teaches. She could give you the names of half a dozen young women who were married and expecting when they were Laura's age . . . and a half-dozen more who were expecting *without* the blessing of the Church. Hopefully, Laura will fall into neither category, but only a fool would fail to recognise that there is more than a spark of something between her and Andrew. However, I have no intention of discouraging it. They could both do far worse.'

That evening Amos was in his room, working on the report he would be sending to the Metropolitan Police commissioner, when he was disturbed by a knock at the door. It was Talwyn. Apologising for interrupting his work, she said, 'You have a caller, Amos. I haven't asked him into the house because . . . well, he is not the most savoury of characters.'

'Did he give you a name?' Amos asked as he used a blotting case to dry the ink on his report before placing it carefully in a drawer.

'No, he would not give a name, but just said that he wanted to speak to "Mr Hawke" . . . and, Amos, I would rather he did not come inside the cottage. It would be difficult to clear the smell afterwards. I don't think he can wash very often.'

'It sounds like Cap'n Billy,' Amos said. 'All right, Talwyn, I'll put on my coat and walk outside with him.'

It *was* Captain Billy. Waiting outside the gate to the cottage, he seemed edgy. When Amos joined him, he said, with no greeting, 'Word is that you've got Pasco locked up as well as Hannibal . . . is it true?'

'Perfectly true, Billy. He appeared before a magistrate today and an army escort took him to Launceston gaol. He'll stay there until the Assizes are held in Bodmin, the week after next. Then they will both be tried – and hanged – for murder.'

Captain Billy seemed to relax at confirmation of Pasco's arrest, but he remained silent for many moments before saying, 'Whose murders are they being charged with?'

'So far it's Detective Inspector Carpenter, Edward Kernow and the two Wheal Phoenix miners. Before they come to trial I want to get enough evidence to also have them charged with the murders of two Excise officers. I don't doubt they are responsible for the deaths of two or three more men, but won't be able to prove it ... certainly not before they come up for trial.'

'Who's giving evidence about the killing of the Wheal Phoenix miners?'

'My pa,' Amos replied. 'He's already given a statement to Sir Joseph Sawle, telling what he knows.'

'So you won't need me to give evidence against them now?'

'Not unless you know anything about the killing of the Excise officers ... although if you *did* want to say what you know of the killing of the Wheal Phoenix miners Sir Joseph would accept a statement from you – but you'd need to clean yourself up before he would allow you in his office. You stink as though you've been sleeping in a pigsty!'

Ignoring Amos's comment, Captain Billy asked, 'What's happening about all those of us who've been involved in smuggling with Pasco and Hannibal in the past?'

'We are getting names from various sources at the moment,' Amos replied. Aware that he was anticipating the fact, he added, 'When the list is complete Sir Joseph will strike off those who have helped convict the Daveys. For the rest? It will be up to him. He might decide to take no action, or he might hand the list over to the new chief constable, who would no doubt order his policemen to arrest them and bring them before the courts.'

This was largely a bluff on Amos's part. The new Cornwall Constabulary would need to rely very heavily on public support for any success it achieved, especially in the early days of its formation. Chief Constable Gilbert would not risk alienating the Cornish people by bringing prosecutions against a great many of them for taking part in something that had for long been regarded as part of their heritage. But it would do no harm for Captain Billy to believe otherwise – and the ruse had immediate results.

'Are you quite certain Pasco and Hannibal are never going to be set free?' he asked.

'Positive. Whatever else happens, there is enough evidence to ensure that they hang for the murders of Detective Inspector Carpenter and Edward Kernow. There can be no doubt of that, but what I want to be able to do is clear up the other murders while I am in Cornwall.'

Captain Billy arrived at a decision. 'All right. I'll get myself cleaned up tomorrow morning. If I come here will *you* take me to see Sir Joseph Sawle?'

'If that's what you want.'

'It is.' Captain Billy spoke as though a weight had been lifted from his mind – but his old ways had not entirely deserted him. 'There's just one thing, Mr Hawke. I can clean myself up, but I've got no other clothes to wear . . .'

With a resigned sigh, Amos reached inside a pocket. Placing two half-crowns into the grubby outstretched hand of the other man, he said, 'Here's five shillings to buy yourself something respectable to wear tomorrow and keep respectable for court. If you let me down and spend it on drink I will personally see that you are arrested and put into a cell with Pasco – do you understand me?'

'I do, Mr Hawke . . . I do.' Backing away, he added, 'I won't let you down. In fact, when we meet tomorrow morning I'll give you the names of a couple of men who know all about the killing of those Excise officers. Now you've caught Pasco I think they'll be relieved to talk to someone about it.'

With that, Captain Billy turned and disappeared into the darkness. Amos called after him to ask more about the men he had mentioned, but received no reply. He went back into the cottage carrying with him the hope that the unpredictable ex-miner would keep his word.

67

When Captain Billy called at the Penrice cottage the next morning, Talwyn failed to recognise him. He had managed to bath, shave and fit himself out with clothes that, while not new, were of a quality that should have been hard to find for five shillings.

When Amos commented on the fact, Captain Billy said, 'That's quite true, Mr Hawke, but it's your reputation and not your money I have to thank for them.' When called upon to explain himself, he said that, at a loss to know where he could clean himself up, he had approached Thomas Stephens at the Rashleigh Arms, knowing that the inn possessed a bathroom.

He had offered to pay for the privilege of using it, but when he explained the reason for his new-found need for cleanliness, Stephens had not only allowed him free use of the bathroom but found him clothes. They came from the store where he kept items left behind by hotel guests. Many had simply forgotten to take them with them at the end of their stay. Others had forfeited them when unable to settle a bill.

When Amos asked why the landlord had suddenly decided to become philanthropic, Captain Billy said, 'He's really frightened of what you might say to Sir Joseph Sawle about him. He is desperately keen to have you think well of him.'

'He probably has more reason than most to fear what action I might take against him,' Amos commented. 'He has been less than honest with me . . . but then, so have you – and at the moment I am particularly interested in what you know about the murder of the Excise officers.'

'In truth, I only know what I've heard,' Captain Billy confessed, 'but I'll give you names and you can follow up what I tell you. Some time ago I was sitting down by the sea wall at Mevagissey with a jug of ale and some bread and cheese when I overheard two fishermen talking. One I recognised as Charlie Kent, who has shares in a Mevagissey boat. He was telling the man who was with him that he and his cousin, Tom Opie – who has a boatyard at Portmellon – had been landing smuggled rum from their boat somewhere along the coast for the Daveys to carry away on their mules when they were surprised by an Excise officer who happened to be patrolling that particular area. He said Pasco shot him without so much as a word being spoken. Kent was upset by it but said what could he do . . . it was the Daveys?'

'This Charlie Kent spoke openly about this in front of you, a complete stranger?' Amos was sceptical.

Captain Billy shrugged. 'I was a tramp – a nobody – sitting half drunk against the sea wall. Looking the way I was, folk don't think you've got ears, or even eyes. You ought to try it sometime – you'd be surprised at what you would learn.'

'Perhaps I will. But let me make a note of those names and then we'll go and see Sir Joseph. I called on him first thing this morning and he says he'll take your statement up at the manor and tell you what you'll need to do when you come to the Assizes.'

At dinner that day in the Penrice cottage, only Amos, Talwyn and Maisie sat down to the meal. Laura was staying at the Charlestown building that was to be the new schoolroom, helping Andrew with the work he was carrying out there – and sharing the food he had brought from his home.

Talwyn had been working there too, but had returned home for the midday meal. 'How did you get on with Sir Joseph this morning?' she asked Amos. 'Is he pleased with the way your investigations are coming along?'

'Very pleased, and with good reason. This afternoon I am going to speak to a Mevagissey fisherman named Kent. If he tells me what I want to hear, we should be able to tie the Daveys in with the killing of at least one of the Excise officers.'

'Would that be Charles Kent you're going to visit?' Talwyn asked.

When Amos confirmed that it was, she offered to go with him, saying she had met Kent, whose son and daughter were both pupils at the Charlestown school.

436

It would be a good opportunity to tell him about the temporary school that would soon be ready to take pupils and ask him to pass the news to the parents of three other Mevagissey pupils who had attended the Charlestown school.

Amos had intended going to Mevagissey on his horse, but he was by no means averse to walking to the fishing village in Talwyn's company. As they walked along the lane together, Talwyn commented, 'By this time in a fortnight the Assizes will be over and you will probably be back in London.'

'I'll be here for the execution and staying on for a day or two afterwards to tie up any loose ends,' Amos said, 'but you're right: it won't be very long before I am on my way.'

'You don't think there is any chance of the Daveys being found not guilty?'

'I am leaving nothing to chance. If this man Kent and his cousin agree to give evidence against the Daveys we will go to the Assizes with proof that they have murdered five or six men – and during the course of the hearing we should be able to hint at almost as many again. Even if the judge won't allow such evidence to be taken into consideration I can't imagine any jury in the land finding them innocent.'

Despite her implacable determination to see her father's killers brought to justice, Talwyn shuddered at the thought of what a guilty verdict would inevitably mean for the two brothers. Trying to dismiss such thoughts from her mind, she said, 'My mother is going to miss having you around the house.'

'Only your mother?' Amos asked, only half teasingly.

'No,' Talwyn replied. 'I know Laura will miss you too, although she has other things to think about at the moment.'

'So it will only be your mother and Laura who miss me?' Amos persisted; then, aware that he was trying to persuade her to admit to something she might not be feeling, he tried to turn it into a joke by saying, 'I shall be quite disappointed if I am not missed by Skellum too.'

'I am afraid that Skellum would only miss something that was lacking in his feeding bowl, but, although I know I can't compete with Skellum, *I* will miss you too.'

It was what Amos had been hoping to hear, but before he could reply an open farm cart came into view behind them, on which were a number of young people from Charlestown, many of whom had been pupils at Talwyn's school.

Singing and shouting happily, they greeted Talwyn effusively and announced that they were on their way to the autumn fair being held in Mevagissey. When they learned Amos and Talwyn were also bound for the fishing village, the occupants of the wagon insisted their teacher and her companion should join them, and for the remainder of the journey there was no opportunity for a private conversation.

68

One of the girls on the farm wagon was a friend of Charles Kent's daughter, and she saved Talwyn and Amos a great deal of time by guiding them up the zigzag path that served the occupants of the houses that clung to the harbourside cliff. The Kent family occupied one of the end houses, which had views of both sea and harbour, and it happened that both Charles Kent and his cousin Tom Opie were there with their wives and a number of friends.

Staunch teetotal Methodists, they were enjoying a cup of tea before going to the village chapel to enjoy a less raucous celebration than the one which would keep the residents of the fishing village awake until the early hours of the morning. They welcomed Talwyn and commiserated with her on the loss of her father and the destruction of the school, but they fell silent when Amos introduced himself and explained the purpose of his visit.

One of the men in the room said, 'If any one of us was to give evidence against the Davey brothers, he would never again be able to hold his head high in Mevagissey. If it wasn't for them there would have been little money coming into many of the houses here.'

'They brought sorrow as well as money into the houses of a great many good Cornish folk too,' Amos retorted. 'That of Miss Kernow for one. Hannibal and Pasco Davey epitomise the evil that the founder of your Church foresaw if smuggling continued. When I was a boy there were men still alive in Mevagissey who had heard John Wesley speak of the evil that could come from smuggling. Can you worship in his chapel and ignore his teaching? Choosing which of his lessons you will follow is nothing short of hypocrisy to my mind.'

Amos looked round the room at the men, but none would meet his eyes. Then, unexpectedly, Talwyn decided to speak.

'I have been watching you while Amos has been talking and, quite frankly, I am appalled that not one of you has spoken up to condemn two of the most evil men we have ever known in these parts. Men who have destroyed a great many lives and, by burning down the Charlestown school, might have blighted the futures of your own children. Even after they are dead, their evil is likely to continue to affect every man who worked with them unless you forget your misplaced loyalties and do something to show you want to shake off their influence once and for all ... but I will let Amos tell you what I mean by that.'

While the men and women in the room were still

looking at each other, puzzled by her words, Amos began to speak once more.

'I had a meeting with Sir Joseph Sawle this morning and we discussed the Davey brothers and various matters concerning them. We have enough evidence to hang them for the last two murders they committed, and also for the murders of two miners on Bodmin Moor which, because of false evidence given at the time, were wrongly declared by a coroner to be accidental deaths. Some of you might say that as the Daveys are going to hang anyway, that should be enough. Sir Joseph doesn't agree – and neither do I. The families of the other murdered men – men like the two Excise officers, whom at least two of you in this room saw killed by the Daveys – need to see justice done. Sir Joseph wants these murders cleared up before he hands over many of his duties to the new chief constable and his county constabulary. There are a number of other unexplained deaths for which I believe the Daveys are responsible and I would like to see the minds of their relatives put at rest.'

One of the women, bolder than the others, asked, 'Why should our men speak up and risk getting themselves into trouble and being cold-shouldered by all their friends just to please you and Sir Joseph Sawle? If the Davey brothers hang then I say that should be an end to it. Let sleeping dogs lie, my mother used to be fond of saying.'

'I think Sir Joseph is willing to do that,' Amos declared, 'but only when he has cleared up these other murders. He is compiling a list of all those men who have been involved in smuggling with the Daveys – and there are a great many local men involved, as I am sure you know. He has already raided the mine adit where the Daveys stored their contraband and at this very moment some of the Excise officers they corrupted are being arrested. Many of those taken into custody are eager to give him names and details of landings in order to save their own skins. Now, Sir Joseph has agreed that if those men who witnessed the murders of the Excise officers come forward, he is prepared to file the list of those involved in smuggling and treat it as just another chapter in Cornwall's colourful history. But if they don't come forward, he intends to hand the list to the new chief constable and order him to bring every man named on it to court. The prison hulks and transports will be crowded with Cornishmen and leave a great many empty places at the tables of homes in Mevagissey. No doubt many of those arrested will be willing to name the men who were with the Daveys when the Excise men were killed in exchange for lighter sentences. By not coming forward of their own free will, the men they name will have shown themselves to be accessories to the murders and are likely to be charged with murder themselves.'

Pausing, Amos looked around the table to see what impact his words had made on his uneasy audience. 'So, you see, it's not a matter of telling tales on two already doomed men, but of sparing your families a great deal of grief. Spread the word among your friends, and warn them that the time when certain authorities turned a blind eye to night-trading has gone for ever. Those of you who witnessed killings should tell me or

Sir Joseph about it, either at the magistrates' court in St Austell or at Penrice manor – but do it quickly. The Daveys appear at the Assize Court the week after next and once the session begins it will be too late. Sir Joseph's list will have been handed to the chief constable.'

'What about your father . . . will he be on Sir Joseph Sawle's list?'

The question came from a man whose face conjured up memories from Amos's childhood. When Amos said 'No' there was an outbreak of derision. Raising his voice in order to be heard above the outcry, Amos said, 'My father's name will not be on the list because he has already given a statement to Sir Joseph and will be standing up in court to tell what he knows of three of the murders committed by the Daveys.'

When the room fell silent, Amos said, 'Think about what I have said – all of you – and enjoy your autumn fair.'

69

The road from Mevagissey climbed a steep hill and Talwyn and Amos had little breath to spare for talking until they reached the top and paused to admire the panorama of blue sea and dramatic Cornish coastline. The cliffs stretched as far as the eye could see until dissipated by distance and an ethereal heat haze.

'Do you think anything I said back there will produce results?' Amos asked as they stood side by side gazing at the view, arms resting on the top of a five-bar gate.

'I don't believe that everything you said fell upon receptive ears,' Talwyn replied, 'but the women in particular were taking everything in. They probably realise more than the men what it would mean to a family to lose the breadwinner. I don't think they will mince their words when they discuss the situation with their husbands.'

Leaving the gate, but not the view, behind, they

resumed their journey homeward and Amos said, 'Wasn't there something we were discussing before the cartload of young people from Charlestown caught up with us?'

Deliberately choosing to misunderstand him, Talwyn replied, 'You mean about Laura having other things on her mind?'

'No, I don't mean that. When the wagon appeared you had just said that you will miss me when I go back to London.'

'That's right, and so I will – in company with Laura, my mother . . . and Skellum.'

The joke was lost on Amos, who had more serious matters on his mind. 'I will miss you too, Talwyn, but we don't have to say goodbye. You could come to London with me and . . . and see if you like it there.'

'Why? Why would I want to come to London? Do you mean I should take a holiday there?'

'No. I thought that if you liked it you might stay there.'

Amos was floundering and he was aware of it. Usually so positive in his approach to things that mattered, he felt uncharacteristically tongue-tied.

'Why should I want to move to London? I like it here in Cornwall, where I have a school to rebuild – and there's my mother. I couldn't leave her alone.'

'She wouldn't be alone,' Amos pointed out. 'She has Laura.'

'Not for long,' Talwyn said. 'While we were away in France, Andrew went up on to the moor to ask Laura's father for her hand in marriage.'

Talwyn's revelation served to jolt Amos from his train of thought. 'Andrew wants to marry Laura? But . . . she's far too young to marry – whatever your mother might think.'

'No, Amos.' Talwyn was amused by his reaction, but annoyed that he had allowed himself to be diverted from a subject she was anxious to pursue – even though she had introduced the diversion herself. 'It is what I thought when I was first told the news, but, as my mother pointed out, Laura will be seventeen next week. She is a young woman, and one who is mature for her age. If she decides she really wants to marry Andrew, then that is what she will do.'

'And has she decided she wants to marry him?'

'Ah! I do not know the answer to that – and neither does Andrew. He only told me this morning what he was planning to do. He has said nothing to Laura yet. I believe she *will* agree to marry him, but she has spent so much time telling people – you especially – that her aim in life is to become one of Florence Nightingale's nurses, she might be embarrassed to say she has changed her mind.'

'She mustn't be concerned about what I think,' Amos declared. 'She has to decide her future for herself. What are your views on such a marriage?'

'I have said many times that she could become an excellent teacher, and a husband and wife teaching team is a very good arrangement. Mind you, I don't doubt she would make an excellent nurse too. She must let her heart and not her head dictate where her future lies.'

'Is that what you would do, Talwyn?'

Talwyn was aware that she had walked into a trap that she had set for herself. 'I think I *probably* would,' she replied cautiously, 'but, of course, one's duty to others has to be considered – and I would need to know that the man I planned to marry really loved me and did not merely believe I might be a competent and compliant person with whom to share his life.'

Amos digested this before saying, 'You are certainly competent in whatever you do, Talwyn, but I don't think anyone would dare to refer to you as "compliant". You are far too strong-minded. That is one of your characteristics that I particularly admire.'

'*You* might,' Talwyn said, 'but it is not something that I would expect a prospective husband to view with complaisance.'

'Is that your way of telling me that I am not to consider myself a prospective husband?'

Talwyn realised that she had walked into a second trap of her own setting. 'No . . . I mean . . . Amos, where is all this foolish talk leading? You know I can't possibly leave my mother, or the school in its present state . . . besides which, I am not certain I could be happy in London – and that is where you have your career. Besides, although we do get on well now, we can hardly say we have had a *romantic* relationship. I may sound like an immature young girl, but that *is* something I think is important in a marriage. I—'

Interrupting her, Amos said, 'What you actually said was that you needed to know that the man you married really loved you. Well, I have thought about that. I believe I actually fell in love with you when I saw you

447

sitting on the muddy ground by the entrance to Penrice, surrounded by groceries and broken eggs, warding off an over-enthusiastic dog and telling me what you thought of me.'

Despite the mixture of confusion and elation that she felt at his revelation, Talwyn could not help smiling when she said, 'I don't think romance was exactly what was on my mind on that day, Amos, but even if I feel differently now – and I *do* – that doesn't alter the situation regarding my mother, the school – or your work.'

'True,' agreed Amos, 'but as you said about Laura, the heart and not the head should dictate the future. We will think of something. In the meantime, come here and let me convince you that I really do love you . . .'

70

The days between his visit to Mevagissey and the commencement of the Assizes were busy ones for Amos. Contrary to his expectations, but true to Talwyn's prediction, the wives of the fishermen to whom he had spoken on that day succeeded in convincing their menfolk that, for the sake of their families, they had no alternative but to tell Sir Joseph Sawle all they knew about the Davey brothers.

Word of what was happening – and the consequences of saying nothing – spread quickly. The number of men who came forward to admit having worked with the Davey brothers astounded the senior magistrate. He had once told Detective Inspector Carpenter that smuggling in Cornwall had ended many years before, but had later been forced to admit he was wrong. Nevertheless, he had not realised quite *how* wrong he had been.

So many men made their way to Penrice manor that

when the Cornish baronet needed to spend time in St Austell on magisterial duties, he insisted that Amos come to the manor house during his absence and interview the ex-smugglers who called there.

Although all the men wished to have it placed on record that they had co-operated with the authorities, most did not possess first-hand evidence of the more murderous of the Daveys' activities, much of their evidence being hearsay. However, even this was of value because it gave Amos the names of some ex-smugglers who had not come forward for fear of being implicated in the murders.

As a result, long before the Assizes began Amos had taken statements from eyewitnesses to the murders of both the Excise officers and, in addition, confirmed that the miners found dead at the Cheesewring quarry and in the ventilation shaft at the Wheal Notter had also died at the hands of the two brothers.

When Pasco and Hannibal Davey stood in the dock at Bodmin Assizes, it would be to answer to charges of murdering no fewer than eight men – and there were unsubstantiated rumours of at least two more. The trial would create a sensation throughout the country.

Colonel Gilbert, Cornwall's chief constable, was delighted with the results that had been achieved, but he would have been happier had he been allowed to prosecute the many self-confessed smugglers who had come forward. However, he accepted the opinion of Sir Joseph and Amos that to do so would not only alienate a great many of Cornwall's residents, upon whom the success of his new police force would largely depend, but would also mean breaking the promises given to them by Amos and the senior magistrate.

Although his days were busy, Amos found enough time during the evenings to take long walks with Talwyn, and would often be at Charlestown to meet her when the day's work on the temporary Charlestown school ended. It was apparent to everyone who knew them that romance had blossomed between the pair – and Maisie was delighted.

When she and Talwyn found themselves alone in the cottage after a midday meal, she said, 'You can't imagine how happy it makes me to see you and Amos getting along so well. I always knew you two would find you had a great deal in common once you got to know each other.'

'We always made a good team when we worked together,' Talwyn replied, 'but that doesn't necessarily mean we were destined to be partners for life.'

'Being a good team is a sound enough beginning,' Maisie replied. 'Many happy marriages have been founded on far less, so if he asks you to marry him, don't turn him down because you think the romance you are looking for is lacking. That very often doesn't show itself until you've been married for a year or two, when you suddenly realise that it's caught up on you without your noticing.'

'He has already asked me to marry him.' Talwyn spoke with an apparent nonchalance that left Maisie staring at her daughter open-mouthed.

'He's asked you . . . ? What did you tell him?'

451

'I told him I didn't think marriage was possible,' Talwyn replied, 'and it isn't. All my commitments are here in Cornwall, while his work is in London – and I just wouldn't be happy there.'

Maisie looked at her daughter suspiciously, 'By "commitments", do you mean me?'

'It's not only you,' Talwyn said, 'although you are very important to me. I would also be letting Sir Joseph down if I left just when we are about to open the new school in Charlestown – and Sir Joseph has been very generous to this family.'

'Amos has more than repaid Sir Joseph for any debt that's owed to him,' Maisie retorted. 'When the Davey brothers are convicted, Amos will have rid Cornwall of the two most bloodthirsty killers it has ever known, as well as bringing smuggling to an end once and for all. If anyone is owed anything it is Amos. He ought to be given a medal for what he's done – and he would be the first to say he could not have arrested Pasco Davey without your help. Indeed, he has said so many times.'

'That's as may be,' Talwyn said enigmatically, 'but Amos knows how I feel about leaving Cornwall and he says he will not try to force me to do anything I really don't want to do.'

She did not add that the well-being of her mother was the major stumbling block in the way of marriage between herself and Amos. She would not leave Maisie to fend for herself so soon after the tragic death of Edward Kernow.

In a bid to change the subject, she said, 'Did you know that Andrew has asked Laura to marry him?'

452

'Yes. She told me last night, when you were out with Amos. It comes as no surprise, Andrew had already told me what he intended to do and said he had spoken to you about it.'

'Did Laura tell you what her answer would be?'

Maisie shook her head. 'She has told Andrew that she needs time to think about it, but I think she has already done all the thinking that needs doing and her answer will be an emphatic yes. But she wants to tell Amos first and explain that she has decided to pursue a career as a teacher instead of in nursing. She is particularly concerned about what he will say, in view of all the support he has given her because he believed she would one day become a nurse.'

'Amos is already aware of the romance between Laura and Andrew,' Talwyn said. 'He is delighted for both of them, so we will probably soon be celebrating their wedding.'

'Not quite yet. Laura has said she does not want to be married until her eighteenth birthday, by which time she feels she will know enough to seriously contemplate becoming a teacher.' Giving her daughter a calculating look, Maisie added, 'So if you change your mind about marrying Amos you can cross me off your list of reasons for not being able to say yes. I will have Laura's help and support for at least another year.'

71

Two days before the trial of the Davey brothers, Doniert and Gabrielle Hawke arrived in Fowey harbour on board one of their newest and fastest schooners, *La Sirène*. The ship, built in an American shipyard, attracted a great deal of attention in a port where such vessels were appreciated.

Although Gabrielle was eager for a reunion with her stepson, and with Talwyn, her trading instinct had not deserted her and *La Sirène* entered the Cornish port laden with a cargo of luxury items that could be expected to return a handsome profit.

There was comfortable accommodation on the vessel and the owners would sleep on board during their stay, but the first thing Doniert did when the ship moored was go ashore and arrange the hire of a horse and light carriage from St Austell for the duration of *La Sirène*'s mooring in the harbour. In this, they set off to visit the cottage at Penrice.

Only Laura was missing from the household and Gabrielle gave everyone a typically warm greeting then enthused about the cottage and its surroundings, much to the delight of Maisie, who took to the Frenchwoman immediately.

It was early afternoon and the midday meal had been eaten and the table cleared, but Maisie quickly produced tea and scones, cooked only that morning. When they had all drunk and eaten enough to satisfy their hostess, Talwyn helped her mother clear away and Gabrielle remained talking to them in the kitchen while Doniert accompanied his son to Penrice manor.

Amos was going to the manor to check whether any latecomers had arrived to make statements about the murderers' activities. Along the way, he told his father of the unexpected success of his campaign to persuade ex-smugglers to come forward and give evidence against the two brothers who had terrorised the local mining and fishing communities for so long.

'Sir Joseph Sawle and I thought that trying to protect witnesses would cause us big problems, so he had fifty special constables sworn in especially for the task, but they are not going to be needed. Far from being reviled, I believe the witnesses are actually being hailed as heroes and urged to tell their stories in alehouses and inns the length and breadth of the county. Ordinary folk have been shocked to discover how murderous the Davey brothers really were, and the killing of Edward Kernow was one too many for most people. They are horrified that a gentle and learned man should have died in such a way, and being able to charge the Daveys with eight murders has certainly turned people against them. It has also meant that Pasco and Hannibal have received no support from those who still believe that smuggling is every Cornishman's right.'

'Talking of the Kernow family,' Doniert said, 'both Gabrielle and I like Maisie – but we are very taken indeed with Talwyn. Pardon me if I am wrong, but I have the feeling you two have moved closer to one another since your return from Roscoff. Would I be right?'

'I have asked her to marry me,' Amos said.

Doniert waited for an amplification of the bare statement. When it did not come, he queried, 'What did she say?'

'She said she can't consider it because it would mean leaving her mother alone, and it's too soon after her father's death for that. She also believes that she and her mother are beholden to Sir Joseph because of all the support he has given them and leaving Cornwall after he has put so much money into the new school at Charlestown would be letting him down.'

'Is there any way we can help resolve the problem?' Doniert asked. 'I am not a poor man any more and I know Gabrielle would love to be able to do something.'

'Thank you for the offer, Pa, but while my future is in London and Talwyn's commitments are in Cornwall there would seem to be little that anyone can do to help.'

At the very moment Amos was discussing the obstacles to their marriage with his father, Talwyn was doing the same with Gabrielle.

The Frenchwoman had asked Talwyn if she would show her round the cottage garden, and, after admiring the shrubs and flowers and making appreciative comments about the neat and productive vegetable plot, she followed the younger woman to the orchard.

After commenting on the heavy crop of apples, which were not yet quite ripe, she took Talwyn by surprise by suddenly saying, 'Has Amos asked you to marry him yet?'

Disconcerted, Talwyn replied, 'Yes, but what made you ask such a question? Has he said something to you?'

'He does not need to tell me. I knew when I saw you both in Roscoff that he is in love with you . . . and you with him. It was going to be only a question of time. When is the wedding to be, and where? But, no, *where* does not matter. Doniert and I will be there to see you married even if you decide to have the ceremony in the heart of Africa . . . but, come, I must give my future daughter-in-law a hug and tell you how happy I am to have gained not only a handsome son, but also a beautiful daughter!'

'I am afraid any such actions would be premature,' Talwyn said before the impetuous and emotional Frenchwoman could carry out her intentions. 'There are far too many obstacles in the way for us to consider marrying at the moment.'

'Obstacles? What obstacles?' Gabrielle demanded. 'Has he not asked you to marry him?'

'Yes, but—'

'Ah! So there is a "but"? That must mean it is you who perceive these "obstacles"?'

'I suppose it is, in a way,' Talwyn admitted, 'but they are not imaginary. There is my mother . . . and my duty to Sir Joseph Sawle, who has put so much money into the school where I teach, and who lets us live in this cottage rent free. He has also been extremely kind to my mother and me since my father was murdered.'

'This Sir Joseph, is he not the magistrate who thinks so highly of Amos? If so, would he not be overjoyed for him to marry the woman he loves?'

'Possibly, but—'

'Another "but"?' Gabrielle interrupted Talwyn once again. '"But" and "obstacles" are not words that lovers should use. I understand your concern for your mother – and I admire you for it – but I am certain she would be very unhappy to feel she is the reason why you will not marry the man you love . . . and who loves you. Why, she could come to live in France, near to me. I own some very nice little houses in Roscoff and we would become great friends.'

Talwyn smiled at the thought of her mother living in a foreign land, trying to cope with a strange language, and she said, 'My mother would never leave Cornwall, and I don't think I would want her to – but here she comes from the cottage now. Perhaps we can discuss it some more when the trial of the Davey brothers is over.'

72

The trial of Pasco and Hannibal Davey for eight murders was expected to be one of the most sensational ever held in Cornwall. More than twenty witnesses had been found board in Bodmin and every inn and lodging house was crammed with as many prospective court-house spectators as could possibly be accommodated. In addition, people flocked in from miles around, hoping to gain admittance to the courtroom to witness the proceedings.

Excitement reached fever pitch the evening before, when a rumour went around that the Davey brothers, brought to Bodmin from the gaol in Launceston castle, had made an escape attempt.

On this occasion, rumour proved to be true. Building work had been going on at the Bodmin gaol for some months and, somehow, proving that the Daveys still had friends, a mason's hammer had been smuggled in to

Hannibal. He used it that evening on the gaoler who brought him his meal.

Fortunately, Sir Joseph Sawle, aware of the dangerous characters of the two brothers, had brought soldiers into the prison as a precaution. The screams of the injured gaoler brought them running to the scene and Hannibal was overpowered and knocked unconscious, but not before the gaoler had sustained a broken collarbone and ribs and one of the soldiers a broken arm.

The soldiers surrounded the courtroom for the trial the following day and the crowd clamouring to obtain entrance were confronted by the giant figure of Harvey Halloran, in the uniform of sergeant major of the Cornwall Constabulary, his already great height added to by the top hat which was part of his dress.

Any thoughts of trying to brush Harvey aside in order to gain entrance to the courtroom were abandoned when word went round that this was the man who had subdued Hannibal Davey in a matter of moments when the older of the two brothers was arrested in Charlestown.

It had been expected that the trial of the two men would occupy the court's time for a full two days. Defence counsel had been appointed and a great many witnesses were due to be called for both defence and prosecution.

Amos accompanied his father to the room occupied by the prosecution witnesses and left him there renewing his acquaintance with men he had not seen for many years. As a prosecution witness himself, Amos would soon be joining them, but first he wanted to check that all witnesses due to give evidence against the Daveys had put in an appearance.

He went to the clerk's office, where he was surprised to find Sir Joseph Sawle, Chief Constable Gilbert and a bevy of bewigged counsel in excited discussion.

When Sir Joseph saw Amos, he pushed his way through the throng to reach him, Chief Constable Gilbert at his heels.

The magistrate's hearty greeting left Amos puzzled. 'Congratulations, dear boy. Many congratulations indeed!'

'Congratulations for what?' he asked.

'For presenting such a strong case against the Davey brothers that they have decided to save everyone the trouble and expense of a lengthy trial and are pleading guilty to all the charges.'

Amos heard him in disbelief. 'Why? The Daveys are not men who would do anything to make things easier for the authorities. There must be another reason why they have chosen not to contest the charges.'

'There is.' A bewigged counsel had heard the exchange and, introducing himself as John Merivale, counsel for the defence, he said, 'You must be Inspector Amos Hawke, from Scotland Yard. I too congratulate you on the presentation of your evidence. There was little I could have contested – not that it would have been possible to win a not guilty verdict for two men arraigned on eight separate counts of murder!'

'But I still don't understand why they have pleaded guilty. It would have been a final act of defiance against authority.'

'No, Inspector Hawke. Hannibal and Pasco Davey spent their lifetimes building reputations of invincibility and strength of character. Had they pleaded not guilty the evidence given by your witnesses would have shown them to be petty men with a lust for killing. Details of the manner of their arrests would have destroyed any hopes they might entertain of history regarding them as men of outstanding strength and cunning. I understand that Hannibal was rendered unconscious by virtually a single blow from one of your colleagues, and Pasco – although armed – was captured largely through the physical intervention of a young woman!'

'That's quite true,' Amos admitted, 'but I hope enough will be said in court to show them up for what they really are . . . two vicious and cowardly murderers.'

'No doubt it will, Inspector. I am going to neither attempt to glorify their activities, nor waste my breath pleading for mercy on their behalf. Few men have been more deserving of the fate that awaits the Davey brothers.'

Inside the courtroom the judge wasted few words on Hannibal and Pasco Davey. After passing sentence of death, he deviated from the official pronouncement to say that rarely, if ever, had it given him pleasure to order the taking of the life of a fellow man. However, on this occasion he would depart from Bodmin with the certain knowledge that he had done the men and women of Cornwall a great service and undoubtedly saved the lives of more than one potential victim.

Pasco and Hannibal Davey were dropped into eternity at noon two days later from a scaffold outside the prison gate, watched by a crowd of men, women and children estimated to number twenty thousand. Two fairs were in the town to celebrate what had virtually become a public holiday, the grisly proceedings being treated as an occasion for celebration.

Sir Joseph Sawle was present at the hanging, as was Chief Constable Gilbert. Amos had been invited to attend, but had declined.

It was not a spectacle he wished to witness and he excused himself by pleading that his father and Gabrielle were leaving Fowey on the evening tide and had invited he and Talwyn to sample the skills of their French chef before they sailed.

On board *La Sirène* the chef was all that Gabrielle had boasted he would be. Although the events taking place at Bodmin dominated the thoughts of the guests, they tried their best to put them out of their minds as the chef used the ship's galley to full advantage. The meal over, father and son went on deck. Doniert looked about him nostalgically. 'You know, I have visited many harbours around the world in the last few years, but I don't think I have ever seen any more beautiful than Fowey.'

'I wouldn't argue with that,' Amos agreed, 'and to my mind there is nowhere else in the world to compare with Cornwall.'

'I think Talwyn would agree with you,' Doniert said. 'And yet you have chosen to work in London!'

'That's just the way things have worked out,' Amos said. 'I *did* return to Cornwall when I left the Marines and was searching for you, but I didn't find you and there was nothing else for me here.'

'But there is now,' Doniert pointed out. 'You have asked Talwyn to marry you. Isn't that reason enough to settle here?'

'As I have said before, my work is in London. I am an acting detective inspector, with prospects of further promotion. I could offer Talwyn a good life there.'

'Possibly,' Doniert said, 'but I don't think she would be happy living in a city – and her mother is here.'

'Yes, and her mother is a problem that appears to be insurmountable at the moment. I am very fond of Maisie too and she has had a very unhappy time in recent months. I wouldn't want to do anything to add to that.'

'She would be delighted if you and Talwyn were to marry,' Doniert declared. 'And very *un*happy if she knew she is the reason why you and Talwyn are not marrying.'

A very similar conversation was being held below decks by Talwyn and Gabrielle, but they too were unable to find a solution. Later, *La Sirène* sailed from Fowey harbour towards the coast of France watched by two young people who were left behind, their futures uncertain.

73

'When do you think you will be leaving us?'

Talwyn put the question to Amos as they sat side by side on the seat of the light carriage that was being returned to the St Austell stables from which it had been hired by Doniert and Gabrielle.

'In a few days' time,' Amos replied unenthusiastically. 'I sent off my report of the trial to the Metropolitan Police commissioner and requested a few days' leave in order to settle my affairs in Cornwall. It may or may not be granted.'

'When do you expect a reply?' Talwyn asked, with a lack of enthusiasm that matched his own.

'Today or tomorrow. Sir Joseph enclosed a sealed letter with mine and he is awaiting a reply too. I understand he entertained the hope that I will be asked to fill the post of Head of Detectives, made vacant by the death of Detective Inspector Carpenter. I believe he also expressed great satisfaction at my investigation into the murders committed by the Daveys, and added that Cornwall's first chief constable endorses his views. Colonel Gilbert says he would be happy to ask Scotland Yard for my assistance should it be needed at any time in the future.'

Talwyn was silent for some time before saying unhappily, 'I wish you didn't have to return to London, Amos.'

'You know I feel the same, Talwyn, but there just isn't anything for me here in Cornwall. It's a great pity we can't persuade your mother to come to London – or even go to France. My pa and Gabrielle would love to have us there with them. They would find work for both of us – and we could enjoy a good life there.'

'I don't doubt it,' Talwyn agreed. 'Quite honestly, the way I feel, I would go anywhere with you . . . but I could not leave my mother now. It would be cruel. She really does need me, Amos.'

'I know.' Reaching out, he grasped her hand, aware of how upset she was. 'But we won't be saying goodbye for ever. As Sir Joseph said in his letter to the commissioner, Colonel Gilbert won't hesitate to ask for me if a detective is needed again in Cornwall.'

It was scant comfort – but even the faint hope it offered them of being together again would soon be dashed.

The letter from London, when it arrived, was addressed to Amos at Penrice manor. Instead of having a servant deliver the letter, the baronet sent a message asking Amos to come to the manor to collect it personally.

When Amos arrived at the big house he was shown

into the study by the butler, and Sir Joseph handed him the letter. 'Read it before we discuss anything, Amos. If it says what I think it does, we will need to have a talk about what can be done.'

Amos opened the letter with some trepidation. Glancing at the unfamiliar signature first, he saw that it was that of a recently appointed assistant commissioner, a man who had been a superintendent in charge of a London police district when Amos had set out for Cornwall with the late Detective Inspector Carpenter.

It began well enough, commending Amos on the successful conclusion of his murder investigation and informing him that a similar commendation had been received from the senior Cornish magistrate, Sir Joseph Sawle. It went on to allow Amos three days' leave in which to settle any personal affairs in Cornwall.

That was disappointing because Amos had asked for a week – but there was an even greater blow to come. The complement of the detective force at Scotland Yard allowed for only one inspector. This had been Detective Inspector Carpenter. After being made up to acting detective inspector when his superior had been killed, Amos had entertained a not unreasonable hope that his acting rank would be made substantive and he would become the officer in charge of the detective branch.

The letter informed him this was not to be so. In view of his outstanding work in Cornwall, he was told that the Metropolitan Police were willing to confirm him as a substantive inspector – but in the uniform branch. If this was acceptable to him, he was to report to the superintendent in charge of 'H' Division (Whitechapel) on his return. If, however, he preferred to remain in the detective branch he would be required to revert to the rank of sergeant and should report to newly appointed Detective Inspector Dyson, at Scotland Yard.

He was ordered to notify the assistant commissioner of his decision by return of post.

When he had read the letter, Amos looked up to see Sir Joseph watching him closely. 'Is your letter as disappointing as I believe it to be?' he asked.

Confirming that it was, Amos told him of the alternatives he had been offered.

'Which of the options do you think you will take?'

'It's something I will need to think about,' Amos replied. 'My preference would be to remain in the detective branch, but I don't think I could work with Dyson. I don't care for him as a person and am not happy with the methods he uses to get results.'

Raising an eyebrow, Sir Joseph said, 'Yet it would appear that someone thinks well enough of him to put him in charge of detectives.'

'It could be something to do with the fact that he is the son-in-law of the assistant commissioner who has written the letter.'

Making no comment on Amos's observation, Sir Joseph said, 'So you will be returning to London to take up an appointment as a uniform inspector, and not as a detective sergeant?'

'Most probably,' Amos agreed. 'When the plain clothes allowance is taken into account there is very little difference in pay between the two . . . but I will need to think about it.'

'Would you like me to write a personal letter to Commissioner Mayne, to reiterate my request that *you* be the one to step into the shoes of the late Detective Inspector Carpenter?'

Amos shook his head. 'Thank you very much, Sir Joseph, but even if Commissioner Mayne heeded your request – which I doubt – it would cause great resentment from both Dyson and the assistant commissioner.'

'Very well, Amos. Come and see me again before you leave Cornwall.'

Amos left Penrice manor heavy-hearted, his mood lightening a little along the way when he realised that Sir Joseph had called him by his Christian name for the first time.

Amos sent only a brief acknowledgement of the assistant commissioner's letter, agreeing to accept the transfer to 'H' Division as a uniform inspector. Then, putting the matter to the back of his mind, he concentrated on spending as much time as possible with Talwyn. However, their increasing awareness of the depth of their love for one another, and the constant discovery of further things they shared in common, only increased their misery at the knowledge that they must soon part and would not see each other again for a very long time.

On the day before Amos was to return to London, Sir Joseph sent a servant with a request that he call on him at the manor. Guiltily, Amos remembered he had promised to call on the magistrate before leaving.

He made his way to the big house, and was surprised to find Colonel Gilbert ensconced in the study with Sir

Joseph when he arrived. The chief constable greeted him warmly and Sir Joseph too made him feel welcome, settling him in a comfortable leather armchair and pouring him a generous cognac.

When Amos was settled, Sir Joseph occupied an armchair between his two guests and said to Amos, 'Have you decided to return to London as a uniform inspector?'

When Amos replied in the affirmative, the chief constable asked whether he was quite happy with the decision.

'Not particularly,' Amos replied, 'but if I turned it down I would need to wait a long time before I was offered promotion again. As it is, if I am lucky, I could make superintendent in ten or fifteen years' time.'

'What is the salary of a police inspector, Amos?'

Surprised that Sir Joseph should ask such a personal question, Amos replied, 'About seventy-five pounds a year, or possibly a few shillings more.'

'I think we might supplement that sum considerably,' the magistrate said smugly. 'You see, the Excise service offered a substantial reward to anyone giving information which led to the capture and conviction of the man, or men, who killed their two officers. You not only discovered the identity of the killers, but also captured them and gained the information which led to their subsequent conviction and execution. The reward is yours – and I have already applied for it on your behalf. You will no doubt be very pleased to know that the sum involved is two hundred and fifty pounds in respect of each officer . . . a total of five hundred pounds!'

For a few moments Amos was speechless; then he

said, 'That *is* a great deal of money, Sir Joseph, but, unfortunately, as a Metropolitan policeman I would not be allowed to accept it.'

'Then leave the London police,' Sir Joseph suggested. 'You can hardly say they have been over-generous towards you in return for the splendid work you have done for us here – and five hundred pounds would represent a great many years' service as a London policeman.'

'It would indeed,' Amos agreed, 'but I enjoy being a policeman – and I could not accept the whole amount anyway. I think half of it should be given to Talwyn Kernow.'

'That is generous . . . *extremely* generous,' said Sir Joseph. Suddenly looking at Amos suspiciously, he said, 'I trust you have not got the girl into trouble?'

'No, Sir Joseph,' Amos said with a smile, 'but I have asked her to marry me.'

The baronet's reaction was a mixture of surprise and indignation. 'You mean you would take my school-teacher away from Cornwall?'

'No, Sir Joseph. That was one of her reasons for refusing to marry me. She realises that she owes you a great debt of gratitude and would not let you down.'

Mollified, Sir Joseph said, 'The girl has a commendable sense of duty . . . but you say that is only one of her reasons for turning you down. What are the others?'

'They also concern her sense of duty,' Amos replied. 'She will not leave her mother after all the problems she has suffered recently – losing her husband, and then her accident.'

'So her reasons for not marrying you are all to do with the fact that she feels she cannot leave Cornwall?' The question came from the chief constable, who added, 'Are you quite satisfied she would marry you if you remained here?'

'Absolutely certain,' Amos declared positively, 'but with two hundred and fifty pounds I don't doubt she will be able to make the occasional journey to London to see me.'

Colonel Gilbert and Sir Joseph exchanged glances before the former spoke to Amos once more.

'What would you say if I proposed an arrangement that would entitle you to accept the Excise service's reward – or half of it, whichever you choose; would allow you to remain in Cornwall and marry Miss Kernow . . . yet enable you to continue with the work you so obviously enjoy – and, may I say, perform so very well?'

'I would say you were a miracle worker, sir,' Amos said, 'but—'

Colonel Gilbert held up his hand to silence him. 'Sir Joseph and I were discussing it shortly before you arrived – and what you have just told us confirms that the decision we reached is the right one for everbody. As you know, I am recruiting men for my new police force. Recruitment is going very well – with one important exception. I am looking for a senior superintendent to work closely with me at police headquarters in Bodmin. As an ex-military man yourself, you would understand me if I said the position would be that of an adjutant – a post that carries with it a great deal of responsibility. The man who accepts the post will be taking on a

472